THE CADRE

By Jack Probyn

For Tom — for giving me the kick up the arse I needed and for reminding me to celebrate the little wins.

MEET JAKE TANNER

Born: 28.03.1985

Height: 6'1"

Weight: 190lbs/86kg/13.5 stone

Physical Description: Brown hair, close shaven beard, brown eyes, slim athletic build

Education: Upper Second Class Honours in Psychology from the University College London (UCL)

Interests: When Jake isn't protecting lives and finding those responsible for taking them, Jake enjoys motorsports — particularly F1

Family: Mother, older sister, younger brother. His father died in a car accident when Jake was fifteen

Relationship Status: Currently in a relationship with Elizabeth Tanner, and he doesn't see that changing, ever

| PART 1 |

CHAPTER 1

GRASS

Up until this point in his life, Lewis Coyne had never felt more alive. He'd once thought extreme doses of excitement came from evading the police by vaulting a brick wall and disappearing down a narrow alleyway, or sprinting away from a horde of armed rival gang members as they pursued him and his mates through the estate. Up until this point in his life, he'd been wrong. Now his body – his toes, legs, fingers, arms – shook with a new type of adrenaline. Rawer, purer, harder. And it consumed him.

What was the word for it? The one someone had used at school?

Unprecedented, he repeated to himself, disregarding the word almost as soon as he remembered it. His vocabulary was minimal – he could count the number of thirteen-letter words he knew on a single hand – and he aimed to keep it that way. Like many others he knew from the estate, he was a failure of the education system, and he didn't want anyone – especially those closest to him – to think he was a bright spark that had been ignited in the classroom all of a sudden because he knew big words. God only knew how much of a ribbing he'd get for that.

And how much that would weaken his standing.

Lewis looked down at his sweaty hands and felt them fight for purchase on the handlebars of his BMX. He wiped them clean on his hoodie, then checked his phone. The latest message in his chats told him it was time to move.

Grabbing the bars and placing one foot on the pedal, he started along the streets towards the estate. Towards the meeting place. It was dark – the clock had just rolled into the early hours of the morning – and he used the street lamps overhead as his only source of illumination. Although it was unnecessary, as from the age of five, as soon as he was allowed out unsupervised, he'd mastered the routes in and around the Cosgrove Estate. The potholes. The dips in the ground. The tree roots jutting out of the pavement which he used to practise his jumps and tricks. The broken pieces of glass that had been left there for years which nobody from the council had bothered to clean up. That came as no surprise; nobody – let alone anyone from the council – came around this way. Especially at night. When the monsters and the lurkers and people's innermost demons came out. It should have scared him, but as a wide-eyed five-year-old, filled with childish ignorance for danger, he'd loved it, and found another place he could call home.

In recent years, the Cosgrove Estate had earned itself a reputation for being home to one of the most notorious gangs in London – the E11 – and Lewis was part of the elite team responsible for upholding it. And tonight, along with some other members, he was about to solidify its position on the map for good.

He snaked in and out of the cars parked on the side of the road. His stunt pegs on the front and back wheels caught the panels and doors of those he passed, scratching them, the sound hissing into the night like a wounded fox. He paid the damage little heed. Not his car, not his problem. He was barely old enough to drive. And if the owners decided to grow a pair of cojones and start something with him, he was confident that the small, matte black Tac Force switchblade in his pocket that Rykard had given him would be enough to make them rethink their action and hurry back inside to their perfect little family, their perfect wife and kids. Because knives had become the new guns. They were more intimate, required more skill, more bravery, greater dexterity. You really got to see what a person was like when you stared into their eyes while holding them at knifepoint. You saw the pain, the fear, the horror, the million and one thoughts racing through their head as you held their life in the balance.

Before the end of the street, Lewis cut left down an alleyway barely wide enough for his handlebars, and at the end, he made another left, this time behind a row of houses and garages. Puddles of rainwater and mud from the brief showers they'd had the other day kicked up in the air and splashed his shoes. Not even the sun was brave enough to venture near the estate. At the end of the alley, he raced past a bramble bush, turned left and drove into an underground tunnel that led to the estate. His home. His office. His playground.

As he reached the centre, he skidded to a halt, swinging the back wheel to the side. Two high-rise buildings dominated the landscape to the north and south, like the king and queen on a chessboard, looking out at the rest of the city. Either side of him was a row of low-rise buildings, boxing him into the prison of society where the lowest of the low were kept away from the rest of civilisation, left to fend for themselves. Hundreds of small squares of light perforated holes in the buildings, making them look like gigantic cheese graters.

A gust of wind ripped beneath the two underpasses that cut through the towers and jostled the bottom of Lewis's damp and dirty jogging bottoms. This time it brought with it the smell of weed, of someone sparking up nearby. Each time was a new scent. Urine. Alcohol. Sweat. Blood. Shit. One of the many reasons they called it The Pit.

To his left was a patch of grass, which was used by many of the lads as a football pitch. Beyond it was a playground, fully kitted out with two swings, a merry-go-round and a climbing frame. Now covered in graffiti and littered with drug paraphernalia, kids of the estate had once flocked to it after school and at the weekends. But after their parents had realised what was going on in there, the place had become desolate.

To his right was a basketball court, and just in front of the patch of grass was a single street lamp; lonely, yet left untouched by the spray can and Sharpie. Fortunately, the light pollution generated from the hundreds of windows surrounding him illuminated the entire area.

A sound distracted him. The ear bursting noise of tyres kissing tarmac.

Lewis snapped his head round and saw a car pull up through the little underpass beneath the south block. The lights were killed, and the doors opened. Two men disembarked from the front, rushed to the back, opened the boot, and pulled something out. In the darkness, it was difficult to discern, but Lewis knew exactly what it was.

Rather, *who* it was.

The two men slammed the boot shut and raced towards Lewis. The body they held in their arms wriggled and struggled to break himself free. His arms were tied behind his back, and as they emerged into the light, Lewis saw a line of black tape across his mouth, stifling his cries and screams, yet no effort had been made to cover the horror in his eyes.

Back at the car, another man exited, made his way to the boot and grabbed a few extra things. By the time he closed the boot again, the two men and the hostage were in front of Lewis.

They dropped the man to the ground, face first.

'All right, Lew?' Jamal asked, his tattooed face and neck bending to look at him, doubling his skin into a second chin. Jamal was by far the tallest man Lewis had ever seen. And it came as no surprise to him that Jamal was always the best player in the estate at basketball – and any other sport they played, for that matter. His legs were twice as long as Lewis's, and, as they'd all learnt after several challenges from some of the lower boys in the gang, Jamal was also the fastest in the estate. As usual, he was immaculately dressed, wearing a dark Nike coat, jeans, and brand-new Air Jordans, the pair Lewis had been eyeing up for weeks. As he reached out to Lewis, the golden ring he wore on his little finger caught the light from the street lamp.

'What you sayin'?' Lewis and Jamal clasped hands and bumped shoulders.

'You been waiting long?' Deshawn asked, standing on the other side of the body. What Des lacked in height, he made up for in width. Not because he was fat, but because he was well built, a solid rock of a man. The only problem was it made him slow. Sometimes too slow. And with the damaged leg he'd sustained after a knife attack by a rival gang member when he was fifteen, Des had no other choice but to stay and fight rather than run away. And he had the scars to prove it. Deshawn was one of the quietest members of the group – reserved and softly spoken. He involved himself only when he needed to, but when the time came, and when he was facing down a small army of twenty rivals, he became a different person, a different type of animal.

'Only a couple minutes,' Lewis replied, greeting Deshawn

the same way he did Jamal. 'No stress.'

The third man arrived.

Rykard was in the middle of the spectrum. Not too tall, not too wide. Just right, like Goldilock's porridge. Father to a daughter of similar age to Lewis, he was one of the most experienced elders in the gang and had been responsible for helping Lewis progress through the ranks. But there was a darker side to him, a Dr Jekyll and Mr Hyde persona where nobody ever really knew which one they were getting. Some days he was fine, calm, reticent. Others he was manic, aggressive, brutish. Many in the estate blamed it on his persistent drug use and the unbridled paranoia it spawned. But Lewis didn't mind. Rykard always treated him with respect and was in several ways another father figure, someone he could look up to.

Rykard dropped a large blue carton of what looked like bleach and a solid metal chain onto the ground. At the sight of it, Lewis's eyes widened, and his skin became even sweatier. Rykard moved around the contents and embraced Lewis. As he pulled away, he said, 'Fucking hell, fam, you getting nervous or something? Hands are sweatier than a prostitute's pussy.'

Jamal and Deshawn laughed, the sound echoing around the estate. Lewis snapped back to attention and gave the man the middle finger.

'You been school today, fam?' Rykard asked once the laughter had finished.

Lewis kissed his teeth. 'Fuck no! School's for waste men and fags.'

'I promised your pops I'd make sure you went.'

'Leave it out.'

'Little man – you do know feds'll come knocking if you don't go, innit? They ain't like it when people don't show up. And you can't have your pops going back in the nick again.

All you gotta do is keep your attendance over fifty per cent and you ain't gonna have no stress. Deal?'

Rykard bent down to Lewis's level and stared at him. The man's eyes were pin sharp, and his forehead shone with a thin sheen of sweat. His mouth was open, brandishing a set of yellow-black stained teeth, and a tongue that dangled like a dog's. Lewis had never seen him take drugs, but he knew the signs of recent activity.

'Deal,' Lewis said, throwing his hand into his pocket, and gently wrapping his fingers around the knife.

'Did you bring what I told you to?' Rykard asked as he stood.

Lewis reached inside his other pocket and produced a mobile phone. Brand-new iPhone 4. Space grey, 32GB storage and 5-megapixel camera. Immaculate condition, not a crack or dent in sight. Six hundred quid to an idiot, or free if you knew how to get one.

'Any issues getting it?'

Lewis smirked. 'Like taking sweets from a baby.'

'Good boy.'

'I ain't no boy,' Lewis said defiantly. 'I'm a man.'

Rykard chuckled. 'You'll be a man after this. Trust.' He turned his attention to the figure on the ground. 'Up you get, you sack of shit!'

Without needing to be told, Deshawn and Jamal raced to the figure's side, hefted him to his feet and dragged him over to the street lamp. Lewis watched on as Des returned for the carton of liquid and chain, placed the carton on the ground and wrapped the chain across the man's chest, underneath his arms and behind his back. Then, Jamal moved closer to the lamp post, climbed to the top using the small struts of metal that had been added a few months back, and hooked the chain around the top. After he jumped down, keeping the chain in hand, he and Deshawn gave a heavy tug. The man on the ground was jerked upwards like a rag doll, screaming behind his makeshift mask, his cries falling on deaf ears. They continued pulling, groaning and wincing under the strain on their arms, until eventually, the body hovered a few feet above the ground. Once the hostage was in position, Des and Jamal tied the slack to the base of the lamp post, wrapping it round several times.

The hostage gasped in agony as the links on the chain bit into his chest and shoulders. The noise continued for a minute, and after it had died down and become nothing more than heavy breathing, Rykard waved his finger in the air.

'Take off the tape – I wanna speak to him.'

Jamal carried out the order.

As soon as the tape was off his mouth, the man suspended two feet in the air spat in Jamal's face. From his expression, it was evident that Jamal was fighting every urge in his body not to retaliate. Punch him in the face. Stab him in the stomach. Shoot him in the head.

'Don't be like that, Jermaine!' Rykard said with surprising enthusiasm. 'I always thought you'd be amicable and gracious in defeat.' He sniffed hard and wiped his nose multiple times as he shuffled slowly towards the victim.

'You don't even know what the word amicable means, you piece of shit,' Jermaine replied, spitting the words between breaths.

'And neither do you, so we've got ourselves an issue. Why don't we talk in a language we both understand?'

Without giving Jermaine a chance to respond, Rykard raised a hand. Jamal nodded his assent, grabbed the blue carton of liquid, unscrewed the cap and held it beside Jermaine's dangling legs.

Then Rykard turned to Lewis and said, 'Get the video sorted on that phone. I want you to learn something from this.'

Lewis's hands shook as he struggled to unlock the phone and open the camera. Eventually, the lens opened and an image of the grass in front of him materialised on the screen. Lewis swiped right and switched to the video function, then prodded the record button.

Everything he saw was through the eye of the camera.

'Sorry it's come to this, Jermaine,' Rykard said. 'I always liked you.'

'Fuck you.'

'But you know what they say: business is business.'

'Your business is dead.'

'They'll be saying the same about yours soon. And you. We know what you've been doing, we know you've broken the terms of our agreement. So why don't you give us the name of your new partner, and then we can forget any of this ever happened.'

Jermaine said nothing.

Rykard reached for his own waist and unhooked his belt. The leather dangled in his hands, jostling as another gust of wind ripped through The Pit, this time carrying with it the smell of fear.

Rykard started swinging the belt buckle like a lasso. Before Jermaine could respond, he whipped him in the face with it. The hostage cried out in pain. But Rykard ignored it. He swung again. And again. And again. Each time increasing the velocity and ferocity of his strikes. Each time landing on a different part of Jermaine's body. And, for a final send-off, he made sure the last landed right where it would hurt the most: Jermaine's crown jewels.

'Stop! Stop! Stop!'

'Ain't no point crying, fam. Ain't nobody gonna save you here. We run this place. This country ain't had a public hanging or torture in a very long time. You could be the lucky one to change that.' He took a step forward. 'Who have you recruited? Who's cutting our shit and replacing it with poison?'

Jermaine said nothing.

Rykard sighed, dropping his gaze to the ground. He looked like he was preparing himself to launch another attack, like a professional footballer psyching himself up before a major derby. But the reality was different.

Instead of bringing the belt down on Jermaine again, Rykard reached into his jacket pocket and removed a knife. He held the six-inch blade against Jermaine's groin. Paying little attention to the man's protestations, Rykard undid the buttons on Jermaine's jeans and undressed him slowly, gradually adding to his humiliation.

'Wh-Wh-What are you… what are you doing?'

'What's his name?'

Jermaine babbled incoherently. Then Rykard pressed the knife deeper into his groin, burying the blade in his inner thigh until a trickle of blood abseiled down his leg. Both men stared at one another. Without saying anything, Rykard gave another signal and Jamal sprang into action, dousing Jermaine with the liquid. And suddenly a new odour wafted through the estate. The smell of petrol.

'Please! No! Please!' Jermaine begged as he tried to kick the liquid from his body. 'Not this, please… not this!'

'What's his name?' Rykard bellowed, taking a step back from the splashes.

'Frank Graham. Frank Graham! He runs the Skull Massive. At Dunsfield Estate. He's just a starter. He don't know what he's doing. But he's got good ideas. Good prospects.'

A blanket of silence descended upon The Pit, save for the raspy sound of Jermaine's heavy, exaggerated breathing.

'Are you still recording, Lew?' Rykard called back, staring into Jermaine's eyes.

'Y-Yeah,' Lewis stuttered, checking the screen to make sure the video was still being captured.

'Good man. Watch this.'

Rykard turned to Jermaine and flashed the bloodied blade beneath his chin. 'We have a particular type of word for people like you, Jermaine. Do you know what it is? Grass. Someone who can't keep his mouth shut. I'm disappointed – I expected more from you. A little bit more fight. Call me a few names. Threaten to set some of your boys on me. But you ain't. In my eyes, that makes you a pussy. But being a grass is worse. It means you can't be trusted. We ain't know what other little secrets might come out if you got arrested or were questioned by the police, do we? We don't like grasses. So they have to be got rid of. And what's the best way to get rid of grass?'

'Wha—'

Before Jermaine had a chance to respond, Rykard pulled a Zippo lighter from his pocket, sparked the flint and held the flame against Jermaine's leg. In an instant, his entire body was consumed in a ball of pure orange. The flames roared and licked the sky and burnt twice the size and height of the lamp post. Piercing screams shot through the air and ricocheted off the building's walls. It was the first time Lewis had heard a man reach such a pitch. He continued to aim the camera at the burning remains, more out of paralysis from the shock of what he was seeing than anything else.

Before long, the smell of cooking skin, flesh and hair drifted through the air. As it rose through Lewis's nostrils, it made him gag, and he lost focus on the camera.

'Come on!' Deshawn cried, tugging at Rykard's arm. 'Let's get out of here.'

'No,' he said, his voice still, calm. 'Ain't nobody going anywhere until I say so. I want to watch him burn.'

CHAPTER 2

SURPRISES

Jake Tanner pressed the button on the tape recorder and concluded the interview, grateful that it was over. They were never easy, and they never would be. No matter how many he'd have to conduct, he always felt an aching pain in his stomach. Six months on from the most difficult case of his life, and he was still investigating it.

Melissa Warren, a thirty-four-year-old hairdresser, was another addition to the growing list of his former colleague's rape victims. She'd told him that, after it had happened, she'd been too afraid to do anything – not just about the rape, but also in her life. She'd once had dreams, hopes, aspirations. But Drew had taken those away from her that night, and she'd never recovered. But now she'd felt confident enough to come forward, to speak her truth and share her story in the hope that others would stand up too. The worst part about it, however, was that Drew Richmond, the man Jake had once considered a friend, would never see any sort of justice for his crimes. Except for the bullet in his brain that had killed him. But in Jake's mind, that wasn't enough.

Jake shoved the witness statement folders under his arm and headed back to the Major Investigation Team's home on the third floor of Bow Green Station in the heart of Stratford. He froze in the doorway moments after the buzzer granted him access. The room was empty and silent, save for the civilian support staff working tirelessly in the background, the quiet, repetitive clicking sound of keyboards and mouses making their way to Jake's ears. They were the people that nobody paid any attention to, even though they probably should have. Jake was used to seeing them around, so much so that he often regarded them as permanent fixtures in the wall. Along with Lindsay Gray, the building's facilities manager, whose office was situated in the corner of the room. Out of sight and out of mind. It was only thanks to a structural flaw that her office was on the same floor as theirs.

She was sitting on her chair, glasses perched on the end of her nose, tilting forward to the screen. She was dressed smartly in blouse and trousers and constantly radiated Jo Malone perfume, whiffs of it emanating through the door into the office at random points throughout the day. Kind-hearted and caring, she made a mean cup of coffee – once she'd learnt how Jake liked it – and she always wore a smile on her face, as though she was permanently happy. Perhaps because she didn't have the same stress levels as the rest of them.

Jake whistled and caught her attention.

'Where is everyone?' he asked, fanning his arms about the room as if he needed to highlight his point. 'They were all here an hour ago.'

Lindsay set her Mickey Mouse coffee mug on the table and shrugged. 'Sorry, love. Haven't seen them all morning. Didn't even notice they were gone. You tried calling them – Stephanie, Darryl?'

Jake unlocked his phone and scrolled through his contacts until he found Stephanie's mobile number, accidentally stopping at C in the alphabet first. Six months on from finding out that her real name was Stephanie and not Charlotte, the undercover name she'd originally given him, and he was still struggling to get the hang of it.

Just as he was about to dial, the screen changed and a photo of Elizabeth, his wife, appeared. He answered the call.

'Liz?'

'Jake! Jake! Oh my God. You have to come home. Please. Quickly. There's something – I can't – I don't know what—'

'Liz! Liz! Calm down.' Jake moved out of the office and into the adjoining briefing room. 'Calm down. Speak slowly. You're not making any sense. Where are you?'

'Home.' She was panting down the phone to him.

'What's happened? Is it one of the girls?'

'No. It's your mum. She's had a fall. She hit her head and now she's not moving.'

Christ. Jake lowered his head into his hand and massaged his temple.

'I'll be there as soon as I can. Have you called an ambulance?'

'Y… Y… Yeah. They're on their way, but I…'

'It's fine. Stay calm. Keep the girls safe, out of the way. Get Maisie to watch the telly with Welly, and I'll be there as fast as I can.'

'Hurry, Jake. Please.'

Jake grabbed his car keys from his desk and raced out of the building. As he jumped into the car, his phone vibrated. Panicking, fearing that it might be Elizabeth updating him and telling him to go to the hospital instead, he glanced at the screen.

It was nothing like that. Instead, staring back at him was an email. Normally, he wouldn't have paid attention to it, but this one caught his attention and made him freeze. The subject of the email read:

15

The world slowed. His body turned cold, his skin sweaty. A lump caught in his throat, and he struggled to swallow, to breathe. *We thank you for your silence.*

He unlocked the phone and opened the email. In the body of the text was an image of his car inside Bow Green's car park. At the sight of it, he snapped his head upwards and scanned his surroundings. Empty. Nobody in sight. Paranoid, and feeling like the confines of the car were closing in around him, he breathed heavily. In, out. In, out. In, out.

And then he remembered the last time he'd received the message. The night after he'd arrested his former boss. The night he'd come one step closer to discovering the identity of The Cabal. The night he'd found a package of drugs in his glove compartment.

Slowly, as if doing so any faster would cause the world to speed up, he rotated his head towards it.

We thank you for your silence.

Jake leant across and unlocked the compartment. A thick block of white powder, tightly wrapped in cellophane, rolled out onto the seat. Shit. He grabbed his coat from the back seat of the car and covered the parcel. A sweet aroma – a hint of strawberry, raspberry, cherry, he didn't know which – coming from the drugs wafted up his nose. Different to the Jo Malone he'd enjoyed only a few minutes earlier. Before he could think about his mum and what might have happened to her, he needed to get rid of the package.

And fast.

Fortunately, the car was a mess and hadn't been cleaned in weeks, and an old wrapper from Maisie's McDonald's Happy Meal was lying in the footwell of the rear passenger seat. Jake grabbed it, placed the drugs inside and hurried towards the public bin on the main road next to Bow Green, where he safely and discreetly disposed of the narcotics.

A short time later, Jake was outside his house in Croydon. He fumbled for his keys by the door and eventually managed to find the lock.

Throwing the door open, he screamed Elizabeth's name.

But there was no answer.

He rushed past the stairs towards the kitchen at the end of the corridor. The door was half open, and he ignored the fact that the house was deathly silent. As his hand touched the door handle, his mind feared the worst. Had his mum suffered a brain injury – a concussion, a haemorrhage? Were they already on their way to the hospital, or was she lying dead in the kitchen?

Jake opened the door. Paused.

Multi-coloured balloons and sparkling confetti littered the floor. Across the length of the kitchen was a banner that sparkled brighter than the confetti under the halogen light bulbs overhead. On the island in the middle of the kitchen was a row of plastic cups, soft drinks, sweets and a cake. Before his mind could process what was happening, several bodies leapt out from behind the island in the middle of the kitchen, each brandishing party poppers and aiming them at him.

'Surprise!' they screamed in unison, pouring out from their hiding places.

Jake staggered backwards, shocked. He counted how many there were. Six in total. Darryl. Stephanie. Ashley. Brendan. Elizabeth. His mum. All wore beaming smiles on their faces and pointy birthday hats on their heads. They began to laugh and clap as a chorus of 'Happy Birthday' unfolded.

'Happy birthday, sweetie,' Elizabeth said after they'd finished and gave him a kiss on the cheek.

'I… thank you… I didn't…' He was lost for words, still dealing with the shock of the surprise. 'How long have you been planning this for?'

'Long enough.'

'Happy birthday, pal!' someone called from beside him, slapping him on the back. It was Darryl Armitage, the new DCI – Liam Greene's replacement. He was a slim individual, with abnormally short arms. His hair was jet black and slicked back to the sides, and his skin was tanned leather – a heritage he didn't know the origin of. Perhaps Italian. Perhaps Spanish. Perhaps Portuguese. Perhaps even further afield. But it was one that he relished every time the sun came out.

'Yeah, Happy Birthday, bud!' DI Stephanie Grayson said, coming up on his other side. In the last twenty-four hours, she'd ditched the blonde look for a dark shade of brown. Jake was still getting used to it, and how much more attractive she was for it.

Next up was DS Brendan Lafferty, one of the latest additions to the team. Drafted in from Surrey Police's Serious and Organised Crime Team, Brendan had been with them for the last six months. He was experienced and didn't mind reminding people of the fact, frequently calling on previous successful cases whenever the slightest opportunity arose – the novelty of which, as it turned out, had worn out pretty quickly. He had thick, wavy fiery hair that was dark at the top and lighter at the bottom. His nose was covered in pencil-mark freckles, and his face looked as though it hadn't grown out of the infant stage. On his cheek, just above his high cheekbone, was a scar from an incident when he was a child; he'd fallen over a gravestone while playing with the family dog. Jake shook his hand.

In the background of the conversation was their newest recruit. Detective Constable Ashley Rivers. On her first day, standing in a stranger's kitchen. Jake had hoped the first time they'd meet would be under more professional circumstances, but it was too late now. She was small yet looked as though she knew how to defend herself without any assistance. She wore her auburn hair in a ponytail and hovered on the outskirts of the group, debating with herself whether to get involved or not. Jake smiled at her and gave her a small nod. She replied in kind, blood rushing to her cheeks.

'Thanks all for being here,' Jake started. 'I'm flattered, to be honest—'

'Enough of that,' Brendan interrupted. 'Shall we crack open a bottle?'

'Of soft drinks, yes!' Elizabeth replied, moving to the central island. 'It's not even lunchtime yet and you've all got work to get back to.'

Elizabeth unscrewed the cap from a bottle of Coke and began pouring the liquid into the plastic cups she'd already arranged. To Jake's left, his mother crept up and kissed him on the cheek.

'Happy birthday, darling,' she said.

'Thanks, Mum. Are you all right? You're not actually hurt, are you?'

'I'm fine. It was all Elizabeth's idea. She's been planning this for weeks, but it's been hard trying to get you all together in one place. You know I've always said she's a keeper.'

Jake smirked. 'She actually plays better in midfield.'

His mum slapped him on the arm playfully. 'Your dad would've been proud of you for that one,' she said and then dropped her head.

Noticing that she was about to dive deep into her own

thoughts, Jake wrapped his arm around her and brought her into his chest. 'I know he would,' he whispered. 'I know he would.'

Today marked his eleventh birthday since his dad had passed in a car crash on the way to pick him up from a Sunday League football match. Jake would have liked to say that each birthday got easier as time passed, but the reality of it was that they didn't. And they never would.

'Ladies and gentlemen,' Brendan shouted, holding a plastic beaker high in the air. 'I'd like to raise a toast… to Jake. Congratulations on making it to thirty-five. You're halfway through life. Officially middle-aged.'

Jake raised an eyebrow. 'Twenty-six,' he corrected. 'Still got a couple of years until I'm as senile as you.' He grabbed a beaker from the table and held it in the air. The rest of the team, Elizabeth and his mum all raised theirs in unison.

'To Jake!' came the chorus of cheers.

'I know it's been a tumultuous year,' Darryl began after the cheers had died down, 'what with DCI Greene and DS Richmond and everything that happened there, but I just wanted to say that I'm happy for you, Jake. I'm happy that you and the rest of the team are in a good place. And without you, mate, none of us would be here, so we've got a lot to thank you for personally. We're only in our infancy, and we've still got a lot of work to do, but I think we're all switched on in the right places and ready for what comes our way.'

'And,' Stephanie added, gesturing to the rest of the room, 'in the unlikely event that you are thinking of becoming a bent copper, you might as well turn yourself in now – it'll be a lot more pleasant than having this guy come after you.'

There was an awkward bout of laughter that struggled to leave the room. The concept of being a bent copper was still too real for some of them. They'd all heard the horror stories, and they were all too familiar with the consequences. Especially Jake.

'Anyway…' Darryl continued, 'I might not get a chance to say it later tonight, so I just wanted to say well done, and here's to the next year working together.'

'Oh, shit,' Brendan said, slapping his forehead with his palm.

'Language!' Elizabeth lambasted. 'There are children still in the house.'

'Sorry, sorry.' Brendan's cheeks turned the colour of his hair. 'Is that really tonight? I'd completely forgotten about it.'

'Yes, Brendan,' Darryl replied, sounding like an unimpressed dad. 'The Met Excellence Awards happen every year. On exactly the same date. At exactly the same venue. It's almost like your birthday – or do you forget that as well?'

Brendan shrugged. 'Sometimes.'

Just as Darryl was about to respond, his phone rang. He held his finger in the air and left the room. Jake, Stephanie and Brendan began a dialogue, but it was over as quickly as it had started.

'Something's come in. We've got to go. Sorry, Elizabeth, I wish we could have enjoyed it for a little bit—'

'Duty calls, I know,' she said, thumbing towards Jake. 'I've been living with this one long enough to know how it works.'

Darryl smiled and turned his attention to the team.

'Ashley, I want you to ride shotgun with Jake.'

'Where we going, guv?' Jake asked.

'Cosgrove Estate.'

A collective groan sounded around the room as everyone set their drinks down and grabbed their things.

'Not The Pit,' Stephanie said, rolling her eyes. 'Anywhere but The Pit.'

Heading out of the door, Ashley pulled Jake's arm and, waiting until it was just the two of them in earshot, asked,

'Why's it called The Pit?'

Jake smirked. 'Because it's a shithole.'

CHAPTER 3

A TALKING TO

For the first few minutes of the drive to the Cosgrove Estate, they rode in complete silence. Jake was usually an outgoing and talkative individual, and he liked to think that he was the first person to make a new addition to the team feel as comfortable and at ease as possible. But, recently, something in him had changed. He'd become much more wary of people and dubious of their intentions. So much so that the little voice in the back of his head – the one that everyone else would have called doubt but he intuition – inhibited him from being himself. The events of the past year had changed him, and not necessarily for the better.

It had been the same with Darryl and Brendan when they'd first joined the team; the standoffish behaviour, the hesitation, the suspicion, the second-guessing of everything they ever said or did, calculating in his mind whether he could trust them or not. And the jury was still out on that one. Anyone coming into the team had a lot to prove. Not just to the DCI, but to him also.

Jake slipped into fifth gear as he merged onto the M25,

keeping a close distance behind Stephanie's car in front. As he moved the stick, his head turned a little to the side, and he caught an awkward glance with Ashley. He feigned a smile and continued driving.

'Happy birthday, by the way,' she said. She spoke with a thin common accent, a hint of which came through when she failed to pronounce the 'H' in happy. To Jake, it sounded like she'd spent years trying to hide her past, her heritage, where she'd come from.

'Thanks,' he replied, feigning an even bigger smile.

'Sorry I didn't say it earlier. First day nerves and all that.'

'You don't strike me as the type of person who's nervous.' He wasn't sure if he believed that. But it was the nice thing to say.

'Usually, I'm not. But it's different when you're coming into a team like this. Everyone's so… close knit. It's difficult. Once you get to know me though, I'm fine.'

'Uh-huh.'

Jake wasn't sure he'd ever get to know her properly. The real Ashley Rivers. After all, he'd thought he knew who the real Drew, Liam and Pete were. *And look how that turned out…*

Jake returned his attention to the road. In the short time they'd been talking, they'd fallen slightly behind the front of the pack, so he put his foot down and within a few hundred yards had reclaimed the distance.

'How long have you been in the service?' Ashley asked, her gaze falling out of the window.

'Why?'

'I just wondered, that's all. I've been a part of the big family for six years; Beat Bobby for two, DC for four. Lewisham. Nasty place. Got a transfer here as soon as the position opened up.'

Stratford's not much better…

Jake said nothing and kept his mouth shut. Before he

knew it, they'd reached their end of the M25 and pulled off onto the A12, the road that would take them into the heart of the Cosgrove Estate.

Beside him, Ashley sniffed hard. 'Is that strawberry I can smell?'

Jake's heart leapt into his mouth. Strawberry. Smell. Drugs. How did she…?

We thank you for your silence.

'What?'

'Strawberry. I can smell it. Have you got one of those car fresheners? It smells really good.'

Jake tried to mask his heavy breathing and the visible rise and fall of his chest by focusing his attention on the road in an attempt to calm himself down. It had little effect. Why was she talking about a strawberry scent? He couldn't smell anything; hadn't been able to since he got rid of the package. Was the smell still there, lingering like the ominous and foreboding message that accompanied the parcel? He didn't think so.

Instead, he decided to change the topic.

'You're in for a treat today. A visit to The Pit on your first day. I've never met anyone as lucky.'

'Is it really as bad as you're making out?'

'Wait and see for yourself. It accounts for about fifty per cent of our uniformed call-outs.'

Ashley flashed a smile, revealing a set of lightly yellowed, tobacco-stained teeth. 'I'm sure with some good policing and good strategies and initiatives we could get that down to thirty.'

Jake scoffed.

'You mean you don't want less crime and an easier life?' She lifted her left eyebrow and looked at him inquisitively.

'You're right. Definitely. One hundred per cent.'

'Are you feeling all right?' she asked him.

'Yes. Fine. I just find it strange welcoming new people to the team.'

'Trusting them, you mean?'

Jake looked at the rolling tarmac in front of him.

'Not everyone's the same, Jake,' she said. 'I don't know what's happened in the past – not the specifics anyway, only what I've seen on the news and heard through the grapevine. But I guess you have to learn to trust again. In Lewisham, we had someone like you. Decent guy. Wonderful detective. But he tried to do it all alone. And couldn't. Ended up killing himself because of the amount of pressure he put himself under.'

Jake pretended like he'd listened and absorbed everything she'd just said. Which in fact he had, but he didn't believe a bit of it. She was just saying that to make him fall for it, make him feel guilty, make him let his guard down so that she and the rest of the team could attack. Well, he wasn't going to. The castle drawbridge was well and truly up, and nobody was allowed in.

CHAPTER 4

PROMISE

The playground bustled with life. Children yelled and screamed frivolously as they chased one another around the benches, in and around the bins at the end of the building. A ball was kicked left and right as the group of cool kids played a game of football. Knots of smaller groups, the social cliques that would follow them from year seven all the way through to graduation, littered the rest of the playground, eating their snacks, talking, flirting, laughing, pretending to get on with one another, making the most of the fifteen minutes they had before they were confined to classrooms and boring lessons about World War Two and algebra. Three hundred kids in a year. Five year groups. That was nearly fifteen hundred kids. And each of them looked happy to be there.

Except for Lewis. He didn't have any time for it. It was all a shitshow, a con, an excuse to keep him away from learning the way the real world worked. He didn't like any of the people in his school, except for one. And that was the only person he needed to like. He didn't need fifteen loose friends who would stab him in the back at the smallest opportunity.

No, he needed one close friend, whom he could trust unconditionally. One who would respect him.

He and Reece Enfield had grown up together on the estate, and they were inseparable. They'd both seen things that none of the other kids could even dream of. Their experiences had expedited the bonding process and they each carried one another's secrets. BFFs – best friends forever – as some of the girls in science called them.

'Hey, man,' Reece said. They were sitting on a set of steps that led to the main foyer of the school. Beside them was a ramp with a railing for disabled access. 'You wanna get outta here?'

'Where to?'

'The usual?'

'Yeah. Calm. Come.'

Lewis lifted himself off his step and started across the playground and onto the playing field, which was out of bounds for break and lunchtimes. Two football goals rose from the dew-soaked grass, and, beyond, was a set of rugby posts. To the left of the field, running along the perimeter of the school, was a line of trees. Their regular haunt. Sometimes they would bunk off during lessons to come and sit down there and talk. Sometimes they'd watch the cars go past. Other times they'd just shout and scream and make passers-by jump.

They climbed through the foliage and found their usual spaces. Lewis climbed higher than Reece and rested his feet on a branch for support. He stretched his back and yawned.

'Bro, I'm shattered,' he said.

'Same, fam.'

'I almost didn't get up this morning.'

'Same,' Reece said.

'Rykard said I had to come though, innit.'

'My mum said I had to come too.'

Lewis laughed and slapped Reece playfully on the top of his head. 'Still listening to what mummy says. Bless you, bro.'

'Least I still got a mum,' Reece said, showing Lewis the finger. It wasn't a new insult, but it didn't stop it from hurting any less. And Lewis knew from experience that Reece only said it when he was upset about something. Or in a mood. He continued, 'What makes you so good anyway? Why's Rykard giving a shit 'bout you coming here? This place is a waste of space.'

'He told me last night, innit.'

'What happened last night?' Reece asked. His attempt at hiding the blatant curiosity in his voice was unsuccessful. 'You was supposed to come online. I got my arse kicked by some foreigners on *Search and Destroy*. Could've used your help.'

Lewis swallowed before continuing. Felt pride rising through himself. 'You see what happened to Jermaine?'

'Course I did. Everyone in the estate knows, but what's that gotta do...' Reece hesitated, surveyed Lewis. '*You* were there?'

'Yeah, man. I was shotting, innit. Then Des, Jay and Ry text me to keep an eye out for when they came down, innit. By the time they got back, The Pit was dead. All I had to do was watch, make sure nothing happened.'

Reece's eyes illuminated with fervour. Now Lewis knew how all the elders must feel every day, having the kids on the estate look up to them the same way Reece was doing now.

'Fam, you messin'? I'm so jealous. I wish I gotta see it.'

Lewis shrugged and twisted himself round so that his legs dangled off the side of the branch. 'You wanna pre the ting?'

'What you think?'

Lewis removed his phone from his pocket. 'Promise me you ain't saying nothing though, bruv. If the teachers find this, I'm dead, fam.'

'Never mind the simps, fam – the feds are the ones you gotta worry 'bout.'

Reece stood on his branch, steadied himself with his arm and leant against the bark. Then Lewis unlocked the phone, opened the camera roll and displayed the video.

'Don't get scared, fam.'

'Fuck off,' Reece replied, prodding his elbow into Lewis's ribs.

Laughing through the pain in his side, Lewis played the video. He turned the sound up to full volume, and for the next five minutes, they watched Rykard beat and batter Jermaine Gordon with a belt buckle, douse him in petrol and set him alight.

'Shit, man,' Reece said moments after the film had finished. 'That's fucked.'

'Heavy, innit. I reckon the feds are already there by now.'

'You reckon that's why Rykard told you to come to school?'

Lewis shrugged. 'Maybe.'

'You reckon the feds'll find out it was yous that done it?'

Lewis shook his head. 'Nah. The pigs don't stay round for too long. Once they've cleared up the body, they'll forget about it. Same shit happened with Kaleed a few years back – remember?'

'Yeah, man, I remember.'

No, he didn't. He was lying. Lewis saw straight through it. The one thing that Lewis hated most about Reece, aside from the jokes about his abandoning mother, was that his best friend was a little bullshitter, a kiss-ass, a yes man who sucked up to him and everyone else in the E11 so that he could get involved and earn himself some recognition.

A moment of silence fell on them both as they watched cars drive past.

'You reckon we'll get more business now?' Reece asked

after a while.

'You and me?'

'Yeah.'

'Hope so, cuz. I wanna keep shotting food, man. The more food we get, more money we can make, and with Jermaine now outta the way, all the customers'll be coming to us.'

'What 'bout this Frank Graham bloke though? The one that Jermaine ratted out. He gonna be an issue?'

Lewis shrugged. Non-committal. 'We'll have to see what he does. I'm sure Henry'll have him wrapped round his finger soon enough.'

'Yeah,' Reece said. He opened his mouth as though he were about to say something else but didn't.

In the distance, the school bell rang, summoning the pupils back to their classes. Lewis darted his head towards the building. Slowly, like a retreating tide, the knots and groups of people that had been playing moments before returned.

'We going?' Reece asked.

'Nah,' Lewis replied. 'Fuck that. Can't be arsed. No one'll know I'm missing.'

Reece grunted, placed his hand in his pocket and removed a packet of cigarettes. Mayfair. The same ones Lewis had introduced him to. He flipped open the pack and offered it to Lewis. 'You want? It's my last one.'

'Yeah, go on then.'

Lewis took the cigarette and Reece, pulling a lighter from his other pocket, lit it.

As he inhaled the sweet taste of Mayfair, he asked, 'What else you got in them pockets?'

Before responding, Reece took the fag from Lewis, sucked on it a few times then kept the smoke in his lungs for a while. They'd both been smoking for several years – Lewis had forgotten the exact age they'd started – and now they'd both

31

become immune to its coarse effects on their lungs.

'You promise you ain't gonna tell?' Reece replied.

'Course.'

Reece reached into the back pocket of his school trousers and pulled something out. It was so small that his hand swallowed it completely.

'What is it?' Lewis asked.

Saying nothing, Reece fanned his hand open, revealing a switchblade. It was small, compact and the same size as a highlighter. Reece flicked the blade open and held it in the air. The light reflected off the blade's perfect edge, underlining its deadliness.

'The fuck you got one of those in school for?'

Reece shrugged. 'Just in case, innit. Jamal said I should always be strapped. You never know when one of your buyers might try something. Or when one of the East Mandela boys might try and jump us. They know our faces now, y'know.'

'Yeah, yeah,' Lewis said, nodding. 'I think you're right, mate. But hey, before I forget – my clothes are gonna stink after this. Can your mum still wash my uniform for me before I get home to my dad tonight?'

CHAPTER 5

MORNING AFTER THE NIGHT BEFORE

The vibration startled him – *bzzzz bzzzz bzzzz* – as the small device on his bedside table shook violently and moved across the surface like it had been picked up by an army of ants. Henry Matheson pinched his nose and rubbed the sleep from his eyes before rolling over and answering the call. He was in no rush. And he didn't care whether the person calling him was either. If it was important, they'd call again. And if it was more important than allowing him time to nurse the hangover that was currently splitting his head in two, then the shit really needed to have hit the fan.

'Yes?' he asked, oblivious to the caller ID. He could still taste the beer and vodka at the back of his throat – along with everything else he'd taken. He grimaced and licked his lips.

'You're a fucking idiot,' shouted the voice on the other end of the line.

'I've been called worse.' He swung his legs off the bed, slipped his feet inside the slippers that were overturned on the floor and shuffled his way to the bathroom. His free hand scratched his genitals and then pulled them over the lip of his boxers.

'What are you doing?' the voice asked.

'Trying to stop my head from pounding,' he replied as he relieved himself into the toilet bowl. 'And you're not making that any easier.'

'Where were you last night?'

Henry pulled the phone away from his ear and glanced at the caller ID. He was staring at a single letter: C. The Cabal. The man who remained elusive, a shadow, a watcher in the dark, an all-seeing, all-knowing thing ready to bring the hammer down on anyone who tried to screw him over.

'I was at a party. *My* party, with about a hundred people there. Doing what needed to be done.'

'That's part of the problem, Henry. It *didn't* need to be done, did it? And now you've left me with a big, gaping arsehole-shaped problem to fix.'

Henry grunted, shook, and then flopped his penis back into his pants. 'Last time I checked, that's what you're good at, and it ain't my problem.'

'It's very easy for me to make it your problem.'

Henry moved towards the sink and peered at himself in the mirror. His eyes were like bloodshot marbles, and his cheeks were flushed red. Christ, he looked like shit and in desperate of a shave.

'You know,' he said as he summoned a ball of phlegm from his throat and dropped it into the sink, 'you should be thanking me. I'm doing you a solid.'

'How's that?'

'That little Bic broke the rules. He suffered the consequences.'

There was a pause, followed by a brief sigh. 'Enlighten me,' The Cabal said.

'Jermaine broke promises. Stepped on my toes. Even had the audacity to find a new business partner. In doing so, he made a deal with the devil.'

'And you're the devil?'

Henry cocked his leg and let one rip, the sound echoing through his bathroom. 'I'm an angel to his entire customer base when they realise he can't supply them anymore.'

'You'd better hope so, otherwise…' The Cabal sighed again. Hesitated.

As he waited, Henry's gaze wandered about the bathroom. Last night had been a blur – a drink-fuelled night of debauchery – but one thing had stuck out to him like a stab wound to the arse: the text message notifying him that the deed had been done. In fact, there had been many deeds, but he was only interested in one. Jermaine Gordon's death. As for the others… well, there was evidence of the night's antics lying around the place. The half-opened snap bags of cocaine and ecstasy inside the bath. The copious amounts of clothing and underwear flung on the floor. He was even surprised to learn the Glock 17 wrapped in a plastic bag was still inside the toilet cistern and not on the kitchen counter like it had been the last time. The night had been fun and for many different reasons. Another legendary party hosted by another legendary man. Like the Gatsby of London—

'How are the month's figures looking?' The Cabal asked, bringing Henry's attention back to the present.

He placed the lid back on the cistern. 'Good. Strong. Very strong, in fact. But there's always room for improvement. I've got a few business meetings planned with the Hellbanianz and Turks in a few days, see what terms we can agree on.'

The Cabal scoffed. 'You make it seem like you're the bleeding CEO. Don't forget your place, Henry.'

Fuck you.

'Before you do any of that, there are a couple more things I need you to do for me,' The Cabal continued.

Henry rolled his eyes. 'Am I not doing enough?' He made

his way slowly back to the bathroom door.

'Just wait, all right. It's a big one, something I think you'll be interested in. Keep an eye on your messages. More details will follow.'

Henry hung up and stopped in the middle of the door frame. All thought of The Cabal – how much of a wanker the man was, how *he* was the CEO of the business and The Cabal was nothing more than an investor – flew out of his mind as his eyes fell on the king-size bed. Wrapped beneath the red-and-gold satin sheets was a woman, naked from the waist up. Her figure was slender, supple, the material hugging the contours of her body.

The girl stirred. A smile beamed on her face as she recognised him. His face replied in kind. And then he glanced down at the bulge in his pants.

If he thought last night was wild, then what did that mean for what was about to happen?

CHAPTER 6

WELCOME TO THE PIT

Jake and the rest of the team stepped out of their respective cars in slow motion, as though they were filming a blockbuster movie. All they needed was an explosion in the background, some high-end cars and designer clothing, and maybe some birds flying overhead, and then they'd be all set. Instead, they'd been forced to settle for Jake's Austin Mini Cooper, Darryl's Volvo and Stephanie's Fiat. Between the five of them, Jake reckoned the most expensive suit any of them was wearing was Darryl's navy one, and that was only because he was on the salary to comfortably afford it.

Jake surveyed the area; the tower blocks overhead, with laundry dangling from the windows. In the distance, he saw a group of kids kicking a ball against a brick wall. At 11:30 a.m. During school hours. On a weekday. He shook his head. Thanks to recent austerity across the country, crime and ASBO rates in the town had increased astronomically. No longer did children have anything to do outside of school hours. There were no after-school activities, no clubs, no leisure centres they could hang out at with their friends, learn a skill, develop their abilities. Instead, they were left like plastic ducks floating in a pond, waiting to be picked up and hooked into a life of crime. It was like a poison, a plague that had spread throughout the estate, and as soon as young people in there reached a certain age, it was almost guaranteed that they were going to become involved with it.

Before they were allowed to go any further, they each stepped into a forensic suit, complete with plastic booties, two pairs of gloves and a mask. Once ready, they entered from the north side, through a small underpass at the bottom of the tower block. The smell of piss, alcohol and vomit hung in the air and assaulted Jake's senses. Puddles of an indeterminate fluid dotted the pavement. Not paying attention to where he was stepping, he trod in one and splashed the liquid over his white suit.

For fuck's sake. Not only did he hate this place, but it scared him also. He had been there only once before, and he vividly remembered the sensation of feeling as though he were constantly being watched by someone, somewhere high above, standing with their face against the window, scrutinising his every move, noting his details, his features, just in case they needed a new victim. The feeling of unease and vulnerability put him on edge.

A blue-and-white police tape stretched from one end of the underpass to the other to establish the perimeter of the scene. Two uniformed officers wearing caps were stationed on the other side of the line. Darryl was first to approach them. He signed his name on the attendance log and then ducked underneath the tape. The rest of the team followed, and Jake allowed Ashley to go ahead of him.

Before he dipped beneath the tape, he gave one last look at his car stationed on the side of the road. Despite the army of officers in the streets and surrounding area, he was still concerned about what damage it would suffer. How many dust-caps would still be there when he returned? How many wheels would have been removed?

Realising there was nothing he could do about it anyway, Jake crossed the threshold into The Pit then stopped to observe his surroundings. The buildings were taller than he'd realised, more domineering, more intimidating, more claustrophobic. Like he was living in a child's Lego set, surrounded by bricks and mess.

As he stood there, he held his breath and listened to the sounds of the estate. It was a microcosm of life. Music blaring a heavy bass from one of the flats. Television sets resting against windowsills spreading the words of Jeremy Kyle and other daytime television shows. The most peculiar thing that caught his attention was the dozens of plastic soft drink bottles littering the ground, rolling in the wind. Coke. Pepsi. Fanta. Sprite.

And then Jake realised exactly why they'd been called in.

In the centre of the estate, thirty or so yards from him, was a black silhouette, dangling from the only lamp post in the vicinity. The body was charred, scorched black and white. At first, Jake thought it was a mannequin that had been hung there to scare and frighten passers-by, but the more he studied it, the more he realised that it was something much more sinister.

'Ah, Darryl, you're here!' a voice called. It came from the small army of scenes of crime officers who were in the middle of erecting a tent over the body. The weather was the worst possible threat to the preservation of evidence, and any measure that could be taken to protect against it should and would be used, regardless of the forecast. In Jake's experience, he'd found that the weather was more unpredictable than the criminals he sought to catch.

He recognised the voice as belonging to Poojah Singh, the forensic pathologist who was frequently assigned to the team.

She was petite in stature, but not in personality and drive. Known for being tenacious and fastidious in her duties, she was a hard worker and a stickler for the rules, although she was frequently described as having a unique sense of humour too, something which Jake had never experienced. And despite having worked with her on several investigations, he still didn't know exactly what she looked like. He'd only ever seen her dressed in her white forensic suit, looking like a ghost that moved rapidly around the place.

'Good morning,' Darryl said, stopping behind the red and white tape that marked the inner cordon which had been erected around the body. 'What are we dealing with?'

Poojah hesitated and turned to the victim. 'Looks like a BBQ or something went severely wrong to me. Do you think they were cooking beef or pork?'

And there it was. The humour he'd heard so much about.

'Do we have an ID on the victim?' Darryl asked, looking up at the body.

Poojah shook her head. 'We don't have a whole lot of anything at the moment. From what I can gather, you're looking at an IC3 male, late twenties, maybe early thirties.'

'How do you know the victim's male?'

Poojah's face contorted, and she looked at the rest of them, unsure whether the question was sincere or not. 'You studied biology at school, right?'

'Yeah.'

She pointed to the victim's charred penis – it looked like a sausage that'd been cooking in the oven for too long. 'Then there's your answer. But apart from that, nothing. Everything else has been decimated. There's not much skin or tissue or hair left to give us a conclusive DNA result.'

'What about clothes?' Darryl asked. 'Was he wearing any before he burnt to death?'

'There are fragments of material stuck to the victim's torso and upper body, but a lot of it perished in the blaze. As for the clothes on his bottom half… well, they were either incinerated or stolen from him before he suffered. The fire services have already found possible traces of an accelerant. Their guess would be petrol, and there are splash marks all over the concrete. So it's likely he would have been burning for some time. If I had to say, I'd suggest he's been here since the early hours the morning. I mean, this place is depraved, but it's not *that* depraved. I doubt they'd burn someone alive in broad daylight, would they?'

'Alive?' Ashley asked, the surprise coming through in her high-pitched voice.

'An unfamiliar face,' Poojah remarked. 'Who are you?'

'DC Ashley Rivers, ma'am. First day.' Ashley extended her hand, but Poojah left it, citing the risk of cross-contamination. 'Nice to meet you.'

'Likewise. But no need for the "ma'am" bit. I'm not worthy of that status yet. I hope you'll be with us for the long run.'

Poojah shot Jake an insipid glance.

'I plan to be,' Ashley replied.

'Back to your earlier question, DC Rivers, our John Doe was burnt alive. There's no evidence to suggest he was physically assaulted or maimed before he was doused in accelerant. At least, I won't find that out until I get him on the table. And even then, we might discover they poured petrol down his throat and burnt him from the inside out.'

'Bloody hell,' Brendan whispered, just within earshot. 'I've always said I'd rather be too cold than too hot.'

'What?' Darryl snapped.

Everyone looked at Brendan.

'You know, when someone asks if you'd rather be too hot or too cold. You can always add layers if you're too cold, but you can't take loads off if you're too hot. Once you're naked, that's it.'

'I don't think you should say anything else. Unless it's useful.'

'Yes, guv. Sorry, guv.' Brendan's cheeks flushed and he looked around sheepishly before quickly taking a step back to the edge of the conversation.

Darryl turned his attention back to Poojah. 'Do we know who found him like this?'

Poojah pointed to two uniformed officers speaking with a woman in her thirties at the basketball court. She was dressed in a black top and a black-and-white patterned skirt. Her hair was tied up, and her face looked heavily made-up. 'Think they're taking a witness statement from her now.'

Darryl thanked Poojah for her time and told her to let him know as soon as the post-mortem had been completed.

As they moved closer to the basketball court, Jake became aware of the jukebox of noises around the estate. Chants, cheers, laughter, a chorus of expletives and aggression drowning amongst the hundreds of random and desultory conversations. Like the low din of football supporters rolling through the streets on match day.

On the outskirts of the estate, kept back only by the territorial support group who'd been called in to help protect the scene, was a pack of civilians, stretching over the cordons, eager to have a closer look at the dead body. There seemed to be a certain excitement in the air. The bewilderment of death had landed on their doorstep, and something told Jake it was heightened because the victim wasn't one of their own.

'Excuse me, officers,' Darryl said, introducing himself, 'I'm the senior investigating officer here. Would you be able to tell me what's going on? I don't suppose we've had any other witnesses come forward, have we?'

One of the uniformed officers scoffed. 'You've gotta be joking, right? In a place like this? You've got more luck finding Osama bin Laden in one of his caves than you would finding someone in this place who'll tell you what they saw.' He spoke with a thick East London accent. Jake placed it as either Barking or West Ham. 'This one was a freak accident. She said she came here because her car broke down.'

'*She* can speak for herself,' the witness said to the officer. Then she turned to face Darryl. 'He's half right. I was on my way to a brunch with the girls, but then the warning light came on in my car, and I had to pull over. This was the only place I could find that was quiet enough.'

'And where's your car now?' Jake asked, jumping into the conversation.

'Over there.' The witness pointed to the south side of the estate. Jake peered behind Darryl and saw a black Golf parked through the underpass. 'I tried calling the AA, but I didn't get a phone signal. So I got out and that was when I saw him hanging there.'

'What time was this?'

'About ten-ish.'

'And you called the police straight away?'

The woman nodded. 'At first, I thought it was a Halloween prank, but then I realised I'm a few months out. Then the lady on the phone told me to go back to my car. She said it would be safe there.'

The irony, Jake thought – thinking she could make a getaway in a vehicle that didn't work.

Jake left the conversation at that. He knew it was a dead end, but checking out the witness would help keep Ashley busy in the afternoon of her first day.

Darryl thanked her, told her that they'd be in touch and then the group returned to the centre of the square, a few metres away from the forensic tent where a handful of SOCOs were photographing the crime scene and canine members of the fire service were busy sniffing around the place.

'Does anybody else feel like they've got a gun aimed at them from a million different angles?' Brendan asked.

'Try a million different guns. And knives. Don't forget the knives,' Stephanie replied sardonically.

'Christ, I hate this place.'

'I bet they hate you just as much,' she said.

'Wasn't expecting a personal attack this early in the morning, DI Grayson, but I can handle it. Just wait until I've had my second morning coffee.'

Stephanie chuckled, and just as she was about to open her mouth, Jake stepped in. Ever since he'd set foot in The Pit, one thought – and one name – had occupied his mind, like dog shit stuck to a carpet.

Henry Matheson. The man in charge of the estate, the gang who ran it, and the drugs that came in and out of it. It was common knowledge within the policing community that, wherever there was a gang-related crime in East London, Henry Matheson was, in some way or another, connected to it. Equipped with an army of dealers, and an even bigger army of solicitors who'd managed to keep him out of jail more times than Jake'd had a good night's sleep, the man was infamous for being the biggest drug dealer this side of the Houses of Parliament. The only problem was, he distanced himself so far from the crimes and logistics of it all that nobody in the force had been able to pin anything on him.

'You reckon?' Darryl replied after Jake had finished explaining his theory.

'I mean, this doesn't look like your average gang killing. It's not a stabbing or a shooting. It's a highly organised and calculated crime. There's no way your average runner could have done this. Not without some specialist help. Nor without Matheson's approval.' Jake scratched the side of his face. 'Maybe this time we'll be able to put him away for something.'

'First time for everything,' Ashley added with a smile that implied she thought she was helping.

'And there are also some things that are impossible,' Stephanie remarked. She placed her hands on her hips and turned to Jake. 'Seems like a bit of a stretch to suggest he's behind it considering we don't know anything yet.'

'You got a better idea?'

Darryl intervened before things got heated. 'I think it's a good place to start. Perhaps we can bring him in voluntarily.'

'Assuming we can find him,' Jake said.

'If he's got nothing to hide, then he should be easy to locate. I'll make a couple of calls.' Darryl turned his back on them and wandered a few paces in the opposite direction, holding his phone to his ear. He returned a minute later. 'Turns out Henry's just been brought in.'

'Already?' Stephanie asked. 'What for?'

'Not sure, but they found him shopping with his sister. Jake, you've dealt with Henry in the past, haven't you?'

Jake shrugged. 'Not him directly. Jermaine Gordon, yes. But not Henry.'

'You've more experience than the rest of us. I want you to lead and, Stephanie, I want you to sit in with him. Once we've got back to the station, Brendan, I want you to arrange house-to-house enquiries. Ask the residents what they were doing between eleven p.m. and six a.m.'

With everyone aware of their tasks, the team filtered out of the estate. As they passed the forensic tent, something caught Jake's eye. It was a small metal object. Square, with a smaller cut-out in the centre. He approached and inspected it.

It was a belt buckle.

He didn't know why, but it struck him as important.

'Poojah!' Jake called, rushing to the tent's door.

The pathologist appeared a few seconds later. 'What do

you want?'

'There's something over there. On the ground. I thought it might be important.' Jake pointed to the item.

'It might be the victim's clothing,' she said dismissively.

'Or it could be the murder weapon?'

She sniggered. 'Death by belt buckle lashing?'

Jake didn't want her to disregard the piece so quickly but knew that if she did, it would be out of spite, rather than any malfeasance or misconduct. Ever since Liam Greene, Jake's former boss, had been arrested for corruption and murder, and sent to prison, Poojah had treated Jake with hostility and disdain. Liam and Poojah had been close friends, and their friendship had been ripped apart by him. For that, he assumed, she would never forgive him.

Poojah sighed and rolled her eyes. 'Natalie – evidence bag. And bring a pen.'

A few seconds later, another SOCO arrived, her features hidden behind the white suit. In her hand, she held a clear evidence bag. She bent down, picked the object up and placed it in the bag.

'NB-180,' Natalie said, scribbling the number on the bag's front.

'Add it to the evidence log,' Poojah instructed and started away from Jake.

'Hey!' he said, holding her back with his arm. 'I think we should have a chat.'

'I'm working.'

'It'll only take a minute.' Jake ushered her to the side, away from the action.

'Listen,' he began, clueless about what to say and where to run with it. 'Everything that happened with Liam and Drew... I never wanted it to happen like that. But I was... I was doing my job. And you know yourself that what they were doing was wrong.'

'I don't care about that,' Poojah said, brushing it away with her hand as though it were a fly. 'I'm more pissed about the aftermath. I miss Liam, I really do. But do you know how many times I've had to try and defend myself and my team to prove that we're not bent as well? I had my entire history looked into. Everything about me. My finances. My messages. My relationships. Everything was investigated. It was a personal attack. And do you know who sanctioned it?'

Jake didn't respond. Poojah looked over his shoulder and gestured with her head.

'Stephanie. Your new *super* inspector.'

'She was just doing her job.'

'Really? You should have seen some of the things she was doing… what she was trying to accuse me of.'

'What do you mean?' Jake asked.

Poojah leant closer. 'All I'm saying is, you should keep an eye on her. And that new girl, Ashley – where did she come from all of a sudden? First day, as soon as you've got one of the biggest gang murders this city has ever seen? Watch yourself, Jake. I've started doing the same.'

With that, his thoughts racing around his head, Jake returned to his car, where Ashley was patiently waiting for him.

'All good?' she asked.

'Perfect,' Jake replied, kicking a soft drink bottle away. He unlocked the car.

'I can't believe all of this,' she said as she gazed up at the tower block.

'What did I tell you? Welcome to The Pit.'

CHAPTER 7

NIGHTMARE

The pounding in his head was reminiscent of the music they'd been listening to the night before. Unending, relentless, heavy and loud.

'Fresh air's supposed to do you some good,' Danielle, his sister, told him, with that smug smile on her face as usual. 'It's better than lounging in bed all day feeling sorry for yourself.'

Said the eighteen-year-old who had never experienced a proper hangover.

'You're annoyingly perky,' Henry said as they stepped out of the car. 'Did you drink much?'

Danielle shook her head. 'Some of us have got things to revise for. Exams to sit. I don't fancy killing all my brain cells with drink like you do. Suppose it helps when you don't have any to start with in the first place.'

Touché.

He wasn't in the mood to disagree with her. The reasons were twofold. One, his mind was still running a few minutes behind, so any quick wit and sarcasm he had left had practically substituted themselves off the pitch and onto the bench. And two, because he would lose the battle with her. It was a given; had been ever since her introduction into the world. As soon as she'd been brought home from the hospital, he'd known he would lose any argument with her. Abiding by the rules of brotherhood and family, she was his world, and he'd do anything for her. And so, when she'd asked him to take her into Stratford City Centre for some shopping, he'd agreed.

'You need uni supplies or something?' he asked, preparing himself to flex his wallet for the ridiculously expensive and overpriced stationery whose most prominent market was people who couldn't afford it.

'Just some folders and notebooks.'

'You run out already? Swear I bought your last set a few weeks ago.'

Danielle shrugged. 'I make a lot of notes.'

'Not the same type as the ones I make. And not nearly as many.' He patted the bulge in his jogging bottoms pocket.

Danielle nudged him in the ribs, and together they entered the small shopping centre in the heart of Stratford. It consisted of roughly thirteen shops, all of which catered to the working class. None of them were the high-end designer stores he was looking for. If he wanted those types of outlets, he was going to have to venture further into the heart of London. And for a man of his stature and notoriety, that was a risky enterprise. His name was on the lips of half of London's neighbouring gang members, which meant a peaceful life outside of Stratford was almost impossible. But with the new multi-million-pound shopping centre, Westfield, opening in a few months, he would be able to spend his money freely without being stabbed.

'What about this one?' Henry asked incessantly, pointing at the various folders, notebooks and assorted pens on the shelves of WHSmith.

Each time, Danielle shoved him and gave him the middle finger. Books and education had never been his thing. The only part of the education system he'd excelled at was maths, and that was only so he was able to calculate the minimum street value of a kilogram of his cocaine as soon as it filtered through the estates and the streets. Apart from that, his mental arithmetic only stretched to working out how much change he'd get from a monkey if he bought a bottle of Grey Goose in the club. The answer was just south of a few quid.

After they'd finished in the stationery store, and after Henry was done paying, they headed towards the exit. Way off in the distance, through the doors at the end of the promenade, was the skeleton of Westfield. Networks of pipes, scaffolding and cranes hugged the side of the building, while small dots of black and yellow flitted around as they set to work on construction, like bumblebees busying themselves on the hive.

Henry felt his excitement bubbling. 'I can't wait for it to open, man,' he said. 'Think of all the things we can buy. The things I can buy you.'

Danielle kissed her teeth. 'And you wonder why you ain't got a girlfriend yet.'

'What you chatting about?'

'Buying things for everyone all the time. You ain't ever gonna get a decent girl like that. She'll be after your money and that's it.'

'Shows what you know. I met a girl last night. She stayed over after the party.' Henry felt his phone vibrate. He checked it and flashed the screen to her. 'That's her now, in fact.'

Danielle leant forward and inspected the screen. 'Lily? As in Lily Ashby?'

'Yeah.'

'Stay away from her, Henry. I heard bad things about her.

Some of the boys on my course said she sleeps around a lot. And she got the clap, swear down.'

Henry chuckled and pocketed his phone. His sister's maternal instinct was sweet but misguided. 'You sound like Mum. Making stuff up when it comes to girls. You know that stuff ain't true. Some boy that she rejected started spreading shit about her – and he was the one who had the clap in the first place.'

In some circles of the E11, chlamydia was as prevalent as the AIDS passed from junky to junky as they exchanged needles and shared the love. Old news. And Henry was certain he'd had it at least once in his life. Still wouldn't visit a doctor, though.

Danielle rolled her eyes and gently tutted. 'Just make sure she ain't after you for the money though.'

'Yes, Mum. Sorry, Mum.' Henry smiled and wrapped his arm around her playfully. 'So what we doing with all these then?' He pointed at the bags of shopping he'd just bought for her. 'You paying me back monthly or you wanna do it all in one go?'

Danielle tilted her head to the side and gave him the puppy-dog eyes. 'You know I can't afford it yet.'

'You know where you can earn yourself some pocket money though. I keep telling you.'

They reached the exit and came to a gradual stop. A figure emerged from behind a telephone box a few feet from them and appeared in the corner of Henry's eye. As soon as Henry recognised him, he shoved Danielle aside and faced the assailant, a smug smile growing on his face.

'You lost, little puppy?'

Charging towards him was Errol Grant, a dweeby kid whose impression of himself was larger than reality. Small-man syndrome, bigger ego than he could handle, that type of thing.

As soon as he was within reaching distance, Errol grabbed Henry by the jumper, then pushed him across the pavement and into the side of the building.

'You're a brave man showing your face right now,' Errol hissed. His face was hidden behind a cap, and a hood was pulled over his head. Henry couldn't see it, nor could he feel it, but he was certain the young man was holding a switchblade against his abdomen. The leftover alcohol in his system was severely impacting his reaction times.

'Get off him!' Danielle said as she started over.

Henry held out a hand and placated her. He wasn't worried. Everything was under control.

'You look lost to me, little puppy,' he said to Errol.

'You'll pay for what you done.'

'Even more so without your little owner pulling the leash,' Henry continued, 'yanking your meat every time you did something good.'

Errol made a little movement, and now Henry was certain there was a knife digging into his stomach. The tip of the blade pierced his coat and scraped against his skin. It wasn't a searing pain but felt more like a pinch. Nothing major. Yet.

'Word of advice,' he told Errol. 'When you decide to come up against the big dogs, you better come prepared.'

'You what?'

'Did you think I didn't know this would happen? That you lot would come over and try and size me up for yourselves? I ain't dumb. There's a reason Jermaine's dead and I ain't.'

Henry paused. A scene was forming around them, a dense wall of confused and concerned faces looking on. 'You're attracting unwanted attention. People have seen your face. People have seen mine. Anything happens to me, a lot worse will happen to you. So why don't you put that little prick down and we can talk about this properly? Sometimes there's

52

a far greater power in our words than in our actions.'

Errol's body was shaking. Henry didn't know the kid's age, but he couldn't have been much older than fifteen. By that age, Henry had already stabbed more people than he had fingers on his hand and established the E11 as a terrifying and formidable movement. But Errol was a rookie, inexperienced. The shaking hands, the heavy breathing, the wild eyes. A boy, not a man.

But there was promise.

'What they teaching you over there?' Henry asked as he shook his head derisively and grabbed the knife. 'Put it away and don't take it out again.'

Errol did as he was told.

'Everything's fine,' he proclaimed to the onlookers, who were clutching their bags close to their bodies and videoing them on their camera phones. 'Ain't nothing to see. You can all go back to what you were doing.'

Reluctantly, and after a little while, normality was restored, and their little run-in had been forgotten about as everyone disappeared and resumed their everyday lives.

'I have a proposition for you,' Henry said, one arm wrapped around Errol's shoulders while the other linked with Danielle's. 'And I want you to think about it before you make your mind up. Without Jermaine anymore, you're gonna need a boss and a supplier to keep your customers happy. How about I be your boss and you come work for me.' Henry posed it as a statement rather than a question, even though he intended on giving the boy time to think.

Errol opened his mouth, but Henry quickly shut him down. 'Like I said. Think about it. Ain't nothing gonna happen to you, promise. I make sure all my boys are well looked after. And I got different contacts than what Jermaine had so I can keep you safe from any heat. Trust me on that one.'

As soon as they reached the end of the road, Henry felt his senses – and his alertness – return in droves. But not for the right reasons. Just as the three of them were about to step off the pavement and onto the tarmac, two liveried police cars pulled in front of them and skidded to a halt. Before he had time to react, four uniformed officers raced towards them. Instinctively, Henry held his hands in the air. Two officers raced towards him, grabbed his hands and thrust them behind his back, while the other two grabbed Errol.

'I am arresting you on suspicion of possession of an offensive weapon. You do not have to say anything, but it may harm your defence if you do not mention when questioned something which you later rely on in court. Anything you do say may be given in evidence.'

'You what?' Henry said as they ushered him towards the back of the nearest uniformed police car.

And then it dawned on him. One of the people in the crowd – one of the Good Samaritans – must have called the police as soon as they'd seen the scuffle outside the centre. Maybe they'd even seen Errol's blade. Which meant…

'Get off me!' Errol's screams pierced the air as he was pinned against the side of the police car and arrested. He tried to kick his way out of it, but it was no use. The police outweighed him tenfold.

Shit.

'Hey, kid!' Henry called as his head was forced beneath the car roof. 'Remember what I told you. Just… leave it with —'

The car door slammed in Henry's face. He kicked the underside of the seat in front of him. Shit. What had been a happy and enjoyable morning was turning into a nightmare.

CHAPTER 8

INSTRUCTIONS

Martin Radcliffe tilted his head to the side and gazed out of the window, trying to do everything possible to delay the inevitable: work. He was a member of the Flying Squad – or The Sweeney, as the hit seventies show had popularised it – and was one of the latest additions to the team, having joined nine months earlier. He liked to say he'd worked his way up the ladder, but that was a lie. Instead, it was a classic case of who you knew, not what you knew.

Alongside him in the corner of the office was an even fresher support officer busy doing all of Martin's work for him. Breaking him in, teaching the ropes – all that sort of stuff. Martin glanced at him, made sure that he was keeping his head down and not giving him any unwanted attention or side glances, then returned to the window. To the cyclists weaving their way in and out of traffic, at the pedestrians displaying a severe lack of personal and spatial awareness as they stepped out onto the road and narrowly avoided becoming a stain on the pavement. *Idiots*. Natural selection at its finest.

His phone vibrated, distracting him from the outside world. A *Kingdom of Empires* notification had just come through.

The only person he knew that communicated via the online game was The Cabal – his benefactor, the one responsible for getting him into this role and position. The one operating everything from behind the scenes. The one who gave him the orders, the one who dictated everything he did, who he spoke to. The Cabal controlled every aspect of his professional life. And he loved it.

Martin stared at the notification a while longer before clutching the phone tightly in his grip and heading out of the building. He needed a cigarette for this.

As he exited, he rounded the side of the building and idled to the smoking area – a small brick wall near a set of bike sheds. A couple of officers in plainclothes whom Martin recognised stood chatting.

Here we go, thought Martin. Bring on the bullshit small talk.

'All right, Mart?' Alain Greenway asked, his yellow-stained fingers shaking inches from his face.

'All right?' Martin said, nodding in Alain's direction as a courtesy more than an invitation to talk further.

'What do you think about this?' Alain began. Beside him was Rebecca Gould, a small woman with a round face that made her look five years younger than her actual age.

'What's that?' Martin asked, trying to mask the disdain in his voice.

'I was just saying to Becks here, don't you think it's a ball-ache we have to wear these body cams everywhere we go now? Especially when they record *everything* we do.'

Martin shrugged, pulled out a cigarette and sparked up. 'Does it matter what I think? Won't change anything.'

'What's got up your arse this morning?' Rebecca asked.

'Am I not allowed to enjoy my cigarette in peace?'

'Of course you can, Your Royal Highness,' Alain said, then pointed at Martin's cigarette. 'Fetch me once you're done – I'll clear the ashes away from your ego if you'd like.'

Martin shot them the middle finger and turned his attention back to his devious and decadent stick of death. The tobacco tasted delicate as it descended his lungs, delicious, like he was drinking from the neck of a bottle. So good that it almost felt like a reward for sinning.

After a few even more rewarding seconds of silence, Alain and Rebecca wandered away, bowing courteously as they went. He stopped paying attention to them. They were nothing. Part-timers. A means to an end in the office. They were part of the large-scale corruption in the service and they didn't even know it. He was aware that his personality – the abrasiveness, the belligerence – along with his close relationship with the governor were the reasons his colleagues seldom spoke to him in the office. But did he care? No. Would he change? Fuck no. Would his behaviour and attitude to his colleagues change anything? No, his job was safe and would be until he was moved on.

Once they were both out of sight, Martin unlocked his phone and opened the *Kingdom of Empires* notification. The online role-playing game opened on the messaging platform, and at the top of the inbox was a message from LG23867 with a red number one beside it.

He inhaled deeply, held it there, contemplated what the message contained and conjured the courage to open it.

Problem in The Pit. Jermaine Gordon. Stratford MIT. Belt buckle locked up in evidence. Bow Green. Evidence number NB-180. Dispose of it. ASAP. Await further instruction, carry on business as usual.

Martin finished reading the message. A paralysing sensation of excitement knotted around his organs. Fantastic. He'd been given a different type of task to do. An opportunity to prove himself capable of something new. To show he was up to the challenge. To remove any qualms the governor might have poisoned The Cabal's mind with.

That bitch.

He could do this. Of course he could. It was no small feat by any means, breaking into a secure laboratory and stealing a significant piece of evidence, but it wasn't impossible.

And Martin revelled in those types of challenges.

He drafted a response, typed it, hit send.

Consider it done.

CHAPTER 9

A DIFFERENT RUPERT

The interview room was possibly one of the most boring rooms Henry had ever had the pleasure of sitting in. And in his time, he'd been in several. In his head he kept a scoresheet of all the rooms, all the stations, all the officers interviewing him, marking them off against one another. So far, this was turning out to be the lowest ranked.

There was no character to it, no personality, no history. A lot could be gathered from sitting inside the confines of four walls, he'd realised. Just think what type of people had been sitting in the same seat as him. Murderers. Rapists. Paedophiles. Burglars. Drug dealers. They all had a past, they all had personalities, they all had histories. But there was nothing to let him know that it was there.

One of his favourites was a small interview room in West Ham's police station, most notably because a hole had been kicked in the wall, and rumour was that to this day, it was still there, serving as a piece of art, a legacy left behind for criminals old and new to enjoy. And the best part was that it hadn't been your usual suspect – it wasn't your average murderer or rapist; instead, it was a schoolboy who'd been caught selling drugs to people twice his age. That boy's name was Deshawn, and he was one of Henry's best recruits.

The door opened, and a man and woman entered. Henry recognised one of them instantly; the other he was going to have to get to know. They pulled their chairs from beneath the table and sat opposite. Shuffled papers on the desk. Opened to the newest pages in their notebooks. Took a sip of water.

They introduced themselves.

Detective Constable Jake Tanner.

Detective Inspector Stephanie Grayson.

Thing one and thing two.

Chalk and cheese.

They both looked the same yet also wildly different in so many respects.

The clock on the wall told him it was nearly 2 p.m. He'd already lost track of how long he'd been in there. Time was irrelevant when he had no grasp of how quickly it was moving. After his arrest, he'd been stripped, searched, and soon absolved of being in possession of an offensive article. It wasn't until he was about to leave that one of the officers in a suit had ventured down and asked him to accompany them for a voluntary interview regarding an investigation they were looking into at the Cosgrove Estate. Voluntary or not, Henry had decided that offering a helping hand was the best thing for him.

Sitting beside him was a woman he knew only by name. Veronica Bateman. His stand-in solicitor, covering for his regular Rupert Haversham, the fifty-something lawyer who'd saved Henry's arse more times than he'd woken up next to a random girl the morning after. She was in her early sixties and wore a navy-blue dress that reached her ankles, with a black blazer wrapped around her shoulders. When he'd first met her, she'd held a handbag at arm's length that dangled by her legs, and she had this air of intimidation and hostility about her that suggested she wasn't ready to take anything from anybody. From that point onwards, he'd known he was in safe hands.

'Shall we begin?' she asked. 'I'm sure we've all got things we'd rather be doing.'

Henry liked her already.

'Yes,' Jake said after beginning the recording and completing the banal formalities. He pulled out a photograph of a burnt body dangling from a lamp post. Henry's handiwork. Spotted in the wild.

'Do you know anything about this incident, Henry? This man was found dead this morning in the middle of the Cosgrove Estate. Hanging. Burnt—'

'Yes, my client can see from the picture, thanks,' Veronica snapped. 'What's this got to do with my client?'

'We believe Henry may have vital information regarding this man's brutal death,' Stephanie said, brave enough to take the reins.

'My client denies having any involvement.'

'We didn't say he was involved,' the detective constable stepped in.

'That's what you're insinuating.'

A brief moment of silence fell over them. The two detectives were rattled, on the ropes, like a football team who'd bottled the last match of the season. And they were only on their first question. Henry pitied the life of Veronica's husband, and children. Must be absolute torture living with a pernicious woman like that, he thought. In a strange way, he found it attractive.

One nil.

'This is your interview, Henry,' Stephanie said, making it obvious that she was trying hard to ignore Veronica's imperious scowl. 'You can answer for yourself.'

Henry pointed to Veronica. 'What she said.'

'Where were you last night?' Stephanie asked.

'Be more specific, Detective,' Veronica replied.

Two nil.

At this rate, he wouldn't have to say anything at all.

Stephanie sighed and glanced at her partner. 'Where were you late last night and early this morning – between eleven p.m. and six a.m.?'

Veronica opened her mouth to speak, but he cut her off.

'At a party,' he replied, deciding that he wanted to have a little fun of his own.

'Whose?'

'Mine.'

'Who was there?'

'Me.'

'And who else?'

'A hundred people or so. I don't know the exact headcount. I was drunk for most of it.'

'Can you give us any names?'

'Sure. Mike. Dan. Steve. Clive. James.'

'Surnames?'

'Oh, sorry, you asked for names. I was just giving you some.'

Jake looked at him, unimpressed. 'We meant names of the people at the party.'

'Should've been clearer, then. But, no, I can't. It was a constant blur kind of night.'

Fucking with the police, in as many ways as possible, was his biggest form of excitement and gratification. Knowing that he was better than them. That he was the biggest seller of class A, B and C drugs in the whole of East London and there was nothing they could do about it. That his business growth and customer base was now expected to double with that little shit Jermaine Gordon finally out of the way. That they didn't have a scrap of evidence to prove he was the one responsible for it.

Henry one, police nil.

He leant forward and pointed at the graphic image. 'Must have been horrible.'

'Being burnt to death?' Jake spoke with venom in his voice. 'I can't imagine he enjoyed it.'

'Do *you* think he enjoyed it, Detective? Do you think there was a part of him that liked what was happening to him?'

'You mean, do I think he was a masochist?'

'Oh my God, you think he was a pervert?'

'No,' Jake said, scrambling to get his words out. 'That's not what I'm saying at all. I… I'll be the one asking questions here, thank you.'

Three nil.

'Do you think he deserved it?' Henry asked. 'I mean, someone who gets burnt alive, especially a man of his stature, must have done something pretty naughty to end up like that.'

Silence.

'Are you saying you know the identity of this individual?'

'No.'

'Are you saying you know what happened?'

Henry shrugged. 'You hear things. You learn things. You pick things up.'

'Do you have any solid evidence against my client?' Veronica asked, jumping in to add some final humiliating blows.

'This was just a voluntary interview, Veronica,' Stephanie responded, her attempt at being authoritative transparent and facetious.

'Well, then, if you've nothing more to add, I think we'll be getting out of here.'

There was a pause. Nobody said anything.

'Perfect. Goodbye.'

And the crowd goes wild. Four nil. The biggest defeat in the establishment's history.

Veronica grabbed her things and left. Henry followed her out of the room and out of the building, feeling the same excitement a child feels when he sets foot in an amusement park for the first time. He suppressed the urge to brandish his middle fingers in the air and point them at the officers as he trundled past them. No point adding fuel to the fire; after that interview, he was more than certain they'd be bringing heat of their own.

Emerging into the light, he made his way to the bottom of the steps then asked, 'Where's Rupert? I was expecting him instead of you.'

Veronica stopped and swivelled on the spot. 'Away.'

'Dead?'

'No. Away.'

Henry appraised her. 'Couldn't take me home, could you? Usually, Rupert drops me off at the estate. You know, all part of the service.'

'I'm not Rupert.'

'I know. Don't worry though, I'll let you off this time.'

Veronica lunged at him, covering the two-metre gap between them with ease, and pointed her finger at his chest, hovering it centimetres away from his ribcage.

'Don't think I'll give you the same treatment as him. You're sadly mistaken if you think that's the case. What was that in there?'

It wasn't until she was right in his face that he noticed her breath smelt of old coffee from earlier in the day. He grimaced and tried to coincide her breathing with his.

'I pay your wages,' he said. He wasn't used to somebody talking to him like that, especially when it was someone he relied on so heavily.

'You're not the only one. I have a lot of other clients in similar positions to you.'

'None of your clients are like me. If there's anything you want, I can get my hands on it. I know what you lawyers are like. Little bit of coke here and there, some baggies of weed after a long hard day. It's cool, your secret's safe with me. But if you want anything, all you have to do is ask, and all I expect in return is some good, solid, sound legal advice.'

'And what about now, eh? Will you pay me double for wasting my time? Or only half because I didn't offer you any "good, solid, sound legal advice"?'

'It wasn't a waste of time.'

'Yes, it was. You knew you had nothing to prove, but you decided to string them along anyway.'

'I saw it as a productive meeting,' Henry said.

He waited for Veronica to ask him to develop his theory, but when she didn't, he continued. 'I learnt who I'm dealing with, and I also learnt that they know fuck all about what happened to Jermaine. And I intend to keep it that way for as long as possible. I'm untouchable in this part of the world. But there're still some who wanna challenge my rule. And now I know that the police have no evidence or information against me, I can make sure my status stays that way, and make sure that I send out a message to those who do want to try and expel me.'

'How are you going to do that?' Veronica asked, lowering her finger.

'You'll have to wait and see, Veronica. Just be ready for the call when you receive it. And before you go, one more thing: there's a kid in there, Errol Grant. Poor bastard got arrested with me. Couldn't do me a massive solid and get him out of there for me, could you? I sort of promised him I would.'

CHAPTER 10

INTO THE WASPS' NEST

Jake was pissed and humiliated. Not just because Henry Matheson had somehow managed to pull their trousers down and bend them over, but because Stephanie had faltered. She'd thrown the interview, stuttered, shown their hand too soon, given away the fact they had no idea what they were doing. She'd made them look incompetent. Jake slammed the folder onto his desk, scattering other sheets of paper and expense receipts onto the floor.

'Went well then?' Brendan asked as he leant forward and picked up the receipts for him.

Jake was still getting used to someone occupying Drew Richmond's former seat. It should have been easy to see a new face every morning, except it wasn't. And every time he looked his new colleague in the eyes, he was constantly reminded of Drew.

The bent copper.

The rapist.

'What happened?' The question came from Darryl, standing in the doorway of his office, one hand in his trouser pocket, the other holding a wad of documents. He looked set for a top-brass meeting somewhere.

'Nothing,' Jake replied. 'That's the problem. Matheson's protesting his innocence, and he's got an alibi.'

'Which is?'

'House party. Hundred people or so there apparently.'

'Is it worth checking out?'

'We can try, but there's not much point, guv,' Stephanie answered for him. 'Waste of time and resources. I would guess that he set that party up on the same night as the murder to give us a deluge of witness statements to get through. And we've already got everyone we can spare conducting house-to-house enquiries in The Pit as it is. Majority of them are already reporting a series of blank walls with everyone they're speaking to.'

'Even if there was no house party,' Jake added, 'whoever lives on that estate will say there was one. Matheson's followers are like loyal little dogs but not the cute kind; the yappy little shit kind. And I don't think they're about to betray him quite so quickly.' Jake tilted back in his chair and placed one leg over the other. 'Has there been any update since we've been gone?'

'Not much,' Ashley responded. She was sitting in the corner of the room, at the desk furthest from Jake. In Pete Garrison's old chair, which still smelt of him, and worse, she appeared to share the same proclivities for a sneaky digestive snack, judging by the half-eaten mulch on her desk.

'We checked out the witness who made the nine nine nine call and she was clean. There's nothing suggesting she's had any connection with anyone in the Cosgrove Estate. She's a nurse, mum of three – nine, fifteen, eighteen – and lives in Waltham Forest.'

'Mums and nurses can be drugs addicts too, you know,' Jake remarked.

'Capable of death by immolation? I don't think so.'

'It's always the ones you least expect,' Brendan murmured, though no one paid his comment any heed. Except Jake – he'd thought the same after he'd found out that his closest friend in the service – Danika Oblak – had secretly been working for The Cabal while funding her own drug and drink habit on the side. He'd felt the bitter sting of betrayal then, and he was gradually becoming immune to its venom.

Jake turned his attention to the conversation again. 'Did the witness's alibi check out?'

Ashley nodded. 'On her witness statement, uniform made a note of the restaurant. I called and they confirmed there was a booking under that name. Apparently, her friends didn't hang around that long.'

Jake sighed heavily, retrieved the receipts from Brendan and dropped them clumsily onto the table. It was the early stages of the investigation, but everyone in the room knew that they were the most crucial. For every hour beyond the first twenty-four, their chances of catching the person, or people, responsible evaporated almost exponentially.

Jake placed his hands on his desk, considering the options and possibilities. The bleak outlook on it was there were none. They had a person that had been burnt to death in the middle of a busy council estate, surrounded by hundreds of people, none of whom were willing to talk nor even admit that they saw anything. In addition, there was very little evidence to go on. Not to mention their biggest suspect was a criminal mastermind who had enough money and power to buy his way out of any conviction.

The Cosgrove Estate was a nest of secrets. Henry Matheson was the queen, and the others inside were the workers prepared to do anything to protect him. The only way to drive the wasp out of its nest was with fire. And Jake had the perfect thing in mind.

'Surveillance,' he said, the idea slapping him in the face. 'We need to conduct surveillance on The Pit.'

'Not a chance,' Darryl said sharply. 'You know how much overtime that is?'

'A justifiable amount surely?'

'Don't call him Shirley,' Brendan added, but now wasn't the time. Everyone in the office let him know their thoughts on the comment by sending him a stern glare.

'I'm sorry, Jake, but no,' Darryl continued. 'The budget won't cover it. And Assistant Commissioner Candy has been on my case about expenses and budgets and spending recently. This is one of the areas he wants to control tightly. It seems that our previous members of the team, who shall remain nameless, took several liberties when it came to expenses. He wants to keep a lid on it all as much as he can.'

'So he'd rather keep his wallet tight than put Henry Matheson where he deserves to be?'

'It's above my head, Jake. And if anything gets by on the sly it'll be *on* my head like a shit ton of shitty bricks.'

Jake opened his mouth to speak but no words came out. A picture painted a thousand words, and in this instance, he could see a thousand tiny daggers of injustice, each of them heading straight towards him, prodding, prodding, prodding.

'Listen,' Darryl began, 'you've all got things you could be doing in the meantime while we're waiting for the DNA and pathology reports. So you don't have any need to be standing around with your thumbs up your arses. Plenty to be doing, plenty to be enquiring about. Now if you'll excuse me, I have a meeting with the assistant commissioner I need to prepare for. Oh, and, Steph, sorry it's late notice, but I'm going to have to ask you to stay back tonight and continue with this while the rest of us are at the ceremony.'

Darryl turned his back on the team and disappeared

behind his office door, leaving them in a stunned stupor.

'Right,' Brendan said, leaning back on his chair. 'Where does that leave us?'

'With your thumb out your arse for starters. But it also means we have to follow the guv's orders. Even if we don't like them,' Stephanie explained, speaking to Brendan but indirectly talking to Jake. She knew what he was like. Disobedient. That he would do what he thought was right because, well… he thought it was right.

And that was the only justification he needed.

'Whatever you say,' Jake retorted.

'Jake, no.'

'What do you want me to do? I'm not allowed to do anything anyway,' he snapped back. 'We'll just have to leave it. Make it look as though we don't give a shit. But I suppose it's OK, because this is a gang-related crime in The Pit, and those are almost instantly forgotten about. So we've done well to get this far.'

Most of the crimes in The Pit, stretching as far back as the new millennium, were still outstanding, pushed to the bottom of the to-do list, and very few had actually been solved. Mostly out of sheer luck than any form of hard police work. There was an epidemic going on inside there, and the people within the Cosgrove Estate needed police support. If they were ever going to stand a chance of building a sustainable and suitable environment for individuals to thrive and develop, something was going to have to change.

'I've got to go,' he said. 'I'll see you all at the ceremony.'

Jake grabbed his things, waved goodbye to everyone and headed home where Elizabeth was waiting for him.

It was time to stick his hand into the wasp's nest and hope for the best.

CHAPTER 11

THE WASHING

'Reece!' his mum called from downstairs, loud enough to reach Lewis on the other side of the estate. 'Have you put the wash on yet?'

No, was the answer. He hadn't. Couldn't be bothered. He had better things to do. Like play *Call of Duty* with his friends. Like watch television. Like wander around the streets, shotting some food to his customers. Anywhere was better than being inside, having to listen to his mum nag him every three seconds.

'Reece!'

'For fuck's sake,' he whispered under his breath as he rolled his legs off the side of the bed. 'What?' he called down the stairs.

'Did you put the wash on?'

'Yeah,' he said, already returning to his room.

'Don't lie to me.'

He stopped in the door frame, sighed, dropped his shoulders and sulked down the stairs, making a U-turn at the bottom of the staircase and then wandering into the kitchen.

Their council flat in the estate was small, narrow and old. Everything he wasn't. The building felt as though it was made out of wood – everything creaked underfoot – and Reece hated it. Hated living there. He saw the sorts of places that Henry and Deshawn and Jamal lived in, the nice furniture, the expensive flat-screen televisions hanging on the wall, the designer gear that accompanied them wherever they went, and he wanted a piece of that life. There were probably words he didn't know that would describe the types of houses they owned, but what he did know was how to get to the top of the food chain.

The oven was roasting his favourite meal: potato waffles, egg and beans. Meanwhile, his mum was in the living room, watching the latest episode of *Countdown*, pretending to be intelligent enough to provide answers for each round, when she could barely complete his homework for him.

Reece wandered up to the washing machine, placed the load in the drum, filled the container with the conditioner and washing powder. He waited until he heard the lock mechanism click into place, then started the machine, before putting the wash basket away in the cupboard under the stairs.

As he headed back to his room, his mum called him.

'Oi!' she said, looking at him through the living room doorway. She wagged her finger at him and beckoned him in. 'How was school?'

'All right,' he lied. He and Lewis had decided they would spend the rest of the day together, roaming the streets, dealing whatever food Jamal and the rest of the elders had given them, and any extras they'd picked up at the phone boxes.

On the menu today, ladies and gents, we have a nice selection of diet cocaine and chips, marijuana salad, and our house favourite – heroin soup.

'You lying to me?' his mum asked.

'No, Mum.'

'You better not be.'

'I ain't, Mum.'

'What lessons did you have?'

'Geography. Maths. English. All the big ones.'

His mum perched herself on the edge of the sofa, looking as if she were ready to bend him over one knee and hit him where it hurt most.

'That's funny,' she said, her voice cool, 'because the school called and wondered why they couldn't find you after second period. Do you know why that might be?'

Reece kissed his teeth and shook his head.

'You better stop lying to me. I'll ask you again. Where were you?'

Reece said nothing. His mum afforded him no time to come up with an elaborate backstory.

'Where were you?'

'With Lewis.'

'Where?'

'Just around.'

'What were you doing?'

'Just chilling, innit.'

'Who else were you with?'

'Nobody, Mum. It was just us two.'

'You been hanging with those boys again?'

'No, Mum.'

'Why didn't you go to school? Someone bullying you?'

'Pfft. No. Nobody's bullying me. Nobody'd even try.'

'Then why didn't you go to school today?'

'Because it's shit.'

'Don't you dare swear in front of me!'

Reece censored himself.

'It's a waste of time.'

'I don't care. You need to go. How else do you think you're going to get a good job and become successful? You need to learn. You won't appreciate it now, but when you're older you will.'

'Then why don't I just do it when I'm older?'

She scoffed, shook her head. 'Because by then it'll be too late. Now go to your room – and no Xbox. Give me your controller.'

Reece groaned, sulked out of the room and climbed the steps before idling to his bedroom, grabbing his video game controller and returning downstairs. One day he wouldn't have to listen to her. One day he'd be able to do whatever he wanted. And nobody would be able to tell him otherwise.

If only that day would hurry up.

'Promise me you'll go to school tomorrow,' his mum said as he handed her the controller.

'Yes, Mum.'

'No, I said promise me.'

Reece rolled his eyes. 'I promise you I'll go to school tomorrow.'

'And what else?'

'I love you.'

'Good boy. Get yourself ready for dinner. And give me a kiss.'

Reluctantly, Reece leant over the arm of the chair, kissed his mum on the cheek and left the room. With absolutely no intention of going to school the next day.

CHAPTER 12

BIG NIGHT

Jake had lost track of time waiting for her. As soon as he was ready, he'd persistently checked his watch for every minute that Elizabeth wasn't, but after the first ten or so, he'd given up and decided to wait at the bottom of the stairs, practising his unimpressed scowl and thinking of the jobs he could tick off from his to-do list. Like tidying the kitchen so it was nice for when they returned. Organising the living room after the girls had finished throwing their toys and pens everywhere. Finally disposing of the broken, almost unrecognisable pair of trainers that were lying by the front door. The same ones he used to take out the rubbish every week – the same ones he'd been meaning to replace for a couple of months but had never got round to. Time was his excuse, or a lack thereof. But he had plenty of it now.

Before he could begin any of that though, the doorbell rang.

'Girls!' he called, angling his head towards the living room. 'Grandma's here!'

Jake opened the door and was greeted by his mum. She

had put her hair up and was wearing her best dress. Jake leant forward and hugged her, kissing her on the cheek.

'You're looking very nice. Suave. Sophisticated,' she told him.

'I could say the same about you. What are you all dressed up for?'

'I like the suit. It fits you well. They used to look nice on your father too. Especially the one he wore on our wedding day.'

Saving him from yet another unwanted conversation about his dad, Maisie burst from the living room. His three-year-old daughter raced along the hallway and leapt onto Grandma's legs, clinging for dear life.

'Have you packed everything?' Jake asked her as he bent down to her height.

Maisie spun on the spot and pointed at her Peppa Pig backpack, which was twice the size of her.

'Looks like you're all set. Come and give Daddy a hug and a kiss.'

Maisie did so with fervour and excitement. She loved going over to Nana Tanner's house. Much more so than visiting Elizabeth's parents, the Clarkes. Perhaps it was because his mum had been a schoolteacher and was some sort of child whisperer, whereas Elizabeth's mother worked in parliament and was always too busy for them whenever they visited as a family. Or perhaps it was that Elizabeth got on better with his mum than she did her own. Either way, it was a win in Jake's book.

Tanner one, Clarke nil.

Jake let go of Maisie, hurried into the living room, retrieved Ellie from her high chair, grabbed her things, and handed everything over to his mum.

'You all set for tonight?' she asked him as she juggled the baby in one hand and the luggage in the other.

'Think so.'

'Nervous?'

'Should I be?'

'You'll be fine. Say good luck to Daddy, girls!'

Maisie screamed the words with an ebullient smile on her face, while Ellie flashed a cheeky grin in keeping with the excitement of the situation. Emotion washed over him, and he kissed them again before waving them off. As he watched them cross the front garden, Maisie disappeared out of sight for a fraction and returned, holding a plastic bottle in her hands.

'What's this, Daddy?'

She brought it into the sliver of light that was cast on the patio by the corridor. As soon as Jake realised what it was, he hurried out of the house and took it from her. She protested.

'You know you're not allowed to drink these things. You're too young,' he told her.

He wasn't as successful at placating her as he'd have liked, but he was grateful that his mum stepped in and offered her a hot chocolate before bed as a consolation. As soon as they were in the car and out of sight, Jake slammed the door shut and hurried to the kitchen.

He investigated the bottle. The Pepsi logo. The rivulets and grooves of the screw top hidden behind the plastic wrapper in the centre.

Henry Matheson's trademark product.

Drugs hiding inside the centre.

He peeled back the label. On the inside of the packet were the words WE THANK YOU FOR YOUR SILENCE.

His body turned cold.

Someone had been to his house. Someone had been within touching distance of his family. Someone had crossed a line.

'Jake?' Elizabeth called from the bedroom upstairs.

He paid her little heed and slipped out through the back

door. He found their rubbish bin and placed the bottle inside. It landed with an almighty clunk that seemed to echo loudly as if purposely attracting attention to his behaviour.

How dare they, he thought. How *fucking* dare they venture near his home. His wife. His kids. His family.

'Jake!' Elizabeth called, her voice teeming with impatience this time.

He skipped back inside the house to find her at the bottom of the stairs.

'What're you up to?' she asked, holding on to the banister.

All thought of the drugs, the bottle, Henry Matheson, the warning – all of it – vanished as soon as his eyes fell on his wife. She wore a black, skin-tight dress that stopped a few inches below her knees, with high heels and held a clutch bag by her side. Her hair was pulled back in a ponytail, her eye make-up smoky and seductive. She'd kept her outfit for tonight a secret, a surprise. She'd said she wanted to see his reaction when his eyes fell on it. He hoped that his open mouth and dangling tongue was the reaction she was hoping for.

'What do you think?'

'I'm struggling to think of anything at this moment.' His eyes climbed up and down the curves of her body. 'I just… I don't even…'

'Did your mum pick the girls up all right?' she asked him.

And then the image of the bottle came flooding back to him, immediately distracting him from the sight before him.

'They're fine.'

The sides of her lips flickered into a smile. She wandered up to him and gave him a kiss on the lips. 'That means we've got the whole night to ourselves…'

'Yeah…' he lied, wrapping his arms around her and lowering his hands until they fell on her bum. He gave a squeeze and felt the blood rush to his genitals.

'Maybe we can try… *without* one tonight?'

Jake held her at a distance. 'Pardon?'

'I've been thinking. I want another one.'

'Another what?'

'Child, Jake. Another mini human.'

Jake looked at her in disbelief. Kids. Another one. Where was this coming from? It was the first he'd heard of it, the first they'd discussed it since Ellie. 'They're not like snacks. You can't just open a new packet whenever you want,' he said.

Then immediately regretted it.

'Are you being serious right now?'

'It's… I… sorry. There's a lot going on in my head. I need to think about it. Now's probably not the night to drop that one on me.' Jake let go of her and grabbed his car keys from the pot resting on the table by the front door.

'Can we at least discuss it?'

Jake reached for the handle. 'Like I said, I need to think about it.'

The aggression and frustration on Elizabeth's face dissipated. 'I don't mean to scare you. I just… want to add to the family, that's all.'

Jake opened the door. 'Shall we?'

Elizabeth looked down at the ground and shuffled past him. He hated seeing her upset. Worse, he hated being the one to make her upset. But a new addition to the Tanner family wasn't what he needed right now. It was the last thing he wanted to think about. His mind was focused on work, on the bottle, on how he was going to ensure he could keep his existing family safe from the threat of The Cabal and whoever was leaving the parcels behind.

'Hey, listen…' Jake said as he climbed into the car with her.

'It's fine. We don't have to discuss it. I understand.

Tonight's your big night.' She placed a hand on his knee. 'Forget about it, please? And maybe later, after you've got your award, I can give you a different treat?'

Elizabeth chewed her bottom lip.

Jake eyed it surreptitiously. 'About that…'

'What now?'

'I forgot to mention, I might not be able to stay too long at this thing. I might have to work.'

'Tonight? But I just said we could—'

'I know.'

'You're not nervous, are you?' Elizabeth stroked his leg, and the blood rushed to his crotch again. 'Because I can help settle the nerves now if you'd like?' Her hand climbed higher. 'But we'll have to be quick – don't want to miss your big night.'

'Don't get my hopes up like that.'

As she cupped him, that wasn't the only thing she was getting up.

CHAPTER 13

GOLD FLAKE VODKA

Rhythm, the two-storey nightclub situated in the busy end of a bustling high street, was one of Frank Graham's regular haunts. A lively, atmospheric place, the usual clientele consisted of the human soup of the population: young women who spent more time getting themselves glammed up than they did on any other aspect of their lives; groups of lads who came out with one intention and one intention only – to score some of the easy local girls – but always found they could only get the stragglers at the end of the night; and finally, there were the groups of friends who didn't really fit in. They weren't from the ends; nor were they from anywhere nearby. Outsiders. Possibly Hertfordshire or Essex, city boys trying to make names for themselves by showing off how much money they had and how much of it they could snort up their noses.

Fortunately, Frank didn't consider himself any of those. He was the one who scoped out everyone in the club and categorised them the moment they walked in. He wasn't interested in scoring or getting high. He was more interested in having a good time, enjoying the music and living in the moment.

That and taking money from the outsiders.

Beside him was Caleb Brown, his number two, propped against the bar, glass of vodka Red Bull in hand. A metal pole ran along the length of the bar and dug into the small of Frank's back. The heavy, repetitive din of the bass coming from the speaker reverberated around his body. *Dun. Dun. Dun. Dun. Dun.* Girls gyrated on the dance floor while hordes of seedy men stood on the outskirts, watching, drooling, waiting for one of the girls to come up to them, like it was some sort of bizarre mating ritual, a flocking of the feathers to see who could stand there the longest and pick up the hottest date. The place was a breeding ground for STDs, poor life choices and absent baby daddies.

A bartender placed two drinks beside Frank's arm. He twisted, picked up the drink and gave a thumbs up. Vodka cranberry. His poison. He didn't care about some of the stick he got for drinking it. He enjoyed it. So what the fuck was wrong with that?

'You reckon she's gonna be here tonight, bruv?' Caleb asked, leaning across and shouting in his ear.

'Yeah,' he called back. 'Girls like her love this place. Think it's the atmosphere.'

Or it was the drugs they sold on the sly. One of Frank's oldest friends owned the venue and, after agreeing to a cut of the proceeds, turned a convenient blind eye to any dealings that took place on the dance floor or in the toilets.

Tonight, the DJ was on fire, playing a combination of Jay-Z, Kanye West, Lil Wayne and David Guetta. The song changed: 'Niggas in Paris', by Kanye and Jay-Z. Frank felt his body ripple and swagger in time with the beat. It was nearing midnight, and the bodies were just beginning to pour in. Within twenty minutes, it was almost a full house, making

Frank's special job for the evening even more difficult.

As he waited for her to arrive, Frank observed the proceedings; every now and then, one of the girls on the dance floor would approach a man wearing a hood, exchange some money for the drugs, and then return to the floor, where they would then disappear into the toilet to snort the cocaine from the cistern. It was a smooth operation, and one that netted them several thousand pounds a night on top of the money brought in from the bar and entrance fees.

Twenty minutes later, Frank finished his drink, placed the plastic beaker on the surface and left it to the bar staff to tidy.

As he turned around, he caught sight of her. Danielle Matheson. The girl he'd been waiting for, accompanied by a friend, both sporting short skirts and crop tops that revealed all sorts of delicious and delicate skin.

'She's here,' he said, nudging Caleb in the ribs and pointing to her in the corner of the room.

'Shall we talk to 'em?'

'Nah. Wait for 'em to come to the bar. They'll need a drink eventually.'

Frank watched Danielle traverse the room, wander past the row of men ogling her and brush them off as though they weren't there. It was clear to see she was a woman of pride, of confidence, of knowing what she wanted. Someone who lapped up the attention she got but wasn't willing to throw it away for some random hook-up. Henry Matheson had raised her properly. Which meant she was intelligent, sophisticated and that Frank had his work cut out for him.

He and Caleb had strategically positioned themselves at the far end of the bar where it was quietest. Theory being that girls like Danielle wouldn't want to fight their way through the crowd to get to the front. They were too highbrow for that. Instead, they'd funnel down to where it was quietest and wait for their good but subtle looks to draw the bartenders towards them; a strange display of power and dominance.

And he was right.

As Danielle and her friend approached the bar, they realised all the servers were busy with other customers and moved down to his side, coming to a stop a few feet from him. She placed her handbag on the counter, reached inside and checked herself in the mirror, showing a complete lack of acknowledgement towards him and Caleb.

So far everything was going according to plan.

Within seconds, Danielle and her friend were seen to, courtesy of a discreet wave from Frank. The bartender took her order of two double vodka Red Bulls and rushed to finish the transaction. When he returned, Frank flagged him down and requested two more vodka cranberries. As soon as the server disappeared again, Frank turned to face the crowd and leant against the metal bar. In the movement, he caught Danielle's eye.

'Is this the part where I'm supposed to buy yours for you?'

Danielle side-eyed him, unimpressed. 'We've got our own money.' She lifted her bag at an angle that suggested she was showing it off rather than threatening to use it as a weapon if he didn't stop talking to her.

Frank took that as a good sign.

'Shame,' he said sarcastically.

The bartender arrived with his drinks, set them down and held his fingers in the air. Five pounds. Frank pointed to the freshly-made drinks. 'If you got your own money, you can buy these for me, if you want?'

Danielle flashed a light-hearted grin but said nothing. No dice.

After paying, he passed Caleb his drink and introduced him to Danielle.

Her eyes widened, the light catching the perfect whites of her eyes. 'And what's your name?'

Hook. Line. Sinker.

'Frank,' he replied, raising his plastic cup.

'I'm Danielle,' she said, and together they touched beakers. 'This is Rochelle.'

'Nice to meet you both. Booth?' Frank pointed to an empty booth to the side of the bar. It was out of the way and offered their ears some respite from the ear-pounding music.

Danielle shrugged noncommittally, but Frank took that to mean yes. The four of them idled over to the booth and sat down, Frank on one end of the girls, Caleb on the other.

'You come here often?' Danielle asked after they'd made themselves comfortable.

'Isn't that what I'm supposed to ask you?'

'I don't like rules. I don't like playing by them either.'

Frank smirked. 'I like that. My friend owns it.'

'And he's still charging you for drinks? You should have a word.'

'I said he was a friend. Not a boyfriend. He's still gotta make money.'

'No shit,' Danielle said, taking a sip of her drink.

'Have you been here before?'

'No. First time.'

I know.

'It's a decent place,' Frank said. 'They've got a nice VIP lounge if you wanna see it? I'm sure I can swing something by the manager.'

'Is that how it works then?' Danielle began. 'Come across all chivalrous and macho, pretend to buy a girl's drink, flirt with her, show her the VIP lounge and use your *mate* to get them into bed?'

Ouch. Just like that, she'd busted him.

'Not at all,' he said as he scratched the underside of his

chin, releasing a new wave of aftershave from his skin. 'I just thought I'd use it to my advantage on this particular occasion. You seem like a one-in-a-million kind of girl. Nobody's forcing you to say yes.'

Danielle rolled her eyes at him. 'I won't then.'

'What brings you and your friend here anyway?'

'Wanted a night out. To get away…'

'The nine-to-five getting too much for you?' Frank jibed.

'Funny enough,' she began, 'it's to get away from arsehole blokes like you.'

'I'm hurt.'

'You should be. You haven't even offered to buy me a drink.'

'Thought you didn't like rules?'

'They don't count when I'm thirsty.'

'Here's an idea: how about I don't buy you one.'

'Why not?'

If his A game didn't work, then it was time for plan B. 'I'll make you one instead.'

'Oh, so you're a barman as well as a fraud?'

'If you want to look at it that way, yeah.' Frank reached into his pocket, produced his wallet and pulled out a business card. 'I own my own club. Just down the road. The Rossiters. You should come check it out. We've just opened, and we've got a big night tomorrow.'

Danielle snatched the card and inspected it. Her fingers ran over the raised lettering, admiring it, confirming that it was legit. Patrick Bateman, eat your heart out.

'We got a deal?' Frank asked, placing his hand on her leg.

Danielle finished surveying the card and lowered it. 'Only if you've got my favourite. Gold flake vodka.'

CHAPTER 14

AWARDS CEREMONY

The Met Excellence Awards were being held at the Natural History Museum. The venue had been cleared and filled with a series of circular tables, evenly spaced between one another, offering ample room for attendees to wander and weave their way through without drunkenly bumping into anyone and disturbing their meal. A high stage stood at the head of the room, with a lonely plinth sitting in the middle. Around the walls were the museum's insights into millions of years of history in the form of artefacts, portraits and Do Not Touch signs. The auditorium bustled with smartly dressed women and men, holding glasses of champagne, and soft drinks for those who were driving, or on shift in the early hours of the morning. Darryl, dressed in the same suit he'd worn all day, was waiting for them at the entrance to the hall.

'I'm so glad you're here… finally,' he remarked as he shook Jake's hand.

Jake and Elizabeth looked at each other and smirked like a couple of teenagers. He placed his arm around her and replied, 'Traffic was a nightmare.'

Without asking any more, Darryl led them to their table, where he was greeted by two familiar faces and several new ones. Brendan, dressed as smartly as Jake had ever seen him, was already nursing his first, or possibly third, glass of champagne of the night. Beside him was Ashley, wearing a black-and-white-checked kimono with white chinos. She was sitting awkwardly, her eyes wandering, looking uncomfortable to be there and keen to take a leaf, or two, out of Brendan's book. As he caught her attention, he gave her a curt nod, and then introduced himself to the rest of the guests.

Adorning the table was a series of crystal glasses, a bouquet of lilies that were probably more expensive than Jake's suit, and jugs of chilled water. It was a grand affair where very little of the taxpayer's money had been spared. Jake wondered what sort of other things the money could have been used for. *Direct surveillance of the Cosgrove Estate for a start.* He grabbed the jug of water and filled his and Elizabeth's glasses, hoping the ice would cool him down.

'Don't you want some of this?' Brendan asked, holding a bottle of wine he'd conjured from nowhere.

Jake hadn't noticed, but there were wine coolers and bottles of red intermittently placed around the table.

'Sorry, mate, I'm driving.'

'Out of all of us, you should be the one enjoying himself. You should be celebrating.'

'I've nothing to celebrate,' he said.

'Don't be so modest,' Ashley added. The earrings that dangled from her ears to her chin sparkled as her head moved from side to side.

Jake shrugged it off and hoped they would move the conversation on.

'What happens at these things?' Brendan asked, pouring more wine into his glass. And once he'd finished, he moved around the table, decanting the liquid into everyone else's.

'We sit and wait,' Darryl replied, placing his napkin on his lap. 'Have a bit of food. Pretend to make polite and general conversation with other people. Announce the awards. And then get out of here.'

Jake liked where Darryl was coming from. Get in and get out. The lower the profile he could maintain, the better. The last thing he wanted was to spend more time there than necessary. He had a wasp's nest to attend to.

Brendan held his glass aloft. 'Sounds like a good plan to me.' And he finished the drink. 'So long as there's more of this, I'm happy.'

'How many have you already had?' Jake asked, his eyebrows raised.

'This is only my second,' Brendan replied. 'It helps settle the nerves in social situations. I'm not good with talking to people I've never met before.'

Jake empathised with that and watched Brendan give an awkward nod to the woman sitting next to him. The detective sergeant was only slightly older than Jake. He'd been in the force for several years, most of which had been spent in the missing persons unit, and for the most part, was a difficult character to read.

Just as he was about to try, Jake felt a firm hand on his shoulder. He flinched and looked up to see Assistant Commissioner Richard Candy towering over him. The man was in his late fifties and was in full police dress uniform, his cap tucked under his armpit. He was tall, had a stomach that bulged out of his shirt, and his hair was short and thin. The light reflected off the thick layers of grease that covered his hair, and he wore square glasses, which made his face look skinnier than it was. The last time Jake had encountered Richard Candy, or Dick Candy as he was affectionately called by certain members of the office, was during the investigation into the Stratford Killer, and the case that had launched him into the limelight and made him subject to public scrutiny. Inexperienced and way out of his depth, Jake had found himself leading press conferences and, eventually, the entire investigation. He'd shown himself to be naïve, and his mistakes had almost cost the lives of the killer's next victims. With any luck, he would have gone up somewhat in the assistant commissioner's estimations since then.

'Assistant Commissioner,' Jake said, hoping the hesitation in his voice wasn't obvious.

'DC Tanner,' Candy replied, holding out a hand for Jake. The man's grip was unrelenting, and he held the handshake for longer than was necessary. 'Pleasure to have you here tonight. I was so thrilled when I saw your name on the list.'

Jake chuckled awkwardly. 'I appreciate it, sir. I'm happy to have been nominated for the award.'

'We pride ourselves on rewarding our best and bravest. The work you did on Operation Jackknife was magnificent. Solving the Cipriano murders while simultaneously weeding out some bad apples in the team. Wonderful. You've shone a spotlight on the force, and I hope your new team are settling in well. As always, we thank you for your service.'

The last few words of Candy's speech failed to register before he wandered off to another table. As soon as Jake realised what the man had said, he watched him move about the room, shaking everyone's hands, greeting them pleasantly, thanking them for coming, and wondered whether the similarity in phrasing to The Cabal's message had been a coincidence, or whether it was something more sinister.

At the head of the room, the Met police commissioner, Cassandra Herman moved to the centre of the stage behind the plinth. She tapped on the microphone and the harsh, muffled noise of feedback reverberated around the open room.

'Good evening, everyone,' she said, pausing until she had the room's attention. 'It's lovely to see so many of you here tonight. I hope you're all prepared for a wonderful evening where we get to celebrate the service's finest officers. We're all colleagues here, and I would like to start by offering a round of applause to every one of you. We are all grateful for your hard work, dedication and bravery. Without you, we wouldn't be able to make the city the safe place it is. You should all be very proud of yourselves. So, please, a round of applause.'

The venue erupted into a cacophony of noise. Everyone in the vicinity started to clap, including Jake. But within a few seconds, the excitement was over as quickly as it had started.

The commissioner continued. 'So, we begin tonight with a few awards, though first come the honourable mentions, then we'll take a break for some food, and then we'll continue, and, at the end, we shall announce the officer of the year.'

Great, Jake thought, I have to be here all evening.

As the night wore on, he allowed himself to relax a little more. He tried not to think of Henry Matheson, of the plastic bottle that had been outside his house, of Jermaine Gordon's killer planning their next victim, of the assistant commissioner's final few words. But it wasn't so easy. Particularly when Elizabeth was a constant reminder of what was at stake, of who would suffer the most if he didn't sort the situation out immediately.

After a few hours, they'd completed the first round of awards and congratulations. The delectable feast of roast lamb, potatoes and vegetables had gone down a treat, while the vegetarian and vegan options seemed to impress the few officers brave enough to eat them in front of their meat-loving colleagues. Now, after what had felt like a lifetime, it was his category. Time to find out whether he would be crowned officer of the year.

'Ladies and gentlemen,' Cassandra said, resuming her position behind the microphone. In her hand, she held a trophy. It was the shape of the New Scotland Yard revolving sign. 'Please may I have silence in the room? It's time for the final award – our officer of the year award. To assist me is Assistant Commissioner Richard Candy.'

We thank you for your service.

'Thanks very much,' Candy said as he clambered onto the stage, taking the trophy from her. For a moment, it looked as though he were preparing to accept the award himself.

'It's an honour to be handing out this award tonight. We know how hard all of you have been working. And we respect and admire each and every one of you. We've been in your position, and we know how tough it is. There may be times when you feel like giving up, or where you feel like you need to stop and you want to quit and you've had enough – we've all been there. But, trust me, it's worth persevering. This job wouldn't be worth doing if that weren't the case. At the end of it all, you'll learn to appreciate when to take the good with the bad. And that's what our officer of the year is doing. They're developing. They're doing what they think is right. Not necessarily for themselves but for others too. Which is why it gives me great honour to announce the winner.'

The room fell silent. Jake lowered himself into the chair.

'PC Angela Davis!'

Jake breathed a heavy sigh of relief as Angela Davis leapt out of her chair in the corner of the room and launched herself onto the stage. She accepted the award, said a few words of thanks and then slipped off. Elizabeth placed a consolatory hand on Jake's leg under the tablecloth.

'Tanner!' Brendan cried from across the table. He was slurring his words and had spilt wine on the tablecloth. 'Sorry, mate. I was really hoping you'd get it.'

Jake chuckled. 'Does that mean you're all going to stop being nice to me now I'm like one of you guys?'

For what was left of the evening, nobody said anything more on the subject. Instead, they spoke about anything and everything. Jake supposed it was because they didn't want to make him feel uncomfortable. It was 11 p.m. by the time the awards ceremony finished. And it would be another hour or two until he could get where he needed to be. Perfect timing. Right when the nocturnal creatures of the Cosgrove Estate would venture out of their holes and incriminate themselves.

After the evening had finished, he drove home in extra quick time, the speedometer nudging the edge of the speed limit, dropped Elizabeth off at home, apologised again for having to leave her on her own and headed back to Stratford, with the last image of her undressing as he closed the door playing on repeat in his mind.

CHAPTER 15

BUSINESS MEETINGS

Henry Matheson was in the back of his Range Rover, fully submerged in the heavy bass blasting from the speakers, drumming his finger and nodding along with the beat. Up in front, sitting in the driver's seat, was Jamal. With Deshawn riding shotgun. None of them said anything while they absorbed the beauty and rhythm of Des's latest song. They'd spent so long making it, it was wonderful to hear it finally playing out.

'Yo, this bangs right here, man,' Jamal said as the song reached the second verse, the verse that Henry himself had written.

'Yeah, man, it pops,' Deshawn replied. 'When can we get in the studio to make some more, Hen?'

'Whenever you want, bro. My guy says it's available any time for us.'

Des and Jamal had lived at the estate when he and his mum had moved in twenty years ago. Back then there were no gangs or drugs, no sense of violence or authority. No single person exerting serious amounts of autonomy and control over the rest of the residents. But that had all changed by the time he was fourteen. He'd started out by bringing drugs into the estate from further afield: South London, North London, Hertfordshire, Essex, through a school friend's brother. And had immediately found success. There was demand, and he was the supplier. Simple economics.

Shortly after, the E11 gang was born, and his notoriety skyrocketed. He became the main source of heroin and cocaine and ecstasy and marijuana in the estate and surrounding postcodes. Anything a junky wanted, he had it. From humble beginnings – packaging the drugs from his mum's flat to dealing on the corner of the high-rises – his business continued to grow.

Now here he was with a small number of his closest friends as lieutenants, an army of dealers, and an even bigger address book of people who either owed him favours or were too afraid to say no to him. Life was—

'They're here,' Jamal said suddenly. He shut off the music.

Henry snapped out of his reverie and leant forward. In the distance, a hundred yards away, he saw a set of headlights approaching. As they waited for the vehicle to arrive, Henry listened to the sound of cars travelling across the overpass above. The area was quiet, desolate and isolated. Ideal.

The car pulled up to Henry's left side. As it slowed, he unrolled the window. The Audi A5 sat lower than his and from his vantage point, he counted two people inside. One driver, one passenger; the latter rolled down the window, slowly revealing themselves.

Henry grinned as his eyes met his next appointment.

'We're here,' Frank Graham said, his voice deep, his expression blank, as though he was higher than his station. Henry knew it was an act, a façade, a persona the man embodied but could only wear for a short amount of time before slipping into the weasel he was.

'Clever boy,' Henry said, flashing his teeth. 'Now be a good little boy and get in the car.'

The muscles in Frank's face distorted. 'Why can't we—'

'I said get in the car.'

'No, I—'

'Get in the car.' Henry lowered his tone and turned his head away. 'I assume you've seen what happened to your little bum boy, Jermaine, haven't you?'

Seconds passed before Frank sighed heavily and stepped out of his car. A few seconds later, the door opened, and he hopped in. He was bigger than Henry had been expecting – taller, a little rounder and more well defined around the edges. He was dressed, as Henry had expected, like a prat. Designer gear, designer trainers, designer watch, designer jewellery. Cartier. Balenciaga. Louis Vuitton. Rolex. The man appeared to be wearing all his money, and it just went to show that there was no price on good taste. But the worst thing about him was the smell. The sweet smell of alcohol steadily evaporated through his pores, laced with a faint hint of One Million Paco Rabanne aftershave that had clearly been applied more than twelve hours ago.

'You been drinking tonight?' Henry asked.

'Just a few.'

'Needed something to take the edge off, did you?'

Neither. Judging by the lack of words coming out of his mouth.

'Don't blame you. Jermaine used to do the same. Although I think his was more of a habitual thing. He let it get to his head, make him do stupid things.'

'Hey, listen,' Frank said, raising his hands in the air in defence. 'Whatever your beef was with him, I don't want no part of it. Trust me.'

Henry shook his head. 'You see, that shit ain't gonna fly. From what I hear, you were his boy, his second in command, his monkey, so now you have to bear the same responsibilities. The beef will stop when I say it stops – when you lot stop cutting our shit with other shit. You know how this business works: we give you the stuff and then you sell it on for a price. You make your cut, I make mine, and the junky gets their fix. Everyone is happy. And in my business, we like it when everyone's happy. Our product is our product. It separates us from all the other products on the market. And the product brings in the business. Without it, we won't survive. But the minute you start to tamper with the product and diminish its quality, you do the same to the business. And this is my business, and I ain't gonna let that happen.'

'Sometimes the biggest businesses change their products. They diversify.'

'That supposed to be funny? Or is that the alcohol talking?'

Frank didn't reply.

'I don't think you understand me,' Henry continued. 'Under no circumstances are you to fuck me over on this. Have I made myself clear?'

'Listen, Hen—'

'Have I made myself clear?' He hated having to repeat himself like he was somehow beneath Frank when the opposite was reality, and everyone in the car knew it.

'I promise you now, it ain't us. We ain't been cutting nothing. It's the dealers, fam, they're the ones—'

Henry cleared his throat, and in an instant, Deshawn turned round and held a gun to Frank's face, inches from the bridge of his nose. Frank panicked, his breathing picked up, and his eyes darted between Deshawn, the gun and Henry.

'Please, I…'

'I'm going to need you to promise me that you'll be keeping your little experiments reserved for the bedroom. Because now you know what will happen if you don't, or do you need another reminder?' Henry pointed out of the window at Frank's driver, who was sitting with one hand on the steering wheel and another on the gearstick.

'No. Honestly. No.'

'Then I need you to promise me. Call me a traditionalist, but I don't like it when people can't keep a promise.'

'I… I… I promise,' Frank said, his forehead covered in a sheen of sweat, rapidly filling the car with more of the alcohol odour.

'Pinky promise.'

Henry held his little finger in the air. Confused, Frank slowly locked his little finger with Henry's, and they shook on it.

Turning to face the back of Deshawn's seat, Henry said, 'Now get the fuck out of my car and get home. It's past your bedtime. We don't want your aunt to be getting worried now, do we?'

'What did you just say?'

Before Henry replied, Deshawn cocked the gun.

'Goodbye, Frank. I hope the next time we see each other will be under better circumstances.'

Frank breathed heavily and opened his mouth as if he wanted to say something else – something brave, something stupid, something that might end up getting him killed. Fortunately, he was smart enough to open the car door and slide out. As soon as he slammed it shut, Jamal started the ignition and roared out of the underpass.

Henry couldn't wait to get home. He needed a cigarette. It had been a long day.

CHAPTER 16

233

They'd elected to use Ashley's battered and beaten BMW 1 Series. It was older than his police career, and the interior was worn. There were scuff marks on the bum of the seat from where years of keys and wallets had degraded the material, and the door handle was smooth and rounded after years of exposure and treatment from the multitude of hands that had touched it.

They hadn't been there long. A brief check on the dashboard now and then told him an hour had passed and they were now well into the early hours of a new day. And the estate was beginning to come to life.

'The nocturnal creatures begin to crawl out of their natural habitats,' Jake said to himself, doing his best David Attenborough impression.

'If your career as a copper doesn't work out…' Ashley said playfully.

Jake grunted. After he'd arrived at the estate, he'd received a call from Ashley, apologising for the disturbance but confessing that she was worried about the investigation and the direction it was headed. She sided with Jake, said that she wanted to conduct surveillance as well, and he'd thought it fit to invite her. Not least because it helped having her along with him. Strength in numbers. But also because it was a good alibi if it all went wrong. So he'd driven back to Bow Green, left his car there, and they'd both grabbed a few snacks from the local twenty-four-hour convenience store before returning to the estate.

'I'm surprised,' she started.

'About what?'

Ashley pointed to the centre of the estate where, only a few hours earlier, they'd witnessed a dead body dangling from the lamp post.

'They got rid of it quickly,' she said.

'In The Pit, you don't hang around. You get in and get out.'

'So, the opposite of what we're doing?'

Jake chuckled and turned to face her. The low orange light from the street lamp illuminated the side of her face and eyes but was absorbed by the leather jacket that hugged her shoulders. 'If you don't like it, we can drop you home? I'll make my own arrangements.'

'I'm fine,' she replied with resolve. He wasn't sure if it was an intentional reaction, but she seemed to straighten her back and hold her head higher after his comment.

On his lap were a pair of binoculars and a camera. It was one he'd borrowed from Elizabeth. State of the art. Top range. Canon 5D Mark I. It was one of the most beautiful things he'd ever seen, and the photographs it produced were even more stunning. He'd begged for permission to use it, and after a brief battle, she'd finally agreed. And, as he sat there, aiming the lens at the surrounding area, he tried not to think of how much it cost, and how much she adored and cared for the device. This was her lifeblood, her career. Photography had always been her passion, and she'd even achieved first-class honours in it at university. The only problem was finding work. Going it alone and trying to find a market to tap into was proving more difficult than they'd both anticipated, and so in recent months, after being scouted by a recruit, she'd become a model. Nothing major. Clothes, shoes and any other sort of fashion for a small start-up that specialised in vegan clothing. It wasn't earning her a living yet, barely enough to cover some of the bills but she was loving it, and he wanted to support her all the way.

Jake peered through the lens. 'I'm surprised you called.'

'Someone had to keep an eye on you.'

'What's that supposed to mean?'

'Nothing. I just heard a few things mentioned around the office today.'

'Like?'

'Nothing major.'

'If it wasn't major, then you wouldn't have said it.'

Ashley cleared her throat and massaged the steering wheel with her hands. 'They said that… just that sometimes you can be a bit of a loose cannon.'

'Did they use the term *rogue*?' Jake surveyed the area with the camera lens as he waited for a response.

'I think someone might have used that word.'

'Who's they?'

'I'd rather not say.'

Jake clicked his tongue. 'I wondered how long it would take for people to have that impression about me.'

'You don't mind?'

'I have my reasons for being the way I am. Reasons for doing things the way I do…'

Silence fell, save for the sound of Ashley's rhythmic breathing. In through the nose, out through the mouth. In. Out. Within a few seconds, it became infuriating, and he lowered the camera and glared at her. A look of apprehension rippled across her face.

'Can I ask you something?' she asked.

'You just did, but sure.'

'Does it…' She hesitated, swallowed. 'Does it have anything to do with what happened before?'

'*Before*?'

'Earlier you avoided talking about something. About your old team.'

'There's a reason for that.'

'Would you mind…' She cleared her throat again. 'Would you mind telling me? I think it would be good to know seeing as the rest of the team do.'

'I thought it was all common knowledge by now, the number of times it's been in the news.'

'I don't want to know everything, just the main points.'

In the months following Operation Jackknife, one of the biggest investigations into police corruption in recent years, Jake had earned himself notoriety. News outlets, journalists, newspapers – all of them had begged him for information on the case. His name had appeared in several headlines and had been front-page news at least once. Uncovering the corruption inside the Major Investigation Team of the Metropolitan Police had highlighted the problems that still existed: the ability to become corrupt and the risks and dangers it posed to not only the police but to society in a wider context. Jake had no problem repeating those sorts of messages to the press. In fact, he openly welcomed them but what he didn't appreciate was having to repeat the same half-story, the same half-truths that the service's press officer had instructed him to because the upper echelons of the Met, for whatever reason, didn't want the world knowing every juicy detail.

So Jake spent the next couple of minutes reeling off the

points that he could mention. Of how his former colleagues, Drew Richmond, Liam Greene and Pete Garrison had been part of a small network of corrupt police officers responsible for orchestrating the deaths of former organised crime group members Danny and Michael Cipriano. Of how they had ruined the credibility of the police and destroyed any notion of trust the public had in them. Of how they had displaced his trust in anyone he ever worked with, past, present or future.

'Now you can understand why I have a hard time relying on people,' he finished.

'And you did it all on your own?'

He nodded. 'Yes.' Stephanie's involvement in the operation, along with that of the directorate of professional standards, had been kept out of the public eye.

'Wow… I'm impressed.'

'Don't be. Just doing my job.' Jake lifted the camera to his face again and watched as a car turned down the road and drove towards them. It made another turn before reaching them and disappeared from sight. 'What about you then? What brings you to the team?'

'Pardon?' Ashley responded.

'I told you my story. Now you tell me yours. Everyone's got one.'

'You want to know how I got involved with the police or how I managed to make it to twenty-seven with all my limbs and features intact?'

Jake shrugged. 'Whichever one you feel comfortable telling.'

Ashley hesitated and tapped her cheek with the back of her thumb before answering. 'I saw a couple of knife-related incidents when I was younger. Made me change my view on things.'

'Someone you knew?' he asked, lowering the camera from

his face once more and looking at her.

She nodded slowly, keeping her gaze pointed out at the world.

'What happened?'

'We were fifteen… sixteen… something like that. It was a school night, and we'd just got back from the park. We were walking along the street, and these guys stopped us. Calvin, the guy who got himself stabbed, hadn't paid the boy's cut of the drugs he'd been selling. I didn't know he was selling at the time; we weren't super close, but we were close enough for him to tell me something like that. And then he said he wouldn't be able to get them the money any time soon because he'd spent it all. So they pulled out a knife and stabbed him in the stomach. They got out of there as fast as I've ever seen anyone move.'

'What happened to him?'

'He died. On the way to the hospital. Officially, he died in the ambulance, but that didn't stop the surgeons and medical staff trying to do everything they could to revive him.' A lump caught in her throat, and she swallowed to get rid of it.

'Is that why you joined?' Jake swapped the camera for the binoculars and held them to his face, squinting and blinking until his eyes adjusted to the darkness.

'That and other reasons,' Ashley said shyly, still directing her gaze towards the window.

'Like?'

Ashley opened her mouth to speak but Jake cut her off with a wave of his hand, flapping it in her face to distract her.

'What is it?' she snapped, seemingly vexed at having been interrupted.

'A deal. Potential drug deal. Two male suspects. One tall, wearing a hood, possibly IC3. The other, younger, smaller, on a bike. Wearing a cap pulled low over his head. Visual confirms IC1.'

Jake passed her the DSLR so she could get a direct view for herself.

'Sighted,' she said. 'Visual confirmed. Another suspect approaching from about three o'clock.'

In the distance, emerging through the underpass on the north side of the building, was the silhouette of a man. Well built, stocky and walking with an air of arrogance about him that suggested he was the one running the place. Except the large duffel coat with collar propped against his ears and rucksack slung over one shoulder suggested he was a bloke who'd just stepped into the women's toilets. Out of place, and far away from where he should be. Clouds of vapour expelled from his mouth as he spoke. His face was hidden beneath the darkness, except for one discernible quality that caught under the street lamp: a tattoo of a scorpion on his hand. The taller, hooded figure shook hands with Scorpion and revealed another insignia. A tattoo on his neck of an eagle catching a fish in its talons.

The men released one another, then Eagle turned to the youngster on the bike, flexing his hands as if asking for something. The kid reached into his pocket and passed a clear plastic bag to the hooded man. Eagle and Scorpion exchanged the bag for a wad of money before each pocketing their new items.

'Are you getting this?' Jake asked, lowering the binoculars from his face. 'Please tell me you're recording this or doing something with it?'

Frantically, Ashley looked down at the device. 'I don't know! I don't know how it works. There are so many buttons!'

Fuck's sake, Jake thought as he snatched the camera from Ashley and flicked it to the right setting.

As he was about to return the camera to her, he noticed the three figures coming closer. His heart leapt into his mouth and his body froze. Had they seen them? Were they on their way to slaughter them now? Or were they…

Jake had his answer almost immediately. The three figures came to a stop at the underpass, and the two adults disappeared through a door that led to the flats above. The kid on the bike lingered.

'Shit!' Jake whispered loudly, smacking the back of his hand on the side of the car. 'Missed them.'

'Sorry,' Ashley said. 'That's my fault.'

'It's fine. I don't know how to use one of these bloody things either. Elizabeth's only shown me the basics. And I still struggle.'

'Did you get a good look at who was involved?'

Nodding, Jake replied, 'I think so. But it's difficult to distinguish them from one another in the light when you've only seen them in the dark.'

Like changing perceptions of someone you'd only heard bad things about.

Then Ashley's mobile rang.

'Oh, shit,' she said, glancing at the screen.

'Who is it?'

She answered the call, ignoring him.

'Hello?' she said tentatively. 'Yes… it is. Yes… we are.' She turned to face him. 'Yes… he is.'

Ashley closed her eyes, lowered the phone to the gearbox and put the device on loudspeaker.

'Am I on?' the voice asked. Jake instantly recognised it as Darryl's.

Shit.

'Yes, you are,' Ashley replied.

'Is Jake there?'

'Yeah,' Jake said, looking out of the window. 'I'm here, guv.'

'What are you two playing at?' Darryl asked. 'You both

know the rules when it comes to surveillance. Neither of you have followed the appropriate channels. And need I mention the fact that we've not got any overtime to sanction this? You two are wasting your own time, and also mine. Both of you need to come into the station immediately.'

'Guv?' Ashley began.

'Someone's just handed themselves in and confessed to the murder of Jermaine Gordon, our unidentified victim.'

Jake's body flushed cold. The skin on his arms pricked. And he snapped his head towards The Pit. If there'd been any doubt in his mind about the possibility that Henry Matheson was behind the murder, that was now diminished.

'Jake?' He heard his name being called. 'Can you make it in?'

'I've not got much of a choice, guv. Ashley's my lift.'

'Good.'

'Quick one, guv. How did you know we were here?'

'The office has ears, Tanner. Now, hurry up and get there as fast as you can. Stephanie's in the office on her own.'

Darryl rang off, and, saying nothing, Ashley started the engine.

'Sorry, Jake,' she said, looking at the steering wheel.

'What are you apologising for?' he asked.

Something outside caught his attention. The young boy on the bike had exited the underpass and was heading around the outskirts of the estate.

'This. It wasn't much of a success, was it?'

'That's not your fault,' Jake said, his eyes following the boy as he went. 'Someone might have grassed us up. There are only a finite number of people on the team, and two of us are sat in this car.'

Before Ashley could respond, he pointed to the kid on the bike and said, 'Follow him on the way out. I want to see where he goes.'

Ashley slipped the car into first, pulled out of the space and idled along the street, keeping her headlights off. As they drove past, the kid stopped outside a small terraced house, left the bike on the grass by the front and bounded towards the door. Jake made a note of the door number.

It held a special place in his heart, making it one he wouldn't forget – 233, the day and month that he and Elizabeth first met.

| PART 2 |

CHAPTER 17

CONNECTIONS

'My client has prepared a statement. We wish to discuss this before we begin with the interview.'

The owner of the voice was Rupert Haversham, a man who no longer needed any introductions. Tyrannical, a bully and officious, Rupert Haversham entered every interview room with a smile and the knowledge that somehow he would be able to get his clients out of whatever situation they were in. A worker for the criminal underworld whose only moral compass was to accept jobs from the highest bidder, Rupert had many friends in many different circles – and any other form or shape imaginable. For that reason, Jake trusted him as far as he could push him which, from the bulge of the stomach that dangled over his waistline like a dog's tongue from its mouth, wasn't very far at all.

The prepared statement had come as a shock to Jake, but not nearly as much as the young man named Rykard handing himself in to the police had. Just before he and Stephanie were due to sit with Rykard and Rupert, they'd discussed their plan of action, and come up with a strategy that would unpick Rykard's confession. But that wasn't to be. Rupert had smothered it before they could even start.

Jake pressed the record button on the recorder, completed the formalities, then gestured for Rupert to read the statement. Rupert's oversized sweaty fingers fumbled inside his blazer pocket and produced a folded and half-scrunched document. He cleared his throat before reading.

'I, Rykard Delawney of twenty-nine Cosgrove Estate, Stratford, admit to the unlawful killing of Jermaine Gordon in the Cosgrove Estate on the night of the twenty-fifth of May. I acted alone, committed the murder alone, and no one else was aware of my plans. I will be seeking legal advice via Rupert Haversham, and if my case is brought to trial, I will be entering a guilty plea. I will now be responding with no comment to any further questions you have at this time.'

Rupert slid his glasses from his nose, set them on the table and looked down at Jake and Stephanie as though they were still on his face.

Jake let out a little sigh and turned to Stephanie, whose expression looked as disappointed as he felt. She gave him a small nod.

'Interview terminated at three oh one a.m.'

Jake leant across the table and pressed the button. Recording finished. He rose from his chair, avoided the smug expression that had formed on Rupert's face and focused his attention on Rykard.

'One of the detention officers will take you back to your holding cell. If, for whatever reason, we require another interview, you'll both be informed via the appropriate channels.'

'I'm only a few minutes away,' Rupert Haversham said with a facetious grin that made Jake's skin crawl.

'What a shitshow,' Stephanie said as they returned to the investigation room.

She slammed her folders down on the table and launched her pen in the general direction of her computer monitor; it bounced and ricocheted onto the floor, rolling to a stop by the wheel of her office chair. On the other side of the room, a member of the cleaning staff was making their way around the floor with a Hoover in one hand and an iPod connected to a set of headphones in the other.

'Don't think that could've gone any worse,' Jake echoed.

'Wrong. He could have shot both of us and then rolled our bodies about in shit. I think that might have made things a little more humiliating.'

Jake slumped into the chair nearest him with so many unanswered questions, he didn't know where to begin. 'What's the plan now then?'

Stephanie joined him in sitting. 'Well, the clock's only just started. I say we give Rykard the full eight hours now and then speak with him at the first opportunity.'

'So we're forced to face a fully fresh and recharged Rupert Haversham when I've had barely any sleep? Joy.'

Stephanie leant over the side of the chair and picked up her pen, her legs hovering off the ground for balance. 'Unless you've got any other suggestions? Or can I just expect some smart and sarcastic comments from you?'

Jake shrugged. 'Probably a bit of both.'

'Well make yourself useful and make me a coffee. Please?'

Groaning as he lifted himself from the chair, he shuffled towards Stephanie's desk, retrieved her mug and then moved back to his desk. Sitting beside his phone was a box of Nescafé's latte sachets. Slightly weaker but tastier than granulated or instant coffee, they were reserved for his midnight-oil shifts.

As he reached for a sachet, his sleeve nudged his computer mouse and awoke the screen. The image he'd taken of Maisie and Ellie at the park, playing on the swings, appeared, and a smile stretched across his face. While he was there, he quickly checked his emails. Just a look to see if there was anything immediate that required his attention.

There was.

An email sitting at the top of his inbox had no right to be there. The subject header read:

WE THANK YOU FOR YOUR SILENCE

The contents of the email were blank; the sender registered as UNDISCLOSED. Jake filed it into his spam folder, grabbed his things and shuffled over to the kitchen, with his mind devoid of thought and a crippling pain in his stomach that felt like an ice pick was stabbing him repeatedly.

Body running on autopilot, he filled the kettle, switched it on and waited. The knot in his stomach tightened, his throat swelled, and the sides of his head pulsated with the same sensation he'd felt when he'd been staring at the end of Liam Greene's gun. Or when he'd laid eyes on Candice Strachan's collar bomb in her Farnham mansion. The onset of a panic attack.

He breathed deep, rhythmic breaths, forcing the rising tides of paranoia back down into their caves. He imagined his happy place: the football stadium with his mum, brother and sister, watching the latest team at Stamford Bridge playing against Tottenham. A London derby. The roar of the crowd. The euphoric atmosphere. The immense performance. With the extra privilege and added excitement of watching his dad race onto the pitch and tend to one of the injured players. The first time Jake had ever seen his dad at work. The coolest dad ever. His hero.

He opened his eyes. The pores on his body had closed and the sweat blanketing his skin had reduced. His breathing gradually returned to normal.

It was done. And so was the kettle.

But his mind and body weren't out of the darkness yet. The words contained in the email header appeared everywhere he looked. The kettle. The mug. Brendan's half-eaten box of cornflakes. The words had even replaced the digits on the clock that dangled above the door.

The warning signs were becoming more frequent. Three in the space of twenty-four hours. He tried to think of why that might be. But then it struck him as obvious.

Henry Matheson. Rupert Haversham. Jermaine Gordon. Rykard Delawney. It's all connected.

And now the threats were feeling more real, more tangible. Had Danny Cipriano received the same packages before he was killed? Michael? Both brothers had known things they shouldn't, and The Cabal had gone to great lengths to get rid of them.

Jake closed his eyes, thought for a moment, and understood what he had to do. Then he looked at his watch, realised the time and headed back to the office. Stephanie was busy working on her computer, a pair of glasses now perched on top of her nose. Jake grabbed his things, and when she asked where he was going, he apologised for leaving her alone to finish all the work by herself.

But there was somewhere he needed to be.

CHAPTER 18

BLINDED

The buzzer inside the bowels of Wandsworth prison sounded, and the man Jake had come to see entered.

'Didn't think I'd ever see your face again,' Liam Greene said as he pulled the chair from beneath the table and sat opposite.

'You say that to all your visitors?'

'Considering you're the first one.'

'Oh?'

Liam pursed his lips and tilted his head to the side. 'Just you so far. Tanya was supposed to make an appearance, but I haven't seen her since the trial. And she hasn't written back. Can't blame her. Her life's pretty much in the shit thanks to me.'

Jake wasn't going to argue with that. The man had been responsible for ruining a lot of people's lives, most of all his own.

He decided to say nothing. Instead, he observed the man before him. It was like Liam was living in the shadow of his former self. The skin on his face had sagged, his clothes hung loose from his body. His hair had completely fallen out, and the area surrounding his eyes was as black as his heart.

'How you coping?' Jake asked.

'You really care?'

'I've got a few minutes to spare.'

'How mighty generous of you.' Liam shot him a grin but soon realised Jake wasn't laughing. Then he broke into a coughing fit. His body convulsed, and for a moment, Jake thought he was having a seizure. After the flurry was finished, Liam reached inside his sleeve and produced a tissue. Wiping away the spittle and blood, he waved his bloodied tissue in the air.

'Suppose that's what you really wanted to know, wasn't it?' Liam started.

'What is?'

'Why I'm not dead yet.'

'Don't say it like that,' Jake replied. 'I still have some need for you.'

'Well, sorry to disappoint you, but it looks like I might be staying around a little longer. The doctors tell me that I'm responding well and that I'm in remission.'

Jake didn't think that was bad news or disappointing at all. No matter how much he despised Liam for everything he'd done – the betrayal, the greed, the murders of his friends and colleagues – cancer was a disease that united people in their desire to defeat it. It was something you wouldn't wish on your worst enemy, so the saying went, and for Jake, that was true. It let them put their differences and their histories aside and get on for a change. After all, Liam was still a human being, and he was suffering a great deal of pain and turmoil, experiencing something nobody deserved.

'I'm pleased to hear that,' Jake said, finding that the smile on his face came easily.

Liam grunted and shoved the tissue back up his sleeve.

'Go on then, out with it – why are you here?'

'I need your help.'

'Is that what you told your inspector?'

Jake dropped his head. Usual procedure dictated that Stephanie should have been the one to contact the prison governor and request the impromptu meeting. But Jake wasn't in the market for following procedure. Especially when he knew Stephanie would straight-up deny his request. The dust between her and Liam hadn't settled, and Jake doubted it ever would.

'My DI's sick,' he lied.

'Is that what you told them?'

Jake shrugged. 'Not my fault some of the people in this place are as bent as you.'

Liam tutted and shook his head disapprovingly, like a parent disciplining a child. 'You'll have to be careful, Jake. If the wrong people see you round here, they'll start to think we're working together. They'll start to wonder if I'm turning you bent or maybe even if you're conspiring to get me out of here.'

Jake wasn't in the mood to be tormented. Time to move the conversation along. He was in charge of the meeting; he was in charge of the outcome.

'I'm being harassed.'

Liam's face dropped, and if it was possible, his skin looked even paler than it had ten seconds ago. Yet the intrigue in his expression rejuvenated him a shade.

'Harassed… *how*?'

Jake explained it to him. Starting with the very first time he'd received the parcel of drugs in his car, on his doorstep; the parcels of money that he would later find in the boot of his car, under his plant pots; and then he described the emails, always anonymous, always saying the same thing.

'We thank you for your silence…' Liam repeated.

Jake confirmed with a nod.

'What do you need me for?'

'Thought you might have some idea who's responsible.'

'I think you know the answer to that one. I warned you, didn't I? Or have you forgotten that already? You need to be careful, Jake.'

'I'm trying.'

'Evidently not hard enough. When was the last time you received one?'

Jake told him.

'And then before that?'

Jake told him again.

'Are they usually that frequent?'

'No. I think they're related to Henry Matheson in some way.'

Shock registered on Liam's face like he hadn't been expecting to hear the name.

'What makes you say that?'

Jake leant forward and lowered his voice. 'Because yesterday morning Jermaine Gordon's body was found burnt to a crisp, dangling from a lamp post in The Pit. Typically, we suspect Matheson may have had a hand in it. Or maybe just *I* do. But when we spoke to him, he gave us a pretty tight alibi.'

'Of course he would. He's not stupid. His kind will do anything to separate themselves from that sort of stuff. That's why they never deal any of the poison they put on the street; they've got their army of runners, or youngers, to do it for them.'

Liam paused, licked his lips and wiped away the excess saliva with the back of his sleeve. 'But these threats are either directly related to him, as in, he's the one giving them out, or they're warning shots from you know who, telling you to back the fuck off from whatever it is they're doing together.'

Jake looked around. His eyes fell on the blank,

nondescript walls, imagining how many times they'd been spat on and shat on in protest; how many stories they could share if they had the ability.

'What do I do?' Jake asked as he turned his gaze back to Liam.

'You do exactly as you're told, kid. Back the fuck off and keep your mouth shut. Don't give them a reason to *stop* thanking you for your silence.'

Liam ran his hand over his head and massaged his scalp. 'I don't need to remind you about what can happen to people that get in too deep with this stuff, do I? Danika… Garrison… Drew… me…'

'I think I get the picture.'

A brief silence fell over them.

'What have you been doing with the parcels?' Liam asked.

'Destroying them.'

'How?'

'Is that important?'

'Yes. More important than you think. For instance, you don't want to dispose of them discreetly, inconspicuously. I know it sounds counterintuitive, but believe me, the last thing you want is to be photographed or seen disposing of a bag of drugs or a wad of cash in the middle of nowhere. The Cabal can do anything, and your career is always going to be one anonymous photograph delivered directly to your new boss away from being over. Make sure that doesn't happen. You have too much going for you.'

'The Cabal and Matheson,' Jake said slowly. 'How closely do they work together?'

'The Cabal's the boss. Matheson only likes to think he is – but that doesn't mean to say he doesn't possess a lot of pulling power. Far from it, especially when it comes to drugs. I liken them to a rock star and their drugs supplier. One of them needs the other to survive. Henry is responsible for keeping The Cabal's business alive, so he gets away with a lot more. And they don't always see eye to eye, which makes for a fractious and potentially volatile relationship. From now on, you need to assume that anything and everything that goes wrong in your investigation is thanks to The Cabal. Regardless of whether or not Henry Matheson's involved.'

'How do I catch him?'

Liam sighed. 'I told you, I don't know who The Cabal is.'

'I meant Matheson. How do I get him for this murder?'

Liam eased himself further back into his chair. So far, Jake had received everything he'd wanted from Liam. He'd been half expecting to have to put up a fight, to battle his way to get the answers he needed. But it had been easy. He hoped that wouldn't change.

'That depends,' Liam said. 'How's the new team?'

'Eh?'

'The new team. Our replacements. *My* replacement. How you finding them?'

'Fine,' Jake said, unsure of himself. 'Charlotte – or Stephanie, her real name is – is still with us. We've got a couple of new additions. Darryl, the DCI is... well, shall we say he's more of a stickler for the rules than you were. Already managed to get myself in trouble with him a couple of times.'

'Do you trust them?'

Jake opened his mouth, but the words dissolved on his tongue. He didn't know how to answer that. Worse, he didn't have an answer for it. It should have been a simple yes or no, but his experiences of corruption and betrayal in the past few years had stained his perception of everyone and everything he came into contact with. His prejudices had tarnished them with the same thick black brush.

'It's not as easy as that,' he said eventually.

'You asked for my advice, didn't you? If you want to

arrest Matheson for the murder of Jermaine Gordon, and the countless other crimes he's responsible for, then you should trust your colleagues. Listen to them, pay attention to them. Go with them no matter what. Whether they're working for you or against you, you'll soon find out. I know that what I did to you has tainted your impression of everyone you've ever worked with, and I'm sorry for that, truly I am, but you won't get anywhere without trust. Think of it as a marriage.'

Jake scoffed. Liam was in no position to be dishing out advice about trust or relationships, considering he'd put one man in a coma and another in a mortuary.

Pot called: kettle, you're black.

The buzzer sounded overhead, cutting their conversation short. Almost immediately, the prison guards who had been stationed on the outskirts of the room stepped forward and reminded Jake that it was time to leave.

'Just remember what I said,' Liam added as he struggled to lift himself out of the chair. 'It's a jungle out there. And, Jake…' He hesitated, placing a hand on the back of the chair. 'Look after yourself, OK? Your family's more important than the job. Don't get blinded by it like I did.'

CHAPTER 19

BE CREATIVE

An hour later, after weaving his way through the unending traffic in the city, Jake returned to the office from Wandsworth with a Starbucks latte and a pack of Nurofen in his hand.

'They for the hangover?' Brendan asked as he entered, nodding at the tablets, looking like death himself.

'No,' Jake said as he slipped into his desk chair. 'They're for the headache I'm about to get today. I can sense a nasty one coming along soon. You're not looking very chipper this morning yourself. You want some?'

Brendan's response was interrupted by Darryl erupting from his office and pacing across to the other side of the room. He didn't say anything, but he didn't need to. Jake and everyone else in the office knew where he was headed.

Jake scrambled out of his seat, grabbing his things – pen, pad, caffeine. As he juggled the items in his hand, Brendan leant in and whispered, 'I think I'll take you up on that offer, mate. Although I think we might need something a little stronger.'

Chuckling, Jake handed Brendan the packet of ibuprofen,

then headed to the briefing room, where they found themselves a seat at the back.

'Right,' Darryl said, kicking a ball of paper out of his way. 'Firstly, morning, welcome. I hope some of you are feeling prepared after last night's after-party. I heard all about it. For those who aren't already aware, twelve hours ago our John Doe became Jermaine Gordon, one of East London's biggest gangland drug dealers, thanks to a confession by one of Henry Matheson's own, Rykard Delawney. Mr Delawney is currently sitting in custody getting his full eight hours while we need to use this time wisely to investigate everything we can to either confirm his account or dispel it.'

Jake raised his hand. 'I'm gonna call it early, guv, but I'm calling bullshit. It's all too convenient. And never in the history of Henry Matheson and the E11 gang have they ever done anything like this before.'

Darryl perched himself on the end of a desk at the other end of the room – the teacher's desk, Jake liked to call it – and folded his arms.

'I'm glad you said that, Jake. I'm even happier you bothered to attend this morning.'

'Sir?'

'Your little excursion last night.' Darryl's eyebrow rose, and in that moment, he reminded Jake of his father; he used to receive the same reaction from his dad whenever he'd done something he knew he shouldn't have. 'How was it?'

'It was good, guv.' He swallowed. 'Saw a drug deal go down. Three individuals. A kid on a bike. IC1 male. A dealer with tattoos on his neck, most notably an eagle. Possibly IC3 male. And then a third male, IC1, with a tattoo on his hand. A scorpion.'

'Any faces?'

Jake shook his head. 'Only the kid's. Looked about twelve years old.'

'Any photographic evidence?'

Jake nodded enthusiastically. This was going better than he'd expected. Maybe Darryl wasn't as much of a hard arse as he'd thought. 'I thought you'd never ask.'

Jake reached inside his blazer pocket and pulled out a small SD card – 12GB worth of storage. He'd taken it straight from Elizabeth's camera in the hope he'd be able to transfer them to his computer at work, but so far he'd struggled to find the time. 'They're all on here, sir.'

Darryl approached and took the storage card from Jake. 'Is there anything else on this?'

'Nope. Fresh out the packet.'

'Good,' Darryl said as he snapped the SD card in half.

Jake leapt to his feet. 'What're you doing?' he yelled. 'They cost thirty quid each!'

'What you did was reckless, not to mention fucking stupid. You went against my orders. You put yourself at risk. Anything could have happened. You're not some rogue warrior with something to prove who can just carry everything on their own, all right. I will not be undermined like that again. Do you understand?'

Jake clenched his jaw, ground his teeth and bit his tongue. There were words he wanted to say, but it was neither the time nor the place. Nor the smartest idea.

'Is there any money in the budget for replacing my *wife's* SD card, *sir*?' Jake pointed to the two pieces of splintered plastic on the floor.

He hadn't realised it, but their outburst had inspired the rest of the office to stand up from their desks and peer around, like meerkats from their holes.

Darryl's expression remained the same. 'I'll replace it for you personally. As a goodwill gesture.'

How mighty fucking generous of you.

Darryl dropped his arms and busied himself with a bobble

on his trousers. 'We need to start from the bottom,' he said after everyone had turned to face the front of the room, unable to bear the awkwardness in the air. 'We have to put our prejudices aside, turn over every rock, and find out who else is responsible for Jermaine Gordon's death. And if our investigations lead to the same individuals as identified by Jake, then by all means we can follow those leads, but for now, I want us to build up a profile of Jermaine Gordon's family. Wife? Kids? Mum? Dad? Brother? Sister? Who?'

The room fell eerily silent. Then it was disturbed by a cough.

'Is this not just a case of a turf war?' one of the young detective constables in the team asked.

'Normally, I would say yes,' Darryl responded, 'but when you've got Jermaine Gordon and Henry Matheson in the same frame – two of the biggest dealers in the city – things stop being about drugs and turf, and they start to become personal. Which is why it's important we look into his family situation, his—'

'Already started that, guv,' Stephanie interrupted.

Jake looked at her with surprise. She had been busy. Was there any midnight oil left for the rest of them?

'After the interview with Rykard, I looked into Jermaine's history. He doesn't have any family. They're all dead. He's never had any kids – at least, as far as I can work out – and the rest of his family were killed in gang crimes. His sister was the last to die: last year. Stabbed in the neck by a junky. His mum was hit by a car, but the circumstances surrounding her death were a little off, and nobody was ever brought to justice for it. Jermaine protested it was a personal hit from Henry, but nobody believed him. And nobody was brave enough to do anything about it.'

'Did he retaliate?' Jake asked.

Stephanie twisted in her seat. 'As far as I can tell, Jermaine didn't do a thing. Treated it as though it'd never happened.'

'Perhaps he was waiting for an opportune moment?'

'Possibly. Maybe he's already done it, Matheson found out, and then decided to take it one step further.'

'All possible things for us to consider,' Darryl said and turned his back on them. He grabbed a pen and wrote the words FAMILY and FRIENDS on the whiteboard behind him. And then after a moment's hesitation, he wrote GANG WAR beside it.

'These are the avenues we need to look into. If nobody in Jermaine's family is alive to tell us about him, then maybe his friends will be able to.'

Brendan scoffed. 'Yeah, like that's going to happen. For these guys, their friendship is as strong as family.'

'Every family has its cracks, Brendan. We just need to exploit them.'

Darryl placed the pen in the small tray that ran along the bottom of the whiteboard. 'Be creative. So long as it's within the law.'

CHAPTER 20

MOVIE BUFF

One thought filled Jake's head as he returned to his desk: that Darryl was as clueless as a nun in a brothel. It was farcical, looking into Jermaine's home life. The absolute wrong place to start. His death was a gang crime through and through. But he wasn't going to say anything. Not after the spanking he'd just received in there.

An idea was forming in his head, all its shapes and contours and nuances coming together like a piece of art on a canvas, and it was all he could think about. At his desk, he logged himself into his computer, loaded the Police National Database and began a search for a property: 233 Cosgrove Estate.

He hit return and the results were instant. At the top of the list was the case number CRZ/760023-M. Jake opened the file and read the summary of the report.

During the early hours of the morning on April 25, 2002, at precisely 1:02 a.m., Mr Aiden Coyne was seen entering the premises of Shree News on the Cosgrove Estate. Mr Coyne then

proceeded to shoplift the following items: Coca Cola x 3, Pot Noodle
x 4, Walkers Crisps x 2.

The proprietor of Shree News caught Mr Coyne and
apprehended him. Police later arrived after being called to the scene.
When questioned, Mr Coyne justified his theft as necessary to feed
his child, Lewis.

Jake stopped reading. He only needed the family members' names. Now, armed with that nugget of information, he entered both names into the database and hit return. His eyes scanned the results furiously, absorbing the information displayed in front of him.

The results didn't surprise him. Both father and son were career criminals. Petty theft, vandalism, public disorder, arson... both of them even had ASBOs. What surprised Jake, however, was the son's age. Thirteen. Young. *Too* young. No age to be lost to the dark side. A whole life ahead of him, but the lures of money and status had invariably poisoned his malleable, impressionable mind.

Jake looked up from his screen, leant to the side and waved at Stephanie opposite him.

'Yeah?' she asked, unimpressed.

'I need company.'

'You learnt your lesson?'

'Don't you start.'

'Where to?'

'The Pit. Where else?'

'What have we got?'

'Two words. Suspects and waiting.'

Stephanie studied him a moment. Sighed. 'This better be legit.' She climbed out of her chair and moved into the lift with him. 'And you'd better've learnt your lesson.'

'Why do you think I've brought you along? When we get back, you can tell Darryl all about how well I'm toeing the line.'

Stephanie folded her arms and puffed air from her nose. 'You know, Jake, sometimes you can surround yourself with so much of what you stand to fight against that you eventually begin to fight for it instead.'

With that cryptic comment in his mind, Jake pressed the button for the ground floor and waited for the lift doors to close.

'I think I've heard that before,' he said finally. 'Didn't Orwell say something like that?'

The doors opened, and together they walked to her car.

'No, not Orwell,' Jake said as he strapped the seat belt across his stomach, 'wasn't it Harvey Dent who said that in *The Dark Knight*? You either die a hero or live long enough to see yourself become the villain.'

No answer. She switched on the engine.

'Never had you down as a movie buff,' she said finally.

'There's a lot you don't know about me.'

If there was anything more truthful in the world, Jake wanted to hear it.

CHAPTER 21

THE DEN

The off-licence in the middle of the estate had, until recently, been the focal point for the Cosgrove residents, the hub of their activity. In its heyday, everyone would be seen congregating around the doors, loitering in the aisles, meandering and deciding what delectable poison to pick. It was even the place where Henry, Jamal, Deshawn and the rest of the elders found themselves conducting their business – supplying the food to junkies, using the goods from the convenience store as a cover whenever any unwanted visitors patrolled nearby. It was like they were in their own economy, and Henry was the Chancellor of the Exchequer. The money would come to him through the dealers, then he'd funnel some of it back into the off-licence, making Arjun, the owner, who had a young family to feed, a very happy man.

But then things began to change. The police presence around the estate increased, and one of the youngers had decided to vandalise and destroy the shop after Arjun inadvertently short-changed him. The younger, whose name Henry had immediately forgotten after he'd disposed of him, had ransacked the shelves and destroyed everything in sight. Bereft, and with his main source of income gone, Arjun couldn't see any way out, so he'd committed suicide shortly after, leaving his wife, newborn girl and three-year-old son behind. It later transpired that he'd been suffering with mental health issues almost all his life, and the actions of one younger had been enough to tilt the chair just off-balance. And so Henry had felt obliged to put it right, making sure Arjun's wife and family were well looked after by giving them enough money for a deposit on a flat outside the estate, and some money to keep them going.

In some ways, Henry felt responsible for Arjun's death. But there was a silver lining amongst the darkness. Following the sudden closure of the off-licence, the police stopped showing their unwelcome faces at unwelcome hours of the day. And then Henry'd had an idea: board up the windows, seal it shut, and create the production line for his entire drug empire. While the youngers and a few of the elders were cutting, bagging and manufacturing his product, Arjun's memory still lived on. Granted, not in the way that he might have wanted, but it lived on nonetheless. And that helped silence some of the guilt in Henry's mind.

Now and then he'd spring a surprise visit on the youngers working in there, check up on how they were doing, like a surprise Ofsted visit at a school; regulating them so they were constantly reminded who was boss.

The inside of The Den, as it was now called, was dark and dreary, devoid of any personality, the shelves now home to row upon row of plastic soft drink bottles; in one half of the room they were full, in the other half they were empty, waiting to be filled. In the middle was a series of tables, and sitting around them were the youngers – boys ranging from eleven to seventeen, dressed in their tracksuits, wearing face masks to protect them from inhaling the chemicals and other cutting agents they used to package the product, each of them working hard at every stage of the production line.

Standing at the other end of The Den was Elijah, one of the elders in charge of overseeing operations, a thirty-nine-year-old man who was still living in his twenties. What he lacked in speed and agility, thanks to the size of his belly and legs, he more than made up for in wisdom and expertise. Elijah had been in the game a long time, and he brought a level of control and knowledge to the operation that was unparalleled. If Henry was the CEO, Elijah was almost certainly the COO.

Henry sauntered towards him, extending his hand.

'What you saying, bro?' Elijah said as they bumped shoulders. 'You good?'

'I'm gonna need you to do me a favour soon,' Henry replied. 'I got the feds breathing down my neck about this whole J thing, so we're gonna need to contain this shit big time. Keep the shipments from the docks to here down to a minimum, and get some of the boys to work longer shifts, but make sure they're paid for it though. Don't want a reason for none of their mums to get suspicious.'

'What about the Hellbanianz?' Elijah asked. 'They're killing us out there.'

The Hellbanianz was the self-titled name for the group of Albanians who'd wandered into the country – literally thanks to the open borders – and taken the drugs industry by storm. They were Henry's direct competition, and they were rapidly becoming bigger than he could have ever imagined. They operated a highly connected network of contacts and supply chains that enabled them to slash their production costs and still provide high-quality, A-grade gear. With junkies being the way they were, if they could get the same quality drugs for half the price, they weren't stupid enough to say no. The Hellbanianz had only been in the market for a year or two, but they were already beginning to push him out of the way and snipe his customers, and with Henry ramping down the business in the next couple of days – weeks, perhaps, until the police lost interest – they were going to get stung financially.

'I can only deal with one issue at a time, bro,' Henry said. 'I got bigger things to worry about. I thought some of the boys were scouting them out?'

Elijah shrugged. 'There's only so much they can do, geez. They ain't standing up to the Hellbanianz's firepower, no way.'

'They not packing nothing? Thought I gave you loads of metal?'

Elijah shrugged again. 'Think they're afraid to use 'em. None of 'em have held a gun before.'

Henry scratched the side of his face and reminded himself he needed to shave. Because they could leave the country with ease and disappear onto the continent, the Hellbanianz weren't afraid to use excessive force to assert their control, and Henry had heard horror stories of gun wars breaking out on housing estates as well as industrial estates in the middle of nowhere. Territory and land was all a gang had, and if they didn't have the power to defend it, then they were at the mercy of those who did.

'They'll learn quicker on the job, trust. If that don't work, then I'll speak to them. I've got a meeting with the Hellz face to face soon. But you leave that with me.'

Henry cast his eye around The Den.

'Before I forget,' he continued, 'there's one of J's youngers I need you to find. Tried bouncing me yesterday morning, but I promised him I'd get him out.' Henry handed over Veronica's business card. 'Give her a bell. She should've got him out by now. When you find him, bring him here and keep him in. He looks like a worker, but if he does anything dumb, you let me know.'

'Course, Hen.'

'Is there anything I need to know?'

Elijah shuffled to Henry's side so he was standing next to his shoulder. He pointed to a young boy with his hood pulled over his face. 'This one's got something he wants to tell ya.'

Elijah whistled, summoning the boy over. Immediately the boy dropped the bag of cocaine he was holding on the scales and hurried over. Henry inspected him. He was no more than twelve, maybe younger. His eyes were big, youthful, and still contained some of that childish innocence he'd seen in a lot of the boys who worked for him. That was a look that quickly disappeared.

'This is Alfie,' Elijah said, yanking back the boy's hood to reveal a set of tightly knitted braids on his head. 'He did his first delivery today shotting some food.'

'Oh yeah?' Henry feigned an impressed smile.

'Only problem was though…' Elijah hesitated and glared at the boy. 'You gonna tell him or me…?'

Alfie took the hint and licked his lips. His eyes fell away from Henry's and landed on his shoes. 'I… I got mugged, innit.'

'Yeah? Who by?'

'My buyer, innit. He must have saw the size of me and thought he could get away with it.'

'And can he?'

Alfie lifted his head.

'You gonna let him get away with it?' Henry asked.

Before he allowed Alfie a chance to respond, Henry held out his hand. As if they were communicating telepathically, Elijah reached into his pocket and placed a small switchblade in Henry's palm. Henry hovered it in Alfie's face. 'When you work for me, you don't let no one step on you like that, you feel me?'

The boy nodded, the innocence slowly fading from his eyes as he studied the metal blade.

'So what I want you to do, fam, is next time you see him, you make sure he learns his lesson, yeah? Make sure he don't step on you again. You understand?'

Alfie took the blade from Henry. He understood perfectly, and as he headed back to his seat, he took one last look at Henry. The innocence in his eyes was gone.

It wasn't Henry's job to corrupt young people. They chose to do it. They were well within their rights to leave the gang and start new lives for themselves, but they were always warned to do one thing: watch their back every step of the way. Former youngers and elders posed a security threat. They possessed knowledge. And in the wrong hands, knowledge could be very dangerous; knowledge could get them killed. Which was why he made a habit of getting them into his debt or getting blood on their hands – whichever came first.

Henry tucked his hands into his pockets. As soon as Alfie was back at his seat, funnelling small quantities of cocaine into plastic baggies, Henry's phone vibrated. He removed it from his pocket and observed the screen. It was a text message from Lily, the girl from the other morning and the night before.

He hadn't realised it, but a smile had grown on his face as he read the message. *I enjoyed the other night. When can I see you again?*

Before he replied, Elijah nudged him on the elbow. 'Fucking hell, bruv, you going soft? First time I've ever seen a girl make you smile. The great Henry Matheson, tamed by some girl he wanted to fuck and chuck.'

Henry kissed his teeth. 'Fuck off, fam. It's different. Ain't expect a player like you to know anything about it.'

He ignored Elijah and replied: *Soon, babes, promise. I'll*

bring the wine and flowers.

As soon as he hit send, the doors to The Den opened. In swaggered Deshawn and Jamal, hands in pockets, puffed up in their puffer jackets that they wore regardless of the outdoor temperature. By the time they arrived beside Henry and Elijah, Henry had placed the phone back in his pocket and forgotten about the message. It was business time.

'All right, boys,' Henry said, greeting them. 'You good? What you saying?'

'Nuffin', fam. What you—'

'Boys, you caught Henry at the wrong time,' Elijah interrupted. 'Think he's got a hard-on at the moment.'

'You what?' asked Jamal.

'Big man's in *looooveee.*'

As soon as the L-word left Elijah's lips, Deshawn and Jamal's eyes widened, and they burst into a flurry of laughter, slapping him on the arms, pointing at him, crying into each other's shoulders.

Henry kissed his teeth and shook his head. He started to walk away, paying them little attention, but as he shuffled his way around the production line, he tripped on a misplaced plastic bottle and staggered into the empty shelving unit a few feet away from him. Fuck. The height of embarrassment. Tripping in front of his friends. They would never let him live it down. The eruption of laughter in The Den was testament to that.

But even worse was what Jamal said afterwards.

'It's Lily, fam. I'm telling you now, that bird's gonna be the death of you, bruv.'

CHAPTER 22

ALLEYWAY

Stephanie slowed the car to a halt. 'Is this it?'

'You see those giant numbers on the door – the two, three, and the other three? That's the house number. Of course we're in the right place.'

'If you're gonna be a dick all day, I'll leave you here and you can make your own way back.'

Jake smirked as he gripped the door handle. 'Didn't my antics last night tell you anything? I *want* to be here.'

Stephanie scoffed. 'Sounds like you've got a death wish.'

The street was empty, save for an overturned bike and a beaten-up Fiesta that had the obligatory 'Fuck me, I'm dirty' inscribed on the back in a layer of dust. Jake chuckled at the classic immature humour. They were on the east side of the estate, opposite the low-rise buildings. The front door of number 233 was made of wood that had once been painted red or maroon in a previous life but had fallen victim to years of decay and bleaching from the sun and was now a dull brown.

'What did you say we were here for?' Stephanie asked,

stepping to the side of the porch to allow Jake a space beside her.

'I didn't. I recognised this address from last night. Thought I'd plug it into the PNC and see what came out. This is the result.'

From the look on her face, she was about to release a torrent of dissatisfied air from her nose. But he beat her to her protestations. 'Relax, all right. I know what I'm doing. Trust me.'

'Sometimes your ego needs to be taken down a peg, Jake,' Stephanie replied, looking at him from the corner of her eye. 'Or several.'

A few seconds later, the front door opened and they were greeted by a man in his early thirties. Jake assumed he and the man were only a few years apart in age, but they couldn't look any more different. The man before him wore a white Lonsdale shirt with accompanying tracksuit that looked as though it had been lived in for several weeks. He had thinning blond hair, and his belly bulged out of his top, the result of a few generous helpings of beer on a weeknight, and double that while the football was on at the weekend.

'Mr Coyne?' Jake asked. He held his warrant card up for the man to see.

'No comment,' Aiden replied reflexively.

'You're not in any trouble, Mr Coyne. We just wanted to ask you a few questions.'

'This about Lewis?'

'Not unless it needs to be, Mr Coyne.'

'How d'you know my name?'

'Well, I'm sure you've heard about what happened to a man named Jermaine Gordon the other day? We're conducting our house-to-house interviews. Your name and address cropped up on our systems.'

'I did my time for that. I'm done with that life.'

'Your son doesn't seem to be.'

'I thought this wasn't about Lewis?'

'Do you mind if we come in? It might be more comfortable,' Jake asked.

Aiden scoffed, but then eventually ceded and stepped to the side. 'It ain't much to look at. You'll have to mind the shit.'

'It's all right,' Jake said, 'we've been to worse places, I can assure you.'

The hall carpet was covered in mud that had been trodden into the house by hundreds of pairs of feet over the years. Wallpaper was beginning to peel from the walls as if escaping the conditions it was subjected to. And the radiator that ran the length of the wall was falling off from one side, revealing a dark-brown stain behind it.

At the end of the corridor, they made a left turn into a passageway which led directly into the living room.

There, Jake froze.

A pair of crutches was propped against the wall to Jake's left, a Zimmer frame positioned in front of the sofa, and, to Jake's right, next to the stairs, was a chairlift.

'Does... someone else live with you both?' Stephanie asked tentatively.

'No,' Aiden said. 'Just us.'

He stopped and turned to Stephanie. He must have read the look on her face because he answered the question that lay there. 'It's for my back. Hypokalaemic periodic paralysis. Fancy name for saying I basically turn into a statue every time it flares up. Sometimes I can't move for an hour, sometimes longer, sometimes less. The crutches are for when Lewis has to help me to the bathroom or bed.'

'I'm so sorry,' Stephanie said.

'No point crying over it. Nothing I can do but live with it. Suppose you could consider me one of the lucky ones. Only affects about one per cent of the population.'

'Makes you unique.' Jake hoped his attempt to lighten the mood was also strong enough to lighten the place up as well.

'That's what I tell myself. I don't get to go out much. Most of the time I'm watching this shit.'

On the television, a repeat episode of *The Jeremy Kyle Show* was playing. The caption along the bottom read, 'I want to prove I didn't sleep with my pregnant girlfriend's mum'.

'You'd be surprised,' Aiden started, 'I've seen pretty much every episode and I've never seen anyone from round here come up. Amazes me considering some of the specimens you find round these ends. Wouldn't mind getting out of here, mind. Less I have to see some of these cretins, the better.'

Jake and Stephanie allowed Aiden to seat himself before they sat adjacent; Stephanie sitting in an armchair and Jake perching on the edge beside her.

'What can you tell us about Jermaine Gordon?' Jake asked once they'd settled.

Aiden shrugged. 'Not a lot. Ain't much I know about him, 'cept his reputation. Never met him personally.'

'Have you seen him around the estate at all recently?'

'Nope.'

'Anyone mention his name? Say they might want to try and harm him in any way?'

'Nope.'

'Has Lewis ever mentioned his name or any people he's associated with?'

'Nope.'

'Anything that might be of any help to us at all?'

'Nope. Sorry. Like I told you, I don't get out much – and this seat ain't much of a vantage point. But I've heard about what's happened. Everybody I spoke to reckons they saw who done it but ain't none of them giving away any names.'

'Do you have the names of these individuals?'

'Nah,' Aiden said, his immediate backtracking noticeable. 'Just a load of people from round the estate. I don't like giving out no names. Never did when I got nicked, so won't start now.'

'Is there anything else you want to tell us?' Stephanie asked, sounding sympathetic. 'We could really use your assistance.'

Aiden dropped his head, apologised and said, 'If I did, I'd tell ya. What they done to that bloke is horrible. Ain't nobody deserves that sort of treatment. If you ever find 'em, make sure you lock 'em away for a long time, yeah?'

'Where was Lewis the other night?'

Aiden shrugged. 'Far as I'm aware he was sleeping. He likes to play out a lot, sometimes late at night, but he was playing on *Call of Duty* I think.'

'And last night?'

'Same again.'

Aiden was either incredulously naïve, or the wool was so far over his eyes he didn't know what year it was.

Jake reached into his pocket and removed a business card. He walked across the room, handed it to Aiden, and their hands locked in a grip. 'If you need anything, please do not hesitate to contact us. We'll always be happy to help.'

Aiden tried to lift himself from the sofa, but Jake and Stephanie told him to stay where he was. After protesting a little, Aiden eventually gave up and waved goodbye.

'We'll show ourselves out,' Jake said, and as he stepped out of the door, he reminded Aiden to call if he needed anything.

'Appreciate it.'

As they idled along the corridor, Jake's curiosity overwhelmed him, and he peered into the other rooms in the house. Into the kitchen that offered views of the narrow back garden – full of overgrown vegetation – and into the bedroom by the front door that Jake presumed was Aiden's. There was nothing of any interest in either.

'What're you thinking?' Stephanie asked, closing the door behind her.

Jake gazed out at the street ahead. 'That he's a man stuck in a shitty situation.'

Stephanie opened her mouth but held back what she was about to say. Nearing the car, she spoke.

'Do you believe it?'

'What?'

'Do you really think he's got that thing? That problem? Hyperplexia or whatever it was. He seemed fine when he opened the door.'

'I… er… yeah, I do. I think he was in a considerable amount of pain; he just managed to hide it well.'

Stephanie grunted. 'It's worth checking out.'

'I'll leave that to you then.'

Their relationship had tightened over the past six months, and Jake had even introduced Stephanie to his home, to Elizabeth and the girls, and they'd all got on as though they'd been friends for years. At first, Jake had worried about how close he and Stephanie were, and how jealous it might make Elizabeth, but his wife adored Stephanie and Stephanie adored Elizabeth.

'Did you find out what you wanted?' Stephanie asked as she readied the keys from her bag.

'Not quite. I need the kid. He's clearly sneaking out when he shouldn't, and if he's running the same sort of shifts as he was last night, then I'm confident he'll have seen the murder.'

Stephanie found her keys and unlocked the door. Just as she was about to climb in, something caught Jake's eye. A child, no older than thirteen or fourteen from his body stature, was riding a bike towards them. His hood was pulled over his face, and he wore a pair of Puma jogging bottoms.

He neared them, swaying left and right on the pavement, Jake observing the kid's every movement.

Lewis?

And then he lost him.

The kid cut down an alleyway that led into the main square of the estate.

It was Jake's chance to act. He bolted from the car, crossed the street, hopped onto the pavement and raced down the alleyway, his legs and arms pumping with blood and excitement. He ran so hard that the balls of his feet landed heavily in his shoes with every step and they soon began to ache.

Down the alleyway, there were three figures in front of him. The kid on the bike and two others, neither of whom he recognised from the night before. The kid on the bike was exchanging something with the two adults. A plastic bottle.

Fanta Orange.

Before Jake could do anything, they caught sight of him and fled. The two adults on foot were quick, disappearing round the corner within a second. But the kid was impeded by the bike. His feet scrabbled for the pedals, and the alley wasn't wide enough for him to turn.

Jake picked up his pace and sprinted towards the boy again. As he stopped by the bike, the kid threw his hand into his pocket, but Jake cut the boy off, grabbed him, and twisted his arm up his back. In the movement, the boy dropped his knife to the ground. It bounced and clattered on the pavement by Jake's feet.

'Fuck off me!' the kid spat. 'Get your hands off me!'

He tried to wriggle and writhe beneath Jake's grasp, but it was no use. The boy looked at the knife and tried to pick it up; Jake kicked it away. At that point, Stephanie arrived.

'Jake! What are you doing?'

He nodded at the blade on the ground. 'This little one

tried to pull that thing out on me.'

'I ain't little!' the teenager screamed. 'Get off!'

'What's your name?'

'I ain't telling you.'

Jake reached into his pocket and pulled out his warrant card. 'What about now?'

The boy's eyes widened. 'I'm sorry! I didn't mean to. Please don't. If they find out I've been nicked, do you know what they'll do to me? I didn't mean to do it.'

'You didn't mean to do what?'

'Pull the knife on you.'

'I really wish you hadn't either. Now come on, you're coming with us.'

CHAPTER 23

BOTTLES

It took them the best part of an hour to process the boy's arrest and sit him in an interview room with a solicitor and a parent, which in this case was the young boy's mother. The boy had given his name as Reece Enfield, and as far as a quick background check on him reported, he'd had no previous run-ins with the law.

First time for everything.

The three of them were bunched against one another behind the small white table like a trio of parked cars on a busy street. On the table, against the right-hand wall of the room, was the recording equipment.

Jake was in the adjoining room, watching them from the CCTV camera positioned in the top corner of the ceiling. It was only his second time interviewing a juvenile. First time one had tried to pull a knife on him though, which added a different dynamic to proceedings.

The door opened and Stephanie peered round it.

'Ready?' she asked, holding a piece of paper in her hand.

'Think so. Everything sorted?'

'Paperwork's complete. Darryl's happy to proceed, so is the custody sergeant. All systems go.'

Stephanie smiled, turned her back on him and left. Before following, Jake gave one last look at the young boy slumped on the chair and prepared himself.

As he entered the interview room, he breathed slowly, then pulled his chair out and sat. His eyes moved from person to person, observing those in front of him. To Jake's left was Sarah McCormack, Reece's solicitor. In her early sixties, she looked tired, as though she didn't want to be there. Jake supposed she was nearing retirement and was slowly counting down the days until she no longer had to pretend like she cared to be at these things. She was dressed in a pink blouse with a burgundy skirt, and her cheeks were the colour of a rose. Today, he mused, she was going for an aged *Legally Blonde* look.

Beside her, in the middle, was Reece's mother, Elaine. She was young, perhaps in her early thirties, and her blood-red hair was in a ponytail. She wore a denim jacket and flip-flops. Dull, black bags hung loosely under her eyes, and the river of veins running into her pupils told him she was fighting to stay awake.

Finally, on the right, was Reece, his body slumped in the chair, staring down at the table below him. He had a double chin and a look of dissent on his face.

'Welcome all,' Stephanie began. It was her turn to lead the interview. 'The time is twelve fifty-seven p.m. Present are Detective Constable Jake Tanner, myself, Detective Inspector Stephanie Grayson, Elaine Enfield, Reece Enfield, and Reece's solicitor, Sarah McCormack. You are all aware why Reece is here. Earlier this morning, Reece was arrested on possession of drugs, possession of drugs with intent to supply, possession of a bladed weapon and affray. The knife has been entered into evidence and is being processed. I want to start this interview by reminding Reece that this is a safe place. Whatever you say here will not be shared beyond these four walls, do you understand?'

Reece grunted and nodded. An unexpected reaction considering his earlier demeanour.

'Perfect. We're going to ask you some questions now, but first I wondered if you had any for us?'

'When can I get out of here?' Reece retorted.

Elaine slapped the back of his hand. 'Don't start with the attitude, Reece,' she said. 'What you've done is serious.'

'It's fine,' Stephanie said, holding a hand in the air to placate Elaine. 'We'll have to work out what's going to happen to you next shortly. But it may not be a case of leaving and going back home right away, you understand?'

'But I ain't done nothing wrong!'

'Unfortunately, Reece, these are some quite serious offences for someone your age. It's a criminal act to carry a blade, especially the one we found on you. Why did you have it?'

'Protection.'

Jake sensed they would only get monosyllabic answers from here on out.

'Why do you have it for protection?'

'Because.'

'Is there someone who wants to hurt you? Or someone who wants to make sure you don't feel safe?'

'No.'

'What were you going to do with the knife, Reece?' Jake asked, unable to stop himself. It still hadn't fully registered that he'd had a knife pulled on him.

'Nothing.'

'If there is someone who wants to hurt you, Reece, we can help.'

'You can't do shit,' Reece replied.

Elaine grabbed her son by the shoulder. 'Have you been hanging around with those boys again? I told you to stay away!'

'Shut up, Mum.' Reece shrugged her away and folded his arms across his chest in an act of defiance.

'What boys, Miss Enfield?' Stephanie asked.

'The dealers. They're everywhere on the estate. They're like a fucking disease. They've been there ever since we moved in when Reece was a baby. They get the little kids to carry out their dirty work for them.'

'What dirty work?' asked Jake. He was already aware of the answer but wanted to hear it straight from Elaine's mouth.

'Drugs. These people – these *elders*, they call 'em – use boys like Reece and others his age, give them drugs to sell on to people around the estate, and some other ones nearby, and they take all the profits. Reece then gets given a tiny cut of it.'

There was something in the way she said it that made Jake think she was slightly disappointed by the fact her son only received a small pay cheque from his illegal activities, like she was advocating child trafficking and slavery in a bizarre sort of way if it meant she could make more money out of it than she currently was.

She continued, 'I caught him the other week with bags of money under his bed, and when I asked him where he got 'em from, he wouldn't say nothing. So I watched him one night and saw him do it. I swear I could have slapped the life out of him, trust me.'

'Elaine…' Sarah McCormack said, placing a gentle hand on her forearm. 'We discussed this…'

'Is that what you were doing in the alleyway when we found you, Reece? Were you dealing drugs to those two individuals?'

'Son of a bitch,' Elaine retorted.

'Reece?' Stephanie repeated when she didn't get an answer.

'No comment,' he replied, looking down at the table.

'Who were they, Reece?'

'No comment.'

Jake leant forward, placed his elbows on the table and swallowed. 'I saw a plastic bottle in your hand. What was inside?'

'I dunno,' Reece replied, the hesitancy in his voice belying his hard exterior.

'Were there drugs in the bottle?'

'Might've been. I don't look inside.'

'Who gave you the bottle?'

'I pick 'em up.'

'From where?'

'They're left in a telephone box with instructions on it.'

'What do the instructions say?'

Reece maintained his eye contact with Jake. 'They tell me where to be and when and who I'm meeting, innit.'

'And then you go to the place and give that person the bottle in exchange for money?'

'Yes.'

'What happens after that?'

'I leave the money in the telephone box, and then the next time I do a drop-off is when I get my cut from the last one.'

Jake absorbed the information and imagined the sequence of events in his head. It was all slowly beginning to make sense to him now. But there were still a myriad questions he needed answers to.

'Do you ever see any faces, learn any names?' he asked.

Reece shook his head. 'No names. No faces. No nothing. That's how they like it. Especially with them junkies. They don't like showing they faces neither.'

'Tell me about the bottles,' Jake said as he tried to force the image of the one he'd found the night before out of his mind.

'They're special,' Reece said, shrinking into the chair, as though trying to escape the persistent round of questioning.

'How?'

Reece suddenly turned tight-lipped.

'Reece, what do they do to the bottles?'

Nothing.

'Answer him,' Elaine insisted.

'He doesn't have to respond,' the solicitor intervened.

'I don't care. He'll do what I bloody well tell him to.' She nudged her son on the arm. '*Answer* him.'

Reece sighed heavily before responding. 'They split the bottles in three bits. Top, middle, bottom. The middle's where the label is, and they put the drugs inside it. Then they fill the top and bottom with the drink, and it all screws together to make it look like there ain't nothing suspicious about none of it.'

The muscles in Jake's back and shoulders relaxed. The young boy had just confirmed what he already knew. Now they could approach the evidence, the gang, and the drugs as a direct result of the interview, rather than Jake throwing more suspicion on himself by coming out of the blue with it.

'How are they doing this?' he asked.

'I dunno.'

'Do you know where?'

'All I know is that that's how they do it. I dunno where they do it. The bottles just turn up like that.'

Perfect, Jake thought.

A moment of silence entered the room and hung there like an unwelcome friend. Jake opened his mouth to speak but was interrupted by Stephanie.

'Thanks for your time here, everyone. We won't be charging you now, and will today be releasing you on bail, pending a further interview. The date will be set when we check you out at the custody suite. We will also have to confiscate and destroy the knife we took from you. You've been a massive help to us today, Reece, so we thank you. And might I remind you that if you need us again, or if you remember anything, then you know where to find us. We'll always be happy to help.'

Stephanie pressed the stop button on the recording device and then instructed the family to follow her to the custody sergeant, after which they'd be allowed to leave. Jake remained behind, tidying the desk of their brief papers.

Five minutes later, when Stephanie returned, he welcomed her with a wide grin. 'Told you it'd be worthwhile.'

'You make it seem like I doubted you.'

'Which is exactly what you were doing.'

It's all anyone seems to be doing nowadays.

CHAPTER 24

THIS LITTLE BEAUTY

Frank Graham had never liked being told what to do. Despised it, had a natural aversion to it, in fact; and he had done ever since he was a child. Rebellious at school, called a little shitbag by some of his teachers when they thought he wasn't listening, he often spent more time outside it than he did in. On the high street or on the fringes of the Dunsfield Estate, he learnt everything he needed to about the world. Life was the biggest lesson of them all, and it didn't take him long to realise that it wasn't all about algebra and history and biology. Although hindsight being a wonderful thing, he could probably have done with paying more attention in biology to save himself the embarrassment of putting things in the wrong places.

But after his encounter with Henry Matheson the night before, he had learnt an even more important lesson. Something that he had almost forgotten about – something he had not needed to remember for so long. That under no circumstance was he to let anyone walk over him. Let anyone tell him what to do. Let anyone think he was a pushover.

Because as soon as they convinced themselves that was the case, nothing would change it.

That shit was permanent.

'Pass me the scales,' Frank said to Caleb.

His friend stopped what he was doing, set his debit card to the side and handed the scales over to Frank. Frank's hand shook under the weight of the three hundred quid scales he'd bought online.

'You still shitting yourself?' Caleb asked, nodding to Frank's poor bicep strength. 'Ain't never seen you so white. Thought I was looking at a fresh chicken breast when you got back in the car.'

'Piss off. Matheson ain't shit. People round here are afraid of him for nothing. Pfft. He won't be saying nothing in a few days.' Frank set the scales down on the table and switched them on.

'You're playing with fire, bruv.'

'Now who's the one shitting himself?'

On the table were tightly wrapped piles of cocaine and assortments of other drugs. Caleb grabbed one and launched it at Frank. The bag soared through the air and, by some miracle, Frank caught it without it exploding all over his face and clothes.

Before the shock of the catch had a chance to register on Caleb's face, Frank threw it back across the desk. The bag collided with his friend's forehead and exploded, spraying the white powder in the air like a plume of smoke.

'Watch it, you fucking reprobate!' Caleb screamed as he frantically clawed at the air in an attempt to stop the drugs from climbing up his nose. His voice echoed up and down the abandoned nightclub that they used as their headquarters, which was just a glorified term for manufacturing warehouse. They'd acquired it a year back and had since been laundering money through it, staging parties with loud music every Friday and Saturday night to keep up appearances.

Frank laughed at his friend. 'Serves you right. Now pass me the E.'

Wiping a clump of cocaine from his eyes, Caleb fumbled for a packet of tablets and lobbed it across the table. Frank caught it and turned his attention to the scales, then grabbed another kilogram bag of cocaine from beside him and poured it delicately onto the device, watching the digital numbers climb and climb until they reached ten grams. Then he removed an ecstasy tablet from the bag Caleb had just given him and began grinding it into a powder next to the scales. Once the pill was pummelled into its finest form, Frank transported it onto the pile of cocaine and mixed the two chemicals together with a Nando's loyalty card.

Nothing like cocaine and peri-peri chicken on a Friday night, he thought.

'Thirteen grams,' he said, finishing up. He wiped his finger along the edge of the card and rubbed the remnants of the drugs into his gums. 'That should be enough to fuck people up, shouldn't it?'

'I thought we were adding more?' Caleb asked, replicating the process Frank had just completed.

'Calm your tits. One thing at a time.'

'What else we adding?'

'Ket, lidocaine, whatever we want. I hear people are going crazy for speed nowadays.'

Frank reached down by his feet, grabbed a cardboard box and lowered the lid, revealing another load of bags containing white powder. 'Plenty to choose from.' He rummaged inside the box, searching for the first substance on the list: ketamine. He found one, set it on the counter and inspected the contents. The chemical looked yellower than the other two products, like nicotine-stained teeth. He grabbed a small spoon from the table, scooped some of the ketamine onto it and poured it onto the scale.

Fifteen grams.

Perfect.

Swirling the mixture together, Frank grinned. With his product, he was going to change the game. After the bullshit spiel Henry had given him the night before, he was even more determined to make the perfect product. Become the perfect competitor. Offer the perfect reason for his clients to repeat their custom.

Three drugs for the price of one.

The smile deepened.

'What you so happy about, Cheshire Cat?' Caleb asked.

Before Frank could respond, his mobile vibrated on the table, the noise echoing around the empty room. Frank ignored Caleb's question and read the message.

'That Danielle?' asked Caleb inquisitively. 'She told you she want to sit on your face yet?'

'Not yet. Still working on it.' Frank read the message. 'But… I don't think it'll be too long until she does. She's still up for coming tonight.'

'And she still thinks this is a real club?'

Frank nodded. 'We better get it sorted out, brother.'

'As well as sort all this mess out?' He gestured to the copious amounts of illegal drugs on the table. 'We ain't have enough time.'

'Trust me. We'll make time. All we need is to set up the lights, get a DJ, give it a clean, spread the word, get some of the boys to come down, and then we'll be sorted.'

'And what are you going to do if Matheson finds out you're partying with his sister?'

Frank smirked. 'He won't set foot in here if he knows what's good for him.'

He poured the mixture of drugs on the scale into a smaller

plastic bag. It bore an image of a skull: their insignia. One day, the skull would surpass Henry's bottles. 'Danielle can be one of the first to try our new product, see what she thinks of the competition.'

Caleb bared his teeth. 'I heard Henry don't let his family anywhere near drugs.'

'You heard her, she's a rule breaker. Tonight, she won't be with him – she'll be with me instead. And everything's fair game. Besides, if she don't know she's taken it, then what's the problem?'

'You're a crazy son of a bitch.'

As Frank sealed the bag shut, he replied, 'If Henry Matheson thinks he can threaten me and get away with it so easily, he's got another thing coming. This little beauty is going to fuck everything up for him.'

CHAPTER 25

DEBT

When Reece returned to the estate, he expected it to be bustling with activity, scores of dealers loitering on the outskirts, Curtis's bulldog yanking on his chain and barking, some of the kids whose relaxed parents didn't care whether they were at school or not either playing basketball or football on the court. But it was empty, dead. Maybe they were all in hiding, he thought as he followed his mum into their flat on the fifth floor.

'Go on,' his mum said, pointing up the stairs. 'Get yourself ready for school.'

'What?'

'You heard me.'

'But there's only a couple of hours left. By the time I get—'

'I don't care,' Elaine replied. 'You're going. Perhaps that'll teach you to carry a knife.' She clipped him round the back of the head and pushed him up the stairs. 'Don't think this is going away any time soon, Reece.'

He said nothing, stomped his way to his room, changed into his uniform and grabbed his school bag. Elaine was waiting for him at the bottom of the steps.

'You and I are going to have a chat about everything later when I get home from work.'

'When's that?' Reece asked, hopeful that she'd say late.

'I'm not telling you. But you better come straight back from school. No more hanging around. And I swear to God, if I see you so much as talking to *anyone*, I'm walking you to school for the rest of the year, coming with you to your classes and sitting with you at the table.'

'You can't do that.'

'Watch me. I can do anything I want. I'm your mum. Now get to school. You're making me late for work.'

Elaine shoved him out the front door. Reece swung his backpack over his shoulder and descended the stairs before traversing the estate and turning down the alleyway where, a few hours earlier, he'd been arrested.

He froze.

Leaning against either side of the alleyway wall were Jamal and Deshawn, two of E11's elders. The ones responsible for giving him the food to sell.

'What you saying, fam?' Jamal asked, pushing himself from the wall with a quick kick.

Reece approached them both.

'Wagwan?' Reece said, fist-bumping each of them.

'Yeah, wagwan, bro?' Deshawn replied. 'Where you been past couple hours?'

'Just about, innit.'

'That right?'

'Yeah, fam.'

'Where 'bouts?'

Reece shrugged. It wasn't a question he had a convincing answer to. 'Been around. You know how it is.'

'You're lying to us, fam,' Jamal said.

'No I ain't.'

Jamal lunged at him, grabbed him by the straps of his backpack and thrust him into the brick wall. 'We know you got nicked, fam. We got eyes and ears everywhere. Ain't no point lying to us. We always find out. Remember that.'

Reece dipped his head.

'And what you tell them, little man?' Deshawn asked as he joined Jamal's side.

'Nothing. You think I'm that stupid?'

'I hope you ain't. Otherwise, you know what happens to grasses, don't you?'

Reece's eyes danced between both men. Their expressions were deadly serious. 'Yeah. I know.'

'Good. So I'm gonna ask you again, little man. And you're gonna tell me what you told the feds. Better you tell us now before Henry finds out another way, otherwise, you'll be in even worse shit. You understand?'

Reece nodded slowly.

'Did they ask about Jermaine?'

'I said I knew nothing.'

'Anything else?'

Reece hesitated. How much should he tell them? He'd grassed on Matheson and the E11. Told the police about their distribution methods. Betrayed them and become everything they didn't like. A snitch. Images of Jermaine Gordon's burning body, etched on his mind thanks to the footage on Lewis's camera, flashed before him. Would they do the same to him? A thirteen-year-old boy?

'Listen—'

'You gotta be shitting me,' Jamal said, shaking his head.

Deshawn gripped Reece by the arm, pinning him in position. 'What you tell them, bruv?'

'I told them about the bottles.'

'Fucking snake,' Jamal spat.

'What else you tell 'em?' Deshawn asked. He moved his

grip further up Reece's body to his neck.

'I told them… I told them… about the phone boxes.'

'You kidding me?' Jamal said, pacing left and right. 'Are you fucking kidding me? Fam, this little yout has fucked up the whole op.'

'Shut up,' Deshawn snapped. 'Shut up.'

'We should waste him, man.'

'No! No! Please, please! I'm sorry. I won't do it again. It won't happen again.'

'You're right,' Deshawn said, his voice calm and controlled. 'It won't happen again. Do you know why? Because we're gonna make sure it don't happen again? You love your mum, right?'

Reece didn't know whether to answer or not. In the end, he said, 'Yeah.'

'Then you'll do everything to stop us from hurting her. You'll do as we say from now on, you understand? You do anything wrong, we hurt her. You mess up, fuck up or do anything like you've just done today, we'll find her and we'll hurt her. You don't want that, do you?'

Reece shook his head, his body cold with fear.

'Good man.' Deshawn kept his eyes trained on Reece as he spoke to Jamal. 'Get Henry. Tell him the phone boxes ain't safe. We need to go back to the old ways of doing things.'

'What we gonna do about this little prick?' Jamal asked, pointing a scarred finger at Reece, evidence of a knife fight gone wrong. 'You want me to tell Hen we've got a rat?'

'Nah. Don't think Hen needs to know just yet. This piece of shit's ours for the next couple days.' Deshawn pinched and pulled Reece's earlobe. Reece squealed and yelped in pain. 'He's just a little boy. A scared little boy. But I think now it's about time we turned him into a man. See what he's capable of.'

CHAPTER 26

CONFRONTATIONS

Jake struggled out of his car. His muscles were fatigued from lack of sleep, and the joints in his limbs ached every time he bent down to pick up either Ellie or Maisie, sometimes both. His body was ageing faster than it should, and, with the added stress of the job, it was no wonder the retirement age was ten years younger than the national minimum.

In front of him was the sign for Rivermeade Secondary School. Across the bottom was an image of a child holding a long balloon that stretched from one end to the other. On the other side, beyond the red metal fencing that circled the building, was a playground. Deserted. Jake checked his watch. It was 2:30 p.m. Just after lunchtime. Lessons were in session.

After the interview with Reece Enfield, Brendan had started researching potential manufacturers of the plastic bottles Henry used to transport his drugs in, and Ashley had sent a handful of uniformed officers to one of the phone boxes outside the Cosgrove Estate. But Jake had other ideas. Other lines of enquiry to follow up on. And Lewis Coyne was at the top of the list. *If* he could find him. Rivermeade had a reputation as one of the worst-performing schools in the borough. Violence, truancy, drugs, teenage pregnancies. The school had it all and was frequented by uniformed police several times a week.

Shutting the car door behind him, Jake approached the school's entrance. He was greeted by two middle-aged women with impassive faces. Both wore glasses on their heads and a set of bags under their eyes. Neither looked as though they were thrilled to be there. Even less so to see him.

'Can I help you?' the woman on the right asked, lowering her glasses to the bridge of her nose.

Jake took out his warrant card. 'I was wondering if you could tell me whether a student turned up for school today and what lesson they're meant to be in right now?' Jake asked as pleasantly as he could manage, then surveyed the reception area. The carpet was covered in black stains from years' worth of chewing gum that had been dropped, trodden on, and buried deep into the fibres of the carpet.

'I…' the receptionist fumbled.

'Perhaps it's something I could help with,' a woman to Jake's left said, appearing from another corridor and standing against the wall. She wore a suit and one-inch heels.

'Who are you?' Jake asked.

'Margaret Armstrong.' She held out her hand. Jake took it. 'I'm the headteacher here. It's my job to know where all of my students are at any given time.'

If that were the case, your Ofsted report would be much better than it is.

'Let's hope you can help me then.'

'I'm sure I have a pretty good idea who this might be about, but please, follow me to my office.'

As they wandered down the corridor in silence, Jake ducked his head and peered into the classrooms, catching brief glimpses of children raising their hands, teachers battling to gain control over their students and paper aeroplanes flying through the air.

Margaret's office was as plain and bland as Jake had expected it to be. Her desk was in the middle of the room, with a filing cabinet visible over her left shoulder. She was surrounded by white walls and a moat of grey carpet. The desk was her castle, and she was the queen. It reminded him of *his* headteacher's office. He'd only been there on one occasion – to be spoken to about a cucumber-throwing incident in which he'd launched the fruit at another student's face – but the images and emotions he felt were raw and immediate.

Margaret lowered the drawbridge to her castle and offered him entry. 'Please take a seat.'

'If it's the same with you, I'd rather stand, Mrs Armstrong.'

'Miss,' Margaret corrected. She moved to her desk, opened her computer and typed on the keyboard. 'Which child was it you were after? Does it begin with an L, and end with ewis? Surname Coyne by any chance?'

'The very same.' Jake put his hands in his pockets.

'I'm afraid to say it may have been a wasted trip for you, Detective. Lewis didn't show up today.'

'And yesterday?'

'Detective Tanner, Lewis Coyne is one of the most delinquent children we have here at Rivermeade and there doesn't seem to be anything we can do to get through to him.'

'I'll see if I can speak with him.'

'If you can find him, I'll give you all the praise in the world.'

Jake smirked. 'Sounds like a reward I could get used to. Any idea where he might be?'

'Sadly, I fear that would mean I start doing your job,

Detective, and I'm already pretty swamped here as it is.'

Busy bullshitting and lying to yourself, it would seem.

Jake bowed his head in surrender, thanked her for her time and then left. Neither of the receptionists offered him a sign of acknowledgement as he waved them goodbye.

As he returned to his car, something caught his eye. On the other side of the road, on the adjacent junction, nestled in a lay-by, was a blacked-out Range Rover. The only car in the vicinity. The same car Jake had recognised from the night before and seen a few minutes earlier when he'd arrived at the school. It had started following him a mile or so after he'd left the station, keeping its distance, but had not been able to avoid his experienced eye's notice. Perhaps they were novices, Jake mused. Or perhaps they were experts that were trying to make him aware that he was being watched.

If it were the latter, then there was only one thing he could do.

He let go of the door handle and scanned the horizon. Nobody else nearby. No cars. No pedestrians. Not even a postman running late on his daily rounds.

Wishing he had a little more security but realising it wasn't the end of the world, Jake wandered over to the Range Rover. He kept his eyes trained on the vehicle, making a mental note of the number plate – RG00 HM1. Jake knew it was probably fake, but it was still worth running through the system later.

He stopped at the kerb, looked both ways and skipped onto the road, brushing his blazer down as he sauntered up to the car, heart beating fast, adrenaline charging through his body. He had no idea what was waiting for him on the other side of the blacked-out passenger's window. It could be a 9mm Glock. A knife. Or nobody at all.

He knocked.

No response.

He knocked again.

Still no response.

As Jake readied his knuckles for another knock, the window rolled down. He gasped slightly and hoped that he covered it well with the facetious, overbearing grin that he flashed immediately afterwards.

He was greeted by two individuals. Both were dark-skinned, and both wore Lonsdale hoodies – the driver's was white, the passenger's black – that concealed a lot of their features. A tobacco-scented wall uppercut him in the nose.

'Afternoon,' Jake said, leaning his elbow against the skeleton of the door arch. 'Looks like you've got a yin and yang thing going on here.' He pointed at the coloured tracksuits. 'I like it.'

His remark was met with two intense, intimidating glares. Their eyes shot knives at him, and he wondered whether they actually had any on them.

'You want summin'?' the passenger asked, his voice gruff and deep.

'I could ask you the same thing. Or is it a coincidence that you've followed me here?'

The top of the man's lips flickered slightly.

'Or am I just being a bit paranoid? Because I'm fairly sure that harassment is against the law. And…' Jake hesitated, sniffed. 'Is that weed I smell? Don't even get me started on that. And what about your parking? From what I can see, this is a double yellow line.' Jake craned his neck to glance at their windscreen. 'And you don't have a disabled parking permit, do you?'

Neither of the two men said anything. The driver started the engine and the passenger rolled up the window. Within a few seconds, they were gone, and he watched as they went, fighting the urge to wave goodbye to them, knowing that he may have just signed his own death warrant.

CHAPTER 27

BIGGEST PROBLEM

The trilling tone sounded in his ears. Ring, ring. Ring, ring. Ring, ring.

No answer.

'Bitch,' Henry muttered under his breath.

He tried again. And this time the person on the other end of the line answered. Eventually.

'Have I upset you?' Henry asked. 'I feel like you're avoiding me. Something I said? Something I did?'

Rupert Haversham sighed down the phone. 'Be quick. I don't have long.'

'You do when it comes to me; I'm the one paying your wages.'

'And I'm the one making sure you stay on the right side of prison.'

Henry snorted. 'That's a lot of fighting talk from the big man with the big briefcase. What news have you got for me, fam? How's Little Ricky holding up?'

'Fine,' Rupert replied.

There was no hesitation in his voice, no apprehension. No

hint that he was lying or hiding something. He just really didn't want to speak with Henry. The two of them had known each other for years, and in that time, Henry had learnt how to discern fact from fiction when it came to the things Rupert said. So far, he was speaking like an encyclopaedia. Their relationship was a lot like a toxic marriage. Henry wanted more than Rupert could offer him, and sometimes vice versa. There were arguments, disagreements but at the end of it all, they depended on one another. And that was what made the marriage work in its own fucked up way.

'He keeping his promises?' Henry asked.

'He's doing everything I tell him, don't worry. He's said nothing. No other names have been mentioned. No details. Nothing.'

'How long's he looking at?' Henry asked.

'Life.'

Henry whistled, grabbed a piece of chewing gum from a pack on the coffee table in front of him and shoved it into his mouth. 'You don't reckon you can get it reduced for him?'

'I've tried, but there's little leeway. He might get a few years knocked off while he's in there if he keeps up good behaviour, but that's still a long way from happening.'

'The boy's done good for me. I'll make sure he's well looked after.' Henry rubbed his nose and thumbed another stick of gum into his gob. 'What about the feds? Where are they?'

The sound of papers rustling echoed through the microphone. 'They're everywhere, Henry. You know that.'

'Funny. But that ain't what I meant, and you know it.'

'Are you asking me how much they know?'

'Bingo.'

Rupert chuckled. It was a haughty, wheezy laugh that reminded Henry of the last dog he'd had before he'd had it put down.

'I'm afraid that's going to cost you extra.'

'Like fuck it is. Where are they up to? They looking into anyone else?'

'Relax. It's like I said, you've got nothing to worry about. Right now, their priority is getting Rykard through the system.'

Henry hesitated, staring into the television screen, the pixels blending and merging into one moving image. 'What about this other one... Jake Tanner?'

'Well, there's your biggest problem, Henry.'

Don't I know it.

'Give me everything you've got on him. I think it's time someone paid him a visit.'

CHAPTER 28

ALWAYS WORKING

He didn't want to think what sort of weapons they had in the front of the Range Rover. He didn't want to think about what they would have done to him if he wasn't reporting back to the station. He didn't want to think what they would do to him now that he'd antagonised them. These were dangerous people, he realised, and even though they hadn't done anything to him yet, he knew what they were capable of, and sometimes it was the knowing that was worse than anything else.

Jake immediately regretted his actions. He had a family to feed and provide for. A wife. Two kids. Maybe a third. Maybe even a dog one day. But they wouldn't be able to afford that luxury if he was dead or being run out of the city.

The thought reminded him of Elliot Bridger and Danika Oblak, his old colleagues from Surrey Police. They'd worked together when Jake had arrested the country's most notorious gang of bank robbers, The Crimsons. They'd also been a part of a corrupt organisation of police officers and had links to the criminal underworld. The only problem was, instead of being the ones in power, they'd been foot soldiers, responsible for carrying out The Cabal's bidding, which meant they'd been forced to live their lives in fear. They knew things, saw things, heard things, got too close to people they shouldn't have. And their outcomes hadn't been pretty. Danika was dead and Bridger was... well, Jake didn't know where Bridger was. Halfway across the world for all he knew. Or cared.

Jake stepped into a hushed office. Everyone was busy working, pounding away at their keyboards, mindlessly swigging endless cups of coffee, destroying their palettes. Ashley was sitting on her foot, her body distorted to one side, facing away from him. Stephanie's face hovered a few inches from her screen, the effervescent light reflecting off her glasses. And Brendan had a set of earbuds buried deep into his ears, his feet and fingers drumming to a silent beat.

Jake tapped him on the shoulder.

'Bloody hell, mate,' Brendan said, flinching and yanking the buds from his ears. 'Couldn't knock next time, could you?'

'Just making sure you're awake.'

'How was it?' Stephanie asked, rising out of her chair. 'Did you find him at the school?'

Jake shook his head. 'No-show. Apparently, he doesn't like turning up. Who'd have guessed?'

'Who we talking about?' asked Brendan.

Jake explained who Lewis Coyne was and why he'd visited the young boy's school.

'Maybe the wee fella was feeling sick and went home,' Brendan said somewhat optimistically.

'Doubt it. He's a drug dealer. I don't think education is the most important thing for him right now.'

'Is it worth checking anywhere else?' Stephanie joined him and placed her hand on the back of Brendan's chair.

Jake shook his head again. 'I'm sure he'll show his face at some point.' He swallowed before continuing. 'There's just something I need to check out before I do anything.'

'Oh, aye?' Brendan asked excitedly, his freckles brightening.

'Run some plates. There was a Range Rover following me. It stopped outside the gates on the other side of the road, so I went up to it and knocked on the window.'

'Are you insane?'

'I asked them a few questions. They weren't forthcoming with any information.'

'Idiot,' Stephanie said beneath her breath, shaking her head. Mother hen was unhappy with the disobedient chick. Again. 'You're not invincible, Jake. One day you'll realise that.'

Jake turned his back on them without saying anything, unlocked his terminal, and loaded up the Police National Computer. He entered the Range Rover's number plates into the search bar and hit return. The results came back with an error message. No registered UK vehicles matching the plates. It didn't exist. A ghost in the machine.

In short, it was a dead end.

Just as he'd expected.

'Does anyone have any good news for me?' he called to the rest of the office.

A door opened; Darryl, standing outside his office with a document in his hand.

'Tanner, how much do you love me?'

'That's a difficult question to respond to, guv. You haven't got Elizabeth in there listening in, have you?'

'Sadly no. But I have just managed to get a surveillance warrant authorised by the powers that be. So you can now carry on your investigations *lawfully*.'

Jake's mouth fell open. He looked at Ashley, Brendan, and

then over to Stephanie. Perfect. Now he could begin the bulk of his investigation without the paranoia that came from acting improperly.

'I don't love you, but I know you're a beautiful human being,' Jake said, rising out of his chair. 'Does that mean the overtime's approved as well?'

Darryl dipped his head. 'Every penny. But your exploits last night can't be accounted for. And you're still lucky you have your job.'

'Understood.'

Jake's phone rang. He looked at the caller ID. Elizabeth. Holding his finger in the air, he excused himself and entered the kitchen at the back of the office.

'Hey,' he said. 'What's up?'

'Is now a good time to talk?'

'Not really. But I'm here now. What's the matter?'

'Tomorrow. I've just had a look and there are a few tickets that've just come up for sale.'

'Which one?'

'*The Singing Kettle*.'

'Sounds like my idea of hell. But I'm sure the kids will love it.'

'You want me to buy them?'

'Are they legit?' Jake asked.

There was a moment's pause. 'Yes. There's a lock icon on the website and everything.'

'Great. What time?'

'It's the matinée. Two o'clock.'

Jake hesitated. That was early. Especially if he was going to be spending the entire evening on a stakeout.

'Jake? Jake? Did you want to do that time?'

'It's fine. But I'll be home late tonight though,' Jake said.

'How late?'

'I'm doing another stakeout. I'm not too sure. Early hours

of the morning.'

'But you said—'

'I know.'

'But it's your day off tomorrow.'

'I know.'

'You've not had one in over ten days. You're always working. You're never home. You hardly see the kids.'

Jake lowered his head and rubbed his temples. Prepared himself for where this was headed.

'I know. But—'

'But it's for a case, I get it. It just always seems to be the same at the moment, Jake.'

He didn't know how many more times he could get away with saying 'I know'.

'I promise I'll be ready in the morning. I promise. When have I ever let you down?'

'You want me to answer that?'

He could think of a dozen things she could use against him. And he was sure she knew of even more than he did.

'Buy the tickets,' he told her. 'Get the kids excited. Pack the bags. I'll buy us breakfast and lunch, and then maybe we could get a takeaway in the evening. I promise I'll be there tomorrow. Even if I have to pump my body full of caffeine. I'll be there.'

That was a promise he intended on keeping, regardless of the circumstances. He wanted to spend time with his family and make up for the precious time he'd lost in recent months and, moreover, prove to Elizabeth that he was just as dedicated to them as he was to the job. That he could manage both of the loves in his life equally.

Jake pocketed his phone and returned to the office.

He clapped his hands together.

'So, when do we start?'

CHAPTER 29

LEGOLAS

Lewis loved his father. The man had raised him from the ground up, cared for him, provided for him even when there was no work. Even when they were struggling to find the next meal. Even when bread was the only thing that they had in the house and it had been attacked by swathes of mould. But their relationship was beginning to tax him. The constant caring, the constant worry that his dad was in pain or discomfort, that he was going to seize up one day and collapse, maybe crack his skull open on the corner of a table.

Ever since his diagnosis, things had changed, become more difficult. His dad wouldn't be able to live the same life, and neither would Lewis. He was growing up and wanted out. He wanted to experience things. Live his own life. He wanted to be able to earn money for himself without having to spend it all on looking after his dad. And he was very quickly beginning to realise there wasn't a world where he could have both.

That it was one or the other.

The two of them were at home, in the bathroom. Aiden

was in the bathtub, while Lewis rubbed him down, scrubbing his back with a two-year-old sponge that desperately needed replacing. His father'd had another episode, and had been incapacitated for the past few hours, paralysed on the sofa.

The episodes were caused by a lack of potassium in the blood, which was mostly due to the diet of salty and fatty foods his dad bought from the shop whenever he was able to. It was also caused by extreme amounts of exercise. In a past life, his dad had been an athlete as a teenager, representing the local community in the 400m all the way up to his early twenties, before he realised he was suffering from fatigue and sporadic paralysis. Overnight, his career had ended, and he'd been living rough ever since.

Shortly after the first few attacks, his dad had discovered that sitting in a hot bath was the best way to combat the condition. Not medically or scientifically proven in any way, but it helped soothe the nerves, relax the muscles and destress both of them.

'I'm sorry, Leg,' his dad said.

Leg was Lewis's nickname. As a child, he'd been an enormous fan of *Lord of the Rings* character Legolas but hadn't been able to pronounce the name properly. Ever since his first attempt, the nickname had stuck.

'Don't apologise, Dad,' Lewis replied.

'You shouldn't have to look after me like this.'

'Maybe soon I won't have to.' Lewis grabbed his dad's arm and started massaging it with the sponge.

'What you talking about?'

'The procedure—'

'No. I told you, it's too dangerous. Too expensive.'

'I've got some money.'

'No, you don't.'

'Yes, I do.'

'From where?' his dad asked naïvely. It was no secret

between them that Lewis was in with the wrong crowd – the crowd that no thirteen-year-old should find himself with. But what could he do about it? There was no known cure, except for the steady dose of potassium tablets prescribed monthly by the doctor. So there was no other option out there for him. With his dad housebound, it was up to him to make sure the bread was no longer mouldy and the kitchen was fully stocked, along with the rest of the house. Lewis might have only been thirteen, but he'd experienced enough to make him act as though he was thirty.

'You better not be dealing,' Aiden said, even though the pain in his voice suggested he already knew the truth.

Lewis opened his mouth to speak but then quickly shut it.

'I told you to stop, but you ain't listening. How long you been doing it behind my back for?'

Lewis shrugged.

'How much you made?'

He stopped wiping his dad's arm, afraid to share the real amount. 'A couple grand.'

'How many?'

'I dunno… fifteen. Twenty.'

'Show me.'

Lewis dropped the sponge into the water, hurried to his bedroom and dived underneath the bed. There, he found an Adidas shoebox. Inside was twenty thousand pounds in notes, divided into different denominations. Fives, tens, twenties, but mostly a lot of fifties. He'd been storing his earnings there for as long as he could remember. Years spent saving what little he made from shotting the food. Enough to buy a car or a deposit on a house, but he didn't even know it.

Lewis dragged the box from beneath the bed and hurried back to the bathroom. He sat on the toilet seat, removed the lid and angled the contents so his dad could see them. Aiden's pupils dilated at the sight.

'Clearly you've been doing it long enough to have this fucking much!' Aiden splashed the water and screamed in agony.

Lewis dropped the box of money to the floor and rushed to his dad's side. The box overspilled and the notes scattered across the tiles. 'It's fine. We don't need that much more money for the op. This is a start. I can get the rest of it.'

And then once I'm done with that, we can start afresh.

Despite there being no known cure for hypokalaemia, Lewis and his father were open to new ideas that could extend the time between each episode. And so they'd started researching private companies online that were working towards long-term solutions, advocating towards building better lives for people with the condition. And then they'd discovered Hyposol.

The team of ten, based in Rochdale in the north, were working on an innovative and ground-breaking solution, a small chip that was embedded into the body, near the heart, that monitored blood potassium levels. It was then capable of emitting signals to the brain, warning an episode was imminent, so people were better able to plan and prepare treatments. But the real benefit of the chip was that it produced and released its own potassium to compensate for the drop, keeping patients at a perfect equilibrium. If all went well, it meant no need for tablets, no need to constantly worry about when the next episode would be.

If all went well, his dad was going to get better.

'H-H-How much is the op?'

Lewis recalled it from memory. 'Thirty grand.'

'How much more do we need?'

Shrugging, he replied, 'Maybe another twenty. Just to be safe.'

'And that covers everything?'

Lewis nodded. 'I want you to get better, Dad. And then

maybe we could use the rest of it to move you somewhere else. Somewhere more comfortable.'

'You'll be coming with me,' his father replied bluntly.

Lewis nodded understandingly. He was secretly counting down the days until he turned eighteen, until he was legally able to do what he wanted. But he had a plan. The first priority was funding his dad's treatments. Hands down. And then they could move on to the next part of his plan – venturing into a new estate. Somewhere a little more salubrious than The Pit. Somewhere he could recreate himself. Somewhere without drugs. Somewhere he could create a cartel of his own and use the tools he'd developed under Henry. Building it from the ground up, just like Henry had done. Maybe Essex. Birmingham. Or Manchester.

There were too many to choose from.

'I don't like you doing what you're doing though, kid,' his father said, breaking Lewis from his reverie. 'It's dangerous. And if you ain't careful, then something terrible's gonna happen to you. I don't wanna see you get put six foot under. You saw what happened to that Jermaine Gordon kid.'

More than you know.

'You ain't gotta worry about me, Dad. I'll be fine. Promise.'

His father reached out of the bath and placed his hand on Lewis's shoulder. 'Tell me you ain't know nothing about what happened to Jermaine. Look me in the eye and tell me you had nothing to do with it.'

As Lewis opened his mouth to speak, his gaze averted from his father's. He couldn't bear to look him in the eye.

'I don't believe this. You're jok… What were you think… I can't… I…' His father paused, his chest heaving. 'The police were round here this morning, asking questions about it. They were looking for you, Lewis! They were looking for *you*.'

'Dad, I didn't have nothing to do with it. I was just there. Watching.'

His dad looked at him as though he'd just slapped a baby. 'Then you're just as much to blame for his death as everyone else who was there.'

Lewis reached inside his jumper pocket and wrapped his hand around the phone that contained the video footage of Jermaine burning alive. The one thing connecting him to the crime. 'It's fine, Dad. We're safe. Ain't nobody gonna hurt us like they did J. It was just business. They ain't got no beef with me or you. So long as I keep doing what I'm doing, we'll be aight.'

'I don't want the money. I don't want the operation. Destroy it. Get rid of it. It's blood money. It's dirty, corrupt. I don't want none of it in this house. And I want you to stop hanging around those people. You'll end up the same way as Jermaine if you ain't careful. And… And…'

His father broke down in tears. The man sobbed in the bathtub, sinking himself lower and lower into the water until his face was submerged and the bubbles covered his hair.

Lewis paused a moment, thinking of what to do. What to say. He wanted to console his father, let him know that everything was going to be all right. But how could he when the man he loved more than anything flat out refused the very help he'd been working so hard to pay for? It was a betrayal, and in that moment, Lewis wanted to punch his dad in the face. Repeatedly. Put an end to all of this grief. Finish it all off so that he never had to worry about it, or him, again.

Saying nothing, Lewis grabbed the pile of money, stormed out of the bathroom and headed to his bedroom, leaving his dad to get out of the bathtub on his own.

CHAPTER 30

THE LEADER BOARD

The trip to Southend had been filled with muted and disgusted stares as other passengers on the 2:52 afternoon C2C train from Fenchurch Street wondered what he and Deshawn were doing on board, and why they weren't at school. Reece wondered, as he returned their judgemental glares with a little more venom, whether they really wanted an answer to their unspoken questions, or whether the new switchblade that Deshawn had given him would be enough for them to keep their thoughts and their fucking prejudices to themselves.

'You gotta be calm about that, fam,' Deshawn told him as they disembarked the train, forty-five minutes after they'd got on. 'You can't just go shanking everyone who look at you funny.'

Reece had never been to Southend before. In fact, he'd never ventured out of the E11 postcode. And his first impressions were great. The coastal town situated forty miles outside London was gorgeous, a step up from the confines of the Cosgrove Estate. The air was fresh, filled with the smell of the sea, salt, and fish and chips. There was so much more room, so much more space. The houses along the seafront were magical and individualistic and spread across the breadth of the seafront. There was no piling, no living atop one another in cramped housing. The high street was replete with his favourite shops and even had a cinema; the nearest thing to a cinema they had in the estate was the seventy-inch flat-screen television and skyscrapers of illegal pirate DVDs in Finchy's flat on the top floor. The bastard even charged entry, but at least your own snacks were allowed.

Southend even had an amusement park: Adventure Island. Dodgems. Rides. Rollercoaster. Spinning machines. The chance for him to win a cuddly toy for his mum as a small consolation for what he'd put her through this morning. He'd never seen a theme park before, let alone been in one.

'Don't get your hopes up,' Des said. 'You ain't setting foot nowhere near one of them things. Not until you've earnt it.'

Reece and Deshawn walked east along the seafront for a couple of miles, Reece feeling like one of the wide-eyed tourists, until they entered a housing estate in Shoeburyness. The buildings were slightly different to London, predominantly low-rises and the only high-rise building Reece had seen was the towering skyscraper in the middle of the high street that peered over the city like a teacher in an examination hall.

At the foot of the estate, a group of kids were playing football, kicking the ball against the wall as hard they possibly could and attempting to control it with their broken and worn trainers. In the distance, birds sang and the sound of the sea lapping against the beachfront reached Reece's ears.

'What we doing here, Des?'

The thought had only occurred to him when it was too

late to turn back.

'Setting up a county line, bruv.'

Reece looked at him, confused. He didn't know what that meant, but from the way Deshawn said it, it sounded like a punishment.

'What's a county line?'

Deshawn sighed. 'Business is getting slow in the E11. Henry wants to branch out, innit. This is the next place we can do that. Lotta junkies and a lotta business down this way. So what we do is come down, set up our mark, our HQ, and then we keep the drug line going, innit, from London to Southend. Anyone needs something, they call the line, and we get them the drugs fast. No problem. You dig?'

Reece did dig. He dug hard.

'You still got that piece I gave you?' Des asked him.

Reece nodded as he put his hand in his pocket.

'Don't take it out yet, fam. Jesus fucking Christ, I know you been nicked once today already but you ain't about to get us nicked again, aight. Keep it in there until I say otherwise.'

'What I need it for?'

A wry smirk stretched across Des's face, his eyes wrinkling. 'You in our debt now, boy. This your errand. There's someone in there I want you to meet. He's the one in charge of this place right now, but he been letting us down. Henry don't like it when people let him down. They need to be taken care of so that we can take this place to the next level. You feel me?'

A cold flush rolled over his body and the hairs on his skin stood in protest. He'd never killed anyone before, never even stabbed anyone. Never felt what it was like to puncture someone else's skin, pierce their organs, their lungs, their liver, their intestines, their heart. Never felt what it was like to rip their life from them in one moment. What was being asked of him was to cross the line into unknown territory. But it was for the best, he understood. He'd made a mistake, he'd been arrested, he'd crossed the line himself when he'd betrayed Henry and everyone else in the E11. It was only fair that he right the wrongs and set things straight, prove that he was worth keeping.

This was his initiation, and he couldn't wait to get started.

Des headed into the low-rise, and Reece followed. They made their way to the top floor of the building and eventually came to a stop outside flat 456. Screams and shouts resounded through the walls and echoed from behind the other flats on the floor, and in a strange way, it reminded him of home. The hubbub, the chaos of it all. The hundreds of independent lives trying to get on with one another but failing. The shouts, the arguments, the marital disagreements, and then the yells of 'fuck yes' and 'harder, harder, harder' and other terms of encouragement he frequently heard on the way to school as life created life. It was an assault on the senses, and he loved every second of it.

But the instant that Deshawn knocked on the door, it all seemed to disappear. Silence fell on the corridor.

The door opened a few seconds later, and they were welcomed by a man twice the size of Reece but half as wide. The skin sagged off his body and he looked malnourished, as if he'd been deprived of any sort of food or sustenance for weeks. Reece scoffed. This wasn't the face or the body of a drug dealer; this was the body of a drug user, somebody who'd allowed himself to fall prey to the lures of their own supply.

Embarrassing.

'Des…' the man said slowly, the synapses in his brain taking a long time to fire. 'What you doing down these ends?'

Deshawn barged into the flat and knocked the man on his back. Reece entered behind him. The property stank of stale cigarette and weed smoke. In front of him was the open-plan living room that connected to the kitchen. Resting on the counter was a pile of crushed beer cans and takeaway boxes. Dozens of plastic packets and needles lay discarded on the floor and buried in the sofa. And there was a spoon sitting on the coffee table, charred and stained black and green. Beside it was a lighter, half full. In the background, the television was playing quietly.

'Fucking shithole you got going on here, Tommy,' Des said.

Tommy composed himself, staggered to his feet and closed the front door. 'What you doing down these ends, bro?'

'Came to see how business was doing.'

Tommy came to a stop and pointed at Reece. 'Who's this?'

Reece wrapped his hand tightly around the blade, his thumb running over the mechanism that switched it from a toy to a weapon.

'This my younger. He's out here on training.' Deshawn shoved his hands in his pockets and stood tall, puffing his chest out. 'How's business? We ain't heard nothing from you in a couple days. Thought there was trouble.'

'No... no trouble.'

'How things moving? You shipping it all out OK, or you need any help?'

'No... it's all... fine. No problem shipping—'

Deshawn dragged his hands slowly out of his pockets, charged at Tommy and wrapped his fingers around the man's neck.

'Don't lie to me, you piece of shit filth.' Deshawn swung a right hook that connected cleanly with Tommy's jaw. The punch was so powerful that it almost sent Tommy to sleep. 'We know you been snorting all the gear up your nose. Look at this fucking place. It's a mess.'

Before Tommy could respond, Deshawn threw him onto

the sofa. The man's almost lifeless body landed on the cushion and rolled onto the floor. There was no fight left, no strength, no energy, no muscles left to defend himself with. The man was a broken wreck, incapacitated by a desire to reach new levels of getting off his face.

Reece looked up at Deshawn in awe. At the violent and terrifying side to him he'd never seen before.

'Get that piece out,' Deshawn told him, flicking his fingers.

Reece did as instructed. The blade felt light in his hand, perfectly balanced.

'You ever heard of the Leader Board?' Des asked as he moved towards Tommy, who lay there dazed and immobile.

Reece shook his head.

Without answering, Deshawn pointed to different parts of Tommy's body and listed their values. 'You get points for each part you stab. I think I got two hundred and ten on my first kill. Henry's was higher. Jam's was shit because the feds nearly caught him. And I think Lewis got something like two twenty – just beat me, the little prick. But this one shouldn't be a problem for you. Nice and easy. He's down and out for the count.'

There was only one part of that explanation that Reece paid any attention to, and it was the fact that Lewis had the highest points out of anyone worth mentioning in the gang. The two of them were friends, best friends, but this was the first he'd heard of it. Now it was making sense that Lewis had been called upon to watch Jermaine Gordon's cremation. Positions in the elders' rankings were scarce, and so competition was fierce. If Reece wanted to make his way higher up the food chain, he was going to have to impress.

He paused a moment to survey Tommy's body. He recounted the points in his head.

Ten for the arms and legs.

Twenty for the stomach.

Fifty for the chest.

Seventy-five for the neck.

One hundred for the head.

Deshawn took a step back and folded his arms, giving him the floor to begin.

Blood and spittle dribbled from Tommy's mouth and pooled around his neck. He tried to speak but the words were incoherent.

Reece smiled and focused on the adrenaline rush in his body. He paid no attention to Tommy's face or eyes. It was just him and the knife.

Him and the knife.

Him and the knife.

He growled like a savage beast feasting on its prey.

In his head, he counted down.

Three.

It was time to earn some respect.

Two.

It was time to hit the top spot on the Leader Board and shit all over Lewis's score.

One.

It was time to kill.

Clutching the knife tightly, he lunged at the body on the sofa, his mind consumed by anger and destruction.

Before long, the entire flat was covered in Tommy the Junky's spilt blood.

CHAPTER 31

CROSS THE LINE

Jake and Stephanie were sitting inside Stephanie's car, with the heated seats on to help soften the muscles in their arses after a long day of sitting on them. She drove a beige Fiat 500 with leather interior. The car was small and cramped, and Jake's knees felt as if they were almost pressed against his chest, but it was better than being squashed into his Mini Austin Cooper, which was half the size – not to mention a little less inconspicuous. It was nearing midnight, and they had, so far, seen nothing. The only thing that had caught Jake's eye was a man wearing a hood walking along the perimeter of the estate with his pit bull.

'What's your favourite dog?' Jake asked.

'Excuse me?' Stephanie replied, lowering the binoculars from her face and turning to look at him.

'Dogs. Do you like them?'

'I have one.'

'Big or small?'

'Dachshund.'

'Sausage dog? I've always wanted a German Shepherd.

Something big and scary. Something that could protect the kids while I'm out or if we're in a park or something.'

'Buy one then. Or is Elizabeth putting her foot down?'

Jake shook his head. 'Too expensive. We can't afford to have one yet. Our finances are still up the shitter.'

'Still?'

'Funnily enough, these things don't go away overnight.'

He wished they did.

'Anything to declare with the DPS?'

Jake scowled at her. He didn't appreciate the question, nor the insinuation that came with it.

'You know I don't.'

'I'm just saying. It would be better for you if you did.'

'You investigating me?'

Stephanie's lips parted slowly, like a crevice ripping the land in two. 'What's that supposed to mean?'

'Nothing.'

'No, go on. If you've got something to say…'

Jake inhaled, held the breath, and then exhaled deeply. 'I know it was you, Steph, who grassed on me and Ashley the other night. What happened? You saw my car and thought the worst? What's Darryl got you doing? Keeping tabs on me. Making sure I toe the line.'

'The line's there for a reason.'

'I think I know that better than most people.' Jake shook his head. Her words told him everything he needed to know. She was now the eyes and ears of the office. Something to bear in mind for future reference. 'You know, I never expected that from you, to be honest. Brendan, someone else, maybe. But not you.'

'I'm just looking for—'

Jake snapped his gaze towards his wing mirror. A flash seen out the corner of his eye had distracted him. And then he recognised it. The black Range Rover. The tinted windows.

The unregistered number plate.

RG00 HM1.

'It's them,' he said, lowering himself in the chair as the car drove towards them.

'What is?'

'The Range Rover. The guys who were following me.'

The car rolled past them, its LED headlights illuminating the entire street like a smaller version of the sun. Then it made a left turn at the junction in front of them and disappeared.

'Follow them,' Jake said, hoping the urgency in his voice was enough to kick Stephanie into gear.

'We can't… we're supposed to—'

'Follow them. Now. Something's telling me it's not a footballer or his wife driving that thing. It's Matheson and his boys.'

'We shouldn't leave. What if something happens?' Stephanie moved her hands towards the key in the ignition, hovered, contemplated whether to turn it or not.

'Maybe it's time to cross the line.'

She shot him a look filled with venom.

'Something will definitely happen if we *don't* follow them,' he told her. 'Trust me on that.'

Stephanie sighed and turned the key in the ignition. 'You don't ask for much, do you?'

CHAPTER 32

ALL AGREED

The black Range Rover due to pick him up was four minutes late. Unacceptable. The third time in as many weeks, and it was beginning to become a problem.

'All right, boss?' Jamal said, looking at Henry through the rear-view mirror as he entered the back of the car.

'I would be if you were on time.'

'Sorry, bro. We were held up.'

'You know the way?' Henry didn't have the time or mental capacity to argue about it. He was still trying to figure out how two of his most senior elders – DripTop and Mars – could be stupid enough to roll down their window earlier in the day and speak to the detective who was trying to arrest him.

'I've got Google Maps to help me, innit,' Jamal said, pointing at the phone plugged into the dashboard. 'Got that new iPhone ting this morning.'

Nor did he have time to give a shit about his friend's new toy. 'How was today?'

Des twisted in his seat. 'Done. County line all set up. Took one of the youngers with me instead. Little yout called Reece. The boy done good, fam.'

'Oh yeah?'

'Scored three hundred on the Leader Board.'

'And?'

'Tommy won't be a problem no more.'

Henry nodded his approval. 'What about tomorrow? Everything prepared? Anything I need to know?'

'The boys are all ready,' Jamal answered. 'Although they ain't had long to prepare, Hen. That's why we was late – getting the last bits sorted, innit.'

It wasn't Henry's fault that he'd received the text message informing him of their next assignment only a few hours ago. The time to prepare had been minimal. But he had faith in his boys. If he didn't, they wouldn't be in the position they were.

'I've changed my mind,' he said, 'I want you both involved.'

'That pushes us up to seven,' Des replied. Henry was certain he sensed fear in his words.

'Seven should be enough.'

'Won't it fuck everything up?'

'If you all follow the same plan, there won't be nothing wrong. More bodies, more money. A lot is riding on this, boys. If we pull this off, we get a shit ton more coming our way very soon.'

A lot was riding on this. The opportunity to make a ton of cash in a short space of time. It was a lucrative venture, but with those rewards came added pressure and extra risk. Usually, when it came to dealing drugs, only one person from the E11 was involved: the dealer. And one outsider: the junky. It was a closed transaction. If there was ever any issue, then there was only one problem Henry had to deal with. But this was different. This was in public, where there were a whole load of unknowns: outsiders. And to top it off, he had seven different people with seven different brains and personalities and ideas of what to do when the shit hit the proverbial. The risk of something going wrong increased tenfold. Now he understood why his predecessors had always spent so long planning their assignments.

He was already beginning to see a few new grey hairs.

Twenty minutes later, Jamal pulled into their meeting place – an underpass just off the A298. The area was surrounded by construction work, mounds of earth and sand, and wire fences running along the perimeter. Deshawn jumped out of the car, moved the fence out of the way and returned to the vehicle.

Jamal proceeded, the gravel crunching beneath the wheels. He rolled the car to a slow stop in the centre of the construction site and killed the engine. In front of them were two vehicles parked facing each other. A BMW and a Mercedes. And there he was in his Range Rover. Germany versus England. Two against one.

'You sure there ain't nothing I need to know?' Henry asked, placing his hand on the door handle.

'Nah, boss. It's all under control.'

Henry opened the door. Brushed himself down. Rolled his head from side to side, felt the sockets in his neck click. Walked purposefully to the middle of the three cars.

Waited.

A second later, the driver's door of the Mercedes opened. A large man, with greasy hair and a belly that made him look pregnant, struggled out of the car. Henry recognised him instantly.

'Rupert!' he yelled, his voice echoing around the area.

'Henry,' Rupert Haversham said.

The two men walked up to one another and embraced, their bodies coming together in a dull but forceful thud. Henry's arms struggled to wrap around Rupert's body and instead got lost in the man's fat.

'Good to see you,' Rupert said as he pulled away.

'It would've been nicer to see you when I needed you.'

'Sorry about that. Family holiday.' He spoke with a thick Queen's English accent, and there was a thin line of sweat buried deeply in a roll of fat on his forehead.

'When did you get back?'

'Earlier. I trust Veronica did everything for you?'

'She didn't need to be there. I just wanted to waste the police's time.'

Rupert rolled his eyes and placed his hands on his hips. 'The more you piss them off, the more they're going to come after you.'

'If you believed that, you wouldn't have told me everything you knew about our pain-in-the-arse friend.'

'We're not allowed to touch him. Not yet. There's too much heat on him right now. Especially after all the media attention he's been getting recently. The Cabal doesn't want anything to happen to him. But apparently he's got something in mind for Jake Tanner.'

'You believe that?'

'He's been saying it for a long time. Maybe he's scared of him.'

Henry scoffed. 'A cop afraid of a cop? Never heard that one before.'

'Stranger things have happened,' Rupert retorted. He sniffed, making a phlegmy sound in his throat, and wiped his nose with the back of his hand.

As Rupert finished, a car door opened. Henry turned his head to see a figure emerging from the BMW. She was dressed in black trousers which were loose at the bottom, and a red-and-blue-petalled shirt that was tucked into her trousers. Her hair was a strawberry blonde that rested at the top of her shoulders and looked as though it hadn't been brushed for at least a week. She pinned the hair behind her ears with a pair of glasses. The only adjustment she'd made to her face was the heavy mascara she wore on her eyelashes.

Her small, slender frame – with straight back and head high – glided across the sand and gravel and stopped beside Rupert. She looked like a breath of wind would knock her over.

'Who might you be?' Henry asked. He'd never seen her before, and he didn't like meeting people he was unacquainted with without prior knowledge.

'Another person you depend upon,' she replied sternly. She was authoritative in the way she spoke. No-nonsense. All the attributes that reminded Henry of his mum.

'There are only a handful of people who hold that accolade. What makes you so special?'

'Because our mutual employer asked me to. If he trusts me, so should you.' Her expression gave nothing away.

'Do I get a name?'

'Not if you want tomorrow to be a success.'

'So no names then?'

'No names.'

'Well, mine's Barbara.' Henry extended his hand. 'Nice to meet you.'

The mysterious woman left it hanging. Already he didn't like her. His mum wouldn't have done that.

'Can I call you Leanne?' he asked. 'No? No? OK. I'll still call you Leanne.' He paused to gauge her reaction; there was none. 'So what is it that you do on a day-to-day basis, *Leanne*?'

'You ask too many questions.'

'I just thought that, given this is the first time we're meeting, and that first impressions count and all, I thought I'd take this opportunity to get to know you a little better.'

'This isn't a date,' she hissed.

'Would you like to go on one?'

Bingo. A reaction. A slight rise in Leanne's left eyebrow. It was only the minutest of movements, but he was sure he'd seen it; slowly, he was wearing her down. Sussing her out. Evaluating her.

'Is everything ready for tomorrow?' she asked.

'What's your involvement in it?'

'I'm the one responsible for making sure there's no *unwanted* police involvement, and making sure you've got enough time to get out of there before they arrive.'

A smirk grew on Henry's face. It was all making sense now.

'I wondered when we'd get another bent cop in on the action. I was beginning to think they were a dying breed.'

She folded her arms across her chest, revealing a thin copper bracelet on her wrist. 'You'd fuck it up if it wasn't for me.'

'I find your lack of faith disturbing.' He was enjoying winding her up. It was important he assert some form of dominance, to let her know that he couldn't be belittled so easily.

'Is everything ready for tomorrow?' she repeated.

'Yes.'

'How many of you?'

'Seven.'

'Why?'

'What do you mean, *why*?'

'That's more than agreed.'

'Plan's changed.'

'Unchange it.'

'Too late. I just told you, everything's sorted.'

'Seven is too many.'

'It was all right for Snow White.'

'We can't account for seven men. That's two vehicles.

We've not had the time; nor do we have the resources.'

'We've had just as much time as you to prepare. Seems like it's more your problem than it is mine,' Henry said. He felt himself smiling, and he didn't give a shit if he was showing it or not.

For a moment, he and Leanne stared at one another, locked in a silent battle, determining who would be the first to break the deadlock and cede. Henry was adamant it wouldn't be him.

'Fine. Seven men,' Leanne replied, sighing. 'When?'

'In the morning at some point.'

Leanne rolled her eyes and turned to Rupert. 'Is he always this difficult?'

'You should try being in an interview room with him.'

Sighing once again, Leanne returned her attention to Henry and said, 'Listen, let me give you a piece of advice. People don't like dicks. It makes you untrustworthy. And the more you act like a dick, the less inclined I am to help. And then all of the men you have on this job will be caught, arrested – by a completely different department, somewhere way out of my control – and then sooner or later they'll be sent to prison. You won't have me to cover for them; nor will you have Rupert. I know you're trying to be cocky and funny and intimidating, but it's not working. I'm twice your age, and in my time, I've experienced many bigger, nastier dicks than you.

'Our mutual employer wants this to succeed. If he wants it to succeed, so do the rest of us, and so do you. I'm sure you're also aware that if this works, there's a whole lot more in the pipeline. Your team could become the next generation of The Crim—'

'Yes, and look what happened to them,' Henry interrupted.

Leanne huffed. 'Listen, what happened to them was

unforeseen.'

'You were bent over and beaten by one man.'

'I'm aware. We all are. And if that same man gets too much involvement in this case, I'll deal with it. You won't have to worry about him.'

'I need some assurances.'

'Assurances?' Leanne's eyebrow rose again.

'I assume you're familiar with the term?'

'What assurances do you need?'

'Deniability. Immunity. If anything goes wrong, it's nothing to do with me. I'm out of the equation. No evidence. Nothing. I've already got too much heat on me at the moment after Jermaine's death, I don't need another excuse for the *real* five-o to come after me.'

'I heard,' Leanne responded. 'I assume you were the one responsible?'

Henry hesitated. Pressed his finger to his chin. 'What's that phrase…? Do bears…' He let the end of the sentence speak for itself.

'You do realise you've just admitted committing murder to a police officer.'

'A *bent* police officer,' Henry corrected. 'Since we're all in the mood for sharing, let me give you a piece of advice, Leanne. It would be a very stupid thing, a very stupid thing indeed, to try and double-cross me in any way. I don't deal with that well.'

'Don't play with fire, Henry,' Leanne said, her body visibly tensing. She buried her hands deeper into her armpits and moved her jaw from side to side. 'Otherwise, you'll get burnt.'

'Are we done here?' Rupert asked, stepping forward to enter the conversation.

'Yes. We're done,' Leanne said.

'Good,' Henry replied.

'So we're all agreed? Tomorrow morning, Royal Hallmark Jewellers, Stratford?'

'Agreed,' Henry and Leanne said in unison, staring at one another.

CHAPTER 33

GRATEFUL

Jake glanced at the anonymous text message on his phone, then at the satnav on the dashboard and then at the clock.

After seeing the Range Rover at the estate, he and Stephanie had followed it to a construction site beneath an underpass where they'd lost visual contact with Henry Matheson and the other members of the gang. It was too dangerous to venture down there on their own, so they'd resigned themselves to sitting in the cramped confines of Stephanie's Fiat 500 until Henry's Range Rover had reappeared just under half an hour later. Once they'd tailed it back to the estate, Jake and Stephanie had decided to call it a night. Gratefully, she'd dropped him off to pick up his car at Bow Green, and that was when he'd received the text message telling him to come here, the middle of nowhere, in the dead of night.

Twenty yards in front of him was the sleepy River Thames, gently lapping against the centuries-old soot and mud and dirt and hidden artefacts of the embankment. Enveloped in a blanket of darkness, without the angelic glow of the city to distract him, he looked out at his surroundings. He was in the middle of a construction site that looked out onto the river. A new build was springing up a few miles east of Stratford, and he was in the heart of it. To his left were the red lights of the Queen Elizabeth II Bridge interspersed evenly in the air, like lights on a Christmas tree, and way off in the distance he saw silver skyscrapers shining against the backdrop of darkness. He rolled down the window and inhaled the salty and dust-filled air, listening for any signs of life, save the distant sound of cars rolling over tarmac overhead.

Nothing.

He was well and truly alone. And suddenly he felt very vulnerable. For a moment he contemplated turning the lights on, heading back the way he'd come and going—

Two brilliant domes of light cut into the gravel and his rear-view mirror, blinding him. Fast approaching over the undulating road surface was a blacked-out Range Rover. The vehicle sidled ahead of him and came to a stop. The rear passenger window rolled down, gradually bringing Henry Matheson's face into view.

'What a coincidence this is, that the two of us should be here together. At exactly the same time.'

Jake looked at the clock on the dashboard. 'I was here on time. You weren't.'

Henry replied by stepping out of the car, slamming the door shut and standing beside Jake's window.

'I think you and I need to have a little chat,' he said, his voice cold.

Jake paused, frozen in his seat. He didn't know where to begin. What to do first. Stay or go? Run or hide? Step out and venture into the unknown? It didn't occur to him that he might be walking to his death until after he was out of the car ten paces ahead of the other man. By that point, it was too late.

They meandered through history as they neared the muddy riverbank. Only God knew how many bodies had been discarded along this part of the river. Dozens. Hundreds. Thousands. It was immeasurable. And Jake thought that he was about to become another statistic. He imagined Henry whipping out a gun and shooting him directly in the head. Fast, instant, painless – hopefully.

'You're a difficult man, Jake,' Henry said. His hands were buried in a thick Adidas sweatshirt, the beaming light from the Range Rover's headlights reflecting off the three white stripes.

'Generally, or…?'

'In every respect of the word.'

'Why does every instinct in my body tell me I shouldn't be here?' Jake asked as he cast a furtive glance back at the Range Rover, preparing himself to see the flash from a gun muzzle any moment now.

Henry stopped and spun on the spot. 'That's because you're a cautious man. And cautious men are only like that 'cause they got things to protect, things that mean something to 'em.'

Jake said nothing. And then he put two and two together.

'Is it you?'

'Is what me?'

'The *parcels*…'

Henry pursed his lips and tilted his head to the side. 'I ain't know what you talking about, Jake. I think you mighta got me confused with someone else, you know.'

Somehow, Jake didn't believe that. There was too much acknowledgement, too much smug derision in his voice for him to be telling the truth.

'I've seen a lot of people like you,' Henry continued.

'Is that supposed to make me feel good?' Jake didn't know

what was coming over him. He was giving teenager levels of sass and backchat to an infamous drug lord capable of strafing him down and slaughtering him right there and then.

'But none of them have been as relentless. They all show a lot of heart. A lot of character, endurance; some of the largest words I know. But in the end, they never make it out the other end alive. Do you understand?'

'Did you kill Jermaine Gordon?' Jake asked, wishing he'd thought to use his phone to record the conversation.

'That didn't take you long.' Henry turned and looked out at the river. 'You know, I'm not responsible for half the murders you think I am in this city. And I definitely had nothing to do with Jermaine's.'

Jake had been foolish to think he'd get a confession that easily.

'Have you ever heard of the term cadre?' Henry asked.

'It's not readily available in my vocabulary, no.'

'The dictionary defines it as a group of trained personnel capable of forming, training or leading an expanded organisation as a skilled workforce.'

'Is that what your gang is then? An organisation?'

'Call it what you want. Organisation. Business. We're a group of trained personnel, just like any type of job. Banks, the police, politicians. And I would argue all of those are bigger criminals than us.'

'Is that why you're on the other side of the law then? Like some sort of modern-day Robin Hood?'

'I don't steal from the rich and give to the poor. Sometimes you have to be a little greedy in this life, fam. Ain't nobody look out for you, so you gotta look out for number one.'

Jake wondered whether this was the usual spiel that Henry churned out, again and again, to convince new recruits to enter a life of crime. He thought it likely.

'And… your point?'

Henry turned his head slowly, revealing a gold chain hidden beneath the rolls in his neck. 'Obvious, innit. We look out for ourselves. Ain't nothing gonna change that. And we protect ourselves whenever anyone threatens us.'

'Maybe you should have named your group after an animal. Sounds much better.'

Henry removed his hands from his pocket. The movement was sudden and only brief, but it was enough for Jake to flinch and panic. A smile grew on Henry's face.

'You're just a baby. So much to learn. Bless you.' He started back towards the car. 'I hope you understand everything I've said.'

'Maybe spell it out for me so it's a little clearer,' Jake said, trying to hide the fear and the catch in his voice.

Henry made it to the car before responding. 'This whole thing's bigger than you, Jake, far bigger. Nobody can bring me down. Nobody. Not you, not your friends. Nobody. You've seen what can happen to people that get on the wrong side of me. Unless you want to end up like Jermaine Gordon, I suggest you stay well away. I'll be very grateful for your silence.'

Henry opened the car door. Just as he was about to hop in, he stopped himself and stepped back. 'I hope you don't mind, Jake,' he said, 'but I've gone to the liberty of recording this conversation on video. And I think we've taken a couple of photographs as well. You're a smart guy. I don't need to explain to you what can happen with them if you don't do as I say.'

There was a pause. Henry looked like he wanted to say more. Jake was too paralysed with fear to stop him.

'Send my love to the family. Oh, and enjoy your time at the show tomorrow. My sister used to love *The Singing Kettle* when she was younger.'

| PART 3 |

CHAPTER 34

ROYAL HALLMARK JEWELLERS

The following morning, after a few hours' sleep, Jake and his family were sitting in one of his favourite haunts – Alinka's. Situated down the road from Bow Green, he and the team frequented it for their early- and mid-morning coffee runs. Sometimes, if things weren't busy, which was a rarity, they'd venture out for breakfast or lunch, sometimes brunch, and Jake would treat himself to their renowned bacon, egg, cheese and hash brown bagel. It was a delectable and delicious treat, and it was even better that he now got to share the experience with his family.

'What do you think I should get?' Elizabeth asked, holding the menu up.

When she didn't like the sound of his bagel, he said, 'For you, I'd recommend the scrambled egg on toast with avocado.'

In the background, the hubbub of the café sizzled, as late risers entered, ordered their coffee and made their way to wherever they were headed.

Jake yawned deeply in an attempt to refuel his brain with

oxygen which seemed more vital now than it ever had done.

Elizabeth scowled at him with a look that said 'serves you right'. And it did. After his meeting with Henry, which was still lingering in the back of his mind like a bad smell, he hadn't returned home until the early hours of the morning, where sleep had then evaded him. All he could think about was Henry, Henry, Henry. How he'd threatened to destroy Jake's career. How he was keeping Jake at arm's length, confident that he was untouchable. How he'd mentioned his family. Jake had contemplated staying at home on his day off and cancelling their plans, but then he'd realised that was what Henry wanted. And by the time he'd eventually figured all that out and gone to sleep, the sun was rolling over the horizon and the girls were stirring from their beds, demanding immediate attention.

'I think I'll get the full English,' Elizabeth said after a while. 'What're you going to get, Maisie?' she asked, listing the possible choices.

Jake's daughter was sitting beside him, while Elizabeth had the luxury of dealing with Ellie in the pushchair. The more he looked at them, the more he realised they looked almost identical in many ways, and more and more like himself and Elizabeth in others. Maisie bore many resemblances to Elizabeth – the eyes, the nose, the mouth – while Ellie was similar to Jake – the hair colour, the jawline and his dark eyes. There was no doubt as to his paternity, that was for sure.

'Scrambly egg and bagoot,' Maisie said, with the ebullience and excitement of a child experiencing new things.

'I don't know if they do baguettes, Maisie. What about having it on some bread instead?'

'I want a bagoot.'

Jake glanced at Elizabeth. 'You spoil them, you do.'

'They're going to have expensive tastes like their mum.

Isn't that right, Mais?'

'Yeah!'

'You're building an army of girls to fight me, aren't you?' Jake asked Elizabeth.

She chuckled, her smile illuminating her face. It was the first time Jake had seen her look happy today, and he hoped it wouldn't be the last.

After some arguments and disagreements, Jake finally allowed Maisie to have her second choice – the most expensive, salmon and avocado – while he enjoyed his bacon, egg, cheese and hash brown bagel. As the time neared eleven, they finished, paid the bill and left.

Walking down the street, hand in hand, Jake dismissed all thoughts of work and allowed himself an opportunity to admire everything around him. His family. His loving, caring wife. His adorable, wonderful children. The sun shining in the sky. The warm air. The gentle breeze. The quiet streets.

In that moment it was all perfect, and nothing could spoil it.

Jamal checked his rear-view mirror for the thirteenth time in less than five seconds, avoiding glimpses of DripTop and Chubz, who were sitting in the back. He didn't want them to see the fear in his eyes. Not even drugs could settle his nerves. He was grateful to Henry for entrusting him with this, but it was all he'd been able to think about since finding out. For the next ninety minutes, he was in charge. Get in, get out, drive to the safe house. And if anything went wrong, it would be his arse and bollocks on the line.

Snap out of it, you little bitch, he lambasted himself. Henry wouldn't have chosen you if he didn't think you could do it.

There was a job on the market, and it was time to show Deshawn, Elijah and all the other elders that he had what it took to manage this side of the business. With Des running the county lines in Essex, and Elijah running The Den, Jamal had been left in the dark, pushed to the side. If he didn't grab this opportunity and twist with everything he had, then he'd stay there.

There were four of them in his car, three in the other. Both vehicles had false number plates, and each man on the job had been forced to wear a ski mask and orange jumpsuit. Each of them had also been kitted out with an MP5 semi-automatic and Glock 15, courtesy of Henry's contacts. The semi-automatics were for show, filled with only blanks, but the Glocks had been armed. Just in case.

Three minutes. Three minutes.

In and out. That was what Henry had told him. In and out in three minutes. Just long enough for them to escape with everything they could grab in that time. Just long enough for the police to arrive too late, moments after they were gone.

'It's here, on the right!' shouted Des beside him. He clutched the MP5 against his chest, the barrel of the gun inches from his mouth. Good job the bloody thing wasn't loaded otherwise one pothole would have sent Deshawn's blood and grey matter all over the ceiling of the car.

Jamal slid the car to a halt on the double yellow lines outside the jewellers. The streets were quiet, save for a few families wandering along with pushchairs or children in tow. Opposite them was a curry house, closed. Jamal kept his eyes trained on the rear-view mirror as he watched the second Range Rover pull in behind him. He became deaf to all sounds around him. The screams. The shouts. The euphoria as the men inside the car disembarked and charged towards the jewellery store.

Jamal applied the brakes, kept both hands firmly wrapped

around the steering wheel and his foot hovering on the biting point like he was Jason Statham in an action movie. He glanced down at the dashboard and initiated the timer plugged into the air vent.

03:00

02:59

02:58

A noise distracted him. Now he could hear the shouting. The sound of glass smashing on the floor. The screams emanating from inside the shop. He was directly opposite the entrance and from his position could see everything.

The youngers who'd been called to the task, the ones Jamal and Des trusted the most, were forcing the shop's employees to stand in the centre of the store, each of them holding their hands to their faces, screaming, suspended in a brief moment of sheer panic and disbelief that something as incredulous as this was happening to them. Meanwhile, the elders ransacked the shelves. Breaking the glass with the butts of their guns, sweeping the jewels and watches into their bags, pilfering everything in sight.

01:21

Time flies when you're having fun.

Jamal drummed his fingers heavily on the steering wheel. Outside, a crowd had begun to form upon hearing the commotion. A group of teenagers wearing shorts and hoodies pulled out their phones and began filming the robbery. They kept their distance, but Jamal knew that it was already becoming too risky. The minute those cameras caught something they shouldn't, it was game over.

He pulled his ski mask over his face and instantly felt his skin itch with sweat. His hands dropped to his lap and searched for the Glock pressed beneath his leg. The fingers of his right hand wrapped around the butt of the weapon and squeezed. The solid metal felt satisfying under his grip. Gave him the sensation he was invincible.

Time flies when you're having fun.

The crowd's size gradually grew, like a cloud rolling over the city. There was still a tangible level of uncertainty in the air. Nobody knew what was happening. Nobody knew why there were screams and shouts and glass smashing, but the onlookers' curiosity knew no bounds.

Jamal would show them bounds. He would show them what was happening. And he would show them what would happen if they didn't evacuate immediately.

Throwing the handbrake on, he shoved the driver's door open, stepped out of the vehicle and, brandishing the Glock at the crowd, screamed, 'Get back! Get the fuck back! Get the fuck outta here!'

As soon as the crowd noticed the gun, panic ensued. Carnage. Chaos. They dispersed and sprinted away. One man fought for survival by pushing another girl in front of him for cover and then charging behind a row of cars.

'Jamal!'

He spun on the spot and saw Felix, the other driver in the raid, stepping out of the car.

'The fuck you doing, fam? Get back in the car!' Felix cried.

Jamal ignored the order and squeezed the gun in his hand, his index finger stroking the trigger.

Before he could do anything, a loud, thunderous crack erupted from inside the shop. Jamal didn't even flinch. He'd been around the estate long enough to know what the sound was. The unmistakable *pop* that had destroyed so many families' lives.

He sprinted towards the entrance and skidded to a stop at the door, kicking up glass and other debris. There, on the floor in the centre of the store, was one of the employees. Her hands pressed to her stomach, a flower of red rapidly spreading across her shirt, a spent bullet casing lying beside her hip. Jamal's gaze lifted, and he saw Lawrence, the group's youngest member, one of their most prominent dealers, holding the Glock in his hand, trembling.

Jamal blocked out the screams around him, grabbed Lawrence by the neck and threw him out of the shop.

'Get back to the car!'

As soon as the boy was out of sight, Jamal returned his attention to the rest of the team. Four left, spread evenly around the shop, piling the few remaining stones and jewels into their backpacks. Jamal didn't know how long they had left, but he decided that too much time had already passed.

It was time to get out.

'Finish it up, lads! Get outta here!'

In an instant, the boys zipped up their gym bags, slung them over their shoulders and raced back to the cars, leaving a trail of broken glass and blood behind them.

Jamal took one final look at the dying girl on the floor. It was an unfortunate circumstance, one he hoped was absolutely necessary, but now that they'd entered into this business like The Crimsons before them, they had to make a name for themselves.

Death was an occupational hazard.

As Jamal hurried out of the shop, he kept his gun pressed against his leg. On his right, the crowd had dispersed like an oil spillage in the sea. But on his left was a man wearing a thin grey jumper and a pair of jeans. He had short brown hair and stubble around his face. Behind him was his family. A woman and two daughters.

The man stepped forward, hands in the air.

'Jake! Get back!' cried the woman behind him. Likely his wife or girlfriend.

Jamal flashed the gun at the man. At once, he froze, holding his hands higher in the air. For a long moment, they stood still, separated by more than twenty feet. Did this bloke really want to chance it? Did he really want to risk his life by being the hero nobody needed?

'Jake!' the woman screamed again, and this time he heeded the woman's calls and inched slowly backwards, keeping his hands in the air at all times.

Smirking beneath the face mask, Jamal lowered the gun and jumped into his car. He kicked the engine into life, slipped the clutch into gear and tore away from the kerb. The tyres screeched against the tarmac, spitting a plume of burnt rubber, smoke and gravel into the air. Then he kept his eyes trained on the road ahead and focused on getting out of there.

The next eighty-five minutes would be the most crucial.

CHAPTER 35

BACK TO THE OFFICE

The first thing Jake noticed about the man wearing the black ski mask was the tattoo on his neck. It was the same eagle, the same fish he'd seen on the individual in the estate from the other night. And there was nothing he could do to catch him. Within seconds, the six individuals that exited the jewellers had disappeared and sped off in their unregistered Range Rovers.

'Jake!' Elizabeth cried behind him. She clutched Maisie against one hip and Ellie's pushchair on the other. 'Jake, get over here *now*.'

Reluctantly, he approached them, pivoting his head left and right, scanning for any further signs of danger.

'Are you OK?' he asked.

In the distance, sirens sounded, growing nearer with every passing second.

'Just about,' Elizabeth said.

Jake bent down to attend to his girls. He stroked their hair, their cheeks, their soft skin, and embraced them.

'I'm glad you're all right,' he said, staring into Maisie's

eyes. 'You're very brave.'

'Why you go towards scary man, Daddy?' Maisie asked. Her innocence was endearing, but it didn't make it any easier to lie to her.

'Because Daddy's stupid. He's a silly man,' Elizabeth said truthfully, her tone laced with scorn.

Jake didn't dare look at her. He knew from the intonation of her voice that she would slap him if he did, and hadn't already for Maisie's sake.

'That's right,' Jake added. 'Daddy's a bit of an idiot sometimes. But he was only doing it to make sure you were safe. If anything like that happens again, I want you to promise me that you'll be calm, sensible, and you'll follow any instructions you're told to, OK? Don't be silly like Daddy. Only Daddy is allowed to be silly because he's older.'

He couldn't believe he'd just had to say that to his three-year-old child.

'I think we should get out of here,' Elizabeth murmured.

Rising to his feet, Jake replied, 'I can't. I need to deal with this.'

'Jake—'

'I'll only be a moment.'

'You're a danger to my life, Jake Tanner,' Elizabeth said. 'We'll be in the café where we had breakfast.'

'I think this might take me back to wo—'

'No, it won't,' she interrupted, giving him one of her trademark 'don't-you-fucking-think-about-it' looks. 'We've got plans. We'll be waiting for you in the café. Just make sure you're not away long.'

Jake couldn't help but smirk. Her willingness to stand up to him was commendable. He respected her more every day. He was a handful, he was aware of that, but it was part and parcel of the job. And he loved her bountifully for putting up with him. He didn't deserve her, what bloke did? Men were all arseholes but even though that was the case, there was something in the back of his mind telling him that, no matter what he did, she would continue to love him. And that, rather selfishly and ignorantly, made him wonder how much he could get away with.

From the sounds of the sirens rapidly approaching, it seemed the entire Stratford emergency response team had been called out. *A few minutes too late.*

He kissed his girls goodbye, told them he would meet them in the café shortly and headed towards the jewellers.

Tentatively, he stepped over the glass, keeping his body crouched and his leg and arm muscles tensed, lest somebody emerge and attack him. To his left, on the other side of the road, another crowd had begun to form, and the people on the outermost layer approached the shop.

'Stay back,' Jake called to them. 'Stay where you are. The police are on their way.'

Preservation of life superseded any other procedure. There was no amount of evidence that could make up for an unnecessary loss of life. Their job was to protect, and how could he do that if he was more worried about contaminating and destroying evidence?

Jake stepped in front of the shop's entrance, glanced down at his feet and noticed droplets of crimson liquid adorning the broken shards of glass like pieces from a stained-glass window. There were red footprints where the liquid had been trodden through the shop and into the street.

He looked up and saw two women standing inside the shop against the far wall, huddled against one another. They were cowering with their hands over their mouths, staring at something on the floor. Jake entered and followed their gaze then froze at what he saw.

He was just able to discern the company's logo on the woman's blouse amidst the flower of blood rapidly seeping from her body. As Jake approached her, he felt a hand clasp his shoulder and pull him to the ground. He stumbled and landed on the glass.

'On your feet!' shouted a voice overhead.

Blinded by the sunlight beaming through the door, Jake squinted upwards, and into the barrel of a SIG MCX 556 Carbine. The man carrying the firearm wore a stab-proof vest and was clad in black protective gear. Adorning his head was a black helmet, and his ID number was demonstrated proudly on his left breast.

Without warning, the man grabbed Jake by the shoulder, hefted him to his feet again, carried him out of the shop and shoved him onto the pavement.

'Please step back!' the armed officer yelled at Jake as he staggered away.

Jake opened his mouth to speak but was cut off by another man. Of similar height and build to Jake, dressed in a suit with an expensive Hublot watch, he looked oddly familiar, like he had one of those faces that you recognised but couldn't remember where from.

'Excuse me, sir,' the man said. 'You can't be here. Please step back.'

'But I—'

'It's for your own safety,' the man insisted. 'The situation is under control. One of my colleagues is currently setting up a perimeter. I kindly ask you to stand behind the tape.'

Jake searched the man's dress for any sign of identification. There was none. He was a police officer, that much was for sure, but Jake didn't know who or what he was. Typically in cases of armed robberies, the first emergency response team, and the subsequent department that the case fell to, was SO11, commonly known as Flying Squad. They were a group of armed, uniformed and plainclothes officers responsible for finding the groups behind armed robberies around the city. Jake'd had minor experience of what life in that part of the force was like after he and a few armed officers had been responsible for arresting The Crimsons, the country's greatest organised career criminals, on board a cruise ship as they prepared themselves to evacuate the country. So he knew how they operated.

And this certainly wasn't it.

Jake was a key witness to an armed robbery and in possession of a litany of evidence. He should have been questioned, examined, his details taken, yet the detective appeared intent on letting him wander off as though nothing had happened.

'Please, sir, move away and stay behind the line. This is an active crime scene.'

Jake continued to observe the man. There was something about him he didn't like, something he didn't trust.

'Sir,' the man continued, 'I don't want to have to ask you again.'

'Right, sorry,' Jake said, blinking himself back to reality. 'I'll just get out of your way.'

Jake didn't know what was happening to him. His mind and body were working on autopilot. He should have announced himself, told the man who he was, but in the end, he left it and decided to walk away and watch the situation unfold from the outskirts. He just hoped he had good reason to do so.

The plainclothes officer extended his right arm in the direction he wanted Jake to go. As he did so, his sleeve rode up his arm and revealed a tattoo. An image of a scorpion. At first glance, Jake didn't recognise it for what it was; his mind simply dismissed it.

'Please,' the man continued. 'Behind the line that my colleague has just set up.'

Saying nothing, suspended in a bizarre daze, Jake wandered away from the crime scene, ducked beneath the white tape and headed back to the café.

'Everything all right?' Elizabeth asked when he returned to his seat a few minutes later.

'No. I don't think so,' he said, staring at the table but not taking any of his surroundings in.

'What's wrong?'

'I think it's happening again.'

'What is, Jake? What?'

He looked up and met Elizabeth's eyes. 'I'm sorry, Liz. I need to go back to the office.'

CHAPTER 36

AS THE ENEMY

'Jake, what are you doing here?' Darryl asked as he stormed into his boss's office. 'Thought it was your day off?'

'Robbery,' Jake began, pulling the seat from behind the table. 'There was a robbery in Stratford.'

'Were you involved? Are you OK? Is Elizabeth all right? The girls?'

Jake held a hand in the air. 'Yes, yes, yes. They're all fine.'

'What happened? Do you want a drink of anything?'

'I'm fine, honestly. It was an armed robbery. Royal Hallmark Jewellers. A group of seven of them. They raided the place with guns and took everything.'

'Did support get there in time?'

Jake shook his head. 'Moments after they'd gone.'

Darryl whispered something underneath his breath. 'Were there any casualties?'

'A woman. Mid-thirties, I think. IC1. Brunette. Shot in the chest.'

'Are you sure?'

Jake looked at him, dumbfounded. 'I saw her with my

own eyes.'

'Oh...'

'But there's something that's bugging me,' Jake said. 'Something you need to hear.'

Darryl's eyes widened and he leant back in his chair as if preparing himself. 'What?'

Jake hesitated before responding. 'Don't call me crazy, but... I think it was a Crimsons copycat.'

If Darryl felt any disbelief at Jake's comment, he didn't show it. Instead, he stayed professional and respectful. 'What gives you that impression?' he asked.

'Because they were wearing orange jumpsuits and had black ski masks over their faces.'

'Bit of a stretch of the imagination, don't you think? It's nothing to do with us anyway. It's Flying Squad's remit.'

Jake had been hoping Darryl would say that; it would make his next point an even harder blow to the stomach.

'Hear me out, guv, but I think it's related to our case. I think Henry Matheson's gang carried it out. I saw one of them, he held a gun to my face. And he had that tattoo on his neck.' Jake pointed to the left side of his oesophagus. 'Of the eagle and the fish. The one I noticed when Ashley and I were on the stakeout.'

'Your *unlawful* stakeout?'

He didn't need reminding, but any opportunity Darryl had to twist the knife in a little deeper he was going to take.

'It's not enough evidence to suggest there's a link,' Darryl continued. 'Hundreds of people probably have that tattoo.'

'That's an even bigger stretch of the imagination, and you know it.'

'I don't want to go stepping on anyone's toes. I've spent the past couple of months trying to build relationships with these people. Ever since what Liam did, everyone seems to think that the people in this team are tarred with the same brush. I don't want to hijack Flying Squad's investigation out of the blue and piss them off. There's a diplomatic way of dealing with this.'

'So it's about politics?' Jake shuffled himself into a more comfortable position, even though internally he was feeling anything but. The adrenaline of being caught in the heist was still ramming his body.

'It's always about politics, Jake. You'd understand if you were in my position.'

In that moment, Jake felt like leaping across the table and slapping Darryl around the face several times, lambasting him for being such a pillock and not listening to him. Instead, he settled for arguing; the diplomatic way.

'But you've been in *my* position before,' he said, scratching the underside of his chin. 'I'm sure there were times when you knew something was right but nobody listened to you. They ignored you. Suppressed you. And now it seems like you're doing the same thing to me.' He sighed heavily.

'What are you proposing we do?'

A smile crept onto his face, and he fought hard to suppress it. He hadn't won the war yet, but the first battle was beginning to look like a clear victory.

'I propose we get a set of eyes in Matheson's ranks. An undercover officer.'

Darryl scoffed. 'You'd have more luck finding the iceberg that sank the *Titanic*. It could take days for the paperwork to be filled out for a UCO. Not to mention the fact that you have fuck all evidence to go on.'

It was a rarity to hear Darryl swear, and Jake always wore it as a badge of honour whenever he enraged Darryl to that point. Like it was the holy grail of policing achievements, drastically surpassing the recognition he'd received for his work on Operation Jackknife.

'Guv, I wouldn't be suggesting it if I didn't think it was

absolutely necessary. If not for the robbery, then at least do it for Jermaine Gordon's death. *Someone* in that gang knows exactly who else was involved. All we have to do is extract that information from someone stupid enough to talk.'

Darryl dragged himself closer to his desk, placed his elbows on the table and knotted his fingers together, making him look like a D-list Bond villain.

'You love twisting my balls, don't you?'

'Only because you let me.'

'That sets a dangerous precedent.' Darryl smirked then glanced at his computer screen and awoke it with a shake of his mouse. His eyes flicked towards the time on the bottom right. 'Listen,' he continued, 'I'll speak with the Home Secretary, see what we can do.'

A knock came at the door, and Brendan entered without warning.

'Guv, there's been a robbery in—' He stopped as soon as he saw Jake. 'Tanner, what're you doing here?'

'Never mind that,' Darryl interrupted. 'Is that the initial report?'

'Yes, guv. It says there were seven individuals in total, dressed in orange jumpsuits and ski masks. They raided the place and early estimates suggest they stole hundreds of thousands of pounds' worth of stock.'

'Any casualties?'

Brendan pursed his lips. 'None mentioned in the report, guv.'

What?

'Thanks for this.' Darryl extended his hand and Brendan placed the document in it. 'That'll be everything. You can go now.'

Brendan turned his back on them and exited, closing the door delicately behind him. Jake waited until the door was closed properly before he released his barrage of questions.

'Guv, why didn't—'

'Because I know what you're like. You love jumping to conclusions. But we only know half of the facts, not even that much. I understand that you're paranoid about this sort of stuff and hell-bent on trying to solve it, but you can't do that alone, and especially not without all of the facts.'

He paused, breathed in deeply and then let the air out slowly, as if intentionally trying to piss Jake off. 'You can't solve this thing in one day, mate, so stop acting like you will. If you're not careful, you'll begin to treat everyone as the enemy.'

CHAPTER 37

CLEAN UP

Henry loved being out in the open, experiencing the fresh air like an excitable dog. For so many years, especially at the beginning of his career, he'd been locked inside, perfecting his product, inhaling nothing but chemicals, wrapping them, and dispatching them to the streets of London, that he hadn't been able to spend any time outside. But now, thanks to his years of effort, hard work and determination, he could afford the luxury of stepping out of the brick jungle and experiencing the salty freshness of the Thames Estuary.

He was in the middle of Tilbury Docks, just east of the city, a few miles from the Queen Elizabeth II Bridge that connected Kent and Essex. He owned a small scrap metal warehouse where he collected old and disused metal and melted it down and then sold it on for a profit. At least, as far as the taxman was concerned. He liked to call it his beard – the front for his criminal activities. There, fifty per cent of his product – cocaine, heroin, marijuana, ecstasy – arrived on the backs of lorries, coming from his extensive network in Amsterdam, Belgium, and further afield in Colombia and

Venezuela. The other fifty per cent contained the plastic bottles, already split into three and sealed with a screw-lid shutter. It had been a genius idea he'd had years ago when he needed to discover a fresh and exciting way to distribute the drugs. Long gone were the days of using small plastic bags. Instead, he wanted something that would distinguish him from the rest, and he was able to charge more for it.

The world had thought Steve Jobs was crazy when he invented the iPhone. Several hundred pounds for innovation, new ideas, ways to change the world.

People had laughed at him.

Every junky who bought from him knew they were getting good quality drugs with the added benefit of enjoying a soft drink afterwards.

Nobody was laughing anymore.

The warehouse itself was dwarfed by the others; so small it looked like it would be the last one to get picked in a school football match. But he was willing to bet his entire empire on the fact that it brought in nearly as much money as the rest of the businesses in the industrial estate. Unofficially, of course.

On the front of the building below the apex of the warehouse roof was the business name he used to launder the drug money. Handy Man Scrap Services. Hardly inspirational, a homage to his initials, but it was simple, discreet and often overlooked. Exactly what he wanted.

A wave of cold air pummelled his body and senses as he entered the reception area, throwing his sinuses into disarray. He sneezed.

'You good?' Rashida, one of Danielle's friends, asked. She'd needed a job, and Henry had been happy to facilitate. All she had to do was sit there, pretend to look busy and get rid of customers as soon as possible, all the while chewing on her gum as loudly as possible and watching the television beneath the counter. Sometimes she even chipped in a helping hand with any of the shipments that needed unpacking.

Henry gave her a flick of the head in acknowledgement and made his way through to the warehouse. It was a vast expanse of space, marginally larger than the square in the Cosgrove Estate. Against the furthest wall, by the large, heavy shutter doors, were two Range Rovers and a row of men clad in orange, holding guns, some holding them in their arms, while others rested them against their hips. In front of them was a table, with several gym bags resting atop it.

'Don't you all look handsome,' Henry said, lifting his hands in the air as he approached in mock surrender. 'How'd it go?'

Silence.

He stopped by the table and placed his hands on the edge, surveying the goods.

'Is this all of it?'

'What do you mean, *all of it*?' Jamal asked. He was the only one who'd kept his mask still pulled over his face.

'Is this everything?'

'Yes.'

'So if I were to ask you all to empty your pockets and undress, we wouldn't find anything hiding up any of your arses?'

Jamal moved his gaze carefully over the men either side of him. 'I fucking hope for their sake that's the case.'

He dropped the gun onto the floor. It landed with a sharp clang that echoed around the warehouse, then he removed his mask and started to unzip his boiler suit. He stepped out of it, kicked it across the floor and emptied his pockets. He was clean, as Henry had known he would be; Jamal had worked too hard to earn his credentials as number two to ruin it by doing something as stupid as stealing from him.

For a while, nothing happened. Nobody moved. Instead,

they all stared at Jamal's overalls on the floor.

'Well?' Henry began. 'What about the rest of ya?'

He clapped his hands, and at once the remaining men started to undress themselves, throwing their coveralls to the floor, emptying out their pockets and dropping their possessions by their feet.

'This is bullshit, cuz!' one of the men said. He stood furthest to the right, and so far he was the only one who'd remained still, arms folded across his chest.

'There a problem, Darius?'

The one Henry trusted least. Duck was his nickname because he always managed to duck out of paying for things.

'This is bullshit,' Darius spat. 'You don't trust us or something?'

Henry rounded the table and sidled towards him, moving slowly, deliberately.

'You're starting to give me a reason not to,' Henry said. 'There's always one person with a problem. And that's because it means they've got something to hide.'

'I ain't got nothing to hide,' Darius said unconvincingly, betrayed by the gold chain around his neck that rose up and down in tandem with the pace of his heavy breathing.

'Then I'm sure we'd all love for you to prove it.'

'Batty boys,' Darius retorted, rolling his shoulders forward.

'I don't think you understand,' Henry said. 'Take your clothes off and prove to me you've not stolen anything. We're all splitting the profits. No reason you should be getting any more than the rest of us.'

As Henry opened his mouth to add a few more choice words, somebody's gun was cocked. Jamal's.

'Don't make me point this at you, fam,' Jamal said.

That was incentive enough. Darius hastily shuffled out of his overalls and kicked them off. Then Henry snapped his fingers and straight away one of the younger boys rushed to inspect the discarded garment.

'Nothing in here, Hen,' the boy reported.

Henry nodded his approval and dismissed the boy back to his position.

'Now your pockets.'

Tentatively, Darius placed his hands in his tracksuit pockets and kept his eyes rooted firmly on Henry. Neither man blinked.

'We've all got things we'd rather be doing,' he added.

Darius rolled the inside of his joggers out and opened his hands. Several diamond rings and bracelets tumbled to the floor, scattering around his feet. The overhead light reflected off them, sparkling like sequins on a dress. Henry gave a quick count. Ten. Fifteen. Twenty. In short: too many.

'Hen—' Darius began.

'Nope.'

'It ain't what it looks like.'

'I think you should apologise.'

'I'm sorry, Hen.' Darius clasped his hands together and started towards him, begging.

Henry waved him away. 'It ain't me you gotta apologise to. I want you to apologise to everyone else. You've let them down more than anyone. You were a team. My best team, apparently, and now you've spoilt it for the rest of them. As a result, none of you are getting any of the proceeds.'

A chorus of groans and expletives directed at Henry erupted from the group of lads. Some even raised their guns at him.

'Quiet!' Henry said, his voice commanding the attention of the entire warehouse. 'It ain't ideal. Trust me, I ain't want it to be this way neither. But a lesson needs to be learnt here. You're all adults, you can accept losses. But you need to understand that if you fuck with me, there are consequences.

And… if you fuck with the team, there are also consequences. Which is why I want you all to give me your guns, and when I say go, you're entitled to do whatever the fuck you want to young Darius over there. Beat him, punch him, slap him, spit on him, tear his bollocks off if you have to. This should stop you from trying to screw me and everyone else over in the future. You lose as a team. You win as a team. And if one of you suffers, you all suffer.'

Henry hesitated a moment. The other boys in the group prepared themselves like a pack of ravenous dogs waiting for their owner's command to feast.

He gave them the order. 'On your marks… get set… go!'

Darius had little time to react, even though he knew what was coming. Within seconds, the four remaining members of the gang, excluding Deshawn and Jamal, raced across the floor and were on him like a swarm of flies around a dead body. Amidst the chaos, Darius screamed and cried as he tried to protect himself, at first kicking his legs and throwing his arms in the air, and then adopting the foetal position. But it was no use. The boys were too vicious in their blows.

Henry grinned as he watched Darius rapidly lose consciousness, then he moved around the table and wandered over to Jamal, who was standing on the outskirts of the attack casting a watchful, wise gaze over the proceedings.

'They'll hate him, you know that, right?' Jamal said, nodding towards Darius.

'Good. They'll learn. And if he survives, so will he.'

'Or he'll resent you and do it again.'

Henry shrugged. 'Then he'll know what the consequences are. Except next time they'll be a lot worse.'

He paused a beat; someone had just delivered one of the final blows to Darius's groin, and the lad curled into a tighter ball on the floor. 'Is there anything else I need to know?

How'd it go?'

'It was good. Quick…'

'But…'

'Something happened,' Jamal said.

'What?'

'Lawrence. He shot one of the cashiers. Killed her.'

Henry's heart stopped and his mouth fell open. One of his best men had jeopardised their first-ever heist. Ruined their credibility. How could Rupert, The Cabal and Leanne entrust them to carry out another one now?

'Son of a bitch,' Henry said, still in a state of shock. He placed his fingers in the corners of his mouth, inhaled and prepared himself to whistle.

Jamal stopped him.

'Easy. Leave it.' Jamal pulled his hands from his mouth. 'I been thinking about it. We're living in The Crimsons' shadow, innit. We need something that makes us different to them.'

'And killing an innocent person is your answer? I never agreed to that. Did you tell him to do it? Did you give him the order?'

'No, no, no, Hen. Honest. But it'll teach people to fear us. Think how much more they'll give us when they know we're prepared to shoot and kill. That was The Crimsons' biggest failing.'

That and putting their trust in the wrong people.

'And what about the police? Do you realise how much more difficult it is for our help to clean up when there's a dead body involved?'

Jamal shrugged. 'That's their problem.'

'It'll be *our* problem when they decide they can't handle us anymore.'

Jamal shrugged again. 'Cross that bridge when we come to it. I'm sure we can find someone else to take the fall for it like Rykard did. For now, mate, leave it.'

Henry turned away from Jamal and looked at the boys, deep in thought.

'Christ sake,' he said, thinking aloud. 'I can't wait for that conversation with Leanne later.'

CHAPTER 38

PROPOSITIONS

Lewis thanked fuck that was over. Six hours of pure dross. Sitting there, fighting every urge in his body to get up and leave so that he didn't have to sit and listen to his teachers babble on about shit he didn't care about, nor would ever care about. When was he going to need to know how plants worked? When would he need to know that World War One started after the assassination of Archduke Franz Ferdinand? When would he need to know that John Steinbeck used Lennie's dog to portray the overall victory of strength over weakness in *Of Mice and Men*?

He hadn't even touched a book in years; the only thing that came close, if the number of words inside was anything to go by, was the instruction manual for the new flat-screen television he'd recently installed in Henry's flat. Because that was where he'd rather be. Out there, earning his stake in the business, making the money to be able to afford the flat-screen television, the designer clothes, the thousand-pound limited-edition shoes. The teachers attempting to educate him could only ever dream of owning such things.

Lewis grabbed his bike from the shed, unlocked the chain, threw it in his bag and cycled out of the playground on his own. He didn't have any friends at school except for Reece. Didn't need them. Had higher friends in higher places. Friends that cared more about him than the pretentious ones at school. Friends who would look out for him, care for him, protect him. Defend him if he was being chased out of the high street by a knife-wielding opposing gang member. Friends who were willing to get his back if things got *heavy*. Those were the friends he wanted in his life. And they were on the other side of those gates.

Lewis stopped at the school's exit to allow a car to pass, and then, after it had gone, carried on down the street. The road was lined with cars either side, and Lewis cycled in the middle, weaving in and out of the road markings. To his left, over fifty yards away, children were playing on a swing in the small playground that sat in the middle of a field. The usual sorts hung around there after school. The cool kids. The smokers and the wannabe stoners. And the kids who were trying so desperately to fit into all of that.

Lewis gave them a quick glance. Slowed down and almost lost control of the bike.

Something in the distance had caught his eye. Frank Graham. Sitting on a bench with one leg placed over the other, smoking what looked like a cigarette. Although Lewis knew it more than likely wasn't.

Taking a detour, Lewis turned into the park and cycled across to him. Since Jermaine's death, all Lewis had heard on the street and inside the estate were mentions of Frank Graham's name, their words filled with praise. Frank Graham this, Frank Graham that. Up and coming, filling Jermaine Gordon's position, gonna take it to the next level, got balls of steel, best product on the market, ain't afraid of Henry Matheson. Ain't afraid of no one.

Now it was time to see if all the rumours were true.

'Aight?' he said confidently as he pulled the bike to a halt and let it fall to the ground.

'All right.' Frank nodded, a cloud of smoke rising from his face.

'You're Frank Graham,' Lewis said, putting his hands in his pockets.

'And you're Lewis Coyne.'

'How'd you know my name?'

'How d'you know mine?'

'Your old mate Jermaine gave it to us before he died.' Lewis wrapped his fingers around the mobile phone in his pocket; it still contained the grisly footage of Jermaine's death.

'Good. I want people to know who I am.' Frank pointed to the seat and ordered Lewis to sit next to him.

'You ain't gonna touch me up, are you? You ain't a nonce or nothing?'

Frank chuckled and threw the cigarette to the ground.

'No, I ain't a nonce. You're brave using that word around me.'

'You've gotta find a better place to meet up, mate,' Lewis told him. 'You couldn't look more like a nonce if you tried.'

'And I'll chop your bollocks off if you keep calling me that.' Frank shook his head and looked at the space on the bench beside him. 'Sit.'

This time, Lewis complied. He placed himself beside Frank, leant back into the wood and surveyed the area. The field beyond the playground was quiet, save for a dog walker way off in the distance. Lewis removed his phone and pretended to scroll through something.

'Decent phone,' Frank said. 'Where'd you get it?'

'Robbed it from some bird. She was with her two kids. In the pram. She didn't even see it coming. They're the easiest, you know: mums.'

'Oh, is it?'

'Someone said it was like a girl lion in the wild, innit. Protecting her cubs. When man comes up to her and she's faced with protecting the cubs or chasing after a wild piece of meat, she's always going to choose the cubs.' Lewis stared at the phone, unable to remove his eyes from the screen. He was lost in his thoughts. 'Sometimes I think about that sort of stuff. How we're not that far away from animals. What's the word?'

'Similar?'

'Yeah! That one. We're similar to the animals.'

At that, Frank burst into a furore of laughter. 'You're dumb, fam,' he said, slapping his knee. 'You seriously think about that type of shit?'

'At least I ain't think about fucking little kiddies like you, nonce.'

Frank's gleeful expression dropped, his laughter dying. 'The fuck did I just say about calling me that?'

Lewis ignored the comment, looking him up and down. 'You know, you're a lot younger than I thought you would be.'

'Why?'

'Your name. Frank Graham. Sounds like you should be about fifty-years-old, but you ain't.'

'You're a mouthy little shit, aren't ya?'

'Piss off.'

'But I like you. I reckon you could go far, kid. How long you been in this game? How long you been shotting product for Matheson?'

'Long enough,' Lewis retorted.

'For what?'

'To learn a few things.'

'Think you're an entrepreneurial type?'

'I'm surprised you know the meaning,' Lewis said. 'Did they have those types of people back in your day or was it just a load of people working in mines and shit?'

'Entrepreneurs have been around longer than mines, mate. Your teacher would've told you that.'

'I don't listen to no teachers.'

'What were you doing in that school just there then?' Frank pointed over Lewis's shoulder.

'Taking the piss,' Lewis replied.

'So you're a clown then?' Frank raised one eyebrow, and the skin beneath his left eye twitched rapidly.

'Piss off. I ain't no clown.'

'Prove it.'

'How?'

'Come work for me. On the side. I give you some gear to shot and we see how you get on.'

Now he had Lewis's attention.

'How much?'

'A hundred grams. Start you off small.'

'I meant what's my cut? How much money you gonna give me to shot it?'

Frank paused a while, contemplating. This was poor business acumen, in Lewis's opinion. Frank should have come prepared with all the facts and figures ahead of their business meeting.

'Ten per cent.'

Lewis scoffed and spat a glob of phlegm onto the ground, inches from his feet.

'Nah, sorry, mate. Don't work like that. I want at least twenty-five.'

'Ten.'

'Twenty-five.'

'Fifteen.'

'Twenty-five.'

'Eighteen.'

'Twenty-five.'

'Twenty. And that's it.'

'Twenty. Five.'

Frank looked away for a moment, observing the group of children playing on the swing. He leant forward, reached inside his bag and pulled out a plastic bag of white powder, wrapped in several more layers of transparent bags and brown tape. Frank extended his other hand. 'You ever see that programme, *Dragon's Den*? Yeah, you should go on it. I reckon you'd be pretty good.'

Lewis took Frank's hand. 'Twenty-five per cent.'

'Twenty-five per cent. Nothing more. Nothing less.' Frank turned to his backpack. 'You'll have to cut it and bag it up yourself. You got scales at home?'

Lewis shook his head.

'Didn't think so,' Frank replied. He shoved his hand into the backpack again and revealed a set of scales. 'Take this. Ten grams. Each time. Put it on the scales. Weigh it. Put it in a bag. Seal it up. Job done. You're all good to go.'

'You got any baggies for me?'

'Produced and branded.' Frank flexed his left arm and pulled up his sleeve, revealing his skull tattoo: his insignia.

'Soon enough,' he continued, 'the Cosgrove Estate will be seeing a lot more of the skull around the place. And nobody will know where it's coming from.'

'Who do you want me to sell it to?'

'I'm glad you asked,' Frank said, another smile growing on his face. 'Your regular customers.'

With that, of course, came the inherent risk of being caught and stabbed repeatedly by Henry and the rest of the elders. But a cut of twenty-five per cent? Damn, that was five times what he was making with Henry at the moment.

'You dumb as well as a nonce?'

'Sell the product to Henry's customers. Let them decide which they prefer. If they want more, I'll give you more. Supply and demand, my friend. And who knows, within a couple of months, a year, you might be finding yourself high up in the rankings.'

'Why me?' Lewis asked, trying to suppress the excitement in his body.

'Because you've got balls—'

'Nonce. Looking at my balls,' Lewis interrupted.

Frank ignored the remark and carried on regardless. 'And I been watching the way you work. You're quick and efficient and that's someone I'd like to have on my team. What you saying? And how 'bout I give you a little something to sweeten the deal?'

Frank reached inside his pocket and produced a small plastic bag; inside was a nugget of marijuana, its aroma already climbing up his nostrils. 'Treat yourself. Celebrate. But be careful, younger, it's got a kick to it. If you don't wanna take it then you can always give it out as a sample; you know, try before you buy.'

Lewis snatched the drugs.

'You got yourself a deal.' He rose from the bench, but Frank held him back.

'Can I trust you to keep this between us, yeah? Little Henry ain't need to hear a squeak about this. You get me?'

'Henry ain't gonna hear nothing.' Lewis stared deep into his eyes. He never said anything he didn't mean, or made any promises that he didn't intend on keeping. 'I promise.'

CHAPTER 39

ACCESS

Jake rapped on the door and waited impatiently for approval to enter.

It came a few seconds later.

He stepped in and was hit with the smell of technology that had been burning dust for several hours, a smell that took him back to his school years when he and his friends had set a piece of magnesium alight in the science laboratory.

If there was any doubt as to whose office he was in, it was removed by the row of desktop monitors stacked neatly on the floor. At the far end of the room, sitting behind the desk, was Roland Lewandowski, the head of the digital investigation unit, his head buried deep in the pixels of his computer screen. Roland had assisted Jake numerous times in previous investigations. Digital forensics. Prying into phone and computer history, discovering people's worst-kept secrets, uncovering the evidence needed to put them away for a long time. He'd helped Jake the most when he and the team – Liam, Drew, Garrison – had been trying to catch the Stratford Ripper. Roland had hacked into The Community, an online platform on the Dark Web for singles and couples to meet and exchange sexual favours for points. It also happened to be the place where the killer had found and groomed his victims. The only problem was gaining access to it. He'd been instrumental in that case and was a vital member of the team.

'It's good to see you,' Roland said, remaining seated. He gestured for Jake to take a seat like a doctor in a surgery, focused on getting you in and out as quickly as possible.

'Sorry I don't have an appointment,' Jake said wryly. 'I wondered whether you could help me with something?'

Roland's attention flitted between Jake and whatever he was working on.

'Of course. Anything. What is it?'

Jake looked at the floor and scratched the side of his face. The dozen computer fans whirring in the background sounded like part of some tiny orchestra, loudly cooling the mechanics and central processing units into a standing ovation. 'I think my computer's got a virus on it. I got this email, and—'

Roland released his hand from the mouse and leant back in his chair, testing the support's strength. Had he put some weight on since Jake had last seen him? If the discarded cans of Red Bull and Monster energy drink all over the place were anything to go by then the answer was almost certainly yes.

'I didn't expect that from you,' Roland said.

'It was an error in judgement on my part. I think I clicked on a phishing email.'

'What was the email about?'

Suddenly Jake felt like he was on trial. A knot in his stomach had formed almost instantly and was crippling him. He should have come to this meeting prepared, but seeing The Cabal's email at the top of his inbox again had panicked him into coming down. He was going against what Liam had told him. He wasn't backing off, he wasn't staying as far away from The Cabal as possible.

Then the paranoia began. What if Roland was in on it too? What if Roland was the one sending them? He'd have the skills and technological know-how to mask his sender information. It would be like breathing to him, second nature.

'You know what,' Jake said, running his finger along the top of his forehead. 'I'm sure it's fine. I can't even remember —'

'What were you trying to access, Jake?' A knowing smile flashed on Roland's lips, putting him a little more at ease. 'Please tell me it wasn't porn. That stuff's blocked beyond comprehension but you wouldn't be the first to try.'

'I dread to think what happened to the bloke who tried that,' Jake said, dropping his shoulders.

'I'm sure you can take an educated guess. I don't think anyone's seen his face around here in a long time. Now, what is it you needed help with?'

Jake dropped his hand to his lap. 'The other week, can't remember when, I got an email from an unknown address. I can't even remember what it was about, but I clicked on the link and then it took me to this internet page. As soon as I realised it was dodgy, I closed it down and deleted the email.'

'You panicked?'

'That's one word for it.'

Roland tapped his fingers together as if he were a maniacal overlord planning to decimate the entire world. It didn't do much to further relax Jake.

'And what makes you think you've got a virus?'

'I keep getting these emails. They're spammy. Each one says the same thing: we thank you for your silence.'

Those last six words sparked something in Roland that made him sit up, tilt forward on his chair, and say, 'I think you'd better show me.'

As Roland laboriously lifted himself out of his seat, he afforded Jake a chance to see the amount of weight he'd put on. The majority of it had gone to his legs, as if it had pooled there with the amount of time he spent sitting down. One particular area though seemed to have enlarged the most. And that was Roland's arse. Not only had it got bigger, it had become firmer, rounder, like a football. As though, despite the obvious weight gain, he'd been squatting a hundred times a day for a whole year. It was out of proportion with the rest of his body, and Jake struggled to tear his eyes from it as they made their way to the Major Investigation Room, watching it jiggle slightly with every step.

When they arrived at his desk, Jake logged into the computer and brought up the earlier email he'd slotted into the spam folder.

'Can you find out where it came from?' he asked quietly as he swapped places with Roland. 'Trace it back to somewhere?'

Roland didn't reply. He was in the zone, absorbed and transfixed by the dancing pixels on the screen as his hands and brain moved faster than the mouse. A few seconds, and over a dozen different screens later, he responded.

'I'll make a copy of your desktop and take a look when I've got some time.'

'How long's that going to take?'

'A couple of days.' Roland put the screen to sleep, slapped Jake on the shoulder and winked. 'In the meantime, stop trying to access things you know you shouldn't.'

CHAPTER 40

HANDY MAN SCRAP SERVICES

Ashley was beginning to love her new job. Her new colleagues. The excitement of it all. The unprecedented adrenaline rush that came with uncovering the truth behind Jermaine Gordon's death. It was addictive, and she was a junky for that sort of thing, had been even when she was a bobby on the beat, and she wanted more and more of it.

Solving crimes and putting people away was her fix.

The past twenty minutes had been the most time she'd spent getting to know Brendan. He was all right. Nice enough bloke. Bit misogynistic, but all right. The first thing she noticed about him was his voice. Soft spoken and intriguing. She listened to his every word intently. And his accent. She loved the Irish accent. The way they rolled their Rs, pronounced their THs. Mmm. Thick and heavy like a creamy coffee. If she could marry any accent in the world, it would be that one.

They were heading towards a remote warehouse in Tilbury Docks. The report that Brendan had run into which manufacturers created the plastic bottles used for Henry

Matheson's drugs had come up with a positive result. It had once been established as a business on Companies House back in 2000 before being struck off the register. Later, the name of the business had changed to Handy Man Scrap Services. And, no surprise to anyone, the owner of the business was one Henry Matheson.

'How far away are we?' Ashley asked.

'Ten minutes. Fifteen tops.' Brendan drummed away to a silent beat on the steering wheel.

Long enough.

Ashley pulled out her phone and opened her emails. Something inside her told her she needed to keep going, to keep the investigation on its toes, at the front of her mind. Like the workhorse she was, she was dedicated to the job. When she wasn't working, she felt guilty about it. And when she was working, she always felt like there was more to do. Another report to compile. Another statement to review. Another action to begin. It was probably one of the reasons she was single and lived alone. She spent more time thinking about criminals than she did anyone else – including herself. Some said it was unhealthy, but it was what made her happy. And sometimes you had to sacrifice one over the other. But she reconciled herself in the knowledge that one day the two would marry and she would experience a new type of happiness.

She scrolled through her inbox, analysing the emails sitting in there. Most of them were junk, people sending out report notices and chasing other people in the department for overdue paperwork.

But then one caught her eye.

She glanced through the email, her eyes scanning the words on the screen. After she'd finished, she opened her address book, found Jake's mobile number and dialled.

'This is DC Tanner.'

'It's Ashley. You got a moment?'

Jake confirmed he did.

'Have you seen the patho and forensic reports yet?'

'No.'

At last, something she knew that Jake didn't.

'The pathologist found bruises and swelling on Jermaine's body, suggesting that he was beaten before he was burnt, although the weapon was never found.'

'Is there any mention of a belt buckle in either report?'

'No.'

'None whatsoever?'

'None that I could see. Why? Should there be?'

'Never mind. Leave it with me. Any mention of DNA found on Jermaine's body?'

'The burns decimated everything. Gordon's fingerprints didn't survive, so it would be a miracle if another person's did.'

'What about hairs? Any of those discovered on the body?'

Ashley shook her head and then realised she was talking on the phone. 'Nothing in the report.'

'OK. Where are you?'

'Stephanie didn't tell you?'

'If she did, I wouldn't have asked.'

Watch that attitude, Jake.

'Brendan found a warehouse that supplies the modified plastic bottles. We're on our way there now.'

'Give me a call if you need me. Nice work.'

Ashley believed him when he said that. Despite Jake's inability to trust and work well with others, she knew that he meant well. After hearing about his past within the department and his exposure to corruption, it was only natural that he be wary of others. But something told her that, slowly, he was beginning to come round.

Ashley hung up, placed the phone in her pocket and

waited patiently for them to arrive. It took them five minutes longer than Brendan's estimations. They pulled into the distribution park where Handy Man Scrap Services was situated, traversed the potholed and gravelled tarmac, and turned into the premises. As she slid out of the car, Ashley observed her surroundings. Barren. Silent. Not a single car or worker in sight.

'Maybe they're all inside,' she said, thinking aloud.

'Or they've gone home for the day.'

Ashley checked her watch. 'It's only three fifty.'

'But it's five o'clock somewhere in the world.'

The reception area inside the warehouse was cramped and reminded Ashley of her local takeaway. There was about a metre and a half's worth of carpet that separated the front desk from the front door, and sitting behind the desk was a young woman wearing large hoop earrings. She had a nose stud planted in her face and wore a pair of telescopic glasses so wide they looked like they could see to the moon.

'Can I help you?' she began, opening her mouth and revealing a piece of chewing gum mid-chew. 'You lost or something?'

'Not quite. We wondered if we could take a look around. Is the proprietor in?'

'Propri… proprie…'

'The owner,' Brendan finished for her.

'Oh…' She hesitated. 'Sorry. He's just stepped out. Is it anything I can help with?'

'What's the nature of the business?' Ashley asked.

'Excuse me?'

'What do you *do* here?' Ashley repeated. She could tell this was going to be difficult. 'What does the company do?'

'Think you must have the wrong place.' She pressed the telescopes higher up her nose.

'I don't think so.'

'Is there a problem or something?'

Ashley lifted the warrant above the counter. 'This document means we can search this entire building. It also means we can seize any property if we have reason to believe it has any involvement in a crime.'

At once, the girl lunged for the telephone, prodded at the digits and held the phone to her ear, clearly out of her depth.

'Yeah, sure, that's not a problem,' Brendan said sarcastically. 'You can call whoever you need to.'

The girl said nothing as she waited for the person on the other end of the call to answer. Within a few seconds, they did.

'Hello? It's me. Listen, we've got a situation down here. Can you come down? No… I'd… I'd rather not say. Yes, it is. I tried, but— Sure. OK.'

She slammed the phone down.

'Who was that?'

'My boss. He'll be here soon.'

'No need. We can do everything we need to without him.'

CHAPTER 41

CONCRETE

Jake made his way down to the SOCO lab as soon as he finished the call with Ashley. Something was clearly wrong with the forensic report, and he intended to find out why the belt buckle had been omitted. If someone was fucking with his investigation, he wanted to know about it. It wouldn't be the first time and he'd be naïve to think it couldn't happen again.

The SOCO lab was situated at the back of Bow Green, connected by a small corridor only accessible to those with specific access. He stopped by the doors, pressed the buzzer and, after a second wait, stepped through. Immediately on his right was a desk where he was required to sign in. He did so, showed his identification, explained why he was there and then made his way through another set of doors. Another hurdle. The place was more heavily guarded than the police station itself.

For the next couple of minutes, he meandered his way through the building until he found a small section on the third floor that was designated specifically for Sandy

Matthews, one of the senior SOCOs in the force. She and her team had a designated laboratory where they were responsible for conducting preliminary investigations and preparing evidence before it was sent off to an external laboratory for further forensic examination. If anything was going to happen to the evidence, it would be here.

Jake came to a stop by another door and knocked, panting like a dog. It disturbed him how unfit he was.

A few seconds later, a SOCO arrived. Jake recognised her as the one who'd picked up the belt buckle beside Jermaine Gordon's dead body. For a while, Jake looked at her with his mouth agape. She was nothing like he'd imagined. The first time he'd seen her, she'd been hiding behind the anonymity of her white-and-blue forensic suit. Now she was in casual clothes with a white lab overcoat hanging freely off her shoulders. She was smaller than Jake remembered, and her hair was a fierce red – something he hadn't even noticed the first time. Her nose and cheeks were pencilled with brown freckles, and for a moment, Jake wondered whether she and Brendan were related. The resemblance was uncanny.

'Yes?' Natalie said, one eyebrow raised. 'Can I help you?'

Her voice shocked Jake back to action. 'You're investigating Operation Deadwood, right?'

She took a tentative step back. 'What about it?'

'I've noticed some errors—'

'*Errors*?' She said the word as though it didn't exist in her vocabulary.

'I watched you pick up a belt buckle at the crime scene, but there's no mention of it in the report. What happened to it?'

'Belt buckle? What do you mean there's no mention of it? I sent it to be examined.'

'Are you sure?'

The woman shot Jake a look as if to ask, Are you

questioning my ability to remember things?

'Then why's it not mentioned in the report?'

'I don't know. Sorry.' She shook her head and let the door swing open.

Jake took a step in and crossed the threshold. He scanned the numerous pieces of machinery that occupied the walls and the rows of desks in the middle. He hadn't noticed it before, but there was a slight humming sound in the background.

'You said you compiled everything to be sent to the external lab?' Jake asked.

'Yes.'

'When was this?'

She searched her memory for a moment. 'No idea. Straight after we'd come back from the crime scene. Same day.'

'When exactly?'

She huffed and then searched through a pile of documents beside her computer. 'Lunchtime. I logged it down as one twenty-eight.'

Half of Jake's brain was logging the information, the other was recreating the scenario as it had happened. Which part of him was listening he didn't know.

'So you picked it up, brought it here for preliminary investigation and then put it away on the shelf somewhere.'

'That's about the half of it.'

'And when was all of the evidence sent to the external lab?'

She checked her notes again, then prodded her finger at a signature and time stamp at the bottom of a document. 'The evidence was released in the evening at seven thirteen.'

'And you can't remember if it was part of the evidence that was sent?'

She shrugged. 'I saw a lot of evidence numbers that day. It was late. I was tired. It may have been there, and I may have

250

glossed over it. I'm not sure.'

The number of minor and avoidable mistakes he'd made while working overtime and running on a lack of sleep was embarrassing and quite possibly more than the number of evidence articles she had locked up somewhere. He could hardly blame her for that. Tiredness and mental fatigue was somewhat an epidemic in the service. It was almost a prerequisite, a job naturally suited to insomniacs and people without personal or social lives.

'Would you be able to do me a favour?' he asked.

'Find out what happened to it?'

'Yes, please. It's important.'

She rolled her eyes. 'It always is.'

'How long's it going to take?'

She shrugged sheepishly. 'I can have it done by tomorrow afternoon.'

'I'll give you until tomorrow morning.'

Jake winked, but it was lost on her. He thanked her, exited, and as he returned to Bow Green, he allowed his mind to wander. It was clear to him that somewhere in the six-hour window between one and seven p.m., the evidence had developed a level of consciousness and wandered out of the building. Either that or someone had stolen the one thing that potentially connected another killer to the crime, someone working closely with The Cabal and Henry Matheson and Rykard Delawney in trying to cover up the murder. The only question was who.

Jake had a name in mind, a hunch, but he couldn't be certain yet. Not until he had something concrete.

CHAPTER 42

FIEND

As a rule, the youngers and runners of the E11 conducted their business on the estate and sometimes the surrounding area. The reasons for which were twofold: it was easier to control – there was less chance of a runner getting robbed inside the estate than if he were out in the open – and because the police stayed well clear of the place. The most anyone had ever seen the feds knocking about was in the last few days, ever since Jermaine's death. It was common knowledge that the Cosgrove Estate was like a sexually transmitted disease to them; the less they knew about it and the more they pleaded ignorance of its existence, the better.

Perfect conditions for the business to grow.

Lewis was waiting in his usual spot, in the alleyway underneath the north high-rise. The passage was barely lit, and he used the enveloping darkness to his advantage. He had his hood pulled over his head and his hands in his pockets. In his left hand, he felt a small baggie of Frank's cocaine, and in his right, the small switchblade Rykard had given him the other day. Shotting Frank Graham's food on

Henry's turf was a dangerous game to be playing, one that he knew the outcome of.

Death. By stabbing. Bludgeoning. Mauling. Burning. Shooting. There were a lot of ways to kill a man, and Lewis had been privy to a few of them. But he felt it necessary. Rykard, in the years that he'd grown up on the estate, had been there for him. Rykard had been the one to teach him the ways of the streets, the pitfalls, the dangers to look out for, how to defend himself if he ever needed to. He'd even been the one to advise him on how to get the highest score on the Leader Board. Rykard had been a different type of father figure. Someone he entrusted with his life; someone with whom he could discuss things his dad would never understand. And Henry's betrayal of Rykard was a betrayal to Lewis.

He placed one foot on the wall and leant against it. Checked the time on his phone. 11:43 p.m.

His buyer was late.

He didn't like it when people were late. Rykard had taught him that. *Instilled* it in him. It was bad for maintaining people's impression of you. If you started being late to every appointment you made, it made you look inferior, unworthy of the product. There were always more customers on the conveyor belt waiting their turn.

Lewis scrolled through the address book on his phone until he found the buyer's number. But just as he was about to call the number, the buyer appeared. His hair was short, bordering on bald. He wore a baggy tracksuit top that hung off one shoulder and tracksuit bottoms that had slid partway down his left thigh. He looked weak, feeble, and walked with a limp. His beard was messy and unkempt and covered in crumbs and grease. His teeth were falling out, and the five that remained were as dark as the alleyway. He wasn't the poster boy for how to live your life, that was for sure.

'What time d'you call this?' Lewis asked, remaining perfectly still.

'I'm… I'm… sorry, Lew. I'm sorry, I—'

'You got the money you owe me? I had to cover for you the other day, man. You owe me big time.'

'I-I-I got it. I got it. Just like you said, Lew.'

The buyer had a severe case of the jitters. He rubbed his arms fervently and wrapped himself in his sweatshirt, then reached into his pocket and pulled out a wad of cash.

'Is it all there? I ain't wanna have to count through it like last time.'

'No… no… it's all… it's all there. I promise. Just like you said, Lew.'

Lewis snatched the money from the customer and pocketed it. He looked up and down the underpass and surveyed the area, making sure that nobody else was watching, waiting for the opportune moment to strike and arrest them. He'd heard about what had happened to Reece, and he was paranoid the same would happen to him.

'What have you got for me?' the junky asked, his voice now pitched with excitement.

'Something a little different,' Lewis replied, struggling to suppress the smile growing on his face.

'What?'

Lewis had never seen someone's eyes light up so much.

'Something new's come onto the market. Top secret. Keep it under wraps for the moment, yeah? And if you like it, which I'm sure you will, I want you here at midday tomorrow. That should be more than enough time for you to be hungry for more. Lots more. Can you do that?'

Lewis removed the packet of drugs from his pocket and hovered it under the junky's nose. 'This one's on the house. But if you like it, the price is slightly higher than usual.'

'Nah. Nah. Can't do higher. I struggled to bring this

money together, just like you asked, Lew.'

'The high's worth the price, fam. Trust me. We got ourselves a deal?'

At the sight of the free drugs, the junky's eyes widened even further, the whites turning phosphorescent.

'Deal.' He snatched the packet from Lewis, clenched it in his hand, sniffed it, then scurried away down the alleyway like a fiend from a kid's cartoon.

Now all Lewis had to do was put his faith in Frank's product and hope that his client returned.

CHAPTER 43

FIRST STEP TO REDEMPTION

The front door felt heavy in Jake's hands, as though it carried the burden of his responsibilities. As he set foot in his house, the smell of dinner hit him in the face. Thai green chicken curry. Home-made. Elizabeth's own version. One of his favourites. It had been a long time since he'd last felt the spice sizzle and dance on his lips.

Just the smell of it made him recall the first time he'd tasted it. The weather hadn't been too dissimilar to today. Normal. No rain. No sun. Not hot, not cold. Just… British. They'd been to the park for a walk, breaking in the new wellington boots they'd bought so they could spend more time on the weekends getting to know the nearby landscape. And then they'd come home to their new house, like the happy little family they were. Their relationship had only been in its infancy at that point, and so far they'd lived on a few basic meals, finding their feet around the kitchen. But on that day, Elizabeth had decided she was going to throw caution to the wind and make a curry. Nothing special, nothing exciting. But it had been one of the best-tasting curries he'd ever had.

And now it was a rare treat whenever she made it.

He wondered what he'd done to deserve it this time.

'Evening,' he said after she appeared in the doorway. He kissed her on the cheek and placed his bag on the floor at the back of the kitchen.

'I hope you're hungry,' she told him as she stirred the boiling pan of rice, accidentally spilling some over the side and sending plumes of steam billowing into her face.

'You have no idea. I could smell it from the car.'

'Don't lie to me,' she replied.

Uh oh. Where did that come from? At first, he thought she was playing, but then he noticed her voice had dropped, and there was something in the way she'd said those words that made it seem like there was more to come.

'How was your day?' he asked, trying to hide the concern in his voice.

'Fine.'

He moved to the other side of the kitchen, keeping the centre island between them just in case she started swinging. Ellie was sitting in her high chair, holding a juice bottle protectively in her hand. Jake stroked her hair, set a hairclip that had fallen out of place back on her head and pinched her cheeks. She looked up at him, eyes wild with bewilderment. In that moment, he thought that she was looking at him the same way she might look at a stranger. Big, wild eyes filled with curiosity. Jake felt a knot in his stomach.

'What did you get up to today?' he asked as he turned his attention back to Elizabeth, forcing his thoughts of Ellie's reaction out of his mind.

Elizabeth ignored him. Continued preparing dinner.

'Liz?'

Keeping her back to him, she set the spoon on the kitchen surface. 'When were you going to tell me, Jake?'

257

He paused, hesitated. The skin on his body turned cold. What did she *know*?

'You're going to have to bring me up to speed, Liz. I don't know what you're talking about.'

He still hadn't developed the art of telepathy, no matter how hard she wanted him to.

Elizabeth disregarded the cooking and strode towards the living room, shoving the door aside so violently as she went that it smashed into the adjacent wall behind her. She returned a few seconds later. In her hands, she held a brown envelope. Jake didn't need to see what was written on it because he already knew. They were all the same, all bearing the same inscription as if it were a mark of pride.

We thank you…

She turned the package over and removed a wad of notes. The smell of legal tender wafted through the air, beating the curry for first place in his nostrils.

'Where did you get all of this from, Jake?'

Shit. There must have been another package. *Think, think, think.*

'Some of the guys in the office,' he told her. 'Playing jokes. Thinking they're funny.'

'By leaving a couple of grand on the doorstep?'

Jake bit his lip.

'Don't bullshit me, Jake. Tell me what's going on.'

He moved slowly across the kitchen towards her. First, to navigate her reaction; second, to take the money and destroy it.

'Honestly, it's nothing you need to worry about. If it was, then I'd tell you.'

Would he? So far, he didn't think so.

'You can't protect us all the time, Jake. No one's making you. We're supposed to be a team, and I need you to be honest with me and tell me where this has come from. I don't believe for a second that it's some of the guys at work. None of them know you well enough; nor would they do such an insensitive thing. And why would they leave it on the doorstep? If they really cared about you, and they really were your *friends*, then they'd know how much distress and pain that side of things has caused.'

She was right. Of course she was. He didn't know how she managed to do it, but she could always see right through him. He was either a terrible liar or she had been born with a sixth sense for sussing out bullshit. Or there was the third option, one that, until now, he'd forgotten. That, no matter what it was, no matter how small or insignificant, women always found out the truth.

The third option seemed most likely.

'I'm giving you one more opportunity to tell me what is going on, otherwise, you can eat dinner on your own and I'll take the girls to my mum's with me. Three… Two…'

Jake held his hands up in surrender. He couldn't lie to her anymore. It had gone on for too long.

'All right, all right. I'm sorry, Liz. It's just…' He dropped his head, collected his thoughts. His palms were sweaty, and his lips felt heavy with the words of truth he was about to speak. 'There are some things I need to tell you. But I promise you, under no circumstance will I allow you or the girls to come to any harm. You have my word on that. I will do everything to protect you.'

The first step to redemption started with being honest.

CHAPTER 44

OPERATION GONE WRONG

The heavy rhythmic beat coming from the dance floor pulsated through Frank Graham's body. The flashing lights and smell of dry ice in the air, combined with the relaxing chemicals of the marijuana currently floating through his bloodstream, created a noxious hit and disorientated him. It was just after midnight, and the club had been open for an hour. And there was still no sign of Danielle. He was beginning to think she wouldn't show. That she was going to embarrass him, humiliate him in front of all his colleagues. Or perhaps that was the weed-induced paranoia talking, and she was just playing with him by being fashionably late.

Well, he didn't appreciate either. He'd put on a show for her tonight, called in a couple of favours from the boys to help him set up and convince her that The Rossiters was a fully functioning venue worthy of her attendance.

'You good, Frank?' Caleb asked, relaxing into the sofa of the VIP section, one hand resting on top of the cushion, the other holding a joint. 'You seem on edge.'

Frank paced from left to right, rubbing his nose. 'I need

me another line.'

'Take it easy, bro. If you go too hard, you'll be too fucked up for when Danielle arrives.'

'Good. I'm better when I'm fucked. Last longer.'

Caleb kissed his teeth. 'You think she's gonna hand over the goods that easy?'

Frank stopped pacing and placed his hands on his hips. Beads of sweat began to drip down his forehead at a frequency that matched his heartbeat. 'I'm gonna make sure she does.' He moved around the table in the middle of the room. 'Now gimme the bag.'

Caleb produced a thin plastic bag of cocaine. It was the same size as a crisp packet, and it was about half full. The rest of the boys had been greedy tonight.

Frank snatched the bag from him, scooped his index finger inside and removed a mountain of white snow on the top of his nail. The light fragrance of strawberry, a trick he'd stolen from Henry's product, wafted through his nose. It was heavenly and made the hairs on his arms tingle. Tonight, he was using the pure stuff, with the exception of the fragrance, and this was the final bag. Getting high off your own supply was one thing, but when the supply was riddled with God knows what else, he was only prepared to take the stuff he could trust, the stuff that didn't contain any poison.

Decanting the powder onto the glass table, he removed a credit card from his pocket and began to chop the substance into thin lines. Once finished, he pinched one nostril closed and sniffed. Hard. The powder stung and grazed his nose as it made its way to his brain. A ball of phlegm formed in his mouth, and he swallowed it down the moment a raw, euphoric energy consumed his body.

'Fuck me!' He pumped his fist into the air and wiped his nose with the other.

'Good?'

'Fucking incredible. The Colombians really know what they're doing. Now wipe this table.'

Caleb groaned, shuffled himself to the sofa's edge, and cleaned up the leftover cocaine with his sleeve.

Frank continued to pace around the room again. Feeling good. Alive. Invincible. Like nobody could touch him. Like he could conquer the world and destroy everyone who opposed him. Like Henry Matheson. Ricky Bricks. Donny Valentino. All those little pricks that'd told him he was no good. One day, he'd show them all.

To the left of the VIP room was his very own bar. It had been left over from the previous owner's tenure and was predominantly used for business meetings and socialising, while the rest of the club was left in a state. Dozens of bottles of different coloured spirits sat in a neat row against the wall, and overhead, wine glasses dangled upside down from the overhead shelf. He grabbed a glass and rounded the bar. As he stood in front of the spirits, contemplating what to have, the door burst open behind him. The room was quickly filled with noise spilling in from the dance hall.

'Frank,' a voice called. One of the boys.

'Yeah?' Frank said on the half-turn.

'She's here.'

'Perfect. Send her through.'

The door closed and stifled the music. It felt as though he were wearing a giant pair of noise-cancelling headphones. By the time the door opened again, he was no closer to deciding what to drink. As soon as he heard the music flood the room, he spun on the spot and spread both arms wide.

'Danielle, you're here!' he exclaimed, beaming at the woman who'd just entered. 'And you brought a friend too!'

Frank rounded the bar and floated towards her. His feet felt like they were moving independently from the rest of his body. When he reached Danielle, he embraced her. A strong whiff of perfume assaulted his senses and tickled the leftover cocaine into action.

'This is Annabelle,' Danielle said, gesturing to her friend.

'Lovely to meet you.' Frank kissed the back of her hand and gestured to Caleb. 'This is my friend, Caleb, the fat fuck who's clearly lost all of his manners, not that he had many to begin with.'

The girls chuckled awkwardly, and Frank took a moment to observe and admire them both. Danielle looked exactly the way he remembered from the night before. The long, dark hair tied in a ponytail with a silver scrunchy at the top of her head The thick black eyeliner and mascara accentuating the darkness of her eyes. The skin-tight black dress that was an attempt at showing some class she couldn't quite pull off. The outline of underwear around her backside. Frank adored it all.

'You're looking *good* tonight,' he said, trying to earn himself some brownie points.

'Just tonight? Not the other night as well?'

Oh, Danielle, you tease.

'Every night,' he said with a wink. 'Can I get you two girls a drink?'

Frank headed towards the bar without waiting for a response. He grabbed two napkins from the side and placed them on the surface, then pulled two glasses from beneath the bar and set them on the napkins.

'You ever worked behind a bar before?' Danielle asked, setting her clutch bag on the counter.

'Can you tell?'

'You seem to know your way around it.'

'I know my way around a lot of things.'

Frank turned his back on them and faced the wall of spirits.

'What d'you fancy?' he asked. 'Gold flake vodka?'

A smile was drawn across her face. 'You remembered?'

'I'm a good listener,' he replied with another wink.

'In that case, I've changed my mind. What do you recommend?'

'Interesting question. My favourite's Jim Beam bourbon. It's smooth. Sweet.' He faced her and looked her up and down. 'The way I like it.'

'Sounds like my idea of fun.'

Danielle eyed him flirtatiously as he poured four glasses of bourbon. He grabbed a bucket of ice and placed a cube delicately in each glass. Each one made a satisfying *dink* noise.

'Cheers,' Frank said, holding the drink aloft. 'To good times and good company.'

The girls and Caleb echoed his sentiment.

'Should we move to the sofa? Might be more comfortable.'

'Lead the way.'

Frank gestured for the girls to sit, and they sat either side of Caleb with Danielle on the right, Annabelle on the left. Frank pulled up beside Danielle, placed his arm around her and squeezed the soft, warm skin on her shoulders. Suddenly the blood rushed to his penis. Either the cocaine was having an effect on him or he was really excited to be with her. Either way, the outcome was the same.

'Shall we get down to business?' he asked, setting the drink on his knee.

'We've only just got here.'

'No rest for the wicked.' Frank reached into his pocket and pulled out a smaller sealed bag of cocaine with the skull insignia printed on it.

Danielle snatched it from him and inspected the packaging.

'It's our product. Going to be the best on the market,' he said enthusiastically.

'What makes it different?'

'Everything.'

'What?'

'As in, literally everything. There's a bit of everything in there. Coke. Mandy. Speed. It's going to light up people's lives.'

'You're shitting me?'

'I wish I was. Cut it so much that we sell half as much for double the price. People are going to go crazy for it. Charge a lot for a little that they'll want again and again… and again.'

Danielle continued to examine the packaging. She ran her fingers along the edge of the packet and pursed her lips. Frank leant forward and placed one hand on her back and the other on her knee.

'Wanna try some?'

'What happened to getting high off your own supply?'

'I say, fuck it. There's only one way to know if it's any good. Did the inventor of McVitie's build his empire not having tasted a single biscuit? I don't think so. You've gotta sample it for yourself, otherwise how else will you know whether it's good enough for the wider population?'

The coke was really doing a lot of the talking now. He'd completely forgotten to keep the ingredients a secret.

'So you've tried it already then?' she asked.

'Had some this morning,' he lied. 'Still on a bender.'

Danielle turned to Anabelle for support before answering. 'A little bit,' she said. 'Not too much.'

'Coming right up.'

Frank took the bag from her, poured a fingernail's worth of substance onto the table and split the pile in half. After forming two lines, he handed Danielle a rolled-up note. She thanked him for it then leant forward and inhaled.

She groaned as the chemicals reacted instantly in her brain. Her head tilted backwards and she fell deeply into the cushions, her eyes rolling into the back of her head. The colour drained from her face, and her freckles looked like flecks of dried blood on a bathroom surface.

'Oh… my… God…' she said, paralytic. Her body remained frozen, incapacitated for a moment. Beside her, Annabelle leant forward and snorted the drugs. She too had the same reaction.

'Good, eh?' Frank asked. So far so good. All systems go. Operation Get Danielle Matheson Fucked Up on Drugs was a success. But there was still a long way to go.

'Un…believe…able.'

'That's all you need. You're set for the next few hours. Trust me.'

Danielle blinked her eyes back in his direction. Her pupils were the size of dinner plates, and rivers of red ran from one end to the other. 'Shall we get down to the second order of —?'

She stopped suddenly as her body retched then convulsed like a worm.

'Danielle?'

Her eyes rolled into the back of her head, her skin turning even paler as her arms fell by her side, and she started shaking uncontrollably, as if she was possessed. Then she began to foam at the mouth.

'Danielle!' Frank shook her, but it was no use.

Within seconds, Danielle Matheson was dead.

| PART 4 |

CHAPTER 45

ARSE-END OF NOWHERE

Frank sobered up faster than was anatomically possible. His feet were firmly planted on the ground, standing over Danielle's dead body. In the time it had taken him to rise to his feet, Annabelle had suffered the same fate. And now both women were lying there, frozen in a snapshot of confusion, pain and euphoria. The triple whammy of any drug taker's hit. During the process of death, their bodies had turned rigid; Frank wasn't sure whether it was because of the copious amount of drugs in their system or because his limited knowledge of people dying told him that rigor mortis might be setting in.

Either way, he knew it meant one thing.

'We're fucked.'

Caleb babbled incoherently. Frank ignored him. He needed to think. Collect his thoughts. Come up with a plan to get them out of this predicament. *Predicament* was an understatement. It was a total fucking nightmare. A disaster. A clusterfuck. And there was only one thing they could do.

Caleb reached for Annabelle's neck, his finger pressed

against her skin, trying to find a pulse.

'What're you doing?' Frank barked. His voice seemed to drown out the sound of the bass coming from the club.

'Checking to see if they're alive,' Caleb replied sheepishly, pulling his hand away.

'Of course they ain't alive! Look at 'em! They ain't coming back from that. They're fucking dead, fam. And there ain't no way you should even be thinking 'bout touching 'em!' Frank pointed at Caleb, and as he held his finger in the air, he noticed it shaking uncontrollably. 'Clean their bodies.'

'What?'

'Get a wet wipe, a flannel, a piece of tissue, anything; I don't fucking care, and begin to wipe their bodies. There can't be none of our DNA left on them. You've seen crime programmes before, right?'

'What we gonna do, Frank?' Caleb asked. The colour had drained from his face, and for a moment Frank wondered whether he was dying as well but then realised it would take a couple more doses of the pure stuff to kill someone his size.

'You do as I say,' Frank told him.

'I mean… about *them*.' Caleb gave a shy nod to the two cadavers.

'We'll have to get rid of them.'

'Us? What about one of the boys? Can't we get one of them to do it?'

Frank shook his head. 'We ain't at that level yet. What happens if they open their mouths? We can't afford for that to happen. It needs to be us.'

Frank placed a hand on his hip and rubbed the sweat through his hair. 'I need to make a phone call.'

He pulled out his mobile and headed towards the door in the corner of the lounge that opened onto a smoking area. It was small, cramped and damp, no larger than a prison cell. Overgrown grass and weeds were growing along the cracks in the tiles and corners of the walls, interspersed by discarded cigarette mountains that were now home to large colonies of ants. The state of the smoking area, however, was the least of his worries.

The call connected.

'Hello?'

'It's Frank.'

A pause as the name registered in the recipient's mind.

'You sure you want to use it now, Frank? You've managed to fix things in the past.'

Frank stared skywards at the moon that was beginning to break free of the clouds. 'Yes. Yes, I'm sure. This is worse than all the others.'

'You said that last time.'

'I know what I said! Just… help. I need help.'

'What's the delivery?'

'Two females. Mid-twenties.'

'Size. Weight. Body dimensions. I need a little more information than that, Frank.'

'Right… er…'

'Come on, Frank. I need to know these things. How tall are they?'

'I dunno!' he screamed. 'I don't have a fucking tape measure with me.'

'You'd better find a solution otherwise there's nothing I can do.'

Frank sighed heavily down the phone. He turned, tore through the door and burst back into the lounge. Meanwhile, Caleb was busy wiping Annabelle's arms down with a wet cloth he'd found behind the bar, soaking the sofa in water and soap. Frank ignored him and observed both girls' bodies.

'I… er…' he stammered, trying to recall how tall they were when they'd been standing. 'One of them… one of them is five-nine. The other was… she was slightly smaller, perhaps five-six, five-seven.'

There was a pause.

'OK. It's not ideal, but I can work with it,' the voice in his ear said.

'Nothing about this is ideal.'

'Remember where the meeting point is?'

'Has it changed?'

'It hasn't.'

'Then yes. How long?'

'An hour.'

Frank checked his watch. It was 1:30 a.m. One hour. Sixty minutes. Three thousand six hundred seconds. That was manageable.

'Fine. We'll see you then.'

'Delays cost money, remember,' the voice said as a final parting gift.

Frank rang off and thrust his phone into his pocket.

'Are you done?' he called to Caleb.

His friend abruptly stopped what he was doing and stared at Frank, looking like a deer caught in headlights.

'Are you done? Are they wiped clean?' Frank repeated.

'I think so.'

'And the glasses? Their drinks? What've you done with them?' Frank answered his own question; he looked down at the table and saw both of the lipstick-stained glasses resting on the table. He picked them up, hurried over to the sink and began frantically washing them until they were spotless.

'What do we do now?' Caleb asked behind him.

Frank finished wiping his hands on a towel and threw it onto the bar's surface. 'Find something to wrap them in. Anything we can use to transport them into the back of the car. I need to get rid of the boys.'

Leaving Caleb to the task, Frank started towards the door. There, he stopped and waited, composing himself, breathing deeply, letting all the tension and stress drain from his face – successfully, he hoped. Then he opened the door and wandered into the club.

People were dancing, most of whom he'd paid to be there and some he didn't recognise, while the rest of his boys were standing behind the bar, serving drinks. In the centre of the room, surrounded by a dance floor, was the DJ, a part-timer to whom Frank had paid an obscene amount of money to come and perform a small set for a couple of hours.

Over a hundred people, drunk off their faces, absolutely oblivious to what was going on around them.

Now it was his job to get rid of them all.

He stormed towards the DJ booth, grabbed the microphone from the bloke's hand, and said, 'Right! Everyone out. Out. That's it. It's over. Time to—'

The DJ snatched the microphone back from Frank and continued to blast the heavy, monotonous music through the speakers.

'What do you think—' Frank started but he was too angry to finish his sentence. He grabbed the DJ by the shoulders and yanked him away from the decks. The man fell down a small step onto the dance floor and landed on his shoulder. Frank found the kill switch and put an end to the music, immediately filling the club with a silence that was quickly evaporated by the sounds of groans and discontent coming from the punters.

'Everyone out,' he said, fumbling for the microphone on the stage, panting.

Nobody reacted. They all simply stood there, gawping at him as if he'd just flashed them.

'Guys, get the fuck outta here. It's over.'

Still nothing. Ridiculous. He needed something that would make them act, and, in his drug-fuelled state, he had it.

'You cretins, get out of here. The police are on their way! The cops! The feds! The pigs! Somebody tipped them off about the drugs in here. They're bringing the dogs.'

That seemed to work. At once, everybody in the vicinity bolted like runners at the start of a race, and within seconds the dance floor had cleared. None of them wanted to be caught with the drugs he'd offered as a token of his appreciation upon their arrival. None of them wanted to spend the night in a piss-stained custody cell.

Frank breathed a sigh of relief, rushed to the VIP lounge and found Caleb in the middle of rolling Annabelle into a curtain net, a thin piece of white material that had been stencilled into a fancy pattern.

'Jesus Christ,' he said, amazed at what he was seeing.

'You got any better suggestions?' Caleb was out of breath, beads of sweat beginning to drip down the bridge of his nose. When Frank didn't respond, he continued, 'You wanna take a fucking picture or something? Don't just stand there. Gimme a hand.'

Frank did, and after a few minutes of attempting to roll both women into the netting, they abandoned it and instead decided to drag their bodies out of the club and into the back of Frank's parked Audi A5. The women's bodies were dead weight, immovable, and felt almost twice as heavy as they had when they were alive. Bending his knees, Frank stood on one side with Caleb on the other, and on the count of three, they hefted Danielle's body into the boot. Anabelle joined her shortly after.

'Get the curtain. Spread it over them,' Frank ordered.

Once Caleb had returned, Frank thrust the gearstick into first and skidded as he pulled out into the street.

They drove for the next hour towards an industrial estate in Kent, crossing the Queen Elizabeth II Bridge, paying the toll charge, and driving towards Bluewater Retail Park with the River Thames on their left.

It was quarter to three in the morning by the time they arrived at the location. Fifteen minutes behind schedule.

They pulled into the car park of a disused warehouse and found a man waiting for them. He wore a black leather jacket and a black baseball cap. In the low light, his face was featureless.

'You sure this is him?' Caleb asked.

'Who the fuck else would it be?' Frank replied sarcastically.

By now the drugs had fully worn off and he was feeling stone-cold sober.

He killed the engine and stepped out of the car.

'You're late,' the contact said.

'Better late than never.' Frank closed the door behind him and strode over the loose gravel, coming to a stop beside the man. Then the contact moved round to the passenger door of his car.

'You want us to get in?' Frank asked confused.

'No. This is for the money. The bodies go in the boot. You go home.'

Fuck. The money. He envisaged it now, sitting under one of the cushions on the sofa in a shoebox.

'I… er…'

'The price is double. Two bodies equals two payments.'

'I… we…' Frank swallowed hard. He struggled to look the man in the eye. 'Do you… would you accept an IOU?'

'No.'

'Bank transfer?'

'You're even more stupid than I thought.'

'Listen, I… I can get you the money, ain't no problem about that. I've got loads of it! I just don't have it with me… here.'

The man said nothing. Slammed the door shut. Rounded

the front of the car, started the engine and drove away before Frank and Caleb were able to comprehend what was happening.

'What the fuck are we supposed to do now, Frank?' Caleb asked.

Frank observed his surroundings, calculating the best possible way out of the situation. For a brief moment, he even considered driving all the way back to the club, but that was ridiculous. Nor was there another contact who could help them. So that meant it was down to them. Two coked-up dealers with no experience in disposing of dead bodies, stuck in the arse-end of nowhere.

Fuck.

Every which way he looked, he was surrounded by walls of black, broken up and dotted by red and white lights way off in the distance. Immediately in front of him, however, just over a few hundred yards away, was a cone of white light that glistened as it rippled on top of the River Thames.

CHAPTER 46

STEP TOO FAR

The noises kept him awake. The cacophony of sound playing and reverberating around his head. The screams. The chatter. The laughter. The shouts and barks and howling as the night turned men into monsters and monsters into devils. The banging of fists on walls. The scratching. The swearing and catcalling and death threats. Everything reverberated around the concrete walls of his prison cell.

Rykard faced the wall with his back towards the sounds. His first proper night in prison. The first night of many. Three hundred and sixty-five days multiplied by however many years he was going to be in there. A sum his stupid brain couldn't even work out.

And at the end of it, what? A daughter who wouldn't recognise him. A daughter who didn't know him. A daughter who'd created a life for herself without him. A daughter who'd forgotten about him, stopped loving him. And for who? Henry Matheson; giving that man a chance to evade the justice he deserved and allowing him to continue his reign as the biggest drug dealer in East London.

No. It wasn't worth it. It wasn't right, it wasn't fair. Not for one second did he believe that there would be a substantial package awaiting him on his release. Henry had already failed to protect him from a savage beating the moment he'd set foot in there.

I can make sure you're well protected, fam. Ain't nobody gonna touch you.

His bruised ribs and smashed kidneys were a *real* testament to that.

Outside his four walls, the screams and banging and barking continued.

He'd heard stories about it lasting all night. Like a prolonged nightmare or sleep paralysis where he was trapped, unable to do anything or protect himself. It was terrifying, and what was worse was that he'd seen things, experienced things. Killed a man. Stood face to face against another holding a knife to his throat. But this… this was horror on a whole new level. And that scared him.

Three hundred and sixty-five days multiplied by however many years he was going to be in there.

He reached underneath his pillow and removed a burner phone that one of the bent prison guards, presumably in Henry's pocket, had smuggled in for him. At least Henry was good on his word about one thing.

Rykard switched the phone on, prayed that it wouldn't chime as it loaded, and when it didn't, allowed the pain in his ribs to dissipate and his body to relax. In the address book were two mobile numbers. One for Rupert. One for Henry. No other lines of communication. Everything during his time in that cell had to be dictated by those two. Rykard had begged for his daughter's number to be added; to hear the sound of her voice, to know that she was OK when he wanted to check up on her – but it had been rejected by Henry, the bastard. And he wasn't intelligent enough to remember it by hand.

He was alone.

Rykard found Rupert Haversham's number and created a message. After he'd finished typing as quickly as possible, he hit send.

Rykard: Ne news? Wot the l8test wiv H?

He waited. And waited. And as he did so, he eventually started to drift off. Just as he was about to fall asleep, the phone vibrated in his hand. The man who never slept had responded.

Rupert: Busy. Southend's done. County line opened. Working on it now with Reece and others. Yours when out.

Like fuck it was. That conniving, backstabbing bastard had gone behind his back and opened up a county line in Reece's name when it was supposed to be *his*. Henry had promised that he would be the one in charge of running the operation from the start, but he'd given it to that little shit instead, the one who probably still pissed himself at night. Rykard's fists curled in frustration.

He'd put up with a lot in the time he'd known and worked for Henry, but now he'd gone too far. Henry had favoured Reece over himself. Had it been anyone else – Deshawn, Jamal – then he would've understood. Those two were elders; they had more experience, more expertise. But giving it to Reece… well, it was a humiliation. And if there was one thing that Rykard wouldn't stand for it was being made to look inferior.

It was one thing to throw him under the bus and make him confess to murder. But it was another to ruin his reputation, and letting a little pissant like Reece Enfield take charge of their first-ever county line was a step too far.

CHAPTER 47

REQUEST TO SPEAK

'You're not going to like me for this,' Darryl told Jake with a hint of solemnity in his voice.

Those weren't the words he wanted to hear first thing in the morning.

'What have you done now?' Jake asked sardonically as he stepped into Darryl's office and found himself a seat opposite the man. He hadn't even had the opportunity to get himself settled and mentally prepared for the mountain of hurdles and obstacles the day would undoubtedly bring.

'I think this is the first time I'm not to blame. And neither are you, which makes a change.'

A nice jibe first thing in the morning. Thanks. Jake added it to the scoresheet.

'I just like to keep you on your toes, guv. What's the issue then?'

Darryl knitted his fingers together and tilted forward, embodying the wealthy businessman he'd perhaps wanted to be as a child. There was a window behind him, and the light that filtered through the slits in the blinds almost gave him an angelic glow.

'It's about the UCO in the OCG,' Darryl began.

Jake remained still, listening intently.

'As expected, we can't have one.'

'Why?' he asked, like an inquisitive child who required immediate answers.

'Because it appears there's already an undercover officer operating within the E11's structure.'

'Who?'

'Mary Poppins. I don't know. You know how CHIS operations work, right?'

CHIS stood for covert human intelligence source and was just a fancy way of saying someone was working undercover. They were a special breed of officer, and were often deployed in organised crime groups and terrorist cells. Their identities were kept secret, known only to a couple of people, and any intelligence was reported through their handler, someone senior who had a close yet discreet relationship with the UCO.

Jake scoffed. 'What are they doing in there?'

Darryl raised a hand. 'I'm gonna save you some time and tell you I don't know anything. That's the nature of the beast with this one. If I had more, I'd give it to you. All I know is that there's one already working within the E11, so that makes life harder for our investigation.'

'Because they're working against us!'

'You don't know that.'

'There's a little thing called intuition. Maybe if you followed yours a bit more you might be able to see through the bullshit you've been fed.'

Darryl flattened one palm on the table, then flexed his fingers so that his hand looked like a five-legged insect.

'You're angry,' he began. 'I get that. But there's no point coming after me. I tried to help, but it didn't work. I've been in your position. I know how it is to be told you can't have something, especially when it's something as big as this. I'm sure I probably reacted the same way, in fact.'

'You're right, guv. I'm sorry. It's just…' Avoiding Darryl's intense gaze, Jake looked down into his lap. Inhaled, sighed. 'It's just… there's no excuse for it. I'm sorry.'

What Jake was really sorry about was not being able to tell Darryl the real reason he was so uptight and tense. That The Cabal was closing in on him. That his and his family's safety was in jeopardy. That nobody would believe him, just like they hadn't all those months ago, and that there was nothing anyone could do about it. Instead, he was left to deal with it himself, bear the burden on his shoulders alone.

'I appreciate the apology, Jake. I know it's not an easy thing to do, admitting you're in the wrong. But I appreciate it, nonetheless.'

Jake feigned a smile, then exited the room and made his way back to his desk, shoulders slumped. First the missing evidence, and now this.

Before he'd had a chance to place his buttocks on the seat, a call came from across the office from one of the new detective constables Jake hadn't bothered to pay much attention to.

'Jake, I'm hearing that…' She looked down at a Post-it note attached to her finger. 'I'm hearing that Rykard Delawney, the arrested suspect for Jermaine Gordon's murder, has made a request to speak with you.'

'I'm busy.'

He wasn't.

'He wants to speak to you alone. He says there's something he needs to tell you about the investigation. Without Rupert Haversham present.'

CHAPTER 48

LITTLE YOUT

The man sitting opposite Jake emitted a rather offensive smell.

It was just the two of them in interview room 4, the last in the long corridor of interview rooms. It was also the one that most detectives tended to avoid. They were all the same, in terms of shape, size, layout and design, but there was something about interview room 4 that warned his colleagues off. Perhaps it was the slight dampness in the light bulb that cast a deeper shade of orange across the rest of the room. Or perhaps it was the temperamental heating that sometimes ranged from summer holidays in Dubai to winter storms at the North Pole. Right now, the temperature was doing nothing to combat the rising tide of body odour currently overpowering the clean air.

'Drink?' Jake asked as he eyed the cup of water that he'd brought for himself.

Rykard shook his head. 'I'm all right for now.'

'I must admit, I didn't think I'd be the first on your list of people to speak with. I imagined you'd want to speak with your daughter. But I hope our discussion this morning can be a bit more productive than the first one we had,' Jake said with a forced smile, really hoping it would be.

'Can we begin or you just gonna talk and waste time?'

Jake reached across the table, started the recording and took a sip of his water. The ice-cold liquid soothed his throat. For some reason this morning it had been feeling quite sore.

'Well?' he began. 'I believe you had something you wanted to tell me…'

'Depends on how much the information is worth to you.'

Jake tilted his head and eyed Rykard suspiciously. 'I don't think it works like that, mate. How will I know if it's worth anything if I don't know what it is?'

'I want some assurances.'

'Assurances?'

'Lighter sentence. Less jail time.'

Jake snorted. 'You know I don't make those decisions.'

'But you know the people who do. You can put in a good word.'

'It's not down to me. It's up to the judge. If you do decide to give us information, and it does prove vital to the outcome of the case, then the judge will acknowledge that when he decides your sentencing. But like I say, if I don't know what the information is, I don't know how much help *I* can be.'

Rykard shifted in his seat, pulled his jumper over his head and slung it over the back of his chair. Jake noticed two dark moons dangled beneath Rykard's armpits. And two blotches of sweat sat beneath his nipples, looking like a pair of eyes on his chest. All he needed now was a line of sweat on one of the folds in his stomach and he would have completed the paint-by-sweat picture.

'Essex,' Rykard said eventually.

'I've heard of it. Never been though,' Jake replied.

'Southend.'

'Are you just naming places?'

'The Hightower Estate.'

Jake hesitated. The name rang a bell. A recent one. But he couldn't recall why.

'There was a murder there the other day, wasn't there?'

Jake nodded slowly as he recalled where he'd heard the name. And then he remembered the details. A brutal stabbing had taken place in one of the estates in Southend, one of Essex's most popular seaside towns. The body of a drug dealer had been discovered, stabbed over twenty times, and left in a pool of blood. Initial reports suggested there were no signs of a break-in, nor any signs that anything had been stolen. The evidence was almost minimal, and the only thing that gave some sort of indication as to what had happened was the stash of drugs that had been left on the coffee table, inches from the deceased individual. It didn't take a genius to work out that a disagreement over the items on the table could have been a cause of the murder. The only question that remained on Jake's mind, however, was how did Rykard know about it?

'The murder took place the other day. You've been in our custody all that time. How did you know?'

Rykard shrugged. 'That's not important. What is important is whether or not it's going to help me.'

'I told you, I can't make those promises. I can't guarantee it.'

'Then what can you guarantee?'

Jake observed the slight movement of Rykard's eyebrows at the small glimmer of hope he experienced. 'I can promise that whoever killed the victim will be sentenced to a lengthy term in prison.'

For some reason, that seemed to placate Rykard more than Jake had anticipated, and a smile grew on the criminal's face.

'Have you ever heard of county lines, Detective?'

'Is that some sort of racetrack?'

'Not even close.'

Rykard scratched the underside of his armpit and then, with his sweaty hand, rubbed the underside of his nose. Grim, thought Jake.

'The drug trade in the city ain't what it used to be,' he continued. 'Lotta competition out there messing with people's business. And there ain't that many more clients neither, so all the gangs start beefing with each other over petty little shit. Some you win, some you lose. But there're places where you ain't even have to fight nobody. You go there, set up your market stall and you're top dog. Once you got your market stall all set, you just need to set up the supply and demand. The demand will always be there, and the supply comes from the city. One thing that connects the two of 'em is a phone line. Hence the term.'

Jake felt like he was in school again, although he'd never expected that one day he'd be learning from a drug-dealing murderer. That was a completely new experience. And as he listened, he wondered how much of what Rykard had just told him had been repeated verbatim from Henry Matheson.

'What's this got to do with anything?' Jake asked.

Rykard rolled his eyes and scoffed. 'It means the county line is now set up. That bloke who got splashed was the man in charge of Southend's drugs. Bit of a useless prick if you ask me. But now he's off the market, it means new business and market stalls can be set up.'

'For who?'

'I ain't telling you that, but it ain't going to take you long to work it out.'

'Who's running the phone, the *county line*?' Jake asked as if he were unsure of it, like it was a bad word that would infect him with hatred and spells and magic.

'You're missing the point,' Rykard said, leaning closer to

the table's edge. 'I ain't telling you none of that. What I am willing to tell you, however, is that I know the name of the yout that done it.'

'You know who killed the victim?'

Rykard dipped his head five degrees south in an imperceptible nod.

'Why would you tell me this information?' Jake asked.

'Guarantees. Plus I wanna see the little shit get put down for it.'

Jake readied himself for his next question. He swallowed then licked his lips. 'Go on then… who was it?'

Rykard made no hesitation in responding. 'A little yout named Reece Enfield. Lives in the Cosgrove Estate with his mum. Close to a couple of boys named Deshawn and Jamal. They was probably the ones who got him involved.'

Jake eased back into his chair, nursing a mild case of shock. He thought of how the boy had gone from wielding a knife to showing remorse and a weaker side, the side you'd expect from a teenager, when being arrested and interviewed, to heading across the country and stabbing a man twenty times a few hours later. It was unfathomable. And for a brief moment, Jake considered himself lucky that he hadn't met the same fate as the man who'd had to be peeled, lifeless, from his sofa.

It wasn't all bad news this morning.

But there was still one question that remained.

'How do you know all of this?'

Rykard flashed a cheeky grin. 'Because I was the one who was supposed to do it. It should've been me instead of Reece. Henry, the little cunt, double-crossed me. So now I'm double-crossing him.'

CHAPTER 49

FRIENDSHIP

They were waiting in Lewis's preferred spot, beside the flight of steps that led to the north tower's twenty floors of flats, resting their feet against the wall, hands in pockets, heads down. In front of Lewis was a bottle of vodka, rolling from side to side in the wind that buffeted through the tunnel.

The night before, Lewis had received a text from his buyer saying that he wanted more of Frank Graham's product and that he would meet Lewis on time, as discussed, at midday. Lewis had been more than happy to oblige and was even happier to have an excuse not to go into school, not that he needed one. On the way to the underpass, he'd run into Reece and offered his friend a chance to join him. It was a good business opportunity for them both. Show Reece some of the goods, show him the possibilities of turning his back on the E11 and venturing into new territory. Of rising through the ranks of Frank's gang.

'What're we waiting for, fam?' Reece complained.

'Just wait, all right. Stop hassling me, man. He's coming.'

It wasn't completely abnormal for fiends to be late for

meetings; they were only ten per cent aware of what was going on around them at the best of times, and that was when they were sober. But this was unprecedented. Ten minutes had turned into twenty, twenty into thirty, and as it was now nearing Lewis's lunchtime, his patience was growing thin, exacerbated by the low grumbling rippling its way through his stomach.

'Maybe he's still on a bender,' Reece said.

'Maybe.' Lewis didn't want to let on that he was getting worried that something might have happened to his buyer. And, more importantly, that his buyer was about to let him down, show him up in front of his best friend and make him look like a right tit.

Another ten minutes passed, as did Reece's tolerance levels with it. 'This is dead, man,' he moaned.

'Allow it. Wait another five minutes at least.'

As Lewis said it, to his left, a group of police officers pulled up on the other side of the estate. Three of them in total. One plainclothes detective, two uniformed. They burst out the cars and charged through the south tower, disappearing up the stairs.

'Shit! They're fucking here for m—' Reece didn't finish his sentence. He clawed at Lewis's arms, and before Lewis could react, Reece sprinted out of the underpass and disappeared round the corner, the sound of his panicked footsteps rapidly receding.

Lewis swore under his breath. *Pussy.* Running away like a little bitch at the first sign of the police. He hadn't run that fast when they'd arrested him the other day. In fact, he'd waxed lyrical about standing his ground, of the police needing three officers to come and pin him down.

But that was all supposed to be over with, forgotten about until he had to report to the police station for his bail. So why was Reece running? Maybe he was a bullshitter as well as a pussy and the police *had* actually struck the fear of God into him. Or perhaps there was another reason. Lewis had only ever seen his best friend sprint like that once before. Way back when they were nine years old, loitering outside Shree News; Reece had just lost a bet, and the forfeit was to jump the next person who exited the off-licence. Which turned out to be an elderly woman, carrying her weekly food and house supplies.

Reece had grabbed the woman, knocked her to the ground and yanked her shopping, all in the vicinity of a police officer. They'd given chase but Reece, having the advantage of being born and bred in the streets, having spent almost every waking hour wandering the roads and learning the lay of the land, had lost them before the chase had even really started.

No, there was something else. Another reason he'd fled.

A day in the estate was fast-paced. A lot of people lived there, and there was a lot to keep an eye on. But in the past day or two, Lewis had been distracted by the fallout of Jermaine Gordon's death, his argument with his dad, and the proposition from Frank Graham, and he'd taken his eye off the ball. Had he missed something when it came to his best friend? Was there something Reece hadn't told him?

And then Lewis recalled something he'd overheard one of the youngers from the south block talking about yesterday.

That the county line had now been set up in Southend-on-Sea.

And that there was a new champion on the Leader Board.

Lewis turned his head and looked up the street after Reece.

He was gone.

As was their friendship.

CHAPTER 50

BLACK CAR

The chassis bounced onto the kerb, tyres screeching to a halt, the nose of the car dipping under the momentum. Jake switched off the engine, disembarked and hurried towards the south tower. Behind him, two uniformed officers erupted from the marked police vehicle that had accompanied him. In his hands, he had an arrest warrant. It had taken him less than twenty minutes to get it all approved; he'd passed the threshold test with ease, and his reasonable grounds had been solid.

Jake looked at the paper and checked for Reece's address.

On the wall by the stairwell of the low-rise building was a placard listing the flat numbers and their corresponding floors. He scanned it. Found the address within seconds.

Thirty-nine.

Third floor.

Perfect.

As Jake started off up the stairs, with the uniformed officers following behind him, he avoided the puddles and cans of cider and beer and the vodka bottles that were strewn across the floor. The air inside the stairwell was a mixture of ammonia, alcohol and anonymous sex. The three As. Worsened by the damp that ran down the walls and made it look as if the concrete was crying.

Fifty steps later, he came to the third floor, stopped in front of another plaque that told him which way to go and turned left. As he swept along the outside of the flats, with a waist-high wall running to his right, he counted the numbers

Thirty-four.

Thirty-five.

Thirty-six.

Thirty-seven.

Thirty-eight.

Thirty-nine.

The Enfields lived in the flat furthest from the stairwell; a maisonette. Eventually, the two uniformed officers caught up with him. It had been decided that, in terms of protection, only a couple of officers could be spared as backup. Darryl saw the increased police presence as a potential threat to the undercover officer's operation, and it irked Jake senseless. But alas there was nothing he could do. He had little to no say in the matter, and there was a reason certain people were paid to make those decisions. If Jake had it his way, things would be very different.

But being a backseat DCI wasn't going to get him anywhere, except perhaps suffering from a disapproval-induced stomach ulcer.

He knocked on the door.

'Miss Enfield?' Jake asked. 'This is the police. Can you open up for me please?'

No answer. Everything went still. He held his breath, listening for signs of life on the other side of the door.

None came.

He knocked again.

'Miss Enfield? Elaine? Reece? Are you in there?'

Still no response. Jake bent down and peered through the letterbox into the hallway. There was a set of wooden stairs on the right, a door to the living room on the left and a bathroom immediately ahead.

'We wanted to speak with you in connection with the death of Tommy Davis. We've got a warrant under section seventeen of the Police and Criminal Evidence Act. If you don't answer, we're within our rights to use reasonable force.' Jake paused a beat. 'Miss Enfield?'

Still no answer.

Jake pushed himself away from the door, stood and turned to the uniformed officers. One of them had been lugging The Enforcer up the steps; the steel battering ram capable of delivering two tons of power in a single swing. It was a beast, and Jake had no intention of ever coming across the wrong side of one. When it came up against an opponent as flimsy as the wooden door in front of him, there was only going to be one winner.

The officer lifted the battering ram and swung it into the door. *Bang*. The deafening sound split the estate in two, reverberating off the large structures as the door splintered and gave way.

Jake and the officers flooded into the flat.

The two constables took the downstairs, while Jake took the bedrooms upstairs. He ascended the steps, checked the rooms and returned to the landing.

'Clear!' he called down.

'Clear!' came the reply.

A second later, the uniformed officers showed their faces at the bottom of the stairs.

'Have a look around. See if there's anything that'll tell us where he's gone. Don't forget your gloves.'

Both uniformed officers nodded their understanding, then

reached into their pockets and donned blue latex gloves. Jake did the same and started about the top floor.

He searched through the young boy's bedroom. But there was nothing to suggest that Reece had ever left. The bed hadn't been made, there was a glass of water on the bedside table that was now home to a few flecks of dust and fibres, and his wardrobes were filled with clothes, some discarded over the back of his desk chair. It was a typical teenager's room. But after a brief search of the wardrobes, the mattress, the bed, the drawers on Reece's desk, he found nothing of substantial evidential value. Nothing indicating that Reece had been involved in the murder. No weapon, no blood-stained clothes. Not even a C2C train ticket. Nothing.

Dismayed, Jake hurried down the steps. The two constables were continuing their search in the kitchen. He left them to it, wandered out of the flat and leant against the wall, looking out over the estate. At the football pitch. At the basketball court. At the small patch of grass. At the lamp post where Jermaine Gordon had been murdered.

But above all of it was the underpass beneath the north tower block. There, he saw a figure leaning against the wall, one leg perched under his backside.

Jake knew of only two boys it could have been. Lewis. Or Reece.

He rushed along the side of the building, down the steps, across the estate and into the underpass, then locked eyes with the boy wearing his hood. Neither of them said anything. A part of him had been expecting the boy to run. But he didn't. He remained perfectly still.

Jake came to a stop beside him, keeping at least an arm's length between them. The last thing he wanted was for a complaint to be filed against him for getting too close to a juvenile.

'Hi,' he said.

'You what?'

'DC Jake Tanner,' Jake said, already pulling out his warrant card. He looked up and down the underpass. 'You waiting for someone?'

'No.'

'You sure?'

'Yeah.'

'What you doing here then?' Jake asked. He tried to keep his voice amicable, but with the kid's monosyllabic answers, it was becoming increasingly difficult.

'Could ask you the same thing. We don't see your kind round this way that much.'

Jake smirked. 'I'm a different breed. What's your name, kid?'

'I ain't no kid. And you ain't no different breed of pig. You're all the same.'

Jake shrugged. 'Maybe you're right. But you still didn't answer my question.'

'I don't need to. I ain't under arrest. Am I?'

Jake inched backwards slightly. 'No. I just wanted to ask you a few questions, that's all.' He twisted towards the square and pointed at the lamp post. 'Suppose you heard about what happened over there?'

'No.'

'You sure?'

'Yeah. Don't know nothing.'

'That's interesting. How's your dad?'

'You what?' Lewis asked. He stomped his foot on the ground, stretched his back so that he looked taller than he was then folded his arms across his chest. 'What you say?'

'Your dad. Aiden Coyne. I spoke with him the other day. I recognised your face from some of the school photos he had on the wall. He said you weren't home a lot; nor were you at school.'

'The fuck you speaking to him for?' Lewis asked.

'He told me about his condition,' Jake said, choosing to ignore Lewis's question.

'You don't know nothing about it.'

'You're right,' Jake said. 'I don't. I can only imagine what it must be like. You must really love him.'

'What?'

'I said you must really love your dad to look after him the way you do.'

Lewis kissed his teeth. 'I ain't gay or nothing.'

'It's not gay to admit you love your dad, Lewis.'

Jake hesitated a moment while he allowed the use of his name to settle. The young boy's face contorted as though he had a hundred questions, or swear words, both of which were acute possibilities, but when Lewis said nothing, Jake continued. 'I had a dad. He died when I was fifteen. It killed me. Similar sort of age to you, I reckon. And I can tell he loves you. He loves you a lot. He misses you every day, and he wishes you went to school and stayed out of trouble. I can relate to that. What I regret most about my relationship with my dad is not spending enough time with him when he was alive. Not appreciating him when he was with us. When I spoke to your dad the other day, he said he'd love to get away from here. Away from what your life is like down here.'

'Yeah?' The intonation in Lewis's voice became more tentative, cautious. More innocent, like a child's. It was clear he was carrying the weight of both their struggles on his small, pubescent shoulders.

'Yeah, and I read up on his file too. The things he used to do to make sure you had food on the table. Probably not too dissimilar to what you might be doing now, or what you might be thinking of doing. What's happened to you both is unfair. I can understand that. But I'm sure he'd want nothing more than for you to be safe. He did those things, the petty theft, the robberies, to put food on the table so you wouldn't have to.'

'What are you talking about, fam?'

The words weren't coming to him easily. Partly because he had no idea what he was trying to say, and secondly because he felt slightly intimidated by this young man. For a moment, he was transported back to when he'd been fifteen, sitting in the living room with his brother Daniel, having to teach him lessons his father had only taught him a few months earlier. It had been hard then, but it was infinitely harder now.

Jake swallowed.

'All I'm saying, Lewis,' he started, 'is ask yourself how your dad would feel if something happened to you. It would kill him. He wants you to be safe and to do the right thing. I'm sure you'll learn to do the right thing in the end, and if you ever need any help with it, you can come to me.' Jake held out his business card, and to his surprise, Lewis took it.

With that, Jake turned his back on Lewis and strolled to his car. Whether or not Lewis would heed his advice, he didn't know. But if he was able to save one person from a fate like Jermaine Gordon's, then he considered he'd done a good job.

By the time Jake reached the car door, his body was covered in a layer of sweat. Feeling like he had several guns and knives and pairs of eyes boring down on him every step of the way, he climbed into his car and exhaled heavily, allowing the tension in his shoulders to dissipate. Something about the conversation with Lewis had been more intimidating than the one he'd had with Henry, and he'd struggled to keep the rising tide of a panic attack at bay. He and Lewis had just had a father-son chat, one he hoped would be the catalyst for Lewis to make some changes in his life.

Jake gripped the steering wheel and breathed in, out, in,

out until his body relaxed.

It didn't last long. His mobile vibrated in his pocket and he held it to his ear without looking at the caller ID.

'This is Jake,' he answered.

'Jake, it's me.' Elizabeth. 'I need you to come home now. There's a black car outside and I think someone's been in the house.'

CHAPTER 51

TILL I SAY

Henry Matheson's breathing was heavy, a weight pressing against his chest, a knot forming in his stomach, constricting with every passing minute. The onset of fear. An alien sensation to him.

Danielle, his sister, his little baby sister, the girl he'd helped raise and mould into a perfect human being, wasn't answering her phone. And every time he tried he was met with her voicemail – *Hiya, it's Dani. Can't come to the phone right now 'cos I'm probably busy, or I don't wanna speak to you –* which worried him. The stupid thing was usually bloody glued to her hands, and it was difficult to get her to focus on anything else. She was a nineteen-year-old university student and had only been on the clubbing scene for just over a year. In that time, Henry had made it his life's mission to make sure she was safe, and that any testosterone-fuelled boys – because, until they could prove themselves to him, everyone who came near her was considered a *boy* – were made aware of who her brother was. As soon as they heard his name or even recognised his face, they knew what he would do if they ever hurt her. She was the thing he cared most about.

He just wished she'd see that it was all for her benefit. In recent months, she'd started to rebel. Defy him. Question everything that he asked of her, pretend she was in one place when she was in another. And he was almost certain she'd started using too.

No matter how hard he tried to keep his business and personal lives separate, he'd known some things would fall through the cracks. Drugs were one of them. First, it had been the bag of weed she'd stolen from his supply in The Den. Then it had been the bag of MDMA…

He didn't want to think what the natural progression of things meant.

Henry tried calling her again.

Still no answer.

Now he was seriously beginning to get worried.

He threw the phone down onto the sofa and punched a pillow beside him.

The door opened. It was Des, which meant it was time to think about other things and turn his attention towards the business.

Bye-bye private life. For now.

'Sorry, bro,' Deshawn said, standing in the doorway. 'I got your message. Wassup? The boys've just seen the feds turn up outside Reece's flat. They charged in and searched the place.'

Henry clenched his fist. Another problem he had to deal with. He breathed rhythmically, methodically, and hesitated before he responded.

'Who told you?'

'Reece did, bruv. Said he got outta there as soon as he saw them.'

'He running scared?'

'Might be after the beef in Southend.'

'You reckon that's why the feds are here?'

Deshawn shrugged and continued to linger in the doorway. Not once did Henry break his gaze from the other man. 'Dunno how they woulda known it was us so soon. And if it's about that, then why ain't they coming after me, knocking down my door?'

'Did they seize anything?' Henry asked.

'I dunno, fam. Like I said, he got outta there asap. He ain't wanna hang around too long, you get me?'

'Where is he now? I wanna speak to him.'

'He's waiting outside. I'll find him, yo.'

Deshawn left the room and allowed the door to close on its own. It wasn't the worst news Henry had heard all day, but it wasn't ideal either. The situation in Southend was just beginning to get underway. Everything had been set up. And the last thing he wanted was some little pissant shithead detective pulling the plug on it before it had had any life to breathe.

Jake, if that's you, I swear I'll release those photos.

Henry pulled his thoughts away from business and Jake Tanner and returned them to Danielle for a brief moment. The short window that Deshawn wasn't in the flat gave him an opportunity. He pulled out his phone, dialled Rupert Haversham's number and held the device to his ear.

'Hello?' Rupert asked in his quintessential British accent.

'It's me. I need you to do something.'

'Glad we're not deviating from the norm.'

'You know Leanne, right?'

'Who?'

'Leanne?'

'You mean *Helen*?'

'She never gave me her real name. But thank you for that. I need a favour. It's my sister. She ain't answering my calls. She went out last night and hasn't come home.'

'She's a teenager. She's got a life of her own. She's probably round a friend's house.'

'Not after the number of times I've warned her.'

'My Erica's the same, and she's only fifteen.'

'I don't need parenting advice,' Henry said. 'I just need you to find her. I need *Helen* to find her, all right? I want her to put a trace on Danielle's mobile number. Find out where she is. Get her to give me an update in an hour once it's done. And tell her to keep them coming throughout the rest of the day.'

Henry hung up before Rupert had a chance to protest. As soon he finished the call, the door swung open. Before him, Deshawn and Reece entered.

Forget about Danielle. Back to business.

Reece was wearing a thick black Adidas jacket, with his hands in his pockets and his collar pulled up to his neck. He stood tall, with his back straight, head up. Proud. Defiant almost.

'Safe,' Henry said, resting himself against the arm of the chair.

'Safe,' Reece responded.

'You got some news for me?'

'Yeah.'

'You wanna tell me or we just gonna stand here staring at each other?'

'It's the pigs, man. They just came and raided my mum's flat, innit. They ain't gonna find nothing though. I got shot of that blade we used, you know. And I got rid of the clothes. Des can vouch for that.'

'I heard what you did. I'm impressed. Getting a new score on the Leader Board as well.'

Reece lifted his little shoulders in a nonchalant shrug. 'It's what I do. Ain't nothing to it.'

'Although now it poses a problem for us. You've turned

into a liability. The feds; we can't have them knocking around the doors all hours of the day looking for you.'

'What you saying, Hen?' The boy suddenly looked like he was about to cry.

'I think we're gonna have to move you outta town, you know. Get you locked down on the Hightower Estate, run the joint down there.'

'And what about my mum?'

Henry took a moment to reflect and consider his answer. Here was a boy who had spent his life without a father figure but with a mother who had done absolutely everything for him. In a way, it reminded him of his own situation. But things had to change. His mother's love was unconditional, and so she would love him regardless of what he'd done, just like Henry's had. Now it was time for Reece to step up and be the man of his family.

'We all have to make sacrifices, kid. She can stay here. You'll go down on your own.'

'No! I don't wanna.'

Henry's lips parted. He admired the kid for speaking up, but he was quickly about to learn why so few did.

'You ain't got a say in the matter,' he replied.

'But you said that if I did something for you then you'd leave my mum alone and forget about my arrest.' Reece's voice reached fever pitch, hovering on the scales between pre-pubescence and puberty.

Henry searched his memory bank. Shook his head. 'Dunno what you talking about, little man. Weren't no deal you made with me.' He gestured at Deshawn with a flick of the head. 'Might've been a deal you done with Des and J, but ain't one you made with me. You don't get to make those sorts of deals with me. So your punishment, fam, for being arrested the other day is going down to Southend.'

Reece kissed his teeth, rolled his shoulders back and stood

taller, stronger. He tapped his foot on the floor and Henry could see that the kid was holding back tears.

'I'm more use to you here, innit,' Reece said, trying to hide the catch in his throat.

'That right? How?'

Reece sniffed hard then wiped the snot free from his nose with the back of his hand. 'Cos I saw the feds turn up, innit.'

'That ain't gonna set the world alight, fam.'

'I ain't finished yet,' Reece retorted. 'I can be your eyes and ears around the estate, yeah. I can let you know when shit like that happens again, you get me. I see things, innit. Hear things too.'

A lot of people bargained for more power in the E11, but they were only granted those permissions if they were good on their word. And many, if not most, weren't.

'That right?' Henry reached over to the coffee table, produced a cigarette from the half-open pack sitting there, and ignited it. He inhaled, held the toxins in his chest, then exhaled deeply. 'Impress me…'

Reece sniffled again, this time keeping his hands by his side. 'The feds weren't there long, you know. I'd say 'bout ten minutes, if that. After I thought the coast was clear and that, I went back to the estate. And then I saw one of the coppers, the one that arrested me, speaking with Lewis.'

'The younger with the crippled dad?'

'Yeah.'

'What else you see?

'I saw the copper give Lewis something. Like a business card. It was small.'

Henry nodded, absorbing what Reece had told him. 'That everything?'

'No,' Reece snapped. 'I was with him before the cops arrived. We was waiting for his buyer. Told me to join because it was important. Said he had something he wanted to show me.'

Henry's interest was gradually piquing.

'What?' he asked.

'I dunno. Didn't get a chance to see it. He wouldn't tell me neither. But his buyer never showed up.'

'What you *think* he wanted to show you?'

Reece shrugged. 'I think he was shotting some new product.'

'What makes you think that, Sherlock?'

'Said he had a business proposition. The two of us. He wanted me to get involved with it.'

Henry's mind raced. He thought of the opportunities that still existed on the market that Lewis could have become involved with. And then he settled on one.

Frank Graham.

Henry sighed heavily. 'I'm impressed. You do have good eyes and ears.' He dropped the cigarette into the ashtray and rubbed the stubble that hugged his chin. 'Maybe we have got a use for you after all.'

'What is it?'

'I need you to do a little reconnaissance. Keep an eye on your little friend and report back what he's doing.'

'For how long?'

'Until I say so.'

'And then I'm done? Out of your debt?'

Henry shook his head and laughed. 'No, no. No. Ain't nobody done till I say they're done.'

CHAPTER 52

SPEED DIAL

Eighteen hours had passed since he'd accidentally killed Danielle Matheson and her friend, and the adrenaline was still rushing through his veins, wreaking havoc with his heart, causing him multiple palpitations. Every time he felt a pain in his chest, he was convinced that was it, that he'd met his end. Probably a faster and less painful way to go than what Henry would do to him. His senses were also on high alert, finely tuned to his surroundings, which meant as soon as his aunt had placed the jerk chicken strips in the saucepan and started frying them, he smelt the sweet taste from the other side of the flat. His mouth salivated instantly, but it did little to make him forget about why he was there.

Aunt Janice, or Janny as he'd called her ever since he'd first mispronounced her name, had allowed him into her home rather reluctantly. Ever since she'd found out about his career choices and what he did to other people's lives, she'd shunned him. But after begging on the doorstep, with a minor threat thrown in, she'd allowed him to stay. She lived on the same estate as him, and her flat was only a few doors down. It wasn't the best hiding spot, but he figured it was just enough for the time being, while he made arrangements for his extrication from the city. He doubted this would be the first place Henry looked. In fact, he didn't even know if Henry had discovered what had happened to his sister yet; his eyes and ears on the ground weren't responding, but this was his best chance of staying out of harm's way for now.

Two minutes. That was all it had taken for his business to come crashing down. One mistake too far. The chemicals in the drugs he'd given Danielle and Anabelle were too strong, too heavily cut. Fuck, he didn't even know *what* was in the mix. How many others had he inadvertently killed? Dozens, he was sure. Handing out the same death packages to those on the estate. Even Henry's customers… Lewis…

The skull was even more literal than he'd originally anticipated.

'Can I get you anything?'

At the sound of Janny's voice, Frank flinched and snapped his gaze away from the living room window. Aunt Janny was standing in the door frame with her apron hanging around her neck. He called her aunt, even though she was his great aunt. He didn't know her exact age, but he was sure she was going to live forever. Growing up, he'd been aware that she was already old, but now he was in his early thirties and she still looked exactly the same.

'I'm fine,' he told her. 'You've done enough.'

'I might not like having you here, but I'm not letting you go anywhere on an empty stomach,' she said. 'You don't know when you're next going to eat.'

Hopefully, as soon as I set foot in 'Dam. The ferry was due to leave the following morning, the earliest he could get a ticket. Many would have seen his disappearance as a true sign of what he was: a coward. But faced with the prospect of either escaping or facing up to Henry Matheson, the choice was painfully simple, and he would challenge anyone who disagreed to face the alternative. Few were brave enough to stand up to Henry, and even fewer lived to tell the tale.

'Food smells delicious,' he said.

'It was your brother's favourite as well.'

'His last meal,' Frank replied, immediately wishing he hadn't.

People in his family seldom spoke about what had happened to Tony. His very existence, decisions in life and choices were a stain on the Graham family name. But not for Frank. He'd looked up to his older brother, saw him as the epitome of everything he wanted to be when he grew up. And then the incident had happened, the day that had changed everything. He wondered what Tony would think of him now, of how he'd destroyed his brother's legacy, how he'd ruined the family name even more.

'I need to go to the flat and collect some more stuff soon. I'll go when it's dark.'

'What stuff?' Janny asked.

'Stuff,' he said, purposely vague as he wondered whether the gun under his bed had a bullet reserved for him in it.

Janny placed her hands on her hips. 'Don't you go bringing none of that filthy stuff here, you hear me! I won't have it. If I see so much as a bag of drugs or the smell of them in my house, I'm calling the police, you best believe me I've got their number on speed dial!'

CHAPTER 53

FULL TIME

Darryl had never been to Mile End Station, home to one of the Flying Squad's satellite offices, and would've preferred to keep it that way given that one of the people he liked least in the force was based there. DCI Helen Clements. A brute of a woman, she was rude, abrupt, abhorrent. And, unofficially speaking, she was an arsehole. There were many aspects of her personality that he despised, and since the second occasion they'd met, he'd abstained from speaking with her. Kept his distance. Now, however, he had no choice.

Mile End, as far as police stations went, was much more modern than Bow Green. The flooring was new, missing the scuff marks that would inevitably stain it within a few months, the walls had been freshly painted and there were even plants in the corners of the room. Leagues above Bow Green, which some had even gone so far as to call a shithole. But that didn't bother Darryl, or anyone else in the team, because it was *their* shithole.

'I'll let her know you're here,' the duty officer said. 'You're more than welcome to wait in the seating area if you'd like.'

'Thanks,' Darryl said, glancing over his shoulder. 'But I'll stand.'

The woman behind the desk flashed him her best customer service smile then turned her attention to the phone beside her and made a call. While he waited, Darryl roamed the entrance, shuffling towards the seating area, where he glanced at the literature pinned to the information bulletin boards. Everything was the same as Bow Green, so there was nothing of interest for him here just yet.

But there was still hope he could get an early lead over Helen before the contest had started. He was dressed in his full police uniform, replete with epaulettes, his cap on his head. If she wasn't wearing hers, then he'd be sitting on the top of the leader board.

Shortly after, a set of double doors to his right opened and there, standing on the threshold, was Helen Clements. Fully dressed, equipped with her police cap. Shit. So far, it was a draw. Her brow was furrowed and the corners of her eyes creased. She looked as though she was done with the conversation before it had even begun.

'Darryl, nice to see you again,' she said.

'Likewise.' He extended his hand.

She took it. Strong, firm. Finished within a second. Like she didn't want to be in his company. At least the feeling was mutual.

He followed her along a corridor, up a flight of stairs, through another set of double doors and into the hundred-square-foot, open-plan office space Flying Squad called home. Darryl made a quick count and noted nearly thirty individuals working. Ten more than he had in his team. On the perimeter of the room was Helen's office. She wandered towards it and gestured for him to enter, closing the door behind him.

'Big team you've got,' he commented, not expecting much

of a response.

'About thirty-six in total. Way more than you've got over at MIT, isn't it?'

Darryl ignored the remark. If it was going to be like that, a tennis game of figures and statistics, then so be it. Let battle commence.

'True, but last time I checked we've closed eight murder investigations in the past year. I'd say that puts us in quite good stead. How're your results? I understand you had a nasty armed robbery the other day.'

One nil. Off to a good start.

She seemed unfazed by his probing comments. 'We're dealing with it. As with all things, they take time, and it certainly isn't a competition, a box-ticking exercise, Darryl. Not when people's lives are at stake.'

Just like that she'd shot him down. Flat on his arse. Face in the dirt. Helen one, Darryl one.

'Did you want anything to drink? Coffee? Water?'

'No thanks,' he lied. He was parched; hadn't drunk anything since his morning coffee. But he wasn't about to let her have the satisfaction of quenching his thirst for him.

'Perfect.' She pulled her chair from her desk and sat. 'I'm glad you could come on such short notice. Especially with how busy you've been, solving those eight murders.'

The sides of Darryl's mouth flickered into an unimpressed smirk. 'When you said it was urgent, you didn't give me much of a choice.'

Helen knitted her fingers together and tilted forward slightly in her chair. The ambient light from outside her window seemed to grow stronger, highlighting her silhouette, making her bob haircut look like she was wearing an astronaut's helmet. 'I must admit,' she began, 'as soon as I became aware of your intention to place an undercover officer inside the E11 gang, I was alarmed.'

'I appreciate that may have come as a shock to you. How long have they been deployed?'

'My guy's been in there for the past nine months, infiltrating the upper echelons of Matheson and his gang.'

'Just the E11?'

Helen shook her head. Scratched her cheek with a long, natural fingernail. 'We've also got an officer in Jermaine Gordon's Stratford Dams.'

More news. More shock. More hindrances towards their investigation. More tail between his legs.

'Why're they even in there, Helen?' Darryl asked, his voice abrupt and matter-of-fact.

'Excuse me?'

'You're Flying Squad. What justification did you have for sending your UCO into one of London's biggest gangs? Do you realise how much of a problem this poses to my investigation?'

The look on her face told him that she couldn't care less, and even if she could, she wouldn't.

'If you must know,' Helen started, 'we've received intelligence from various reliable informants that one of these gangs has, in the past, had several connections to the group formerly known as The Crimsons. We believe that they were working together and that one of the gangs may be responsible for the raid on the jewellers in Stratford the other day.'

'Do you have any idea which one? I'd like to find and arrest the people who murdered Jermaine Gordon pretty quick, but I can't do that with you blocking my investigation.'

'Bit rich, don't you think?'

Darryl flinched in surprise. Their conversation had taken a sudden change of direction. She was going on the offensive. Darryl prepared himself.

'I don't follow,' he told her.

'My guys have had to go into hiding. They've had to lie low for a while because *you've* put their lives in jeopardy.'

'I fail to see how.'

'Well, your failure to see how might result in their deaths. Ever since you started Operation Deadwood, several officers from your team have been seen conducting surveillance on the Cosgrove Estate. That in turn puts my UCOs under a very real threat, the outcome of which could be fatal. This is why I asked to meet with you, Darryl. I need you and your team to stay the fuck away from the estate and my investigation.'

For a moment, Darryl sat there and blinked. It was the only thing he could think to do.

Helen had been throwing him off the scent at every turn, and now she was keeping him from digging deeper into Henry Matheson and the rest of the E11, delaying Operation Deadwood at every opportunity. She had the upper hand, and she was using it to full advantage.

Inevitably then, the game was drawing to a close, with Helen's team looking like they might score a last-minute winner, but Darryl still liked to think he had an ace up his sleeve.

'We've got a murder enquiry that we need to investigate,' he said.

'That's not my issue. The safety of my officers is my priority and my concern. You must have other lines of enquiry that you can be pursuing, surely? Other pieces of evidence you can investigate.'

'I wasn't referring to Jermaine Gordon, Helen.'

'What murder investigation then?'

Striker, please step up to the spot.

'The one that took place at the same time as the jewellery heist. The poor employee who was fatally shot in the chest and died on the shop floor.'

Silence as the ball travelled through the air. Helen sat

there, fingers still knitted, her expression giving nothing away. Yet Darryl knew the cogs in her brain were working on an answer. A way out. That silence was all he needed to confirm his suspicions. Jake was right, a murder *had* taken place at the heist. And now Flying Squad were covering it up.

'How did you know about that?' Helen asked.

'Is that important?'

'We haven't revealed that information to the public just yet. We were keeping that out of the press until absolutely necessary,' Helen said.

Bullshit.

Just as Darryl opened his mouth to counter, she raised a hand to stifle him.

'The death that took place has no effect on anything,' she continued. 'It is still our investigation. The murder is linked, yes, but I can't allow you to have any involvement with it. If you want to argue the toss on that then I'm more than happy to take it to the assistant commissioner, but with the way your department's been run in recent months, I can't imagine he's going to take a keen look at it. We've got some fantastic people in my team, who have had plenty of experience in dealing with major crimes, so there's nothing for you to worry about. But what I will say is this: *you* will have to worry about *me* if you do not listen to what I'm telling you.'

Her voice dropped a few pitches. 'I don't want anyone from your team anywhere near my undercover officer. I don't want anyone near Henry Matheson and the Cosgrove Estate, and that especially applies to your man DC Jake Tanner that I keep hearing about. His actions and your actions could jeopardise everything and I am not willing to let that happen. Am I understood?'

Darryl kept quiet for a moment longer. Myriad thoughts raced around his head. He'd failed. He'd failed to regain control of his operation. And he'd even failed to keep Jake's name out of the conversation, something which, he now realised, was becoming increasingly difficult.

Without even batting an eyelid, Helen had managed to save the spot kick, run up to the other end of the pitch and score, concluding the game in the final few minutes.

'Yes,' he said quietly, making no effort to hide the malevolence and reluctance in his voice. 'You've made yourself abundantly clear.'

Darryl showed himself out of her office, out of the building and back to the car.

Full time result: Helen two, Darryl one.

CHAPTER 54

DISPOSAL

Jake burst through the front door and immediately headed towards the kitchen, where he found Elizabeth feeding Ellie in her high chair. His sudden appearance and the loud bang from the front door slamming against the wall startled her.

'I came as soon as I could,' Jake said, hurrying towards her and embracing her. 'Are you all right? The kids?'

'Yes, yes, we're all fine. What's going on, Jake?'

Jake took a step back and glanced around the kitchen and out the back window into the garden, his eyes wild with alertness and adrenaline.

Turning his back on the kitchen, he paced about the house, hurrying to the bay windows in the living room, drawing the curtains, overturning pillows, checking the drawers in the bedroom, inside the toilet cistern. His mind was awash with worry and fear. Images of someone breaking into his house and touching his things, moving them, planting drugs and money and warning signs in the most innocuous of places flashed into his mind on repeat like a scene from a thriller movie. If he were a criminal, and he were trying to plant drugs in someone's house, where would he—

'Jake!' Elizabeth screamed behind him. She was standing in the doorway to their bedroom with her arms folded across her chest. Her mood had now changed from panic and fear to anger and frustration. 'Tell me what the hell is going on.'

'I'm sorry, Liz. I'm sorry. Come on, let's go downstairs. I'll explain everything.'

In their absence, Ellie had thrown her bowl of food onto the floor. Jake bent down to pick it up.

'No,' Elizabeth told him. 'That can wait. Explain. *Now*.'

Jake sighed, swivelled on his hips and leant against the island in the middle of the kitchen.

'I don't want you to worry, OK. But… I didn't tell you *everything* last night.'

This didn't seem to come as a revelation to her, as if she'd already been expecting it. Even he would have been dubious at how little he'd told her; that it was only a lower-level thug with a vendetta coming after him.

'It's the case we're working. Some serious and dangerous people are involved. We're talking organised crime groups. Gangs.'

'Do they have guns?'

Jake didn't respond.

'Are we in danger?'

Jake shook his head. 'Of course not. I would never let anything happen to any of you. I just need you to tell me everything that you saw. Let me deal with it.'

Ellie started crying. Jake reacted first, bending down to pick her up out of the high chair. But as soon as he had her in his hands, Elizabeth swooped in and snatched her from him.

Jake looked at her in disbelief and opened his mouth to protest but couldn't bring himself to say anything. In that moment, she'd just crushed his heart. She didn't trust him to hold his own daughter, to protect her. She didn't trust him to be near her. She didn't trust him to protect her. Why did she look so afraid of him, as though *he* were the threat?

'Elizabeth…'

'A Range Rover. I saw a Range Rover.'

'And?'

'A man stepped out. He came towards us.'

'Did you get a good look at him?'

She shook her head, bouncing Ellie on her hip.

'Can you remember what he was wearing?'

Another shake.

'Any identifiable features?'

And another.

'Anything?'

'No.' A lump caught in her throat.

'What about the car, did you get a look at the registration?'

'No. I'm sorry.'

Jake sighed and ran his fingers through his hair. 'What have I told you? Pay attention to the details. Be observant. All of these things are designed to protect you.'

'I know, Jake. I'm not fucking stupid. I panicked.'

'It's fine.'

It wasn't fine. First, she'd taken their daughter from him, both literally and figuratively, and now she'd failed to remember the few pieces of training he'd given her to secure the house if anything bad happened. That was a lazy Sunday afternoon well spent.

'I need to go,' Jake declared.

'No,' she said. 'Please… what about us?'

Jake told her to visit his mum's, and she agreed. It was for the best. While Elizabeth frantically gathered her and the kids' things together, he made a call to his mum, confirmed they could visit, then went to help pack.

'It'll just be for a couple of hours,' he told Elizabeth. 'As soon as I've finished work you can come back. All right?'

She nodded, eyes wild, almost as if she were under the influence of a mind-altering drug.

He placed his hands on her shoulders. 'You're going to be fine. Both you and the girls, all right?'

'But what about you?'

'I'll be safe. I'm with a dozen other officers all day, locked inside a building most of the time. Nothing bad's going to happen to me.'

'Promise?'

'I promise,' he lied.

'And don't go looking for danger like you did outside the jewellers the other day.'

To that, he had no response. The events of the past few days had taught him nothing. He was still making mistakes, lying, acting selfishly. He'd failed to come clean about the severity of the situation, something he was now regretting. But his justification was that he was only trying to protect them. The less she knew, the less she'd worry. But now he realised that he couldn't keep the two apart. Henry Matheson and The Cabal were getting closer and closer, and Elizabeth and the girls were now intrinsically linked to it all.

It took them another ten minutes to pack everything for his family's short stay at his mum's, and after he'd waved them off, Jake returned to the house and began checking everything again. Every nook and cranny. Every place that somebody may have hidden something. Of course, he didn't know for certain that someone had been inside the house while everyone was out, but he didn't want to leave that to chance. Audio equipment, visual equipment, drugs, money; he searched for it all. After an hour, he'd found nothing.

When he returned to his car, he surveyed each and every stationary vehicle up and down the street, including those on his neighbours' driveways. He recognised all of them. Nothing was out of place. Nothing was untoward.

The drive back to Bow Green was filled with despair and paranoia. What if something happened to Elizabeth or one of the girls, or all of them? He remembered how he'd felt after he'd learnt that Liam had photographed his family in the park and approached them in his home. He'd felt ashamed, afraid, a failure, and pure anger towards Liam. Anger so strong he'd wanted to rip the man's head off and make him suffer the same fate as those he'd killed.

Jake pulled into Bow Green car park, scanned his ID at the barrier, found his usual parking space, and reversed in. Then he sat there for a while, still. Thinking, calculating, preparing himself. Activity at the station was sparse. Very little movement in and around the area. But that didn't stop him from feeling like he was being watched. Like a dozen eyes were monitoring his every movement.

Jake closed his eyes and rested his head against the headrest. Thought. Conjured images of inside the house. Where had he forgotten to check? What had he overlooked?

And then the smell hit him.

Strawberry.

The answer had been in the car all along.

He opened his eyes and slowly tilted his head towards the glove compartment. It was only poetic that he find something in there, coming full circle from the first time he'd found a package.

He reached across, hooked his hand underneath the handle and released the catch. The compartment door fell open and a cold tendril wrapped its arms around Jake and strangled him.

The contents of the glove compartment had been emptied and replaced with a bottle of Pepsi, a kilogram of cocaine hermetically sealed in plastic, and a brown paper bag containing stacks of notes sticking out the end of it.

Someone had been at his home at the same time that he

was there. And he'd missed them.

Someone had set him up again.

But this time felt different. This time it felt like there was more to come. Intuition, instinct, the sensation in the bottom of his gut was telling him so.

For the first time in a long time, he remembered Liam's advice and resolved to follow it. The only problem that remained now was where to dispose of it.

CHAPTER 55

BUSTED

Flustered and out of breath, Jake slipped into the incident room and returned to his desk. As usual, Brendan had his earbuds in and was nodding along to a silent beat. Meanwhile, Ashley was on the phone, head bent to the side, scribbling away on a piece of paper. Stephanie was sitting at her desk, head down, in the middle of completing a form. None of them paid him any attention. Miraculously. For once they were all getting on with their work, and it didn't feel like they were keeping tabs on every step he made.

And then paranoia knocked on the door. What if they were all pretending to get on with their work when in reality they were trying to corrupt him? What if they could smell the drugs and the money on his hands, on his person? What if one of them had been responsible for placing the packages in his car?

Absurd. Of course not. It was impossible; he lived so far away that they would have only just beaten him back to the station. It was the work of one man and one man alone.

Jake shook his computer mouse and woke the operating

system from its restful daze.

'All right, mate,' Brendan said, distracting him from his screen. 'Back at long last. Where you been?'

Jake ignored Brendan and cast his eye across the room.

'Where's Darryl?' he asked.

'On his way back from a meeting.'

'With who?'

Brendan shrugged. 'Need to know. Need to know.'

Before Jake could give much thought to what that meant, the double doors to the incident room opened and Darryl stepped in. He looked solemn and beaten, as though he'd recently discovered the death of a loved one but had still been forced to work his shift.

'Can I get you to stop what you're doing please,' he said – a statement more than a question. 'I've just had a meeting with DCI Clements over at Flying Squad. The short of it is that, as of now, we are to go nowhere near the Cosgrove Estate. In any capacity. That includes our existing surveillance warrants.'

Jake's mouth fell open; he was lost for words. First the package, now this.

Somehow The Cabal and Henry Matheson were tightening the rope around the investigation, cutting off its oxygen supply. Soon enough, there'd be none left and it would be dead in the water.

'Any interference with the estate, and those around it, would be detrimental to their operation and could potentially prove fatal. DCI Clements was insistent on that point. I know it's not what you wanted to hear, but I'm sure you can all appreciate the complexities surrounding this investigation.'

Nobody said anything, each of them taking their time to process the news. After a brief pause, Jake raised his hand.

'Can I have a word, guv?'

Darryl looked around the rest of the office as if waiting for any objections. When none came, he said, 'My office?'

'Perfect.'

Jake climbed out of his seat, followed Darryl into his office and closed the door behind him.

'What's on your mind, Jake?' Darryl asked as he strolled to his desk.

Jake steadied his breath, controlled himself. He had to be careful about how he went about this. Stepping on eggshells wasn't his forte. Neither was toeing the line, as it turned out.

'Lots,' he began.

'Never good. What's the issue?'

Where do I begin?

'For starters, guv, Jermaine Gordon's forensic report.'

'What about it?'

Jake paused before responding. Cleared the thoughts from his mind. Pushed Elizabeth and the package and the girls away. Focused on work. 'How do I put it? There was… there was an omission.'

'Go on…'

'At the crime scene, I saw a belt buckle on the ground. I asked one of the SOCOs to collect it for examination. I watched them pick it up and add it to the catalogue. But on the forensic report, there was no mention of it.'

'You think one of Poojah's team omitted it? I don't think they'd do such a thing, especially something as blatant as that.'

'I don't think they did it either,' Jake continued. 'But I think someone knew about the evidence, and someone either erased that part of the report or disposed of the evidence before it ever got examined.'

'Is this just conjecture or have you got solid evidence?' Darryl asked.

Jake smirked. 'I'm glad you asked. It gives me an opportunity to prove myself right, that I'm not just being paranoid.'

'Go on…'

'The buckle's no longer in evidence. It's gone missing.'

The colour in Darryl's cheeks faded slightly. He leant forward and placed his elbows on his desk. 'You're aware that you need to substantiate all of this?'

'Naturally. Wouldn't be doing my job if I didn't understand that was a prerequisite.'

'Then I suggest you go away and investigate it, but I don't want it taking up too much of your time. Raise it with Stephanie as well and she can oversee it. Given her history, she might be able to help, offer a few bits of advice.'

'Thank you, guv.'

The conversation had come to a natural end, yet Jake remained where he was, convincing himself to bring Darryl up to speed about the packages, about the way his family were being haunted by his actions. But in the end, he decided to keep Darryl out of it. He could sort it on his own. He didn't need any help. Not yet.

As Jake made his way out of the office, Darryl called him back. 'Just a minute there, Jake. Close the door to.'

Jake did as he was told.

'Before you go, who?'

'Excuse me, guv?'

'I'm sure your little grey cells are working away in the background and you're beginning to come up with a list of suspects. I want to know who's top of that list.'

Jake licked his lips. The seed of doubt had well and truly been planted into Darryl's mind. 'I'm sorry, sir. I couldn't possibly assume, not without obtaining the necessary evidence.'

Jake shut the door behind him and hurried back to his desk. As he manoeuvred his way across the office, weaving his way around the desks, the television on the wall caught his eye. Breaking news on the BBC.

BODIES FOUND IN THAMES

Jake shuffled closer and turned the volume up.

'This morning, the bodies of two young females were found on the bank of the Thames Estuary near Kent. And only moments ago, the bodies were identified and their images released to the public. The police are urging anyone with any information to come forward.'

The screen split in two, and two images appeared. On the left was a girl Jake didn't recognise. Young, youthful, vibrant, looking up at the camera with her whole life ahead of her. As for the image on the right, Jake recognised it instantly.

'Danielle Matheson,' he whispered. He recognised the photo from his investigations into Danielle's social media accounts as part of the wider investigation into her brother. 'I don't believe it.'

'What's that, Jake?' Stephanie asked, spinning round on her chair.

'This.' He pointed at the television.

'Yeah, it's been on the news all day,' Stephanie replied.

'Terrible,' Ashley added. 'It's Kent Police's problem now though.'

'I wasn't worried about that,' Jake said, this time pointing at the image of Danielle on the screen.

'Is that who I think it is?' Stephanie asked.

'Yep.'

Stephanie propelled herself out of the chair and rushed towards him. 'You reckon he knows?'

'I can't imagine the family liaison officer had the balls to tell him.'

'Don't blame them,' Brendan called from the other side of the office, holding both earphones in his hands.

'Does this change anything for our investigation?' Ashley asked innocently. She was looking up at Jake for the answer, as if he knew everything.

He turned to Stephanie, who looked just as confused as he felt. 'Hopefully not,' he replied. 'If anything, it gives us greater reason to monitor his activities. His sister's death could turn out to be a freak accident, or it could be revenge for Jermaine. Gordon's gang have been quiet about the entire thing so far. I imagine when Henry finds out he'll be apoplectic, and he might just do something to incriminate himself. We need to be ready for when he does.'

'You just heard what the boss said, right? That we're to go nowhere near The Pit, under *any* circumstance.'

Jake shrugged. Danielle's death meant the dynamic of the investigation had changed. 'I don't remember hearing that.' Selective hearing was a wonderful thing. He turned his back on the television and started towards the exit.

'Where are you going?' Stephanie called after him.

Jake paused, his key card gripped tightly in his grasp. 'Out.'

He didn't make it very far. He was just getting out of the lift on the bottom floor of Bow Green when both Darryl and Stephanie caught up to him.

'Where do you think you're going?' Darryl asked. His face was flustered from the rapid three-storey descent, and he was out of breath.

'I was going out.'

'I need you to come with me.'

Darryl took a step back and gestured down the corridor to Jake's left. Cautiously, feeling like he was under arrest for something, he started down the corridor. A few seconds later,

Darryl instructed him to enter the first interview room and asked Stephanie to wait outside.

'Guv?' Jake asked as Darryl shut the door behind them. 'Everything all right?' Even though he knew it wasn't.

'I think you've got some explaining to do…' Darryl took a step closer to Jake. His brow was furrowed, and now Jake was beginning to realise he'd misconstrued the rosy cheeks for unfitness when it should have been anger.

'I don't follow you, guv. What's happened?'

'After you left my office, I checked my emails. What do you think I found in there, Jake?'

The photos. Of him and Henry Matheson, out in the open, in the middle of nowhere, getting along like a house on fire.

'I don't know, guv. Honestly, you've lost me.'

Sometimes playing dumb was the best way to go.

Darryl lost his patience, reached into his pocket and produced his phone. Already loaded on the screen was an image of Jake entering his car. The photo had been taken in the middle of the day, outside his house. Just over an hour and a half ago.

'Guv…' Jake began but didn't know what more to say.

'I need to look inside your car, Jake.'

'Darryl…'

'I need to look inside your car. Give me your keys.'

'What for? Why?'

But he already knew the answer. He just wanted to hear Darryl say it, confirm that someone, somewhere was trying to set him up and that the threats now contained an extra dimension. They were real, and they were dangerous, and everything he loved was at risk because if he didn't act quickly enough or dispose of the parcels in time, there would be terrible consequences.

'I'm sorry, Jake,' Darryl responded, sounding as though he actually meant it, 'but I have to. Someone seems to think you've got drugs in your car.'

CHAPTER 56

ALONE

Jake was noticeably quiet as he shuffled towards his car, accompanied by Darryl, PC Edwin Arrons, an officer Darryl had roped into coming with them as a witness, and specialist searcher Lauren Haines. At first, Jake had thought about kicking up a fuss, about shouting, about lamenting the fact they were doing the search in the first place, but then he realised that it would only increase the suspicion around him. Instead, he was going for the silent, smug, in-your-face reaction, while, inside, he was absolutely shitting it.

'I can't believe you're making me do this,' Jake said, deciding that he needed to say *something*.

Darryl ignored him.

They made it to the car. Jake reached inside his pocket and produced his keys. In his haste, and with the loss of grip from his sweat-soaked skin, he fumbled the car keys to the ground.

Fuck. Off to a good start.

As Jake bent down to retrieve them, Darryl stepped in.

'Let us do that, son,' he said. That was the first time Darryl had ever called him anything like that, and he didn't know how to take it. 'I think it's best if we have a look inside ourselves.'

Jake stepped aside and folded his arms across his chest so he wouldn't be tempted to do or touch anything.

Darryl and Edwin stayed by his side while Lauren donned a pair of rubber gloves, unlocked the door and started rooting through the vehicle. Despite knowing that the car was clean, that he'd disposed of the drugs and money in a skip a mile down the road, Jake's body shook with fear and a knot formed in his stomach, constricting tighter and tighter with every second.

And then he realised that in his panic after finding the drugs and package, he'd completely forgotten to check the boot.

Shit! How could he have been so stupid?

Fuckfuckfuckfuck.

Lauren climbed into the driver's seat, reached underneath, then moved about the vehicle, foraging through the passenger's side, the glove compartment, and even reaching into the back of the car. She found nothing.

Then she moved to the boot, standing over it as if preparing herself to find a dead body inside.

Jake tensed.

'I'm sorry we've had to do this, Jake,' Darryl said as if he knew now wasn't the right time to be talking to him. 'But if there's anything in here that shouldn't be, I need you to tell me now.'

Jake's eyes flitted to Darryl's. He opened his mouth but said nothing. Shook his head.

With that, Darryl gave the command and Lauren opened the boot. Jake held his breath. Waited. And waited.

A few seconds later, which felt like a lifetime, Lauren dropped the boot with an almighty slam and gave Darryl a quick shake of the head. Jake allowed himself to breathe a deep sigh of relief. It was over. Twenty minutes of excruciating pain in his stomach and chest. But they'd found nothing. And he was able to keep his job for the foreseeable future. Whoever'd put the stuff there had made a blunder, and so had he. But he didn't think they'd make the same mistake next time.

Darryl thanked Edwin and Lauren for their time and then sent them on their way.

'Like I said, Jake, I'm sorry I had to do that. But I can't take these things lightly. If it was anyone else, I would have done exactly the same thing.'

Of course you would. That was exactly the sort of thing that someone who wouldn't have done the same thing for someone else would say. Jake was dubious and hesitant to listen.

'Who told you it was there?' Jake asked, deciding he was going to go on the offensive.

'I can't disclose that.'

'Of course you can. They lied. They made a false allegation against my name. They're trying to discredit me. I'd like to make a complaint against them. I'm being set up. Someone's trying to frame me. It was The Cabal.'

Darryl exhaled derisively and shook his head. 'Jake, please. I thought we'd been through this.'

They had. But not recently.

'I'm telling you.'

'Jake…'

'Why won't you believe me?'

'It's just—' Darryl's phone started ringing. He held a finger in Jake's face and then answered the call. 'Sorry, I have to take this.'

And then, without warning, he handed the keys back to Jake and disappeared into the station, leaving the question unanswered. And in that moment, as Jake watched him go, he'd never felt more alone.

CHAPTER 57

TIME OF ENTRY

For the past few hours, Henry Matheson had been sitting in his mum's old flat on the top floor of the north tower. It was small and, in recent years, ever since her passing, had become derelict, unkempt and uncared for. It was a second headquarters, a second place to hide, if absolutely necessary. And that was what he needed right now. A place to get away from it all. From Jake Tanner. From the heist. From the feds knocking on Reece's door. From them knocking on the warehouse door. From the heat that was, for the first time in his life, getting too hot.

Since he'd first spoken to Rupert Haversham about his sister, he'd heard from the lawyer only twice. Once to confirm that a trace had been set up on Danielle's phone, the other to confirm that the last ping on a phone tower had been in Kent in the early hours of the morning before the signal was lost. After hearing the news, Henry had trawled his mind, wondering why on earth she'd been in Kent at that time of night and trying to figure out who she could have possibly been with.

He'd drawn blanks at every turn.

Rupert had given him strict instructions not to call her, saying that it would raise alarm and suspicion, and potentially delay the investigation into her disappearance. And, for the first time in a day of firsts, he'd heeded Haversham's advice. The video game flickering on the television screen now was a welcome form of distraction.

Die, you zombie scum. Die. Die. Die.

There was a knock on the door.

Deshawn and Jamal entered. They were bringing him soft drinks and snacks, like they were all about to have a slumber party in his mum's bedroom. Henry snatched the offerings from his friends and decanted them into bowls.

'How you doing?' Jamal asked, folding one leg over the other as he got himself comfortable on the sofa.

'Fine.'

'You ain't been watching the news have you, bro?'

'No,' Henry replied. 'You know I ain't do that shit.'

Just as Jamal was about to speak, on the other sofa, Deshawn pulled out a cigarette and sparked the end.

'No. No, no,' Henry said, setting the controller down on the coffee table. 'Out. Put it out.'

Lowering the cigarette from his mouth, Deshawn said, 'Come on, fam. You've let me do it before.'

'Yeah. That was before. Not today. This's my mum's place. Have some respect.'

Deshawn tilted his head in acknowledgement and tenderly placed the cigarette back in its box.

'What's the latest on the street?' Henry asked, trying to make himself comfortable. But the situation and the concerns in the back of his mind made it nearly impossible.

'Not a lot, bruv,' Jamal said. 'Youngers've been shotting all day, no problems there. That new kid you roped in from Gordon's gang – what's his name, Errol? – he's doing all right from what I hear. We've moved the jewellery and money back into the docks, but other than the beef with Reece and that Lewis kid, there ain't been no trouble.'

God worked in mysterious ways. Not usually devout, he'd relied on hard work and intuition to help him get to where he was. But on that day, Henry was certain God, or even Lady Luck, had been on his side, looking out for him. Moments before the police had turned up at the scrapyard with their search warrant, he'd decided to move the money and jewels from the heist to Shree News, where it would be under closer watch and less vulnerable to attack or seizure. Without that decision, he and the other seven gang members would have been looking at jail time. But since their earlier arrival, searching for Lewis, Henry had decided to move them back again.

'What about the cops?' he asked. 'They been hanging around the estate anymore?'

'Nah. They cleared out long way back. Ain't seen Mr Bean in that Mini Cooper neither, so don't think we're being watched.'

'Good. Keep an eye out for me though, yeah?'

'Calm,' Jamal said. 'Paid a visit to our Little Piglet's house as well. Left his surprise parcel like you asked.'

Henry dipped his head. Jake Tanner, or Mr Bean, or Little Piglet, as they liked to call him, was the thorn in his side that was, as time went by, probing deeper and deeper and deeper. If he didn't sort it out soon, the thorn would eventually travel through his bloodstream and pierce his heart.

And ruin his entire empire.

'Anything else?' Henry asked for the final time.

Another bout of silence fell over them. This time Deshawn swayed from side to side on the balls of his feet and dropped his gaze to the floor. He couldn't bring himself to look at Henry.

'You… you ain't been watching the news, have you?'

'No. Don't want to.' Henry hesitated. 'Why? What's the—'

He was interrupted by the doorbell.

Someone was at the door.

Jake killed the engine, shut off the lights. The early stages of darkness had fallen on the city and his face was illuminated by the hundreds of individual lights coming from the windows in the two tower blocks in front of him, each light offering a window into the owners' lives, their habits, their routines. He'd spent the past half hour getting to the estate. Throwing off suspicion and still furious with the invasion of privacy and the allegation made against him, he'd idled in and out of the streets, pretending to stop outside off-licences for some snacks, allowing himself to calm down a little. Now he had a selection of his favourites beside him. Pepsi Max. Kinder Bueno – two packs. Walkers Cheese & Onion crisps. And a twin pack of Twix.

He was set for the night ahead.

All he needed to do now was wait. Jake didn't care about the instructions Darryl had given him. Aborting the surveillance around the Cosgrove Estate was the worst possible decision they could make. It would play perfectly into his enemies' plans and allow them to cover up the murders of both Jermaine Gordon and Emily Harris, the Royal Hallmark employee. After the raid, Jake had made a point to track down one of the other employees, find out the woman's name and send her family a bouquet of flowers. No one else was willing to remember her in death, but he was.

Within minutes of his arrival, a car drove past him and parked farther along the road. A few seconds later, a figure emerged from it.

Jake lowered himself in his chair as he watched the man cross the road and disappear into the estate.

He made a note of the time of entry.

CHAPTER 58

KENT POLICE

Henry hadn't been expecting anybody else. But it wasn't uncommon for randoms and strangers to turn up unannounced at the door. There was something about him being in his mum's flat that meant they felt they could approach him and talk to him and ask him for money, like he was some form of charity. Perhaps it was because a lot of the people who made those unannounced visits were old and had known his mum well enough that they thought they could come to him. And when it wasn't them asking for money, it was some of the up-and-coming youngers asking to do business with him, to let them into the ranks of the E11. But a lot of the time they were too young, too dumb and too naïve. They didn't know anything about the business, and they were full of shit. He showed them the door pretty quickly.

'Open it,' Henry instructed Deshawn, who was nearest.

Des groaned, turned and then meandered towards the door. He kept his right hand by the back of his leg, lest he have to use the Glock tucked tightly beneath his waistband.

The door opened.

'Yeah?' Deshawn said, his voice flowing through the corridor. 'Who is it?'

'It's me,' came the distant, quiet response.

'What you saying? You good? Come in.'

A few seconds later, Deshawn returned to the living room, followed by Martin Radcliffe, the man he and the rest of the elders had grown suspicious of over the past few days.

The man was moonlighting as a bent cop, pretending to be undercover so that he could report back to his bosses behind their desks and inform them of Henry's latest movements, the majority of which were fabricated and false. When Martin wasn't lying to the pencil pushers, he was, with Henry's prior approval, handing over the names of the youngers who weren't pulling their weight. What happened to them, he didn't know. But they were either arrested and sentenced or sent to another part of the country.

It was a mutually beneficial agreement: Henry was able to lean on Martin whenever he needed to, and Martin was able to shift his share of the drugs himself and take a tidy cut of the profit at the end of it. Something to keep him onside, make sure he didn't start rolling over and telling the police the truth about Henry's movements. In a way Martin Radcliffe was running his own business; his bosses were the shareholders, while the youngers and runners that he helped put behind bars, as well as the false information he leaked on Henry, was the product.

There was no doubt in Henry's mind that Martin Radcliffe was weaselling his way into The Cabal's team, trying to earn himself some extra notoriety so that he sat above Helen in The Cabal's rankings. And Henry was acutely aware of Martin's involvement with the jewellery shop raid they'd carried out the other day. That was both good and bad. If Henry was able to keep him onside, continue buttering him up, then he could use Martin as leverage against Helen if the middle-aged woman decided to throw him under the literal and metaphorical bus. And, if the time ever came, he could sever all ties and dispose of the man with ease.

Tonight, Martin was dressed in his usual large trench coat, his hair slicked back off his face, revealing a mole just beneath his hairline that Henry had never noticed before.

'You good?' Henry asked, remaining seated.

Martin shrugged. 'Can't complain.'

'What can I do for you?'

Martin reached into his pocket, produced a package wrapped in a brown paper bag and placed it on the table.

Payday.

'Is it all there?' Henry asked.

'Of course. Weighed and counted by the machine itself.'

'God bless modern technology, eh,' Jamal noted, as he reached over and snatched the bag, unfolding the top and inspecting its contents. A six-inch-thick wad of money. Of varying denominations. Approximately fifteen thousand pounds sterling. From half a kilogram of cocaine. 'I'll sort out your cut tomorrow.'

'Light work, if you ask me,' Henry said, snatching the money from Jamal's hands and assessing it himself. Quickly bored, he set it aside and turned his attention back to Martin. 'Speaking of work, there anything we need to be aware of?'

Martin leant forward, elbows on knees.

'On the balance of probabilities, there's nothing you need to worry about. But…' He paused. 'The jewellery job; we've had to come clean about the murder.'

'What!'

'One of the witnesses reported it.'

'Can we get rid of them? Pay them off?'

Martin shook his head. 'Honestly, it's been a fuck-up from start to finish. But it's nothing you lot need to worry about.

341

There's no way we can pay them off.'

'Why not?'

'Because it's another cop. He was on leave when he saw the job take place. I should've recognised him, but I was shitting bricks so I didn't even notice. And, trust me, he's as far away from being bent as anybody I've ever known.'

'Who?'

'Tanner. Jake Tanner. In fact, I saw him outside when I came down just now. Sitting in that pissy little Mini Cooper like he's some sort of modern-day Michael Caine.'

Deshawn growled. 'That son of a bitch, man. He ain't going away.'

Martin waved his fingers in the air like an excitable child. 'There's good news as well.'

'You wanna tell us, or you gonna make us guess?' Henry asked. Meaning: tell us now or get out.

Martin shuffled to the edge of the sofa cushion. 'You lot haven't gotta worry about the fallout from that job no more. Good news is soon we're gonna be making a few arrests.'

'Who?'

'Gordon's boys. Nobody's heard a peep from them since Jermaine's death. Bet you guys were planning for some all-out turf war after you topped him, weren't you? I'm sure we can make it look like they were planning the heist in that time.'

'Feasible.'

'And what about Jermaine? What's the latest with that?' Jamal asked, coming to the fore. Ever since that night, Jamal and Deshawn had been paranoid, constantly worrying about how safe they were, how much Rykard's surrender had helped them. Henry's attempts at calming them down had been ineffective. Hopefully, Martin could tell them something that would shut them up.

Martin pursed his lips. 'Hands are tied on that one, I'm

afraid. It's not our investigation. But they've not got any evidence pointing to any of you. I've made sure of it. It's all under control.'

'We're relying on you to keep it that way,' Henry said. 'You know what can happen if things go wrong, regardless of whether we're in prison or not. You fuck this up for us, we'll fuck this up for you.'

'I appreciate that as my warning,' Martin said, trailing off. He twiddled his fingers around one another. It looked as though he wanted to say something but was too afraid. 'There's… there's also something else you should know,' Martin began.

'What?' Henry's eyes remained fixed on Martin's.

'Your sister. There's been… there's been an update. Have you, um, uh… have you been watching the news?'

'Why does everyone keep fucking asking me that?'

'Right…' Martin looked at the two men either side of him. 'Well, I hate to be the bearer of bad news, but what I'm about to tell you, you could have learnt a little earlier. And you would have saved me the ball-ache of needing to have this conversation with you.'

'Just get on with it.'

'It's about your sister, Hen. Kent Police found her body washed up in the River Thames this morning.'

CHAPTER 59

ON THE LADDER

Henry was in shock. That much was clear. Martin had only known him for just over half a year, and this was the first time he'd seen the drug kingpin speechless. In a way, it unnerved him. Here was this guy who was supposed to be ruthless, tenacious, untouchable, deprived of any sense of humility or emotion, the Michael Corleone of East London, and yet now he was trapped inside his own body, pinned down by grief.

'You…' Henry started but trailed off. 'Wh—'

'It's a lot to take in,' Martin said. He was cautious not to slip into work mode and offer his usual script to the loved ones of dead relatives. They were no longer strangers, and were now, in fact, friends, compadres, amigos, comrades, and that demanded a different type of respect. 'Tomorrow, you'll have another officer come to find you and tell you the same thing. A family liaison officer. I think they've already tried your home address. But I assume you've been here all day?'

Henry nodded gently, his expression blank.

'OK. Well…' He paused. 'I'm sorry, mate. Truly, I am.'

'What do you know? Tell me everything.' Henry's voice was soft, almost a delicate whisper, as if he were talking to a sleeping child, trying to rouse them from slumber.

Martin bit his lip and tentatively responded, 'She was found down by Margate. With her friend, Annabelle. Someone on a boat saw them floating along the shore.' He coughed and cleared his throat, fighting down his own grief. 'Danielle's body has been taken to the pathologist and they're inspecting her now. From what I'm hearing through the rotten grapevine, it doesn't look like she'd suffered any form of wounds or received a beating, so I'm ruling out a stabbing or a bludgeoning for you. In my professional opinion, from what I've been able to gather, this looks like it could have been drug or drink related. An overdose, perhaps.'

'Drug overdose?' Henry asked, his voice noticeably louder and clearer this time.

'She could have been spiked for all we know.'

'What was found in her system?'

'Early reports indicate lots of different things. Coke. Mandy. Ket. Speed. Lidocaine. Whatever it was she took, she couldn't have suffered long. All those drugs in her system would have killed her almost instantly.'

'Is that supposed to make me feel better?' Henry pulled at the gold chain around his neck, clenching it into his fist.

'I'm just saying. She wouldn't have suffered.'

Henry lowered his head and stared into the coffee table. 'That cunt. That fucking useless…' Henry caught himself before he let out a tirade of abuse directed at an inanimate object on the coffee table. 'I bet it was him. Graham. Frank fucking Graham. That's his product coming onto the market. He's mixing everything into one.'

Henry looked up and caught Martin's quizzical look. 'Yesterday, Deshawn found some on a junky and took it from him. We've been testing it ever since. That snake.'

Henry's voice returned to a state of calm; it unsettled Martin how quickly he could switch between pathological killer and calm business owner. 'I bet that prick thought he could use my sister to get to me. Big mistake.'

'What you want us to do, bro?' Deshawn asked, already pulling the Glock out from behind his back.

'We're gonna find him, and then we're gonna fucking kill him.'

'J-style?'

'Yep. Bring some of the cavalry as well. I want them to see this.'

Henry lifted himself out of his seat and charged towards the door. Martin reacted first and stepped in front of him, cutting him off, holding his hands against Henry's chest to keep him at bay. The expression on Henry's face told him that it was a stupid thing to do, but he continued regardless.

'Wait,' he told Henry. 'You're going to need help.'

'Nah, this one's all on me.'

'You've got a copper out there, with a back straighter than a steel rod, already watching this place. Already waiting. The minute he sees you going somewhere in a hurry, you don't think he's going to call in the rest of his posse and start hunting you down before you get to Frank? He will. I don't blame you for being angry. But you need to think clearly.'

He lowered his hands from Henry's chest. 'So here's how it's going to play out. I'll get rid of the copper, then you guys get in your car and go round the back. I'll use one of the youngers to act as a diversion if I need to.'

'It's on you. Deal with Tanner yourself. If he sees us leaving, it's your problem.'

'Can't you wait until I've done it?'

'No. I don't want Frank running away.'

Martin sighed. There was no point fighting it. Henry would get his own way, and everyone in the room knew that.

But he was about to relish another opportunity to prove himself and earn his status with Henry and the rest of them.

And prove himself to The Cabal.

To get one step higher than Helen Clements on the ladder.

He cleared his throat. 'Leave it with me.'

CHAPTER 60

EVENTUALLY

In the hours he'd been surveilling the Cosgrove Estate, Jake had abstained from delving into any of the snacks calling out to him. But now, as the grumbling in his stomach reached fever pitch, he accepted defeat. First on the menu: Walkers Cheese & Onion crisps. Unrivalled.

He reached for the bag, opened it and shoved a handful of crisps in his mouth. The tanginess hit his lips, instantly satiating his hunger. Then he opened the bottle of Pepsi Max and drank fervently to quench his salt-induced thirst.

As he set the bottle on the seat beside him, a figure emerged from within the estate.

Flustered at the sight of his target, Jake dropped the crisp packet into the gap between his knees and grabbed his notebook. He made a note of the time the figure exited the estate, this time making an effort to add any extra details that could be of use. What he was wearing. What he was holding. His countenance. His walk. His stature. Was he afraid? Proud? Defeated?

Jake lifted his head from the pocketbook and his heart

leapt, his body frozen. In the time that he'd had his head down and focused on the page, the figure had deviated from his original path out of the estate and was now standing in the middle of the road, arms by his side, staring directly at Jake. Perfectly still, save for the wisps of hair flicking over his face in the light breeze.

Like he was some sort of murderous villain on a killing rampage.

Like he was in the middle of a Halloween slasher thriller.

Thirty seconds passed.

A minute.

Eventually, the man idled up to Jake's window, the street light nearby illuminating the smile on his rugged, well-groomed face. The rest of his body was well built, suggesting he'd once been in the armed forces, or he was just a massive gym junky who lived and breathed iron. Jake didn't know who the man was, but there was something in his face that struck him as familiar, as if they'd met before. Reluctantly, Jake lowered the window a fraction.

'Evening,' the man said. He bent forward and rested his arms on the door frame. 'Fancy seeing you here. Hope I'm not spoiling your dinner.' He pointed at the half-eaten packet of crisps.

Jake followed the man's arm but stopped halfway. The sleeve of the man's coat had pulled further up his wrist, revealing a forearm as thick as the barbells that had been used to produce it – and a tattoo. Jake's eyes glanced over it, inspecting it from left to right.

A scorpion.

And then he realised where he recognised the man from.

'You?' he said, thinking aloud.

He and Martin Radcliffe had met twice before. The first time had been when Jake was working in Surrey, during The Crimsons' final heist on a jewellers in Guildford. They'd taken a hostage and travelled to Southampton where a cruise liner was readying itself to ship them out of the country, while a group of corrupt officers were doing everything in their power to help them get there. Martin Radcliffe had been one of the authorised firearms officers from Hampshire Police that fatally shot Luke Cipriano, the youngest Crimsons member, with lethal force.

The second time they'd met had been a few days ago, outside the jewellers. Martin had yanked him out of the store and shoved him as far away as possible. Martin was the one covering up the murder. Martin was the one working undercover for Henry Matheson and his gang.

Jake didn't want to know what sort of career progression he'd managed to wangle to move from Southampton to the Flying Squad, but he was sure that there was someone behind it, exercising their influence over every aspect of the journey.

The Cabal.

Martin pulled his arm away from Jake's view. 'Finally figured it out?'

'I never forget a face. Nor a name,' Jake replied. 'What are you doing here?'

'I could ask you the same thing,' Martin replied. 'I've got an undercover operation to run. Your presence jeopardises that.'

'I find that difficult to believe.'

'Well, it's the truth. And if I'm not mistaken, you shouldn't even be here, should you? Last I heard, your direct surveillance warrant was rescinded earlier this afternoon.'

Jake fell silent.

'No?' Martin insisted. 'If I'm mistaken, please let me know. No? Didn't think so. Go on then.' Martin slapped the inside of Jake's car door. 'Off you pop. Don't want your new guv'nor finding out about your reckless behaviour, do we? Don't want any performance regulations coming your way.

Again.'

Jake bit his tongue.

'We'll find the killer,' he said defiantly.

'Eventually,' Martin added.

'Both of them.'

Jake started the ignition and depressed the clutch. Slipping the car into first gear, he continued, 'And I wonder, when we find out who's responsible for Jermaine and the jewellery heist, where you'll fit into it all.' Jake turned to Martin. 'The centre?'

Without giving him any time to respond, Jake pulled away from the kerb and headed out of the estate. It was time to go home to his wife and kids and make sure they were safe.

CHAPTER 61

RUNNING

Lewis had no idea where he was. Nor where he was going.

His friend had messaged and asked to meet him, dragging him away from the spaghetti Bolognese he'd made for dinner. His dad was in the middle of another episode, and with the way they'd left things last time, Lewis was more than happy to get out of the house. After meeting with Reece in the underpass, they'd wandered through to the other side of the estate then hopped into Henry Matheson's Range Rover.

There were three of them in the back: Lewis, Henry, and Reece, and two in the front: Deshawn and Jamal. There was complete silence in the car, save for the sound of Henry's furious breathing through his nose.

'You ready, boys?' Henry asked after a long time of nothing.

'Course, fam,' Reece said. 'We got this.'

Lewis saw straight through Reece's false sense of bravado. When he'd seen Reece in the underpass, his friend had been shaking nervously, and when he'd asked if he was all right, Reece had blamed it on the cold. Except Reece was in a jumper, and the temperature was in the teens.

'You're both gonna learn a few things tonight. See a few things.'

'Calm,' Reece said. 'We got this.'

'What about you, Lewis?' Henry rotated his head towards him. 'Ain't heard much from you. You ain't scared, are you? You two about to become men. You need to be ready.'

Lewis swallowed hard. 'Yeah,' he replied. 'I'm fine. Just concentrating, innit.'

'Making sure you don't piss yourself?'

Lewis snorted. 'No. The only place I piss is in your mum's house.'

A resounding cheer sounded from the others in the car, followed by a cacophony of laughter. It had been an instinctive reaction and defence mechanism. Fortunately, it didn't garner the beating he was expecting.

'You're a funny little cunt, aren't you?' Henry said. He reached his arm up and over Lewis's head and placed it on his shoulder. 'I'll let that one slide. This time. But don't get smart, kid. Bigger men than you have tried, and people don't like it. Jermaine thought he was smarter than me and look at him. This place we're going, the man involved thinks he's smarter than me, and now something similar's gonna happen to him.'

Lewis said nothing for the rest of the journey. They drove for another fifteen minutes, heading north, leaving behind the sparkling skyline of Central London until they came to a stop in Walthamstow. Frank Graham's estate. To his left was a large tower block. Smaller but wider than the Cosgrove Estate. Kids on bicycles snaked their way up and down the road before eventually disappearing out of sight. Meanwhile, a group of teenagers were sitting on a brick wall in the distance, their black jackets and hoods turned orange by the street lamps.

Henry whistled, gesturing for everyone to alight from the car.

'How d'you wanna play this, Hen?' Jamal asked as they met by the bonnet. He had his hands in his pockets, and, for a moment, Lewis wondered what was in them. But then he realised he already knew the answer. Protection. The same went for Deshawn, Henry, probably even Reece. Which meant he was the only one without any. Which meant they all knew something he didn't.

'I want you to find him. Bring him out. And then hand him over to me.'

'What about us?' Reece asked, pointing at himself and Lewis.

'Speak to those youngers over there. See if they know anything. And if they kick off, deal with it.'

'Aight,' Reece said. He looked over at Lewis and added, 'Come then. What we waiting for?'

Lewis grunted in response and reluctantly followed Reece towards the group of kids sitting on the wall. He didn't feel comfortable being there. It was a betrayal of Frank's trust. But there was no time for him to back out now. He was in too deep. He had his loyalties to Henry. But also to Frank. And now he wondered which one he favoured more.

'What you saying?' Reece called over to the group as they bowled over.

'Who the fuck are you?' the tallest member of the group asked. He was dressed in a grey tracksuit and wore a pair of brand-new black Nike Air Force trainers. His face and any other identifiable features were concealed by the low light and the collar of his hoodie, which was pulled flush to his chin.

'Was wondering if you knew where Frank was, innit? Got a message for him.'

'Frank don't wanna deal with you. He don't even know

who you are,' Air Force said.

'Yeah,' Reece replied, 'but he knows who this is.'

Reece prodded Lewis in the shoulder. And in that moment, he felt vulnerable, out in the open. His best friend had just exposed him, and if he was willing to do that in front of a bunch of strangers, what else might he do?

'You his bodyguard or somethin'?' Air Force asked.

'You could say that,' Reece replied, rustling his hands through his pockets. 'Now where is he? We wanna talk business.'

Air Force wandered up to them, his frame growing drastically in size as he drew nearer. He was much larger than Lewis had realised, and with only one knife between them versus an arsenal of perhaps four, Lewis wasn't liking their chances.

'Fuck outta here,' Air Force hissed. 'I said Frank ain't wanna see you.'

Reece let out a breath and stepped back. 'Lewis, show him your pockets, bruv.'

Lewis hesitated a moment, realised what his friend was asking of him, then removed the small bag of Frank Graham's cocaine, making sure to show the skull on the front of it.

'Where'd you get that?' Air Force asked.

'He ain't tell you? I'm shotting food for him now. I'm one of you lot.'

'Bullshit. A scrawny little shit like you? You're mad, fam.'

'It's *his* food. Not *my* food. Not *your* food. His. Now tell him I'm here or tell me where I can find him.'

Air Force's eyes crawled over every part of Lewis's body, surveying him, sussing him out, until eventually he tutted, flicked his head in approval, and said, 'Fine. Flat twenty-four. But one of my youngers comes with you.'

Lewis nodded, saving his sigh of relief for later. 'Calm. Do what you gotta do, innit.'

They weren't safe yet.

Their escort was a girl, a fifteen-year-old who didn't look like she could hold her own. Her frame was slender and slight, her trousers baggy and loose around her thighs. And if it hadn't been for the hooped earrings and the hair, Lewis might have mistaken her for a boy.

They didn't get a name.

Nor did they wait for their escort to guide them. Instead, they set off towards the estate and allowed her to catch up. As they made their way around the place, he saw Des and Jamal following behind, keeping their distance like they were stalking their prey.

Finally, Lewis and Reece stopped outside Frank's flat. The girl knocked on the door and the three of them waited. Out of the corner of his eye, Lewis saw Jamal and Deshawn deftly emerge from behind a brick wall.

As soon as the door opened, the two elders charged down the corridor and jumped Frank, placing a bag over his head and punching him repeatedly in the solar plexus, winding him, incapacitating him. At once, the girl screamed. But her cries for help were soon stifled by Reece, who wrapped his arm around her neck and held a knife against her throat.

'Don't say a fucking word,' Reece hissed.

Meanwhile, Lewis watched on in horror. Everything had happened so quickly, so quietly, he couldn't believe it.

Before he could consider it any further, Jamal gave the command, and at once, he, Deshawn and Reece, with their hostages in tow, made their way down the stairs and into the centre of the estate, where they dropped the bodies onto the ground.

A sound behind Lewis distracted him; Henry, lugging a can of petrol in one hand and a length of thick chain in the other.

No! Lewis thought.

History repeating itself.

They were going to burn them alive.

The thought made him feel sick.

He needed to get out of there. Run. Run away. Save himself and let these other people die at the hands of Henry Matheson.

But he was stuck, firmly rooted to the spot with fear. His gaze followed Henry as the man came to a stop beside Frank, who was still being held at knifepoint. There, on his knees, bag still wrapped around his head, Lewis noticed how small the man really was, how skinny and insignificant he appeared in comparison to Henry and the others. How, in the few seconds he'd been lying there, he looked as though he'd already resigned himself to his fate; there was no fighting back, no bitchiness, no verbal retaliation.

Nothing.

As for the girl, she was currently pinned to the ground by Deshawn, who was savagely beating her round the face in an attempt to subdue her and stifle her screams, which echoed around the estate.

Lewis hadn't noticed it, but that left—

Reece. Where was he? Lewis cast a quick glance round, and then—

The first thing he noticed was the temperature of the blade. Freezing at first, but as it dug deeper into the fat around his neck, it began to sizzle and burn like a hot piece of metal in cold water. Then he felt his friend behind him, locking his arms into place. Then came Reece's excitable and heavy breathing on the back of his ear and hair.

'Reece! What are you—'

Reece kicked the back of his legs, causing him to buckle under his own weight. Lewis collapsed to his knees, his head falling naturally into his chest. Then Reece grabbed a tuft of his hair and yanked his head back, forcing him to watch the events unfolding in front of him. To watch the conveyor belt of execution until he was next.

In the short time Lewis had been incapacitated, the girl's and Frank's hands and feet had been bound together with cable ties.

And now that they were finished, it could only mean one thing.

He was next.

Checkout number three is now open.

'No! No! Please no!' he screamed, the blade perilously close to his throat. 'Please! No! Don't—'

Another yank of the head, cutting him off. He stared skyward into the blackness. Overhead, stars punctured the night sky, and he wondered how many punctures he would receive – twenty, thirty, forty? – or whether his death would be like the sun coming over the horizon, going up in flames.

The next thing Lewis heard was the sound of footsteps. Then Henry appeared in his vision, evil stretched across every inch of his face.

'You fucking snake,' he hissed aptly. The E11 leader grabbed his face and pinched his cheeks, squishing his lips together. 'You thought you could fuck me over by selling someone else's product on my estate?'

Lewis babbled, but his attempt to speak was silenced by a slap in the face. Henry gave him a shove and then strolled away. As he returned to Frank Graham's side, he whistled, raised his hand in the air, turned on the spot and called, 'Time for you to up your score on the Leader Board, Reecey boy.'

Lewis's body flushed cold, like he'd just been submerged in an ice bath and was being held under by an insurmountable force, the water suffocating him, the shock paralysing him. His eyes wide open, staring at the blankness in front of him, Lewis thought of his dad, of how he'd neglected him and treated him in the past few months, of how much stress and strain he'd put him under, how much of a wanker he'd been. And then he thought of Reece. Of how it had come to this. Best friends since they were kids, playing together, growing up on the streets together, navigating the politics and treachery of gangland lifestyle together. Only for it to end like this?

'Reece, please! You don't want to—'

Reece hugged Lewis more tightly and pressed the blade deeper into his skin. One false move and the blade would tear open his neck and spill the contents of his body onto the pavement. One false move and he'd die.

'You silly little prick,' Reece whispered in his ear. It was the first time Lewis had heard his friend say anything in a long time. Was that a catch in his throat?

'Reece, please!'

'Why'd you have to go and fucking do it, fam!'

Yes, it was a catch. Possibly a tear in his eye too, although he wouldn't show it.

'Reece, fam, come on! My dad! He needs—'

Reece adjusted his grip, loosening it slightly. It was only brief, but it was enough. An opportunity not to be missed.

Lewis thrust his backside into Reece's sternum and jabbed his friend in the ribs with his elbow, causing Reece to buckle over. The movement wasn't as fluid as he'd have liked, but it was a start. And it was just enough for him to turn to his friend, notice the shimmering guilt in Reece's eyes and recognise that it made absolutely no difference at all. There was still a desire to fight, to get revenge, to kill. And Lewis needed to do everything he could to make sure he was the one who came out on top.

Reece lifted the blade in the air and brought it swinging down. Lewis stepped to the side and grabbed it, severing the skin on his hand and fingers. Using all his body weight, and with a little help from the adrenaline coursing through him, he barged into Reece and shoved his friend to the ground. Gravity took hold of him, and he fell on top of Reece, his weight pinning his friend to the concrete. In the collision, the blade dropped and clattered away from them. Clenching his fist, Lewis punched Reece in the face. Once. Twice. Three times. Until his face became a bloody mess.

Reece, cowering on the ground, shielded himself, allowing Lewis a brief opportunity to decide what to do next: he jumped to his feet, grabbed the blade and turned to see the rest of the retribution. Henry and Jamal were hovering over Frank Graham, kicking him and beating him on the ground, while Deshawn was atop the girl, his fingers wrapped tightly around her throat.

Three against one. No chance.

The option was simple.

Turn his back on everything and run.

And so he did.

He turned his back on it all and sprinted out of the estate. As fast as his legs would carry him before they buckled under the pressure.

'Hey, you piece of shit!' came a scream from somewhere.

Distant.

Far away.

Close enough for them to catch up with him?

He didn't know.

But he kept on running anyway.

CHAPTER 62

BLAZE OF HISTORY

Lewis's arms and legs pumped ferociously as he turned the corner of an empty street. Then his foot caught some loose gravel underfoot and he slipped, slamming onto the pavement. He landed hard on his right shoulder, and his head smashed onto the concrete, his bloodied and lacerated hand tearing through the gravel and dirt. He yelped in pain and then quickly clambered to his feet, scurrying towards the nearest wall.

It was then, gasping and panting against the brick, that he felt the wetness, the warmth, spreading across his chest. He pulled his jumper and shirt down from his neck, revealing his collarbone. There, he saw a four-inch laceration across his breast, a wound he hadn't known he had.

Breathing heavily, panicking, feeling nothing at all thanks to the adrenaline masking the pain, Lewis looked around him.

He had no idea where he was.

A residential street somewhere. There were cars and houses all around him, and the sensation made him feel vulnerable. As though he were out in the open. Susceptible to attack. He preferred the looming towers of the estate; he knew them well and knew where the nearest and best possible escape routes were. It was his brick jungle, and he couldn't imagine a life where he lived somewhere that was as open as this desert around him.

As he stood there, chest heaving, he contemplated his next move. The options were twofold: run or hide. But then there was a third option, the one which his subconscious brought to the forefront of his mind.

The police. Jake Tanner. The man had been kind, offered him friendly advice. Even given him his card.

Jake Tanner needed his help.

And Lewis wanted to help him.

With Henry Matheson off the streets, the estate would be a much safer place. Mums and dads wouldn't have to worry about where their children were and what sort of things they were getting up to. They wouldn't have to worry every time the doorbell rang, afraid it was a police officer coming to inform them that their son had died. They wouldn't have to worry every time their child stepped out of the house.

Lewis inhaled deeply and held the breath before letting it go, allowing his body to calm, again and again until he felt normal once more. Once he was OK, he lifted himself to his feet and stalked back towards Frank Graham's estate, lurking in the shadows with his hand wrapped around the blade, lest anyone attack him.

As he neared the centre of the estate, the sound of voices and screams and shouts grew. He slowed to a halt, just on the outskirts of the high-rise. In the distance, forty yards away from his position, were Henry, Deshawn, Jamal, Reece, the girl and Frank Graham. Their voices echoed around the area.

'We can talk about this!' Frank screamed. 'What's this ab —'

Jamal delivered a blow to Frank's stomach, winding him and bending him double.

'You know what it's about,' Henry replied.

Frank collapsed to the ground on all fours, the bag still on his head, his limbs still tied together like he was a pig on a spit roast. Immediately after, Jamal and Deshawn kicked and punched him until he was cowering in a ball.

Lewis watched on, helpless. There was nothing he could do, not unless he wanted to end up exactly the same way.

But *there was* something he could do. He just didn't realise it yet.

The phone in his pocket.

It could be used as evidence.

To get Henry off the streets.

To make them a safer place.

Lewis carefully removed it, cautious not to smear blood over the lens, and started recording. The phone was now his eyes and ears, and he made sure to keep his breathing to a minimum in case it distracted the microphone from picking up Henry and Frank's conversation.

For the next twenty minutes, Lewis crouched against the wall, watching as a blaze of history burst into life and repeated itself in front of his very eyes.

CHAPTER 63

ORANGE AND RED

'Pick him up!' Henry screamed at Jamal and Deshawn, his voice breaking under the strain in his throat.

At once, the two elders crouched down, hooked their arms underneath Frank's armpits and hefted him to his feet. Without needing to be instructed, they carried him towards the nearest lamp post, wrapped the chain around his body and hoisted him a few feet in the air.

Henry smirked at the sight. *So this is what Jermaine looked like.* Weak, defenceless, completely at his mercy.

He strolled towards Frank and lifted the bag from his face. 'Scared?'

Frank said nothing. His left eye was badly bruised and blood swelled from his lips, streaming down his chin and neck.

'You look like you're in a bit of pain,' Henry continued. 'Did my boys hurt you?'

Frank spat a glob of blood onto the ground.

'I'm going to make you suffer,' Henry said, feeling oddly calm. 'I don't want it to be quick and easy like it was for

Danielle. No way.'

At the mention of Danielle's name, Frank's half-open eyes widened slightly.

'How did you…' His voice was weak. 'I didn't do… It wasn't…'

'Don't bullshit me. I know what you done. And the police know it's you as well. You're in the unfortunate position that I managed to get to you first. They would have been much kinder.'

'Please…'

'No!' Henry screamed in Frank's face, his finger hovering inches away from the man's nose. 'You don't get to beg. First you ignore me and continue to sell your poison on *my* streets. Then you start selling your food to *my* clients. And then you kill *my* fucking sister with it. You're not getting out of this one alive, fam. You're a fucking cretin… shit-stained piece of… shit!'

'I didn't mean… I didn't mean to,' Frank whispered, wincing in pain as each breath caused the chain to dig deeper into his ribs. 'It was an accident.'

'And what's about to happen to you will be considered an accident as well. Oops, sorry, Mr Police Officer. It looks like I accidentally hung Frank Graham from a lamp post, and accidentally doused his body in flammable liquid, and accidentally set his body alight with a lighter, and accidentally didn't lose any sleep over it.'

Frank spat another glob of blood on the ground, strands of it dangling from his lips. 'Please.'

Henry ignored him, took a step back and gave the order. Deshawn and Jamal jumped into action by pouring the liquid over Frank's limp, feeble body, and within seconds, it covered Frank from head to toe. The man wriggled and writhed, trying to shake off the fuel. But it was useless. There was nothing anybody could do to save him now.

'Why'd you do it?' Henry asked. 'What did my sister do wrong?'

Frank shook his head. 'Nothing.' His voice was drowned out by the liquid, and as he spoke, he inhaled some and choked on it.

'Why were you with her?'

'To… to…'

'Yes?'

'To… to get to *you*.'

That was it. He'd heard enough.

Henry reached into his back pocket, removed a lighter and sparked the flint.

At the sight of the flame, the girl under Reece's control screamed, her high-pitched cry piercing the air. Henry spun on the spot and told her that she would be next if she didn't shut up.

Then he turned to Frank.

Took a step closer.

Held the lighter under the soaked man's face.

Lowered it beneath his feet.

And watched Frank Graham's body be engulfed in a blaze of orange and red.

| PART 5 |

CHAPTER 64

THE CAMERA SHUTTER

His rapid breathing disturbed the still air, legs and arms pumping as fast as he could possibly move them, ignoring the pain in his chest and hand. He was heading back to The Pit, racing against an invisible countdown. For all he knew, Henry could be a minute away, a few seconds behind him, bearing down on him at fifty miles per hour with the headlights of his Range Rover illuminating his every move.

Twenty minutes after setting off, Lewis eventually arrived home, his legs faltering and turning to jelly, his body exhausted, its oxygen levels depleted. Nausea assaulted his senses. He bent double and rested the palms of his hands on his knees. Breathing heavily. A raspy, wheezy sound. Too many cigarettes and not enough exercise.

In. Out. In. Out.

Until he caught his breath.

Reaching into the back pocket of his jeans, he approached his front door. All the lights in the house were off, but experience told him that that didn't mean anything. On too many occasions, Lewis had come home in the early hours of the morning to find his dad sitting in the living room, waiting for him, the room illuminated a pale shade of blue by the television screen.

For the first time in his life, Lewis hoped tonight was one of those times.

He shoved the key into the lock, twisted, opened and stepped inside tentatively. He was cautious, and blatantly aware, that there could be someone in the house. One of the other elders. Tremaine. DripTop. Elijah. Silently waiting for his return, a gun tucked into their waistband, a knife in their back pocket. So they could either shoot him dead or abduct him and take him someplace else.

He'd betrayed them. Turned his back on them. There was no coming back from that. It was too late. Damage done. His life in the Cosgrove Estate had irreversibly come to an end.

And all over one stupid mistake. One stupid decision that had now left him running for his life.

He had a wrong to right.

Lewis closed the door behind him and froze in the hallway. Listened for any sign of life. But there was nothing, save for the sound of his father's heavy, rhythmic snoring.

Deciding it was safe to proceed, Lewis crept through the house until he reached his father's bedroom, his knuckles white around Reece's blade. His dad was lying atop the duvet, head facing the other wall, spread-eagled across the bed. Peaceful.

Before entering, Lewis surveyed the room quickly.

It was clean.

Loosening his grip on the blade, he entered and hurried towards his dad.

'Wake up!' he whispered, shaking his father awake. 'Dad, get up. It's important.'

Aiden groaned and slowly stirred, then turned on the bed to face Lewis.

'What the…' he said blearily. From the sound of it, he'd been having his first decent night's sleep in a long time. 'What time is it?'

Lewis didn't know. 'Three o'clock maybe. That don't matter right now. We need to get outta here. Quickly. We need to go.'

'Where?'

'Anywhere. A hotel. That place you were looking at. Houses up north. We can find somewhere.'

'We ain't going nowhere,' Aiden replied, propping himself onto his elbows slowly. As he did it, he winced in pain. 'See what you've done? My back. It was…' He grimaced and said through his teeth, 'It was fine while I was asleep.'

Lewis dropped the knife onto the carpet. The sound was buried beneath his dad's groans.

'Come on!' Lewis implored. 'We *have* to get out of here. It's not safe.'

'Why? What's happened?'

Lewis didn't respond.

'Leg, why isn't it safe? What've you done?'

'Nothing. I…' Lewis grabbed his dad's arm and started to yank the man out of bed. But it was no use. His body was too heavy and Lewis too weak. 'Dad, please. We have to go. I can call a cab. They can get us out of here.'

'Not until you tell me what's going on. Why are we running? *What* are we running from?'

'I can't tell you. Because then they might come for you too.'

His father's face dropped. Slowly, he said, 'Who might, Leg?'

Lewis stared at the floor unable to look his father in the eyes.

'Henry Matheson.'

Aiden sighed and shook his head. 'I don't… I don't

believe… this. You.' He paused. 'I told you to stay away from them. And you didn't listen, did you?'

Lewis shook his head.

'Right. Well, we ain't going nowhere. Not until you tell me what's going on.'

Lewis sighed indignantly. 'We don't have time for this. I'll tell you later. Please, Dad. You have to listen to me. I wouldn't say it unless I absolutely meant it.'

As he waited for his dad's reaction, he scratched the back of his hand, a nervous tic he'd developed on the first day of school as a way to battle his nerves, until he'd scratched too hard and the skin had started to bleed, forcing him to go to the nurse. Right now, the scratching alleviated some of the other pain in his body.

A minute passed of nothing, of staring at one another, each silently waiting for the other to break. But then something in Lewis's expression must have finally got through to his dad, a drop of the eye, a disconsolate twitch of the eyebrows because Aiden looked out of the window then lowered his expression.

'Go to your room,' he said finally. 'Grab your bags. Pack the essentials for both of us. I'll see if I can get us a cab.'

Lewis didn't need to be told twice. He spun on the spot and sprinted to his bedroom, threw open his wardrobe and yanked the suitcase resting at the bottom out onto the floor. The contents spilt out over the carpet. Clothes, shoes, his old primary school uniform, the outfits his mum had bought him when he was a child that his dad had never wanted to throw out.

All the history, all the memories.

For a while he stood there, paralysed by something, staring blankly at the suitcase. Thinking of her. Mum. The woman that had left them when he was four. Where was she? What was she doing? What would she think of him now?

How would *she* handle the situation?

Run away like she did before. Leave it all behind as soon as things got a bit difficult. And that's exactly what you're doing now. You're running. Running like a bitch.

Stay and fight. That was what a real younger would do. That was what any of the members of E11 would do.

But not him. He wanted to run, hide. Because he wanted to *live*. Nothing was worth dying over. He had his money, and he had enough for both of them.

Enough that they could make it work.

But…

The voice in his head was telling him to stay, defend himself, perhaps even explain himself. They'd let him off, wouldn't they?

Then he slapped himself round the head, banishing the thoughts from his mind. He was stressed; needed a cigarette. His heart was pumping, his breathing becoming increasingly irregular, and the bleeding from his slashed hand had worsened.

He looked down at the perfect circles of blood on the carpet; they looked like raindrops on the pavement. How much had he lost? A litre? Two? How much more could he lose before he passed out and collapsed?

The wave of nausea that rolled over him answered his question. He was hyperventilating. Panicking. Freaking out. Whatever you wanted to call it. He needed something to calm himself down. Mellow him out.

But he didn't have any cigarettes left.

And then he remembered he had just the remedy. A backup.

He dropped the suitcase, rounded the bed and reached underneath, pulling out a shoebox. Inside it was the drug money he'd secured over the past few months. Wrong one.

He reached in again and pulled out another shoebox. This

one contained the bag of cocaine that Frank had given him. Beside it: the small bag of marijuana, his free sample. Lewis grabbed the papers, rolled the weed into a joint and moved to the window. A rush of cold air blasted him in the face and he heard the sound of police sirens and dogs barking in the distance.

Lewis sat on the windowsill and sparked the end of the joint. The orange tip ignited and crawled closer to his face as he inhaled. The smoke descended to his lungs, and he stifled a cough. The hit was almost instant, and at once he felt better; calmer, smoother, more relaxed.

And then he remembered why it tasted so good. Something Frank had said after he'd given it to him. That there was a little extra ingredient in it.

An extra couple of ingredients.

Lewis took another toke and then it was too late. The chemicals took control of his body, sending him into a vortex of delirium. The world danced in and out of his vision, like the shutter of a camera when pressed repeatedly, until someone let go and everything switched to black.

Lewis's eyes rolled into the back of his head and his body slumped to the side, landing heavily on his bedroom floor.

The camera shutter was permanently closed.

CHAPTER 65

SECOND DATE

The car skidded round the corner, and Deshawn fought for control of the rear of Henry's beloved Range Rover.

'Fucking watch it!' he lambasted from the back seat. 'Thought I said drive normally, you tit.'

'Sorry, bro,' Des replied, planting both hands on the steering wheel in the ten-to-two position. It was unusual for him to be in the front seat, that accolade usually fell to Jamal, but they'd had little time to worry themselves about the seating arrangements after they'd been spotted by an elderly woman holding a phone to her ear while leaning against the barrier outside her flat. Desperate times called for desperate measures.

'It's all right,' Henry replied. He rubbed the flash burn on his hand caused by igniting the fuel on Frank Graham's body, trying to allay its sting. 'Like I said, innit. We're all good. Them kids ain't gonna be troubling us no more...' He turned to Reece beside him. 'Are they?'

Moments before the elderly woman had turned up, Reece had chased after a group of youngers who'd had the misfortune of interrupting them.

'Nah, fam,' the younger responded. His voice sounded deeper, as if the events of the past twenty minutes had aged him, turned him into a man. 'Ain't nobody gonna be saying nothing about what they saw. I got you.'

For the next five minutes, they continued driving closer and closer to The Pit, all four of them high on the adrenaline of what had just transpired in Frank Graham's estate. Henry had instructed them to drive around the north side of Stratford and then come back from the west side. It was a precaution they sometimes took whenever there was an issue that needed solving immediately.

'Where d'you want dropping off, Hen?' Des asked, glancing in the rear-view mirror.

Henry looked down at his phone. He scrolled through the address book, found the contact called Lily, and sent her a message. He received a response a few seconds later.

'I've got an address for you,' he said and proceeded to give him the details.

'You hoping for round two?' Jamal asked, twisting in his seat and flashing him a wink.

'If I need to get my alibi straight I am.'

After another ten minutes of driving around the city to throw anyone off their scent, Deshawn rolled the car to a stop down a quiet residential street, just a way off the road that ran through the heart of the town. At the other end of the street was an off-licence.

As Henry hopped out of the car, he caught himself and leant back in.

'Don't forget,' he began. 'Get your alibis straight. Reece, get yourself down to Essex, hide out in the estate, but keep a low profile. Des, lock yourself in The Den for a day or two. Kick Elijah and the rest of the boys out. And Jamal... what about your aunt? Can you see her?'

'No problem, bro,' Deshawn replied, giving Henry the thumbs up. 'What you want us to do 'bout Lewis?'

Henry considered a moment. 'Leave him until the morning. It's too hot for us to go anywhere near him right now. Don't do nothing until you hear from me. And I mean *nothing*.'

'Aight.' Jamal leant back in the chair to shake Henry's hand. Meanwhile, the others nodded their acknowledgement and waved him off.

As soon as the car was out of sight, he started towards the off-licence. Inside, he bought a chocolate bar and two bottles of wine. After paying the owner and leaving a generous tip for his services, something to add to the alibi if he ever needed it, he pocketed the chocolate and started towards the house.

Number ninety-two. The year Danielle had been born.

The house was lost amongst the row of other terraced buildings, and his eyes struggled to find the right number. Eventually, after wandering up and down the road, fighting the temptation to call Lily and ask her to help him, he found the front door.

A few moments later, the hallway light turned on and the door opened. The person in front of him was small, had her hair pulled off her face and was dressed in a jumper that hung loosely off one shoulder, revealing a bra strap and a cute lonely mole on her arm. He remembered it fondly from the other morning, stroking it as they'd lain in one another's arms. Slightly raised, soft, tender, a small blemish on otherwise perfect skin.

Right now, as she stood in front of him, he noticed she looked nothing like she had the other night with her face full of make-up and dressed in a pair of tight jeans and linen shirt – but he didn't mind. She was still attractive without any of that shit on her face. In fact, he decided, she looked better.

Wasn't that the true test of love?

'I was wondering how long it would take you to get here,' she said, crossing one leg over the other and tilting her head to the side shyly.

'You missing me that much already?'

'You wish.'

'You gonna let me in? The chocolate's melting against my arse and this wine is gonna go off if you're not too careful.'

The decision didn't take long.

She smirked. 'Suppose you can come in. But you better not be expecting none of that Netflix and chill stuff,' she said, stepping aside and letting him through.

Henry chuckled. 'You got Amazon Prime instead?'

As he brushed past, she scowled at him and elbowed him playfully in the ribs.

'Get your arse in the kitchen and shut up. What are you doing awake this early in the morning anyway?'

Henry stopped in the middle of the hallway. 'I don't think that's second date territory.'

'Oh really? Too dangerous, are you? An international man of mystery? If you tell me, you're going to have to kill me – that kind of thing?'

He shrugged. 'Ain't far from the truth.'

Lily laughed to herself. As she closed the door, she realised what he'd said and yelled, 'Wait! What do you mean, *second date*?'

'I thought the meaning was obvious. I told you I'd bring the chocolate and wine. And I'm always true to my word.'

Coy and pensive, she glanced down at her feet.

Henry held the wine in the air and said, 'Want me to put one in the fridge for now, or is there not much point?'

CHAPTER 66

PERFECT EXECUTION

The call shocked him awake at five a.m. It wasn't the first time he'd received a call that early; nor would it be the last. And somehow he already knew what it would be about as soon as he held the phone to his ear.

'We've got another hanging furnace,' Brendan said on the phone.

At first, in his semi-conscious stupor, Brendan's accent made it sound like a prank call and confused Jake, but then, after closing his eyes and applying himself, he realised who he was talking to.

'Another one?' Jake stepped out of the bedroom and closed the door behind him.

'Afraid so.'

'Where?'

'Dunsfield Estate.'

'Any idea who?'

'No definitive answer yet, but some witnesses are saying it's Frank Graham.'

Jake froze on the landing and pinched the bridge of his

nose.

'All right,' he said. 'I'll be there as soon as I can. Does Darryl know?'

'He's on his way there now.'

'OK. Fine. Send me the address.'

As Martin Radcliffe watched the shadows, he became painfully aware that, in the grand scheme of corrupt things, he wasn't at the top of the food chain. He wasn't where he needed to be. There was one person in front of him, a minor hurdle, a small obstacle for him to overcome and push to the bottom of the ladder.

Helen Clements: his boss. She'd been the one to put the pieces in the correct positions and help him transfer from Hampshire Police all the way through to Flying Squad. And she'd done a good job of it too, there was no denying that. In fact, she'd made it pretty seamless.

After the incident involving the fatal shooting of Luke Cipriano on that summer's day, he'd thought that his career was over, both in the police and in The Cabal's clandestine network, that it was time to pack up his desk and find another job stacking shelves somewhere. But she'd come through, followed her orders and done him a solid. It was just a shame that she resented him for it.

It wasn't his fault The Cabal saw something in him, a resilience, a determination, a merciless desire to become as corrupt as possible. He'd caught the bug, and now it had consumed him. And it was that bug that had made him realise, despite her help, that Helen offered him no loyalty, that she was willing to stick the knife in as soon as he wasn't looking.

He'd already begun hearing rumours that she'd been

passing on feedback about his mistakes, about the cock-up involving Jake Tanner at the armed robbery crime scene. That had been a fuck-up from start to finish, and he blamed himself for not having noticed Tanner earlier. It was a mistake, a momentary lapse that, if not dealt with soon, would prove costly. That was on him. There was no mistake about that. But now he was hoping he could make amends, prove that he was capable of dealing with issues, of proving himself once more, of putting wrongs to right.

The sky was pitch-dark, and it was that time of night where everything was still, everything was silent. No planes soaring through the sky. No heavy traffic on the streets. No youngers loitering on the estate. No lights on in the flats, no music bursting through windows, no house parties keeping neighbours up. Everything, for the time being at least, was perfectly silent, perfectly balanced.

Just the way he liked it. *Needed* it.

There were thirty-five shadows in front of him. Authorised firearms officers. Members of SO19, the Met's elite firearms squad. All waiting for his orders. All waiting to fly into Jermaine Gordon's estate and ransack the homes of those closest to him. And with the help of the territorial support group keeping any stragglers and onlookers at bay, he was hoping for a swift, easy and undisturbed arrest.

Ever since Jermaine's death, his number two and number three had gone into hiding, sheltering themselves from the might of Henry Matheson. Martin thought it was ridiculous but also a blessing in disguise. They called themselves a gang, one of the hardest and most revered in East London, but how was that possible if they didn't act like it? If they didn't retaliate and avenge their leader's death? It was an embarrassment. And for that they deserved the salt he was about to rub into their wounds.

Martin was leaning against the back of his car, police vest

on, radio in hand. He held the device to his lips.

'Everything ready?' he asked PS Shawcross, a man standing by the front of an armed response vehicle over a hundred yards away. His lower half was physically larger than his top half, yet he was still a powerful man, despite being the smallest out of all of them.

'Ready when you are,' Shawcross replied.

'Remember. Hit them all at once. Disorientate them.'

Shawcross slowly rotated and glanced at Martin. If he could see the man's expression, Martin knew it would be telling him to fuck off right now. 'You don't need to tell me how to do me job, mate,' he said. 'Save it for Helen.'

'One of these days, man. One of these days.'

As they finished, someone called from across the street, beckoning Shawcross over. The man hurried away, his black protective gear bouncing up and down on his body, the Glock 17 and the rest of the bells and whistles swinging from side to side on his hip. Shawcross stopped in front of the man, had a quick discussion, then hurried over to Martin.

'We're all clear,' he said.

'Then let's get to it. I wanna get home at a respectable time this evening. The sooner we do this, the more time I have for filling out paperwork.'

'Understood.' Shawcross nodded, pulled his goggles from the top of his helmet and over his eyes, and turned.

With that, the armed officers set off, hurrying away in single file along the street that led to the estate, crouching low, keeping their bodies pressed against the side of the road. And then, just like that, they turned left down an alleyway and disappeared out of sight.

A muffled, distorted sound echoed on the radio receiver in Martin's hand. He turned the volume up and held the microphone close to his ear. The sound of heavy breathing grew.

After a few seconds, several of the AFOs came into view, appearing through a thin gap between two houses. They'd split up into seven groups of five, spreading across the estate like a virus, and were now adopting their final positions.

'Foxtrot one in position.'

'Foxtrot five in position.'

'Foxtrot two…'

'Foxtrot four…'

A couple of minutes later, everyone was ready. And then there was a prolonged silence. For the majority of it, Martin wondered whether he'd lost signal. But then, moments later, Shawcross's voice returned.

He heard a whisper –'Three. Two. One.'– followed by a series of loud bangs splitting the silence in two. Screams and shouts of 'Armed police!' erupted through the microphone and around the estate, immediately succeeded by a ringtone of surprise.

Martin held the radio away from his ear and quietened the feedback.

He waited.

Waited.

Waited.

Then: 'Martin, do you receive? Over.'

'Receiving you.'

'Raid executed perfectly. Seven individuals, seven arrests. Bringing them back to you now. Time for you to complete that paperwork.'

CHAPTER 67

GENIUS COLLEGE

It was light by the time Jake arrived at the Dunsfield Estate, the sky an incongruously cheerful blue given the scene he was about to walk into.

Setting foot on this estate was a new experience for him. He ambled along the street, made a left turn through an alleyway, passed a knot of police officers who were standing around discussing the previous night's Champions League action, and approached the police constable whose unfortunate job it was to stand there on the outer cordon. Already wearing his forensic suit, Jake signed in on the log. Just as he was about to duck beneath the tape, a news van arrived. The camera crew and reporters immediately disembarked from the vehicle and set up their apparatus on the outskirts of the perimeter.

Great, Jake thought. The vultures are here.

'Morning,' Brendan called from Jake's left. He was standing beside Ashley, both of them looking like a pair of vampires who'd been caught in the sun.

'Morning.'

'Where did you go off to yesterday?' Ashley asked. She had her hands by her side and stood with her legs pressed together like a toy soldier standing to attention.

'The Pit.'

'Did you see our friend?'

'Which one? We know so many of them on first-name terms I'm beginning to lose track.'

Brendan entered the conversation. 'Matheson?'

'No-show. Elusive as ever.'

'Do you know if he's found out about his sister yet?'

Jake shook his head. 'Stephanie'll know. But I imagine he'll have found out by now. Could explain why he didn't show his face last night.'

'I wonder what his reaction's going to be.'

Jake turned to the centre of the estate, where the majority of the activity was taking place. Then he turned back to face his colleagues. 'I'm going to hazard a guess and say murder…'

'You reckon?' Ashley asked.

'I don't think you have to graduate from genius college to work it out.'

Brendan raised a hand in the air, placating Jake. 'Now, now, Tanner,' he said as diplomatically as possible. 'You're jumping the gun massively there. For starters, nobody knows who killed Danielle Matheson. Kent police haven't been able to solve that one just yet.'

'Again,' Jake began, this time tapping the side of his head, 'genius college.'

The entire estate had been shut down. Nosy residents were being shepherded back to their homes, protesting and spewing venomous words at the territorial support group officers who were pushing them away. The fire service, accompanied by their dogs, were in the middle of searching the area, sniffing for signs of accelerant.

And in the centre was the reason they were all there.

The crime scene itself looked worse than Jermaine's. As though the deceased's body had burnt harder, faster, more vigorously and ferociously. The blaze had decimated everything. There were no distinguishable marks, no noticeable features. It was as if the fire had melted everything away. The only significant DNA evidence they had to go on were the patches of blood on the ground.

'Where's Darryl?' Jake asked, inspecting the congealing puddles.

'On his way,' Brendan replied.

'Still?'

'Stephanie's in charge in the meantime.'

Almost as if they'd rehearsed it, from the corner of his eye he saw Stephanie appear. He wondered whether she'd emerged from a trapdoor in the concrete somewhere. As ever, she was looking vibrant and excitable, her eyes wide and mouth beaming. Yet the two dark clouds under her eyes suggested that it might not last long, that her ebullience was gradually fading.

'Morning,' she said, touching Jake on the arm.

'Fill us in,' he replied, cutting straight to the chase.

'Well, as you can see, another one. *Believed* to be an IC1 male. Mid to late twenties. Too early to identify the body yet. I've spoken with the first responders, and they've said that they received the call at around four this morning. Not like last time, where we had to wait ages for the Good Samaritan to come to the rescue. Instead, it was one of the homeowners in the area. They said they smelt something burning outside. As they approached their window, they noticed the body burning and called it in. Whoever it was, they were dead by the time the paramedics arrived.'

'Did the witness know the deceased?' Jake asked.

'Possibly. But we're having trouble finding the caller. They didn't give their name. And they didn't say where they lived.' Stephanie looked skyward at the flats towering over her. 'It could be any one of them. Like a speck of dust in the cosmos.'

'What now then?' Ashley asked, taking Jake by surprise.

'The priority right now is conducting the house-to-house enquiries. Speak with everyone and everything. Someone somewhere knows what happened, we just have to find out who. It's a large area, so I want you to split the buildings into three and decide amongst yourselves who gets what.'

Very diplomatic, Jake thought. Winning us over by allowing us to make our own choices. I like it.

In recent weeks, Jake had seen more and more of Stephanie's abilities to perform and conduct herself as a deputy senior investigating officer. She was a credit to the team, hard-working, fair, and not afraid to listen to others' opinions, and he thought she'd make a good DCI one day. But right now, she was the detective inspector, and he was going to make her work hard for that promotion. If she could put up with him, she could put up with anything.

'Well, if we're doing that, what're *you* doing?' he asked. 'Putting your feet up?'

His heckling didn't seem to faze her. 'I'll be shoving my foot up your arse if you're not careful. Now, go on, get to it.'

CHAPTER 68

BAD INFLUENCE

As Henry rolled over to the other side of the bed, the entire world continued for another ninety degrees. He hadn't even opened his eyes yet and already he felt the incipient, unrelenting pain focusing on his head, readying itself to pull the trigger like an assassin eyeing up its target. The Double H, he called it. The headache from hell. Groaning, he lifted the covers from his body and swung his feet off the side of the bed, using the headboard for stability.

Somebody stirred behind him. And then he realised where he was. And who he was with. And what had happened the night before. And how many times.

'Morning,' Lily said, pulling the duvet closer to her chest. Her smile illuminated her face and she had a reason to be so happy. He'd given her one. Several times.

'What the fuck is wrong with you?' Henry asked abruptly, hiding any emotion or playfulness in his voice. He blinked several times, thought about shaking his head but then decided against it; the carpet looked new and didn't need a vomit stain on it.

'What do you mean?' she asked, sounding worried.

'Are you an alien? You look too good in the morning. You're outta this world. Everyone else looks like a fucking mess. Me included. And I feel like one too.'

Lily flashed a smile at him and his eyes were drawn to her mouth. Those lips… Those soft, warm, tasty lips were calling out to him. He had to refrain from lunging over and kissing her face off.

'You don't look that bad,' she told him. 'Hair's all over the place, but other than that, nobody would know you've just spent the night here.'

Henry shrugged. 'I don't mind if people know. We can go to the rooftop and shout it to the world if you'd like?'

Lily giggled and lifted herself onto her elbow, resting her head against the headboard. 'What's got into you this morning? You weren't like this last time. And you can't blame it on the alcohol either.'

'I'm just happy to see you, that's all.'

It wasn't a complete lie. As much as he'd tried denying it, he had, in fact, developed feelings for Lily. She was funny, interesting, intelligent, able to hold a conversation on her own, and she was great in bed. But he was also excited to see her for one important reason: so she could provide him with a watertight alibi for the last twelve hours. And that was worth more to him than anything.

Henry turned his attention to the bedside table. On it were his watch, his wallet and his necklace. But there was something missing: his mobile. 'Have you seen my phone?'

She rolled over to the other side of the bed, reached onto the floor and grabbed something. 'You mean this?' She waved the device in the air. 'I took it off you last night after you started getting panicked.'

Henry's body tensed. He forced a smile, while his alcohol-induced mind tried working out what he'd done. 'Why…

why was I getting *panicked*?'

How much had he drunk? How much of the night had the booze erased?

'You don't remember?'

Henry shook his head. *If I did, I wouldn't have asked.*

'Frank Graham. Your sister. You told me everything.'

He swallowed hard. Oh fuck. *Oh fuck, oh fuck, oh fuck.* What the fuck was he thinking? What was he playing at? He'd spent years mastering the art of keeping his mouth shut, manipulating, lying, betraying people's trust in him so that he, Des and Jamal could continue what they were doing. Years of deceit had come crumbling down in one night. His cardinal rule broken.

'I… I…' he stuttered.

'It's fine,' Lily said. 'Your secret's safe with me.' She shuffled closer and placed a hand on his. 'I won't say anything to anyone. You had to do what you had to do. You explained that for pretty much the entire evening. Christ, I would've done the same thing if someone killed my sister.'

She paused, squeezed his hand. 'Did you really think I didn't know who you are and what you do, Henry? You're not the enigma you think you are. And I'm not naïve like all your previous girlfriends. I've got my head screwed on a little bit tighter. But do you know what, it doesn't bother me nearly as much as it should. Because I like you and if anyone comes round here asking where you were, I'll tell them you were with me the whole night. From seven till seven.'

'I… I…' he started, but his brain was a few seconds behind.

'I've put your clothes in the wash as well, by the way. You came here stinking of smoke and petrol, and you were covered in blood. Like, honestly, it was disgusting. Hopefully, it should get rid of any evidence that was on you. But I don't know how you didn't notice, or how you thought *I* wouldn't notice. Perhaps I should be part of the gang. Keep you lot in check. You got too much testosterone in there at the moment. You need a woman around the place. Run you better than you can run yourselves.'

For the first time in his life, Henry Matheson was speechless. 'I… I honestly don't know what to say,' he told her. It was an alien concept to him. Having someone like her he could trust, rely upon, depend upon. She was one in a million. 'Marry me?'

Lily laughed, her cheeks flushing. 'You wish. You're gonna have to do a lot more work than that. You owe me. Big time.'

'I do. Honestly, I do. But first, I need to make a call.'

Without needing to be asked, Lily passed the phone to him. He unlocked the screen and checked the notifications. Fifteen messages. Twenty-one WhatsApps. Thirty-five missed calls. All from Deshawn and Jamal.

Fuck's sake. Sometimes they were like kids, requiring constant attention and mollycoddling. It was probably just them being paranoid. Calling him for advice and guidance.

He tried Jamal first.

'Yo?' he said into the phone as soon as Jamal picked up. 'What's up?'

'Mate, I'm going out my mind over here. I keep thinking about that woman, man. And Frank's youngers, fam. What if Reece fucked up again?'

'Keep it down, would you? My head's pounding. What did I say? I thought I told you both to keep your mouths shut until I got in contact with you. I've got a ton of missed calls from you both, and do you know who I ain't heard a peep out of, fam? Reece, the same kid you're worried about. Imagine that, a kid following orders better than two of my closest boys. Embarrassing.'

'Hen, I—'

'Nah,' Henry said. 'Shut it. If I need you, I'll call you.

Don't do nothing stupid in the meantime.'

Before Jamal had a chance to respond, Henry cut the call off. Without wasting any time, and paying Lily little attention, he found Reece's number and dialled.

'Hello?' Reece said. His voice sounded different from the previous night, as though the hours since the burning had reverted it to the innocence of pre-pubescence.

'It's me, fam. You good to talk?'

'Yeah, bro. Course.'

'Good man. I need you to do something for me.'

'What?'

'It's time to take care of your little friend. Something needs to be done about him. For good, this time. You reckon you can handle that?'

'What you got in mind, Hen?'

Henry lifted his gaze. His eyes fell on Lily. He contemplated before responding. 'I'll let you decide. Be as creative as you want. Just make sure he ain't gonna be a problem no more. You know him better than anyone else. So you know where it can hurt him the most.'

'I got an idea. Leave it with me. What about the others?'

'If you need other help, call Jamal. He needs calming down, something to distract him.'

'And then we're done?'

There was that maturity in his voice again, the one that Henry liked; it almost made him forgive the young boy for being arrested.

'Does this put me out of the debt so I can start making proper gains?'

Henry hesitated before responding. 'I ain't making no promises, but I would say that's a fair deal.'

'I'll hold you to that,' Reece said and hung up.

Henry lowered the phone from his ear and held it against his leg.

'Everything all right?' Lily asked, shuffling herself across the bed. She stopped by his knees, keeping the duvet in place with a hand across her chest.

'Do you ever wonder whether the things you do in life are wrong?'

Amnesia, meet the Double H, meet the existential crisis.

'I think you have to look out for number one. You can't be held responsible for other people's actions. Everyone has their own choice, or choices, to make.'

'But what if I've told them to make those decisions?'

She placed her hands on his shoulders, letting the duvet fall from her body.

'They're adults. They're able to make their own decisions. If they didn't like it, they'd do something about it.'

She was centimetres from his face now. Lips ready.

'Is that what you're doing?' he asked, eyeing them surreptitiously. 'Making your own decision?'

She nodded, keeping her eyes locked on his. 'I'm making my own choices. Just like that little kid is. And only I can be held responsible for my actions.'

'Oh, Lily,' Henry said as he leant in. 'I can tell you're going to be a bad influence on me.'

CHAPTER 69

GOOD RIDDANCE

Jake pounded his knuckles on the wood of number fifty-six. It was only the third flat he'd been to, but he knew already that he was in for a long, long day. On his way to the first house, he'd made a quick count. Six floors in the building. Each floor consisted of ten flats. That meant there were sixty residences to visit. At least sixty individuals. Which meant there was a lot of paperwork to complete.

And people say policing sounds like fun.

A few moments later, the front door opened, revealing an elderly lady. Her hair was lined grey, the curls tight against her head, and she wore a pair of glasses that rested on the top of her nose. She had a set of dentures plugged into her mouth and a thick, dark-blue apron hung around her neck. The pervading smell of spicy chicken wafted through the door and made Jake's empty stomach grumble.

'Good morning.' Jake pulled out his warrant card and hovered it under her nose. 'I'm with the Metropolitan Police. We're investigating the incident that took place last night. I was wondering if I could ask you a few questions about anything you might've seen?'

'Fifteen times…' the woman began.

'Excuse me?'

'Fifteen times I've called you guys in the past month, and nobody's ever bothered to return my calls. Nobody wants to listen to me.'

Jake all of a sudden got the suspicion that he was about to be forced to.

'I'm sorry, Miss…'

'Graham.'

'What sort of things were you calling about, Miss Graham?'

'The boys down there. In the middle of the street. Playing music late. Riding on their bicycles. Shouting profanity at nobody. Dealing drugs.'

'You saw them dealing drugs?'

'Course I have. I know what it looks like. I might be old but I'm not dumb.'

'Of course not, Miss Graham,' Jake said, calculating how he was going to play this. 'Do you know the names of any of the boys that were dealing drugs?'

'Yeah. I found 'em on Facebook and everything.'

Jake flicked to a new page in his pocketbook and began to scribble.

'Do you have any information for me regarding what happened last night? Anything you might have seen? Any of the boys that you've seen about the estate, the ones you know the names of?'

'I saw the whole thing,' Miss Graham said, her face moving animatedly as she geared herself up to release a torrent of pent-up information. 'I started hearing these noises in the middle of the night, so I had a look out of my window and saw a car pulled up outside. It was a big thing. You know, like, one of those big black cars. Range Rovers, I think they're called, you know. Hold on, I wrote the number plate down. Give me a second.'

Miss Graham turned her back on him and returned a few seconds later, holding a Post-it note in her hand.

Jake took it from her and glanced at the scraggly writing. He recognised the registration at once. The same one that had followed him outside Rivermeade school, that he'd sighted on countless occasions, that he'd run through the database, that was unequivocally associated with Henry Matheson. All of a sudden Jake felt an invisible knot tightening around Henry's neck, and he was the one applying the pressure from both ends.

'Who did you see exiting the vehicle, Miss Graham?'

'Three guys and two little children.'

'Children?' Jake interrupted, already making the jump in his mind.

'Yeah,' she said. 'There were two of them. With the older guys. None of them were from round here. I didn't recognise any of their faces. They got out of the car and started wandering down the street, where some of the kids from this estate were playing. You know, making noise and keeping me awake. At first, I thought, "Oh, no. Here we go. There's going to be trouble."'

'Have they caused trouble before?'

'Never seen them around this way before, you know.'

'Did you hear any names?'

'Henry, I think one of them was called. They were shouting in the street at one another. I think he was the big one, you know, the one who was in charge. But they were all wearing hoods over their heads so I didn't get a good look at their faces.'

'What else?'

'They went over to the group of kids by the lamp post. I couldn't hear what they were saying, but then one of them kids took them into the estate. It was a girl. She was taller than the little kids.'

Miss Graham hesitated to catch her breath and swallow. 'They disappeared for a while. I didn't know where they went. While they were gone, I thought they'd left the estate. I thought maybe they'd gone somewhere else. Home. The graveyard. I didn't care. So long as they were out of my way and not keeping me awake.'

'But they didn't leave, did they, Miss Graham?'

She shook her head.

'They came back. And this time they had a man with them, shouting. Two of the guys from the car were holding him in their arms. I rushed to my other window to watch.'

'What time did you call the police?'

'I don't know. You must have that on record somewhere. I tried to get through to someone, but nobody answered. I think maybe you guys have blocked my number. You see it and think, "Oh, here she is again. Calling to complain about something else."'

Jake tried to hide his smirk by licking his lips. 'I can assure you that definitely isn't the case. We value every emergency call we receive, no matter how serious it may or may not be.'

Miss Graham scoffed. 'The other officer told me that the last time I mentioned it, but I don't believe it. You know why? Because I called again and had to pretend I was someone else. Didn't even give my name. Just acted like I was a random person. Funny how you guys listened to that instead of a concerned citizen.'

Jake was conscious that the conversation was taking a detour. And not a good one. So once she stopped, he said, 'As you were saying…'

'Yes. The two guys. Holding that man. I didn't see their faces, but I recognised him…'

Jake's ears perked up. 'You recognised the victim? The

man who was burnt to death?'

'Course I did. He was my nephew, great-nephew actually. Hadn't spoken to him in months, years even. Ever since his brother died and he started dealing drugs, I wanted nothing to do with him. But now all of a sudden he comes round here needing a place to stay, somewhere to hide. I couldn't say no, could I? Had to pretend we were all happy families again. That boy's always been trouble, just like his brother was, getting into danger and stuff they shouldn't have been. My niece wasn't raised like that. I don't know where it all went wrong for them, I really don't. He must have done something wrong for that to happen to him, but when I asked him what was going on, he wouldn't tell me. But good riddance, if you ask me. I'm sure he did something to deserve it. All those lives he's destroyed by fuelling their filthy habits… it's wrong, and people like him shouldn't exist.'

Not wanting to appear rude, Jake had been chewing his tongue while he waited for her to finish. When she did, he asked, 'What was his name, Miss Graham?' Even though he already knew the answer.

'Frank. Frank Graham. Those bastards burnt him alive. Good riddance.'

CHAPTER 70

IN A HURRY

Reece wrapped his fingers tightly around the Higonokami SPE2 switchblade he'd bought online the other night using his mum's credit card. The weapon was lightweight, thin, and nimble in his grip. The handle was finished with tortoiseshell, one of the reasons he'd purchased this specific model, and the entire thing looked as though it wouldn't appear out of place in a Quentin Tarantino movie. The blade was just over seven centimetres long; long enough to pierce the skin then twist to cause a lot of damage.

He kept his head down as he stalked across the Cosgrove Estate, determined, paying his surroundings little heed. It didn't matter to him if there was a younger pissing about with another younger on the football pitch. Nor did it bother him that there was a random old woman whom he didn't recognise on the other side of the estate, wheeling her granny trolley behind her.

He was focused. On a mission. And he wasn't going to let Henry down.

Reece knew what he had to do, and he knew exactly how

he was going to do it.

He travelled through the underpass beneath the north tower block, made a left turn and headed towards Lewis's house on the road opposite. At the house, he moved the front gate aside and wandered up to the front step. Clenching his hand into a fist, he knocked on the door.

There was no response.

He waited a few moments before knocking again.

Beside him, a figure emerged from the house next door.

'You all right there, Reece?'

It was Debbie, colloquially known as Deb to him and the rest of the youngers. She was one of the nicest people he'd ever met. Attentive, caring, wholesome, she often fed some of the boys if they were struggling with food. And she never asked for anything in return. But the boys always paid her back whenever they could. Never a bad word against her, everyone in The Pit adored her. She knew everything and anything, and Reece had always joked that, if anything happened to Henry, she'd be the one to succeed him.

'I'm all right, thanks, Deb,' Reece replied. 'Just waiting, innit.'

An awkward moment danced between them, Reece shuffling from side to side while he waited for her to go back inside. When she didn't, he contemplated asking her what her problem was. But she was first to break the deadlock.

'Haven't you heard?'

Reece said nothing and hoped that his silence would provoke a response from Deb.

'Lewis…' she began. 'He… he went to hospital this morning. He passed out and his dad found him. Didn't nobody tell you?'

Reece decided it was in his best interests not to play dumb. 'Oh, you mean that! Yeah. Course I knew 'bout that. His dad told me. Said he needed me to come and get some little bits for Lewis. Think he said they were going to keep him in for the rest of the day, maybe overnight as well. Aiden said that there might be some family members home who could help. You seen anyone?'

Debbie shook her head. 'Nobody's come round this way. I've been watching, keeping an eye on the house for 'em.'

Course you have.

Aside from being close with the youngers and kids on the estate, the other reason that Debbie knew everything and everyone was because she was The Pit's resident busybody, nesting herself in other people's affairs, making sure she knew what was going on in her estate before anyone else did.

'Never mind,' Reece added. 'Maybe they're on their way and'll be down in a bit. Anyway, you have a good day now, Deb!'

As he turned his attention back to the front door, he had one final thought. Something to sweeten her up, make sure she didn't suspect anything.

'Actually, is there anything you'd like me to pass on to Lewis when I see him?'

'Oh, yes, please. Er…' She hesitated. 'Send my love and give him a hug from me. Tell him that he's got a plate of biscuits waiting for him when he comes back.'

Reece told her that he would then crouched down. Under his feet was a doormat. Beneath that, a spare key. He reached under, grabbed it and used it to enter the deathly silent house.

He froze. Hesitated. Listened.

Nothing.

Reece moved along the corridor, brushing his fingers against the wall. He held the blade in his other hand, clutching it so tightly that his palm started to sweat.

At the end of the corridor was the living room where Reece had spent many an afternoon watching television in silence with Lewis and Lewis's dad. Pretending he was interested in daytime television. Making it look like he was there to play, rather than go out and collect the drugs they needed to sell.

Just before the living room, Reece climbed the stairs and ducked into Lewis's bedroom at the top of the landing. In the middle of the room was Lewis's bed. Reece shuffled to the other side, keeping his body beneath the window and using his hands against the wall for support. There, he allowed himself to let go of the blade. He pulled his hand from his pocket and reached beneath Lewis's bed. Before long, he found what he was searching for.

The shoebox of drugs felt heavy in his hands. He removed the lid and glanced inside. Sitting in front of him was a handful of Frank Graham's poison. Next to it, tucked down the side, was a handful of small plastic bags. Reece grabbed one and poured some of the powder into it. Then he closed the lid and slid the shoebox back to its previous position. And as he pulled away, his knuckles brushed against something else. Another box. Intrigued, Reece fumbled for it and yanked it out then sat on the floor with his legs crossed. He didn't know why, but there was a lure about this box that the other didn't have. Reece had known about the first one. But this one… it was almost as if it was meant to be kept a secret.

He removed the lid. Then his eyes widened and a grin grew on his face involuntarily.

Wrapped tightly into small rolls, sealed with elastic bands, were thick wads of money. So much. Too much. It was inconceivable for there to be that much. Reece could scarcely believe it. It was way more than he'd ever got for working with Henry and Des and Jamal and the rest of them. What the fuck? How could Lewis make this much money while he was still begging to be considered part of their larger plans? Angered, Reece grabbed the money and started shoving it in his pockets until they were filled to the brim.

Weighed down by the thousands of pounds, the drugs and the switchblade in his jumper, Reece headed out of the house and started the long walk to the hospital, wondering what sort of things he might buy with his new riches.

And then wondering how he was going to make his friend suffer for lying to him all this time.

Fortunately, he had the journey time to decide. He had nowhere he needed to be in a hurry.

CHAPTER 71

PLAIN AND SIMPLE

Jake slid out of his car, breathed in the tepid air and held it there before shutting the door behind him. He'd taken it upon himself, with Darryl's *loose* approval, to visit the Cosgrove Estate, under the provision that he was there to attempt another arrest on Reece Enfield on behalf of Essex Police. After the information that Miss Graham had given him, they were now confident that Frank Graham was the deceased, that a man named Henry was responsible and that two younger individuals were accompanying them. And Jake was almost certain that Lewis Coyne and Reece Enfield were involved. So much so that he was willing to bet his pension on it.

Now all Jake had to do was speak with either of the boys and hope that they came quietly.

The first destination: Lewis Coyne's house.

Jake arrived at the gate, moved it aside, approached the house, then rang the doorbell and waited. A few seconds later, a neighbour arrived on his right, her head peering around the side of the building. Her back was slightly hunched, and her eyes were wide from the extra-strength lenses in her glasses.

'You all right there, love?' she asked accusatorially, as though he had no right being there.

'Good afternoon, ma'am,' Jake said, removing his warrant card and showing it to her. 'I'm from the Metropolitan Police. We're investigating a few incidents around the area recently and I was just looking to speak with Lewis or Aiden if either are available.' He pressed the doorbell again. 'Have you seen them?'

'They went to the hospital this morning.'

Oh, God. Aiden. His condition.

'Is Mr Coyne OK?'

'It wasn't the boy's dad, dear. It was the boy. Little Lewis. I'm not too sure what happened, but he was passed out and he was covered in blood when I saw him. Paramedics took him to the hospital early this morning. One of Lewis's friends just dropped by; you just missed him. Think he came to pick up a few things.'

'Reece?'

She nodded.

Perfect. The pieces were falling into place. Jake's intuition one, everyone else's zero.

'Excellent,' Jake said, already on the half-turn. 'Do you know which hospital?'

'Whipps Cross.'

'Perfect.'

Jake thanked her, said goodbye and ran back to the car. As he stepped into the road, a car shot past, narrowly missing him. But he didn't have time to process what'd happened. He was in a rush, and a young boy was waiting in a hospital room like a sitting duck.

Entering his Mini, Jake closed the door behind him, fastened his seat belt and thrust his key into the ignition.

He glanced out of the windshield.

Froze.

'Hello!' came the distant voice from outside the car.

Jake sighed. Tensed his body. Wound the window down.

'Thought I told you this was a no-go zone?' Martin Radcliffe asked, sauntering towards him like he didn't have a care in the world, as though the dinner menu for tonight was the most pressing thing on his mind.

'What're you doing here, Martin?'

'Could ask you the same thing.'

Jake rolled his eyes, placed his left hand on the gearstick and depressed the clutch, prepared to slam on the accelerator if necessary.

'We're not having the same conversation again, Martin.'

'It's beginning to feel like Groundhog Day. Maybe there's something in the air?'

Jake raised an eyebrow. 'Smouldering remains, perhaps?'

'What you talking about?'

'You haven't heard?' Jake asked. 'Someone we believe to be Frank Graham was burnt alive last night. Same way that Jermaine Gordon was.'

Martin's face remained expressionless. If he knew anything about what had happened, he gave nothing away. He was either a good liar, which Jake was still yet to see supporting evidence for, or he'd been left in the dark about Henry Matheson's latest exploits.

'The plot thickens,' he said. 'But I'm sure you'll solve it. The great Jake Tanner.' Then he gave Jake a knowing, condescending smile. 'Shame you won't be able to solve it quicker than our investigation though.'

'Your ghost murder victim?'

Martin glanced at his watch. 'As of five hours ago, we arrested seven individuals in connection with the crime *and* the murder and they're all being interviewed and put through the wringer as we speak. Funny how things work out, isn't it?'

'Incredibly. Who did you pin it on?'

'A couple of Jermaine Gordon's cronies. The way I see it, and the way my governor and the Crown Prosecution Service see it, after their little leader died, they needed some cash. Maybe there was no one to take the reins after Gordon, and they needed money fast, so they branched out, robbed the jewellery store to see them through to the end of the year. Unsuccessfully, I might add. But they did it all without their revered leader. A little like what you're trying to do now, Jake. One man against an immense army.'

Jake ignored the comment and focused on feeding his intuition with information. He was making mental notes of everything that came out of Martin's mouth, storing it for future use. He didn't know how or when he'd need it, just that he inevitably would.

'What led you to them?'

'Oh, you know,' Martin replied. 'This and that. Evidence here and there. I can't tell you how we did all of it. I don't want to help you with your investigations since you're so intent on jeopardising mine.'

'If they're being dealt with, what are you doing here then? Surely you can't be here to police me? Not when there are real criminals out there.'

'Sometimes they're the ones staring you right in the face.'

Ain't that the truth.

'You don't have any kids, do you?' Jake asked, not realising he'd said it with an evil smile. 'Family? A wife?'

Martin's expression changed. The image of a man who had nothing to fear disappeared and was replaced with someone who had, all of a sudden, as though by some divine intervention, realised he had everything to lose.

'Why?'

'Just wondered. Might be useful to know.'

'I don't have anyone that you can hurt, Jake.'

'Who said anything about hurting anyone? It was just a question. Plain and simple. Pretty harmless. Unless you've got a reason to be suspicious? Perhaps getting a little paranoid? Now that we're going to be seeing a lot more of each other, I thought I'd get to know you. That was all. No need to read anything into it. Besides, it's probably for the best if you don't tell me, because I already know what it's like to have my home life invaded, my privacy and family's safety removed. And if you're anything like me, you'll know that some things are just off limits. And that if those lines are crossed, you'd be willing to do *anything* to make sure it didn't happen again.'

Jake shrugged nonchalantly and started the engine. Slipping the car into gear, he said, 'Just a little something for you to think about, Martin. Take care of yourself. I'm sure I'll be seeing you soon.'

CHAPTER 72

A CHAT

The first thing Lewis felt when he opened his eyes was pain: the fluorescent lights overhead splitting the crack in his skull even wider; the suffocating pressure crushing his chest, worsening with every exhausted breath; the unending numbness in his legs; the tubes buried in his skin, stinging like cigarette burns deep in his muscles.

He'd known pain before: the beatings, the fights, even the flesh wound he'd sustained from a small knife fight with one of the youngers while they were play fighting, but for the first time in his life, *everything* hurt, and he'd never known anything as agonising.

Lewis groaned himself awake, rolling his head from side to side, blinking reality back into existence.

'Dad?' he whispered. His vision was still hazy and took a couple more blinks to return to normal. 'Dad?'

As his eyes adjusted and fell on his father, sleeping peacefully on a chair beside him, head tilted forward, clutching his walking cane against his chest, the pain in Lewis's body dissipated. He was safe. Protected. They had each other, looked out for one another. Like a caddy and a golfer. One needed the other, their relationship symbiotic.

Lewis reached out an arm and tapped his dad awake. Within seconds, Aiden stirred and tried to lift himself into a standing position. But it was no use. The pain in his back was too severe.

'It's OK,' Lewis said softly. 'Stay there. I'm fine. Stay.'

'Are you…' His dad winced again as he lowered himself into his seat. 'Are you OK? How are you feeling? I was so worried, Leg. I thought you were having a heart attack or something.'

'What happened?' Lewis asked. His voice felt weak, and he could feel the lump in his throat beginning to swell. 'The only thing I remember is opening the wardrobe and finding all of the clothes Mum bought me in a suitcase.'

'You went to your bedroom. You started to pack. A few seconds later I heard a noise. When I found you, you were on the floor having a fit. Your body was jerking up and down like you were possessed or something. I've never seen you like that before. I was so scared. I called the ambulance and they brought you in. You've been out all morning.'

His father leant forward, despite the pain, and grabbed Lewis's hand. 'How are you feeling?'

Lewis felt a squeeze. 'I'm… I'm OK. Just… sore.'

His dad's eyes began to glisten beneath the light. Lewis had only ever seen that change in him once before – all those years ago when he'd told him that his mum had walked out on them and left them to be a team on their own.

She's gone, Leg. It's just you and me. And I'm going to make sure you have everything you need in life.

'Lewis…' his dad started. 'I need you to tell me what happened. What were you doing with those drugs? What happened to your hand? What happened to your chest?'

'I…' Lewis trailed off. A lump formed in his throat and

grew to the size of a walnut. 'I…'

'Lewis, if you listen to me, I can help you. We can work through it together. Like a team. Like we've always done.' He paused to rub the snot from the underside of his nose. 'Where did you get the drugs from?'

'A friend.'

'Reece?'

'No! No! His name was… his name was Frank. He's one of the dealers in the city. He gave me some stuff to sell. The weed was just for me, a little taster in case I wanted it.'

'Jesus,' his father whispered under his breath. 'And what happened here?' As he pointed to the bandages on his hand and across his chest, the wounds flared up in a flash of pain, like a poor version of Harry Potter's scar. 'Did you get involved in a fight because of the drugs?'

Lewis's gaze dropped to his ribcage and images of Reece holding the blade flashed in his mind. He decided, for now, it was better to keep the real cause of it a secret. 'Yes,' he began, 'it was just one of my buyers. He was on something. Got real crazy when I told him the price had gone up. Whipped a knife on me.'

His dad sighed and dropped his head again; there was that look for the second time. Except it was filled with a paralysing disappointment. 'You should've told me about all of this. I could have helped you. Why didn't you come to me? Did you feel like you couldn't?'

'No!' Lewis said, his voice breaking into a shout. 'Yes. No. Yes. You told me I couldn't do it, so… it was all I wanted to do.'

'We don't keep secrets in this family. I've never kept one from you. I've told you everything about everything. Your mum. Me. What I've done. Everything. We don't keep secrets, OK? Maybe once you're out of here we can look at moving to a different place. A different part of the city. Further north maybe. Would you like that?'

Lewis nodded as fast as he could manage.

And then panic flashed through him.

'Where's my phone? Dad? Do you have my phone? Dad? The iPhone.'

Aiden said nothing but reached into his jacket pocket and pulled out the device. 'I wondered where you'd got this from. Did you buy it with that drug money of yours?'

At the sight of the device, Lewis breathed a heavy sigh of relief. The deep exhalation invoked a pain in his ribs, but he ignored it. The evidence on the phone was worth it.

'It doesn't matter where I got it from.'

'Yes, Lewis, it does. Remember, no secrets. Tell me. Where did you get it from? And what's on it that's so important?'

Lewis turned away from his dad and faced directly ahead, at the blank grey wall staring back at him. His body tensed, and he became aware that he was clenching his jaw. He eased the tension in his mouth and closed his eyes as he forced himself to tell the truth.

'I stole it. From some random woman. I needed a new phone. My old one was broken. And I… I wanted to have a nice one like the rest of the elders do.'

'OK,' his dad said slowly and plainly. There was no emotion in his voice. No anger. No frustration. No resentment. 'And what about what's on it? What's on the phone that's so important, Lewis?'

'I… you know… nothing.'

He couldn't do it. He couldn't make it as far as telling his dad the whole truth. That he was there at the time of both Jermaine Gordon and Frank Graham's deaths. That he had documented both their assassinations on camera. That he was complicit in both acts. That as a result of his inactivity, he may as well as have lit the fire himself.

He couldn't do it.

'I'm going to ask you one more time. Tell me what's on this phone.'

'Videos,' Lewis whispered, barely audible, the pressure too much for him to bear.

'Videos of what?'

Just as Lewis opened his mouth to explain, there was a knock on the door. Both of them snapped their heads towards the source of the noise.

Before either of them could respond, the door opened.

'Reece… what are you doing here?' Lewis asked, shocked to see his best friend. Only a few hours ago, they had wrestled on the ground, intent on killing one another.

Reece stepped in, wearing a casual grin on his face. He was dressed in the same clothes he'd been in last night, and to Lewis's surprise, he wasn't covered in blood. The only thing that looked different about him was that his pockets and jumper was bulging in odd ways.

'I came to see my best mate, innit,' he said. 'That not allowed or something?'

'Yeah… I…' Lewis began.

'Good to see you, Reece,' his dad said with a friendly smile. 'Would you like to sit down? I can get you both a drink if you want? Give you two some time.'

'But, Dad, your back! You need to be careful.'

Without saying anything, Aiden hefted himself out of the chair, struggled and wandered to the door.

'You boys have a chat. I'll be back in a minute.'

CHAPTER 73

JAKE

'What you doing here, Reece?' Lewis tried to shift himself further up the bed, but his muscles were too weak to support himself.

'Wanted to make sure you're all right, innit. That's what friends do. They don't leave each other, do they? Especially not best friends…'

'You tried to k—'

Reece lunged towards him and placed a hand on Lewis's wrist, pinning him down. 'I weren't gonna kill you, bruv. Honest. You musta knew that. It was all for show. I had to make it look like I was. They wanted to teach you a lesson, innit. They wanted you to watch what happens when you betray Hen.'

Reece tightened his grip and a brief smile flashed across his face as he began to get excited about the thought of inflicting pain. Something in his friend's expression made Lewis distrust everything that came out of his mouth.

'You shoulda seen it, bro. Fucking magnificent, watching his body go up in flames like that. Ain't never seen nothing like it.'

'Now we're on one each,' Lewis said weakly. He decided to stop resisting and wasting what precious little energy he had left.

'Think my score on the Leader Board says otherwise.'

The scores. The Leader Board.

Lewis's recollection of last night's events was hazy at best. But there was one thing he could recall with crystal clarity – Henry Matheson telling his best friend to use him as a means to progress his score on the Leader Board. He hadn't managed it then, so now he was here to finish the job off.

The muscles in Lewis's body tightened in preparation for an assault. But it was pointless. He was too weak to do anything, too weak to defend himself, like a lost lion cub in the wild, vulnerable and susceptible to attack from Reece, Henry, Des and Jamal; the pack of hyenas currently gunning for his blood.

Lewis began to sweat, a thin film of liquid forming on his forehead. His chest rose and fell rapidly, the bandaging bouncing in and out of his view. 'You gonna kill me?'

The sides of Reece's mouth rose slowly into an evil smile. 'Nah, fam. You ain't worth the effort.'

If he wasn't here to kill him, then what was he here for?

'What you gonna do to me?' An invisible force crushed Lewis's chest and spread to the rest of his body, trapping him beneath the white linen sheets. Beside him, he was aware of the beeping sound coming from the ECG monitor as it registered his racing heartbeat.

'Just gotta make some assurances.'

'About what?'

'That you ain't never gonna set foot in the estate again. And that you ain't never gonna tell no one about what happened, innit.'

'Like I would,' he lied, hoping the bravado in his voice

was enough to fool his best friend.

'Words don't mean much coming out your mouth no more, fam. They want me to make sure you ain't gonna do or say nothing.'

Lewis opened his mouth, but his throat was dry, and every time he swallowed it felt like a thousand blades scraping against his skin. Where was his dad with those drinks?

'How?' he asked.

'Couple of ways.' He tapped the side of his temple knowingly. 'But first I wanna know about that video you showed me the other day. That's the one thing that links Deshawn and Jamal to Jermaine's murder, and none of us want that getting into the wrong hands.'

'No, I…'

'Where's the phone, Lewis?'

Lewis didn't respond. Now his throat had sealed shut with fear.

'Lewis? Don't make me hurt you, fam.'

'I'm not! I don't have the video anymore. I don't have the phone either. I dropped it last night.'

Reece's head turned towards the chair where Lewis's father had been sitting a few moments ago. The phone, as blatant and obvious as the fracture in their relationship, was resting on the seat right in front of them, glistening under the overheads.

Shit.

Smirking, Reece pounced on the phone. Lewis reached for his friend, trying to grapple the device from him, but it was no use. He was too far away and the sudden movement sent a blinding spasm of pain up and down his spine, around his chest, and then all the way up to his head.

'Reece!' he yelled, fighting off the dancing stars in his vision. 'Give it back!'

Reece didn't reply. He was too busy trying to get into the phone.

'What's your password, fam?'

'I ain't telling you.'

'What's your password?'

'I'm not—'

Reece lunged at him again. This time he grabbed Lewis's hand, dragged him halfway off the hospital bed, rendering him defenceless, and started prodding the screen.

'What's the code?'

'I ain't saying.'

Reece entered Lewis's birthday. Nothing.

'What about your dad's?' Reece asked, thinking aloud.

'You don't know it.'

'Course I do. The number of times I had to come over for it, fuck's sake.'

And then he had it. He was in. Bingo.

'Fam…' Lewis said, his voice a raspy whisper as he dangled there upside down. 'Come on.'

Reece remained silent. His friend was too focused, and all Lewis could do was watch him scroll to the camera library, find the video of Jermaine Gordon burning alive, and then delete it.

'There,' he said, twirling the phone in his fingers proudly. 'All done, mate. And it's deleted from your deleted folder as well. Ain't nobody gonna find it. Gone forever.'

Slowly, riding the wave of disbelief at his friend's actions, Lewis used all his energy to climb back onto the bed. But before he could open his mouth and beg Reece to leave and never come back, his dad charged into the room, followed closely by a nurse.

'What's going on in here?' Aiden asked, holding a cardboard tray of plastic cups.

'Nothing,' Reece said.

'Nothing,' Lewis echoed, trying to hide the exasperation on his face. 'I was just showing Reece something on my phone, Dad.'

His dad set the tray on a chair beside him and, under the strain of the situation, his back spasmed. He cried out in pain and buckled.

'Are you OK, sir?' the nurse asked. She wrapped her arms around him, helped him round the bed and onto the seat beside Lewis. It hurt him to see his dad like this. And the sensation was magnified when he realised there was nothing he could do about it. That his dad was at the mercy of the nurses and doctors, people who didn't know the methods he'd used to make him feel better.

'Dad…' Lewis said weakly.

'I think Reece should go. Give Lewis his phone back.'

For a long while, Reece stood there, staring at Lewis, and Lewis returned the gesture with a defeated expression that said, 'Come on. You've done everything you came here to do. Now leave.'

But he didn't budge. It wasn't until the nurse said something to him that he finally paid attention. Perhaps it was because the only maternal voice in the room had spoken. Or perhaps it was because Reece knew that he was outnumbered. Either way, Lewis was relieved to see his friend relinquish control of the phone.

'I'm outta here,' Reece said on the half-turn. 'But I just wanted to let you know, some of the boys from the estate are coming over later to see you. I told 'em you're here.'

Lewis didn't like the sound of that. Not one bit.

After Reece had left, nobody said a word. The only sound that remained was the noise of Aiden's heavy breathing.

'Are you all right, Dad?'

Aiden turned to the nurse and said, 'I'm fine. Could you give us a couple of minutes?'

After checking his pulse, the nurse gave a curt nod and started out of the room. As she reached the door, a looming figure appeared beside her, clad in black protective gear, with fluorescent epaulettes on his shoulders and the word POLICE stitched onto his breast. Lewis's eyes followed the nurse and stopped immediately on the face of the figure. The tattoos. The thin stubble around the side of his face. The sheer height of him as he struggled to fit into the door frame.

Jamal.

Some of the boys from the estate are coming over later to see you. I told 'em you're here.

What Reece had failed to mention was that they'd be dressed as police officers, the perfect disguise.

'Is everything all right, officer?' the nurse started, taking a step back.

'Everything's fine, miss. Would it be possible to speak with the patient? I have a few questions I need to ask him about an incident last night.' Jamal spoke in his most eloquent voice, the best Lewis had ever heard, which unsettled him enormously.

'Certainly. I'll just be down the corridor.'

Without asking any more questions, without interrogating this man in front of her – because why would she? – the nurse exited, leaving Lewis and his dad with Jamal. Alone.

'Good afternoon, both.' Jamal stepped into the room and flashed an ID that Lewis had never seen before. It looked fake, but Lewis's dad was in no fit state to pay much attention to it. 'I was wondering if I'd be able to speak with Lewis regarding an incident we have reason to believe he was involved in last night.'

'Seriously?' Aiden asked, wincing through the pain, grinding his teeth. 'Is that necessary? Is it urgent? You can see he's not feeling very well.'

Jamal dipped his head. 'I understand, sir. But it will only

take a couple of minutes. I just want to establish Lewis's whereabouts during the early hours of the morning. Normally, I would allow some time to pass, but this is our top priority. I hope you can appreciate the urgency of what we're dealing with. I'll be in and out in a matter of minutes.' Jamal paused, licked his lips, pointed at his dad. 'You look like you could do with a drink. Why don't I get you one? Coffee? Water?'

His dad settled into the seat, visibly put at ease by Jamal's calming demeanour. 'Black. No sugar. There's a machine down the corridor. I meant to get myself one but they didn't have a tray for three or more cups.'

Jamal nodded politely, as though he were meeting royalty, but just before he exited the room, he gave Lewis a look that filled him with a dark premonition; something bad was about to happen.

'What's going on, Lewis? What's this all about?' his dad asked as the sound of Jamal's feet echoed down the corridor.

Lewis didn't know what to say. He didn't know what to think. It was as if he was out of his body. Floating further and further away from the situation, finding himself more and more unable to do anything about it.

'Lewis! Answer me. What is that officer talking about? Last night? Lewis!'

He was deaf to the sounds around him. The butterflies in his stomach worsened, and his chest heaved. This was it. It was time. To tell the truth. The whole truth. And nothing but the truth.

He twisted his head.

'Jermaine Gordon. I was there, Dad. I watched him burn to death. And I did nothing about it. Now Frank Graham's dead. The same way. Burnt. I was there last night when it happened too. I watched it. And that's what this is about.' He pointed to his chest and hand. 'I tried to stop it. We got in a fight, Reece and me. I ran away as soon as I could.'

'Lewis—'

'But, Dad, that man, that officer… He's—'

There was no time to finish his sentence. Somehow, the space of a minute had flashed by, and now Jamal was standing in the doorway, holding a cup of coffee in one hand and a transparent cup of water in the other.

'Here you are,' he said, moving through the room and passing the coffee cup to Lewis's dad. Elegant ribbons of steam escaped from the top, drifting randomly through the air.

Aiden took the cup from Jamal and sipped.

'Please,' he began. 'If you could get this over with quickly. I'd prefer my son to have as little stress as possible.'

Jamal moved about the bed and passed the cup of water to Lewis, keeping his gaze locked on him.

'Certainly, sir. Nice coffee?'

Slowly, Lewis turned to face his dad, who was indulging himself in another sip of his drink. And another. And another. Bouncing the cup up and down. When his dad was finished, he lowered the mug and breathed heavily. Wiping his lips, he said, 'I needed that, thanks. Just what the doctor ordered. It's impressive what a coffee machine can do nowadays.'

Jamal said nothing.

For a long time, a terrifyingly long time, he continued to stare at Lewis's dad.

As if waiting. And waiting. And waiting.

For something to happen.

And then it did.

His dad coughed violently, suddenly, abruptly. Spitting his lungs onto his chest. The cup fell to his lap and his hand flew to his throat, grappling it. Gasping for breath. Eyes widening. Coughing. Convulsing. He slipped lower and lower into his chair until his body collapsed to the floor, as though the linoleum was sucking the life out of him.

Lewis watched on, helpless, in horror, rooted to the spot in fear. His brain couldn't comprehend what was happening.

His dad was foaming at the mouth, pinned to the floor by an invisible attacker. He reached for Lewis's hand. Lewis caught it, clung to it, savoured the sensation of his father's touch. His calloused and coarse fingers worn down by years of using the cane and walking sticks. The bump and groove of the scar he had on his right palm from a knife attack when he was nineteen. The little mole on his thumb that he'd been meaning to get checked out but had never been well enough or brave enough to manage.

All those pieces of history that made his dad who he was. Stories shared with him. No secrets, no lies. Only truth.

But within seconds, the man's grip felt limp, weak, lifeless.

Lewis dragged himself over the side of the bed. By the time he reached down and touched his dad's face, he realised the man who'd raised him from the ground up, the man he loved more than anything else, was dead.

A lump swelled in his throat. Tears filled his eyes.

'Dad…' he whispered. 'Dad…'

'You've been warned, Lewis,' Jamal said, making his way out of the room. 'If you know what's good for you, get as far away as possible from everything.'

Angered, Lewis crawled off the bed and started after him. But Jamal was gone. He'd slipped out of the room almost as fast as the life had drained from his dad's eyes.

Lewis cried for a nurse, and within moments, the same one that had been there a few moments earlier charged towards him.

'You should be back in bed,' she told him.

'My dad. The police. I need the police. My dad. He's dead!'

'What are you talking about, Lewis? What's wrong? Where's your father? Calm down.'

And then the woman noticed his dead dad lying on the linoleum. She pressed a button and an alarm sounded.

'Jake Tanner,' Lewis screamed over the noise. 'Jake. His name's Jake.'

'Whose?'

'Police. He's a police officer. I want to speak to Jake Tanner!'

CHAPTER 74

HURDLES

Jake barged through the hospital doors, holding his phone against his ear. He was talking with Stephanie, updating her on where he was. She was asking him questions, lots of them. Questions he didn't know the answers to. Questions he wouldn't know the answer to until he was there.

All he knew was that a medical emergency required his attention.

That *Lewis* required his attention.

'He's in the east wing. Hemingway Ward. Room 34E,' the nurse at the reception desk told him in his other ear.

Around him, the hubbub and hustle of A&E bustled with life and urgency. Doctors and nurses and other medical professionals darted from one corner of the room to another, wheeling patients through, carrying them on gurneys, supporting them as they hobbled, while family members and loved ones remained in their seats and watched them disappear behind the double doors.

Jake scanned the placard overhead and followed the small arrow directing him towards Hemingway Ward. He raced along the corridors, weaving in and out of the staff and patients and family members opposing him in the other lanes of traffic.

A few minutes, and a few flights of stairs, later, Jake made it to Hemingway, room 34E. There was a knot of nurses huddled in the doorway. One of them held the door frame for support.

'Excuse me,' Jake said as he approached them. The nurse holding on to the door frame turned to face him. 'DC Jake Tanner. One of your colleagues told me to be here as soon as I could.'

'That was me,' the nurse said. 'Did you come alone, like I asked?'

Jake nodded. It had been an odd request, but one he'd respected nonetheless. Besides, Stephanie and the team were on standby back at the station, ten minutes away – five, if the blue lights were on.

'Yes. What's going on?'

'Do you have your ID? Something to prove you are who you say you are?'

Jake sighed but didn't let his exasperation show on his face. He reached into his back pocket and produced his warrant card. The nurse snatched it from him and inspected it scrupulously.

'I'm sorry,' she said as she handed it back to him, 'I have to be cautious. You'll understand when you see him. Please follow me.'

The nurse slipped into the room. There, in the middle, sitting upright in the hospital bed, was Lewis Coyne, dressed in a gown, hooked up to machines. At once, Jake felt a paternal instinct flush over him. The compulsion to protect the young boy as though he were his own. Like a bear protecting its young in the wild.

In a way, Lewis reminded him of Maisie, of Ellie. How

they were sometimes mischievous, naughty, reckless, rebellious, but deep down they were good kids that just needed to be told when to behave and when not to. There was no malice in Lewis, Jake could see that. Only a lost child in desperate need of help, and willing to do stupid things to get it. A boy that had been in this situation for so long he'd forgotten what was wrong and what was right.

'Lewis…' Jake began. 'Is everything OK? What are you doing here?'

Lewis was silent. Both Jake and the nurse stood either side of him. Slowly, he turned to the nurse and gave her a look. The nurse must have known what it meant because she glanced at Jake and said, 'If you need me, I'll be outside.'

Before departing, she told them that she was going to guard the room and that nobody else was allowed in.

Jake waited until she closed the door before starting. 'What's going on, Lewis? What's happened?'

Lewis's head dropped. He wiped his eyes. 'Can you keep promises, Detective?'

'Of course I can. But only if they don't involve breaking the law, Lewis. Do you understand? If someone has put you in this hospital, then you can tell me. I'll make sure you're looked after, and I'll make sure nobody can hurt you anymore. OK? Are you going to tell me what happened?'

Lewis nodded.

'Great. Let me grab a chair and then you can start.' Jake pulled the nearest chair up to the bed without waiting for a response. He sat and removed his pocketbook and pen from his blazer. 'I'm going to have to make a few notes. Is that OK?'

Lewis nodded, still keeping his head down. Jake made a note of the date, time, who was present and where he was. It was like second nature to him now. Everything about the job was. You either had to learn fast or sink even faster.

'Where's your dad, Lewis? Will he be joining us?'

At the mention of his dad's name, Lewis lifted his head, said, 'He's dead,' and then dropped it again. Like a robot being switched on and off. 'Twenty minutes ago. Before you got here. I… I was in the hospital bed. I…' Something caught in Lewis's throat and he coughed.

Jake placed his hand on the mattress. 'Take it easy. Take your time. Start from the beginning. What happened? I've got all day. I'm not going anywhere.'

Lewis swallowed hard. His child-sized Adam's apple convulsed up and down.

'Last night… Frank Graham. I was there. I was there when he died. But I had nothing to do with it. I watched *them* do it.'

Jake opened his mouth to ask who but decided against it. Now was the time to listen.

Lewis continued, 'I watched them kill him. Burn him alive. Just like they done Jermaine. I was there for both of them. A few days ago Frank asked me to start dealing some stuff for him, so I said yeah. He was paying better and he promised his product was better than anyone else's on the market. But last night, when we was on the way to pick up Frank, Henry and his boys, Jamal and Deshawn, were talking about something to do with Frank killing Danielle, Hen's sister. I overheard them say Frank killed her with the drugs he was selling on the streets, the drugs *I* was selling for him. And now I know why my buyer didn't turn up yesterday. He's probably dead too. And I killed him.'

'You don't know that, Lewis,' Jake said, feeling compelled to interrupt. 'Please, carry on. Tell me what else you know.'

Lewis stuttered before continuing.

'I… they… *we* picked Frank up. They kidnapped him out his flat at his estate, took him downstairs and then tied him to the lamp post. I think they found out I was shotting Frank's food, 'cause Reece, my best friend, held me at knifepoint so I could watch. But I think they was gonna take it one step further. I think they was gonna kill me. I managed to get away but nobody followed me. A bit later, I went back and recorded them kill and burn Frank to death on my phone. I ran home afterwards. I tried to get my dad to come with me. I wanted to get out of there. Move to another city. I started to pack, but that's the last thing I remember. I passed out.'

Nodding, understanding, taking it all in, Jake said, 'And you've been in here ever since?'

'I woke up a few hours ago. Dad was here. I told him everything that'd happened. But then Reece turned up.'

'Reece Enfield? Your friend?'

'He wanted to delete the video I had of them killing Jermaine. Jamal or Des must've told him to do it. They was the only ones who knew I had the video.'

'Did he delete the footage?'

Lewis nodded, and immediately Jake's hopes of hammering the final few nails into Henry Matheson's coffin disappeared.

'But then Jamal…' Lewis sniffed, coughed and wiped away the tear in his right eye. 'Jamal came, pretending he was one of you lot. He disappeared for a bit and made my dad a cup of coffee. Dad drank it, then a few seconds later, he died on the floor right there.'

Lewis pointed but Jake didn't look. His mind was struggling to comprehend what had taken place. He found himself staring at Lewis, absorbed by his story; he hadn't made a single note in the few minutes he'd been sat there.

'They musta gone into my house, spiked it with some of the drugs Frank asked me to sell for him.'

Now that explained why Reece had been at Lewis's house moments before him. If only he'd arrived a few minutes before, he could have caught Reece in the act, arrested him for the murder and possession of drugs, sent the little shitbag to prison where he deserved to rot. But more importantly, he could have saved a life. A tsunami of guilt rolled over him, drowning him.

He decided to keep that information to himself.

'Are you sure it was Jamal?' Jake asked. 'Are you sure it was him?'

Lewis nodded.

'And…' Jake swallowed before continuing, approaching the question with caution. 'Do you… What happened to the phone, Lewis? What did they do with it?'

Lewis reached under his pillow. Slowly he removed the iPhone from behind his back. As he held it aloft, the screen illuminated, revealing a screensaver of a photo of Lewis and his dad. 'I hid it when they moved me to this room.'

'You're very brave, Lewis.' Jake reached out for the phone and squeezed it. Finally. At long last. The evidence they needed.

'You said Reece deleted the video of Jermaine Gordon's death. Did he delete the video from last night?'

Lewis shook his head, a small, wry smile growing on his face. Jake respected the boy for finding the courage to smile amidst a devastating situation. 'Nobody knows I took it.'

Brave and a genius. Not bad, kid.

'Well done,' he said aloud and unlocked the phone. He scrolled through the pages and found the camera library. At the bottom of the screen was a black square. Jake selected it and rotated the phone so it would play full screen. And for the next five minutes, he watched Henry Matheson burn Frank Graham from a lamp post.

Got you now, you son of a bitch.

Except there was one small problem, a slight hurdle to overcome.

Jake didn't have Henry Matheson at all.

For starters, he didn't even know where the man was.

CHAPTER 75

A LONG NIGHT

'We need eyeballs around every single known location associated with Henry Matheson,' Jake shouted into the phone as he slipped the car into fourth gear. 'The Pit. His house. His mum's house. His sister's house. Jamal's. Deshawn's. Lewis's. Reece's. The Dunsfield Estate. The Hightower Estate. Handy Man Scrap Services. Everywhere. The slippery bastard is out there somewhere, and we need to find him before he disappears off the map. He's used to his twin towers, so he's not going to have ventured into the countryside. What about that list you said Ashley was putting together? We need their addresses too. Start there.'

Stephanie waited a while before responding. 'So you've realised you've got a team now then, have you?'

Typical.

Trying to get one up on him.

Yet he couldn't let her know she was right. 'What's that supposed to mean?'

'You've finally come to terms with the fact you can't do this on your own?'

Jake bit his tongue. In the past few days, as the investigation into Henry Matheson grew, he'd become less and less wary of Stephanie, Ashley and Brendan. They'd proven themselves capable of the job. Stephanie by coming with him to Aiden Coyne's house; Ashley for updating him on the missing belt buckle; and Brendan for finding the bottle warehouse in the first place, and as a result they'd earned his trust. Yet he couldn't let her know she was right. 'I don't think we have long to act. He knows the pressure's too hot for him right now, so he needs somewhere to lay low.'

'You'll have to be patient. Darryl hasn't seen the video yet. He doesn't even know it exists.'

Jake slammed on the brakes and dropped down to third gear. 'What difference does that make?'

'Procedure, Jake,' Stephanie replied, a strange calmness to her voice. 'You've already cut more than a few corners during this investigation. We can't afford any more. Not when it's something as vital as this.'

Corners were cut because no one else was prepared to listen.

'I suggest you come back to the office. Show us the video. And then we can discuss the next course of action. Get the necessary warrants.'

Jake gripped the steering wheel in frustration until his knuckles turned white and the leather pinched his skin.

'All right,' he said reluctantly. Ceding control was a foreign concept to him, one he hoped he wouldn't become too familiar with. 'You're a ball-buster, you know that.'

'So I've been told.'

'Can you hurry up and become the DCI so I can get away with more.'

Stephanie chuckled. The sound echoed around the car. 'You'd be so lucky. Now hurry up and get back so we can sort these warrants.'

'Why don't we deal with that after the fact?'

'Darryl doesn't want to risk it, Jake. This could be our one big chance to get Matheson off the streets. We need to be as prepared as possible. Especially if Haversham's going to represent him. We can't afford for him to find a hole in *anything*.'

'Is that you speaking or Darryl?'

'Both of us, if you must know.'

His current DCI and his future DCI.

Jake slowed as he approached a set of traffic lights. He'd spent all morning and afternoon with Lewis, comforting him, consoling him, ascertaining all the facts. Due to the sensitivity of the case, the individuals involved and the level of organisation already demonstrated against him, two armed officers had been stationed outside Lewis's room, keeping a constant watch over him. Jake was glad he was able to relax in the knowledge that, so long as they were there, Lewis was untouchable, safe. The only people who weren't safe were the idiotic drivers in front of him, holding him up. Jake slammed his fist on the horn.

'Where are you?' Stephanie asked as he navigated the junction.

'I'm five minutes away.'

Four minutes later, Jake arrived at Bow Green, entered the Major Incident Room, showed Darryl and the rest of the team the video, and then they reconvened around the desks in the middle. The atmosphere in the room was tense, the idea of Henry Matheson being arrested becoming more tangible with each passing minute.

They were so close, but they couldn't afford to slip up now.

Everything had to be immaculately planned.

Darryl stood at the head of the room, proud, dominant. If anyone chose to speak before him, he shot them down. If anyone breathed too loud, he let them know about it. In this moment, he was fastidious, and he immediately demanded attention from everyone in the room. It was the first time Jake had seen him in a situation like this, where the tyres met the track, and so far, he was impressed.

'I want uniform sent to every known location that Henry Matheson has ever spent time at,' Darryl said.

Exactly what I said.

'Someone of his stature and prominence isn't going to just disappear. He's got contacts. And his contacts have got contacts. So he's going to use them. Ashley, can you look into Rupert Haversham's associates as well? Stephanie, as media liaison officer, I want you to speak with whoever you can and get Matheson's face on the television somehow; the news, social media. Maybe even put him on a sky letter banner. Along with Jamal Bennet and Deshawn Aubrey. They might all be holed up together somewhere.' He held his index finger in the air and shook it fervently. 'One. That's all we need. One of them. One of the cards in the house and they all come crumbling down. If we find one of them, we'll find them all.'

'And what about the rest of us?' Jake asked, folding his arms.

Darryl lowered his finger. 'Call your loved ones. It's going to be a long night.'

CHAPTER 76

FROM THE TOP

If there was one thing Jake hated more than not being able to see his girls, it was telling them that he wouldn't be home to tuck them in. The sense of guilt he felt was profound. They were growing up so fast; Ellie was already beginning to talk, and he didn't want to miss anything. But he had a job to do.

The worst part of the call was telling Elizabeth. Sure, there were times when she was understanding, but there were also times when he could have lied and told her he was having an affair and she'd be less incensed. The only trouble was trying to gauge which reaction he was going to get. Sadly, the predeterminers were never clear cut, so he was entering himself into a lottery every time he had to break the news. This time round, however, she decided to lay it on him. Thick.

'Ever since you stood in front of that gun, Jake, we haven't seen you,' she'd said. 'Maisie's scared every time she goes out into the street now. Every time I take her to nursery, she thinks someone's going to come at her and start shooting. She's worried about you getting yourself killed. She's worried every time she sees a black car. She's a child, Jake.

She shouldn't be worried about things like this. She should be having a normal childhood. One where she doesn't wake up afraid that some madman's going to come at her daddy with a gun.'

Jake exhaled deeply after she'd repeatedly knifed him in the stomach with her words. They cut deep. That wasn't a life for a three-year-old. Nor was it a life for anyone. He'd become too reckless, too chauvinistic, too myopic in his endeavours. Oblivious to the pain and suffering he was causing them and his extended family, his colleagues.

His only explanation, his only justification for it was that it was his job and, like a dog after a bone, he was going to get what he wanted, regardless of the destruction caused.

Times of such deep reflection seldom came to him, and this realisation was one he was going to heed.

He hoped.

'Listen,' Jake began, 'Liz, I'm sorry. Maisie'll stop being scared one day. The nightmares will stop, and then they'll be replaced by something else. As long as I'm doing the job that I'm doing, you're always going to worry. It's natural. But it's something you signed up for. You knew what I was getting into from way back. You knew the risks. We both did. And we took a gamble. And I know it'll pay off in the end. I promise it won't be like this forever. When the kids are old enough, they'll understand, and they'll be much more resilient for it.'

'They'll resent you.'

Those three words felt like a knife to the throat, cutting off his air. She could have posed it as a question, a counterargument, but instead, she'd decided to twist and twist and twist until his oesophagus had become severed and tangled around the blade she held in her hand. She'd opted for the matter-of-fact approach, and as a result, it made him resent her just a little bit.

'Don't say things like that. Please. After tonight's done,

hopefully, we'll have one of the city's biggest criminals behind bars where he should be and no one will be hassling us.'

'And what then?'

'I come home, and then we can spend some time together. Quality time. As a family. We can watch a film maybe. *How to Train Your Dragon* has just come out on DVD. The kids might like that.'

A pause. Jake prepared himself for another tirade of home truths: that their troubles couldn't be fixed in a day, that it would take more than a movie and a takeaway to solve their issues, that he was going to need to be fully committed to working on their relationship.

Everything he knew, but nothing he'd had the courage to admit to himself.

Her reaction surprised him.

'Come on, Jake. Don't pretend it'll be for the kids. I know you secretly want to watch it more than they do.'

'Jay Baruchel's got the voice of an angel,' he replied.

Elizabeth chuckled, and the warm sound of her laughter brought a smile to his face. Just like that their little spat had been forgotten about. For now, they were back to normal.

'I'm sure we can find something else that's more suitable,' Jake said.

He finished the conversation, told her he loved her, sent his love to Ellie and Maisie, and then rang off. Then he exited the briefing room and returned to the MIR.

The room bustled with life and energy. The sound of keyboards tapping and computer fans whirring reverberated around the walls. Jake started to make a quick count of the bodies in the room and then swiftly gave up. There were too many. Easily thirty or forty people, all of whom had been roped in. Special constables, as well as civilian staff, were situated in one corner of the room, completing and filing the necessary paperwork. Even Lindsay Gray was offering a helping hand, though there was very little she could do operationally.

The entire operation had been upgraded to gold status.

Jake caught sight of Stephanie, who was leaning over Ashley's desk, pointing at her screen.

'What've I missed?'

'We've deployed uniform and a few plainclothes officers to Henry Matheson's most frequented addresses: his mum's, sister's, the estate. But we've had nothing come back since.'

'What about the warehouse in Tilbury?'

'Uniform are on the way now. They're going to scout the place out. It's out of hours at the moment, so nobody will be in.'

'I think one of us should be down there permanently. Just in case anyone else turns up.'

'Who are you expecting to turn up?'

Jake shrugged. 'Anyone that's of interest.' Which, in Jake's mind, extended as far as Martin Radcliffe and the band of corrupt officers he was working with.

'Fine,' Stephanie said, accepting defeat. 'It makes sense. Just because we didn't find anything the first time round doesn't mean we won't this time. I'll get it sorted.'

'Any other updates?' Jake asked.

'We're putting the word out about Matheson's disappearance and connection with the murders. If anyone finds him, they've got the number to call.'

'His mobile phone?'

'Put in the warrant for a trace already. Going to take some time for it to come through. Darryl's giving it to the judge himself. Look at that, the guv doing your dirty work for you.'

'And yours,' Jake said with a mischievous smirk.

He turned his attention to a scrap of paper on the desk. On it was a list of Henry Matheson's closest friends, family, acquaintances, anyone who'd ever been associated with him, and anyone who'd ever come across him, no matter how briefly. Compiled by Ashley and another DC, the list was almost the length of the page, front and back.

Jake observed the names.

'Who's working on this?'

'Uniform,' Ashley added, removing her glasses from her nose to speak to him. 'They're slowly working through it. Last update I had was that they were ten addresses in and there was no sign of them.'

'Starting from the top?'

Ashley confirmed they were.

'Lovely,' he said. 'I'll start at the bottom and work my way up.'

CHAPTER 77

ANY IDEAS?

The problem with getting older, he'd found, was that the hangovers lasted longer than usual. Last night's antics were still having an adverse effect on him, and no matter how much coffee he injected into his system to try and wake himself up, he still yawned continuously and felt a constant brain fog descending over him. The poison of cheap wine, a combination of both his and Lily's, was still coursing through his system, mocking him for getting as drunk as he had.

Henry stretched on the sofa beside her, reaching his arm around her. They were watching the latest nature documentary on the Discovery Channel. But Henry wasn't paying any attention. His mind was elsewhere. Lost in thoughts of Frank and Jermaine and Jamal and Deshawn and Reece and Lewis. Last night had been a flash in the pan, a miscalculated, illogical decision, rash. There'd been no forethought or planning, which meant it was left open to holes. With the jewellery heist, there'd been a plan, a backup, an escape route, a band of corrupt police officers helping them escape. But with this... nothing. And as he sat there, staring into the flickering pixels of the television screen, he wondered whether they'd covered every angle. Whether they'd done enough to ensure they weren't caught. Whether there was any need to involve The Cabal and get him to help cover it up.

And then Henry received the phone call he'd been dreading.

The screen illuminated, and the small device began vibrating on the coffee table in front of him, shaking violently on the surface. Rupert Haversham's name appeared just above the answer button.

Here we go. Henry lifted his arm away from Lily, placated her with a smile and exited the room. Stepping into the hallway and closing the door behind him, he answered the call.

'Yes?'

'You good to talk?' Rupert asked.

'Depends what you need to talk about.'

'Don't play dumb. You know what I'm speaking to you for. What the fuck happened?'

'We paid Frank a little visit,' Henry said as he moved down the hallway and into the kitchen by the front of the house.

'More than a visit from what I hear. It's all over the news. You nearly set the whole place alight.'

'Any mention of my name?'

'No mention of any names,' Rupert replied. 'It seems you're clean. For now.'

'Best news I've heard all day.'

'It should be. But now I'm about to give you the worst news you've had all day.'

Henry hesitated, held his breath.

'You need to get out of town for a while. A *long* while. Until I say it's OK to come back.'

'You been smoking something?' Henry asked. 'I ain't going nowhere. What makes you think I'm gonna leave the estate, everything behind, my *business*?'

'Because if you don't, sooner or later they'll find you. Your days are rapidly becoming numbered, Henry, especially with the amount of shit you keep pulling. I don't have the time or the resources to come up with a solid enough defence case for you.'

Henry scoffed. 'You're the best in the business. What's The Cabal paying you for? What am *I* paying you for?'

'The Cabal and I go way back. He doesn't need to pay me for anything. You, on the other hand, are getting out of control. You're drawing too much attention to yourself.'

'Is that coming from The Cabal or Helen? I got the feeling that woman didn't like me.'

'Neither,' Rupert responded. 'It's coming from *me*. You'll be pleased to know that Helen and Martin and her team arrested Gordon's boys this morning. They're charging them with the robbery and the heist murder. So that's one less thing for you to worry about.'

'See, there's a solution for everything.'

'You've got all these people looking out for you, making sure you stay out of where you deserve to be.'

'And…?'

'You thank them by crucifying another man on a lamp post?'

Henry didn't dignify that with a response.

'The police aren't going to stop there, Henry,' Rupert continued. 'They're still going to come for you. Which is why I need you to tell me what happened last night. Is there anyone who saw Deshawn or Jamal?'

Henry moved to the other end of the kitchen, furthest away from the door, and rested against the oven. 'It's been sorted. We won't have any whistle-blowers getting their lungs full.'

'Are you sure?'

'Yes.' He hoped.

'I'd still like to know what happened.'

Henry shook his head. He wasn't about to be bullied by Rupert. Especially after the way he'd just been spoken to. Who did Rupert think he was?

'It's sorted,' Henry told him. 'I've dealt with it.'

Rupert sighed down the phone. 'You know, Henry,' he began, and already Henry knew he wasn't going to like what he was about to hear. 'You know, one day I won't be there, and that'll be the day you need me most. You already had a taste of that when I was on holiday. But the more you tell me now, the better I can help you. The less you decide to tell me, the less I'll *want* to help. I don't owe you any loyalty. I don't owe anyone any loyalty. There will be more kings of the criminal underworld, just like yourself, but there won't be anyone like me. At least, not for a long while.'

'Are you threatening me, Rupert?'

'No. I'm helping you or *trying to*, at least. If you want to misconstrue that as a threat then so be it. But if you don't tell me what happened, I can't best prepare a case for you. And I might have to call it a day on our relationship.'

Someone's obviously had their spinach this morning and grown a pair.

'You'd do that?' Henry asked. 'Do you think that's wise? You've seen what happened to Jermaine and Frank, right? So you know what I'm capable of. You want the same to happen to you, to your family?'

'Now who's makings threats?' Rupert replied. 'The one thing you've failed to consider, Henry, is the amount of knowledge I possess. All those times I've had to bail you out, I've got a record. Locked up in storage somewhere, as well as what I'm capable of keeping in my head. You want to cross me like that, I leak everything to the press. And police.'

'Smart,' Henry retorted. He didn't believe for a second that Rupert would make good on his threats. They were empty; they always were. 'But there's one thing *you've* failed to remember, Rupert: you're not a fucking saint in all this either. The moment you send that information to the police, providing Helen or someone else doesn't intercept it first, you're convicting yourself of perverting the course of justice.'

'If the information falls into the wrong hands, yes. But in the right hands… well…'

The right hands? Whose hands? Henry had lost count of the number of bent coppers on The Cabal's payroll. They were all as straight as a ruler until they saw a sum large enough, and a taste of the life they could live, to convince them otherwise.

All except one.

'Tanner?' Henry said. He heard a sound coming from the living room that distracted him momentarily.

'There's nobody better. He's the one who could see it through to the bitter end.'

'Not if I get to him first,' Henry said instinctively, only partly conscious of what he'd said. And then his attention turned back to the conversation. 'Why would you want to do that anyway? I mean, morally. Ethically. The man stands against us in every aspect. If you tell him everything then he's won.'

Silence.

Neither of them wanted Jake Tanner to know too much. It would shatter their careers and their lives as well as the lives of those working for them. And they would undoubtedly be looking at a lifetime behind bars. Jake Tanner was the epitome of the wrong hands, and if certain information fell into them, there was no knowing how far he'd take it.

'Where do we go from here?' Rupert asked eventually. There was reluctance in his voice, and Henry admired him for it, respected him even.

'We carry on as usual. Like nothing's happened.' Henry hesitated to swallow. 'You don't know anything about what happened last night because you don't need to. And you're not going to find out. It's been taken care of. And that's all anyone needs to know. And if the time comes, I'll call on you and together we'll sort the problem out. Whatever it may be. This is it, Rupert, there won't be no more killings like that. At least not in the near future.'

'Don't say things you can't guarantee, mate.'

Mate. That word. He hated it. Especially when it was coming from someone like Rupert. A business partner. An associate. Someone who had no right to call him friend. Henry knew next to nothing about the man, except for the fact that he had two daughters and a smoking-hot wife, and he intended on keeping it that way.

Henry asked, 'Is that everything?'

'For now. I'll be in touch if I need you.'

Henry rang off, feeling aggrieved. The conversation hadn't gone the way he'd expected.

Just as he was about to pocket the phone, the device vibrated again. Perhaps it was Rupert calling to apologise. Wrong. It was a notification from The Cabal.

Henry looked at the screen and unlocked the phone with his finger. It was a *Kingdom of Empires* notification. He opened the app, tapped the message notification in the top-right corner and read:

Get out. They're coming for you. Too late for Helen or Martin to save you.

The last sentence hit him. In the past, he'd been able to rely on Liam or Pete or Drew to get him out of difficult situations. But now, the people whose job it was to keep him out of prison couldn't even do what they were supposed to. What was happening? Henry remembered a time when the bent coppers in the Metropolitan Police were able to protect anyone, keep anyone out of a life behind bars. Now they were beginning to crumble, their infrastructure falling to its knees.

And it was all thanks to one man.

Jake fucking Tanner.

As he stood there, staring at the screen, the kitchen door opened.

'Everything all right?' Lily asked. 'I couldn't hear anything and thought you might've collapsed or something.'

'I have to go.' Henry started towards the door. 'I'm sorry.'

'That's...' She stepped aside to let him pass. 'That's OK. Where?'

Henry tore through the hallway and stopped at the foot of the stairs. His mind wasn't thinking properly, cohesively. He needed to get out of there. But to where? With what? And with whom?

He frisked his pockets, searching for his valuables. Phone. Wallet. And his keys. He had them all.

'Where are you gonna go?' Lily asked again.

Henry stared into her eyes blankly. 'I honestly don't know. You got any ideas?'

CHAPTER 78

THE TEA

Henry had no idea where he was. Except that he was in a house. A friend's house. One of Lily's. She'd dropped him round there, and after a brief discussion, followed by their first-ever argument as a couple, she'd left him alone with the friend.

The friend, whose name he'd learnt was Zara, was currently in the kitchen, making him a cup of tea, even though he'd politely refused and told her he detested the taste. Give him a Coke or a beer. But not tea. It made him need a piss every ten minutes, five if he'd already had a glass of water. It wasn't conducive to a productive day in any way.

He was in the living room, swallowed between the cushions of Zara's black faux-leather sofa. In the corner of the room, the television played, but he paid no attention. Instead, he scanned his surroundings, taking in the rows of books and photo frames sitting on the bookshelf. The mirror hanging on the wall above his head. The forest of houseplants oxygenating the room. The patio doors that led to the small, well-kept, square garden outside.

His gaze returned to the bookshelf. Something had caught his eye. A photo. Henry struggled out of the sofa, shuffled towards it and picked up the picture frame. Smiling up at him were Zara and her son. Next to them in the photo was Mickey Mouse, the Disneyland castle towering in the background. The young boy was no more than ten, eleven at the very most, and the inscription on the bottom left dated the picture from two years ago. Which meant her son was approximately twelve or thirteen. A ripe age. Turning into a man. Building his confidence in the world, becoming increasingly aware of the way things work. School, class, social structures. Drugs, money, women. The video games on the floor – *Call of Duty, Grand Theft Auto* – suggested he already had a foothold in the Game of Life.

The thought made him turn round to see if Zara was standing behind him. She wasn't. She was still making the tea. Somehow. He was no expert, but it didn't take ten minutes to boil a kettle, did it?

Ignoring that thought, he turned his attention back to the young boy. Wondered whether perhaps he'd like to make some money. With Lewis out of the equation, Henry could do with some more youngers around the estate to help him, take over some of the business so he could stay well away from it for the time being. The more bodies Henry had between himself and Jake Tanner, and the rest of the police, the better. The youngers were the foot soldiers, the front-line heroes sent into war to be decimated and obliterated on the first row of—

'Here you are,' Zara said, interrupting his thoughts, carrying a mug in each hand.

Finally. The tea.

Henry accepted the drink and thanked her. Zara sat on the armchair beside him and grabbed the remote. After setting the photo frame back on the bookshelf, Henry returned to the middle of the sofa.

As he watched Zara flick endlessly through the channels, trying to find something to numb the silence, his surroundings suddenly conjured images of a family life he'd never had. A once-loving wife who now resented him. A disobedient adolescent who spent all his time locked in his bedroom playing video games. A life of mundanity and banality sitting in front of the box, wasting away six inches deep in the sofa. It was an alien concept to Henry, and it scared the fuck out of him.

'Lily tells me you spent the night together last night.'

Henry took a sip of tea to delay having to answer. Why did he feel like he was about to be berated and interrogated by a woman he'd never met about a relationship that had only just started?

'Yeah, that's right,' he responded.

'She's been through a lot, that girl. She's got a kind heart on her too. Big one. Will do anything for anyone. I mean, look what she's done for you now.'

Sent me into the lion's den for a shredding, to test my boyfriend-iness.

'And I'm grateful for it,' Henry said, keeping the stubbornness out of his voice.

'You should be. I'm doing *her* a favour, not you. This is only temporary while I try and find you somewhere more permanent. I know who you are, and I don't want you staying anywhere near my son. Do you understand?'

He did understand. But that didn't necessarily mean he was going to listen.

'Where is he, by the—'

'No. We're not talking about him. I don't want you knowing anything about him.'

Surprised, Henry held his hands in the air in surrender. 'Of course,' he said reluctantly. 'This is your house. Your rules.'

'If I had it my way, as soon as I closed the door on Lily, I would have let you go off on your own. Into the wild. Let whatever you deserve come and find you.'

Henry took another sip. 'If you really wanted that then you would have already called the police by now.'

As he finished speaking, the doorbell rang.

CHAPTER 79

THE WORDS

Jake held his breath, waited for the door to number forty-nine to open. Standing beside him were two uniformed officers, poised, tensed, one hand placed on their hips, the other curled into a ball. A few minutes after leaving Bow Green, he and the officers that had been assigned to accompany him, courtesy of Stephanie's dubiousness, had received a tip-off. That Henry Matheson, in all his criminal glory, was in number forty-nine. Alone. With a mother and her son.

Reinforcements were on their way, but Jake had made an executive decision, even though he was in no position to do so, to exact the arrest, and catch Henry when he was least expecting it and at his most vulnerable.

Their one opportunity to catch him and the task fell to Jake.

No pressure.

A few seconds later he heard the sound of footsteps hurrying towards him, followed by a brief scream. Jake glanced at the officers, indicating that they should brace themselves.

None of them knew what was on the other side of that door. They had to be prepared for anything.

Jake tensed his body, took a step back.

The door crashed open, drowning them in light, momentarily blinding them. A woman appeared in front of them, hobbling. Her jumper had been pulled off her shoulder, and her eyes were wild.

'Quick!' she screamed. 'Quick! He's getting away. He's going through the back door!'

Jake peered round the woman. At the end of the hallway was the living room. Jake saw a black faux-leather sofa, with a mug tipped over on the carpet. Beyond that was a set of patio doors that led into the garden. Bounding through them was the figure of a man on the run.

At the sight of it, Jake leapt into the house, shoving the woman aside accidentally.

'Go round the back!' he called to the officers.

This was it. Jake's chance to catch Henry Matheson. He was pumped and ready, and he wasn't going to let anything get in his way.

He tore through the hallway, into the living room, and rounded the sofa, slipping on the liquid. He staggered slightly but remained on his feet; nothing was going to stop him.

The patio doors were open. In the garden, the motion-sensitive lights had activated, illuminating Henry Matheson in a cage of near broad daylight. He looked like a zebra in his black-and-white-striped tracksuit.

'Henry!' Jake bellowed, his voice splitting the still air. 'Henry!' Still no response. 'Henry! Stop right there. It's over!'

Henry continued regardless towards the end of the garden. Reaching high into the air, he grabbed the top of the fence and started clambering over the slats, the soles of his feet desperately searching for purchase.

'Henry!' Jake gave one last warning shot.

After that, game on.

Henry had made his decision. And so had Jake: by any means necessary.

Jake sprinted across the garden towards to the fence panel, hopping over an overturned BMX. Henry's foot dangled over the lip of the fence briefly before disappearing. Too late.

A second behind.

Retreating from the wooden panel, Jake prepared himself to vault the fence.

Counted down in his head.

Three.

Two.

One.

He charged. Leapt.

His hands caught the top of the panel, splinters pricking his skin, and using the momentum behind him, he hauled himself over. By the time he was on the other side, Henry had already crossed the road and was heading left, up another street. To his right, the two uniformed officers appeared, their baggy police vests arriving two seconds behind them.

Jake gave chase again, paying little attention to his colleagues. He was carrying a much lighter load than them.

Henry made a right turn down another street, skipping past a lamp post. In the distance, cars and buses sped from left to right and right to left. Jake had never been to Ilford before, and he was becoming disorientated the further he ventured from the security of the car. In the back of his mind, he mapped out where he'd been and where he was going.

'Henry!' Jake called, letting the other man know that they were still coming after him.

They reached the end of the road, tore through a small alleyway and emerged at a major junction. Cars streamed past across two lanes of traffic. Buses. Taxis. Cyclists. Vans.

But Henry continued sprinting as if he were made of rubber. Jake skidded to an abrupt halt, images of his family immediately coming to the forefront of his mind as he drank in the dangers of the highway. He didn't want to die. And he wasn't about to risk his life to catch the drug kingpin.

Fortunately, he didn't have to.

As Henry jumped into the second lane of traffic, some five metres away from Jake and the officers, a silver Renault Clio crashed into him. The man's body rolled up and over the roof, then onto the tarmac beneath, his limbs splayed out like a rag doll. The windscreen shattered upon impact, and the driver skidded to a stop a few feet from where Henry had landed.

Jake hurried over. Henry was lying on his back, clutching his stomach, wincing in pain. His tracksuit was dirtied and ruined, but there were no bloodstains; the only blood Jake could see was a trickle of crimson running down the side of his head.

Jake bent down by his side, told him to relax, calm down, breathe slowly, in and out, in, out, that there was nothing to worry about because he was first aid trained, that he was in good hands.

After unzipping his coat and inspecting Henry's stomach, Jake determined there were no major injuries visible. But that didn't mean there was nothing internal. Rapidly spreading through him. A silent killer.

Jake ordered the uniformed officers to call for an ambulance. One of them made the call, while the other kept the traffic at bay. Within a few moments, a crowd of onlookers had formed, and several mobile phones were pointed at Jake, documenting the scene. Possibly uploading it to social media while he protected a man who didn't even deserve it.

That was something that had always baffled Jake: the

extent to which emergency responders, himself included, would go in order to protect and save the lives of individuals who didn't deserve it; who, given the opportunity, wouldn't have done the same if the shoe was on the other foot. That they didn't just leave them to die, as payment for their previous crimes. But then he realised that was the fundamental difference between himself and the people he sought to catch. That, no matter what they'd done, he believed they still deserved to live, to have a life, a career, a family, a chance. Because it was their right.

Four minutes later, the ambulance arrived, and two paramedics disembarked, swiftly attending to Henry and putting him in the back of the van.

As he watched them fasten Henry in the vehicle, Jake's emotions were bittersweet. Yes, they finally had him, but now his imminent hospitalisation would delay and prolong the investigation and the interview process; nobody could touch him unless he'd been given the all-clear by a medical professional.

Which meant more waiting, more time.

But Jake wasn't going to make it that easy for him.

'I'm going with him,' he said to the paramedic, hopping into the back of the van before she could protest.

As the cabin swayed from side to side, Jake leant forward, looked into Henry's dark eyes and said the words he'd been waiting a long time to say: 'Henry Matheson, I am arresting you for the murders of Jermaine Gordon and Frank Graham. You do not have to say anything, but it may harm your defence if you do not mention when questioned something which you later rely on in court. Anything you do say may be given in evidence.'

| PART 6 |

CHAPTER 80

NO COMMENT

It was four a.m., and after hours of painfully waiting, Henry Matheson had finally been discharged from hospital and sent to the station with a series of broken ribs and a sprained shoulder. Injuries far less serious than he deserved, Jake thought.

When Henry had arrived at the station, checking in at the custody suite, he'd been informed of his right to obtain legal advice. To no one's surprise, he'd asked for Rupert Haversham's services, but after several attempts, the custody officer had been unsuccessful in contacting the solicitor, and was instead instructed to appoint free legal advice courtesy of the Criminal Defence Service.

What a fall from grace. One second you were cock of the walk on the top floor of your estate, the next you were at the bottom of the shit pile like everyone else.

Kevin Rowney was an idiotic-looking man, someone who looked as though he could barely tie his own shoelace let alone successfully inform someone when to talk and when not to. Dressed in a scruffy light-pink shirt that looked as if it hadn't been washed for weeks, he stood with his shoulders slumped and his back curved. His collar was undone, and his black tie hung to one side like a flag flying listlessly in the wind. Around his crotch, the end of his belt dangled loosely, phallically, and in one hand, he carried a bottle of water and in the other a rucksack, like a schoolchild ready for the first day of a new term. On the face of it, Jake and Brendan seemed in for an easy ride.

The four of them entered the interview room. It was artificially lit, airy and warm. The table was in the middle, propped against one side wall, with a tape recorder on top. There was also a video recorder in the top corner of the room, over Jake's right shoulder.

Between them, it had been decided that Jake would lead the interview and Brendan would assist where necessary. Having been fast-tracked through the ranks to DS, Brendan didn't have as much interview experience as Jake so was happy to let him take the reins.

'Interview commenced at four twenty-three a.m. at Bow Green Station, Stratford. Present in the room is DC Jake Tanner, DS Brendan Lafferty, Henry Matheson and his solicitor, Kevin Rowney. Please could you state your names for the tape.'

One by one, they went round the room.

'Henry Matheson,' Jake continued, 'I'd just like to remind you that you are under caution and that you do not have to say anything, but it may harm your defence if you do not mention when questioned something which you later rely on in court. Anything you do say may be given in evidence. You have already exercised your right to legal assistance, and at the custody desk, you waived your right to make a phone call.

'I'd also like to remind you that you are being charged with the following counts.' He grabbed a piece of paper that contained the list of associated offences. 'Two counts of premeditated murder. Conspiracy to commit murder. Money laundering. The dealing and supply of class A, B and C drugs. Perverting the course of justice. And, finally, carrying an offensive weapon. There are other things we'd like to charge you with, and further charges may follow once our ongoing investigations are completed.'

Jake took a moment to catch his breath, savour the moment, digest and soak up the atmosphere after speaking the words he'd never thought he'd say, followed by the blank expression on Henry's face as he was forced to listen to them.

Once he was satisfied that the pause was enough to make Henry shift uncomfortably a little more, Jake rested his arms on the table and continued. 'We'd like you to corroborate things, give us a better understanding of what took place.'

'If you're so certain I done them, what do you need me for?'

'The very reason I just stated. But remember you don't have to say anything if you think it will harm your defence.'

'You've told me enough times.'

'Just want to make sure the message is crystal clear, like a diamond.'

At the mention of the last word, Jake noticed a sudden change in Henry's expression. Small, almost minute, but present nonetheless. The flick of an eyebrow unearthed by the allusion to the jewellery heist the other day.

Gotcha.

'There's no need to belittle my client, Detective,' Kevin said, reaching across the table, revealing a hairy, almost bearlike forearm. 'He's aware of his rights and doesn't need to be told every five seconds. We've discussed this at length.'

'Perfect. Then I think we're in a position to begin, don't you?'

Jake didn't bother waiting for anyone to respond. He

didn't care whether they were ready or not. It had been a long night, and he was tired. There was only so much the coffee in his system could do at this time of day.

'I'd like to start with the first item on the evidence list.'

Jake turned his attention to the desk. In front of him was a pile of paper, a folder and, beneath it all, a tablet. Jake reached for the tablet, unlocked the device and opened the image library. He loaded the latest file in there and spun the device across the table so that it faced Henry and Kevin.

Intrigued, Henry tilted forward. 'You guys share that one between all of you? Bet you must fight over it a lot. Me and my boys, we have one each.'

'Oh yeah, how'd you afford to pay for those?' Jake raised his eyebrows.

'Some secrets stay with us until we die.'

'Let's hope that's not the case for all of them, eh,' Jake continued, moving the conversation along as quickly as possible. 'As I was saying, the evidence here was given to us a few hours ago and has been forensically examined. I'm going to play it now.'

Jake tapped the play button.

The video started.

At first, there was black as Lewis fumbled the camera into position, and then it remained still. Light dominated the video. In the centre of the screen was Frank Graham, dangling from the lamp post. Before him, Henry, holding a lighter, hovering it beneath Frank's foot. To his right were Jamal and Deshawn suspending Frank from the lamp post. On the ground was a girl, cowering, screaming, pinned to the concrete. And then, in the next frame, the dangling man's shoe was aflame. Within seconds his body was a furious fireball, illuminating the square and the faces of those caught in the shot.

Jake paused the video. He glanced up and inspected

Henry's face: the man's eyes were wide and the colour had drained from his cheeks. His head turned towards his solicitor, but he said nothing.

'Do you know who that man in the video is?' Jake asked. 'That's you, isn't it?'

Kevin nodded at Henry, silently telling him what to do.

'No comment,' Henry said, easing into his chair and folding his arms.

Jake cursed himself. He'd played his trump card too early and shown his hand before he'd even had a chance to know what he was up against. He knew that, from here on out, it would be an uphill struggle to get Henry to say anything other than 'no comment'.

'Are you able to identify anyone in this video? No? What about the man that's being burnt alive, do you recognise him? The two guys beside you? Or what about the young boy who's holding a girl at knifepoint on the ground? Who's he, Henry? And where is that young girl? According to our investigations, nobody's seen her since she was last with you and the rest of your gang.' Jake paused a beat, preparing himself to deliver a powerful right hook. 'Are you responsible for what's happened to her as well? Are you?'

'Detective!' snapped Kevin, bringing his sweaty frame into Jake's eyeline. 'Please stop harassing my client like this. Quite frankly I find your attitude abhorrent and vindictive. This is beginning to feel like a bullying session. Either ask him a proper question or move on.'

A bullying session? As though the man who murdered one and ordered the killing of another didn't deserve it. The world really was one fucked up place.

He deserves everything he gets.

Breathing heavily, allowing his blood to calm, Jake tilted his head towards the suspect. 'Henry… anything to add?'

'No comment.'

Fine. So that was the way it was to be.

CHAPTER 81

CONSEQUENCES

The mobile phone rang, disturbing him from his sleep. In the years he'd been doing the job, answering the early morning phone calls had never grown any easier, especially as his already-sleep-deprived body often struggled to dip its toes into the lagoon of unconsciousness in the first place. Sleep was a commodity for him, and his pattern was almightily fucked as a result of his career choice. Rupert Haversham rolled over, stretched his arms and legs across the empty double bed and reached for the phone.

'Hello?' he answered with his eyes still closed.

'Rupert?'

The Cabal's voice shocked him awake.

'Are you free to talk?'

'Yeah. Karen's on one of her girls' nights. What's the matter?' He swung his legs over the side of the bed, picked up his dressing gown from the chair in front of him, where he usually liked to read before going to bed, and donned it.

'You need to get yourself down to Bow Green.'

'Why?' he asked, pretending he hadn't already seen the

four missed calls from the police station.

'It's happened.'

'Matheson's day of reckoning?' Rupert asked as he tied the robe around his body, juggling the phone between his hands.

There was a long pause.

'You knew this would happen?' The Cabal asked.

Rupert shrugged, even though he knew The Cabal couldn't see. 'I warned him to be careful. He wasn't. This is what happens.'

'What are you talking about?'

'I tried to warn him. Told him to tell me what had happened to Frank Graham so that I could help. But he wouldn't. Instead, he said there was nothing to worry about. Nothing that I needed to worry myself over. So I'm not.'

'He needs you there with him, defending him now!'

A flash of anger coming from The Cabal, the first time he'd ever heard such emotion in the man's voice.

'I know,' Rupert said, getting comfortable in his chair, enjoying this rather sadistically. 'I've received all the calls from the police station. They've been trying to get hold of me for hours. It's been ringing non-stop.'

'Excuse me? He asked for you and you turned him down?'

'I warned him…'

'Who's paying you? What are they paying you? You know I can—'

'It's not about the money anymore, D. It's about the respect. He pays me none. And I've had enough of it. He uses me only when he needs me.'

'Because that's your fucking job!'

'But he doesn't make it any easier for me. You'd have thought that he'd have learnt how to cover his tracks a little better by now. He's been doing this for so long, he should

462

know the ins and outs of it. The loopholes I can get him through. But there are only so many situations that I can bail him out of. Inevitably, there was going to be one where it was too big, too grand for even me to overcome. And this is it.'

Henry Matheson's day of reckoning.

'Is this it for him?' The emotion in The Cabal's voice had changed from anger to anguish.

'From what my sources are telling me, yes. I've got one of my good friends in there with him. Apparently, there's video footage of him killing Graham. They've also got another video of three of his right-hand men murdering Jermaine. Their digital forensics unit somehow managed to retrieve the video after it was deleted. So they're all doubly fucked.'

'Idiot.' The Cabal sighed. 'I told him to go nowhere near Graham.'

'Yeah, but when you're in front of the man who's just killed your sister, you'll do whatever your anger tells you to do, no matter the outcome.'

The Cabal hesitated again. It was a thoughtful silence. 'Out of ten?'

'The likelihood he'll get out?'

'Yeah.'

'One,' Rupert replied without hesitation. It was an arbitrary number, a guess, with no guarantee that it would be as bad as that. 'With the evidence they've got against him, he's looking at life. And without me as his solicitor, they'll try and get him for everything else as well.'

'Including the heist?'

There was a sudden change in The Cabal's voice. From anger to anguish to detachment. As if there was no emotion left. All care and affection towards Henry Matheson had gone. Now it was all about business.

'I thought everything'd been tidied away?' Rupert asked.

'I... I'll have to find out.'

'That's one loose end that could seriously complicate everything you've got going on. If Helen and Martin haven't done their jobs properly, then you're going to have a problem.'

'We, Rupert. *We're* going to have a problem. You're involved with this just as much as everyone else is.'

'Yes. But I can only help after the fact. There's nothing I can do now, except instruct you guys on how to proceed.'

'Then fucking tell us instead of giving me your riddle shit and keeping your dick out of trouble.'

Rupert sighed. Rupert the oracle. Rupert the superhero. Rupert the one with all the answers. Coming to the rescue.

'My recommendation would be to speak with Martin and Helen first,' he said, making no effort to hide the disdain in his voice. 'Find out where they're up to, what they've done, what they haven't. Then come back to me. Until then, I'm going back to sleep.'

As Rupert hung up and threw the phone down onto the bed, a seed of doubt crept into his mind and made him wonder whether he'd done everything that was required of him. Whether he'd done everything possible to protect The Cabal, Henry, their mutual interests. Because if he hadn't, and he'd left them vulnerable in any way, then he knew the consequences.

Everyone working for The Cabal did.

CHAPTER 82

WE NO LONGER THANK YOU FOR YOUR SERVICE

The early morning sunrise illuminated the Cosgrove Estate's towers a lighter shade of grey, and brilliant balls of light reflected off the windows, turning them into spires of cat's eyes reaching into the sky. The estate was sleeping, and there was an air of solemnity around the place. As if everyone inside felt lost, alone and without a thought of their own now their great leader was missing.

Jake stepped out of the car, brushing his jacket down. He closed the door behind him and glanced at Brendan on the other side.

The past few hours had been unkind to them both. Henry Matheson was in a cell, currently getting his eight hours of uninterrupted rest. This time was usually spent conducting follow-up interviews, investigating new lines of enquiry following the evidence they'd gleaned from interview but the problem was Henry hadn't said a word. He'd been tight-lipped about everything. No names. No dates. No locations. No events. Simply replying with 'no comment' to every question that was thrown his way.

Everyone in that interview room knew Henry Matheson was going down for a long time, so it was a matter of damage limitation. The less he answered, the less he incriminated himself.

All that remained now, for Jake and the rest of the team, was to build an arsenal of evidence against him. At the top of that list was finding Jamal and Deshawn, the two associates wanted in connection with Jermaine Gordon and Frank Graham's murders. But there was an ulterior motive for Jake too. If he and Brendan also managed to find the jewels he believed were hiding in the estate somewhere then not only would they have the people responsible in custody, they'd also be able to prove that Martin Radcliffe had arrested the wrong individuals and that he was part of a new wave of corrupt officers; more dangerous, more deeply involved, less afraid to get caught and suffer the consequences.

'You ready?' Brendan asked, breaking Jake from his thoughts.

'Yeah,' he replied. 'You sure we don't need backup for this? You know what some of these guys carry, right?'

'They won't do anything. Not when they haven't got Matheson around, telling them what to do.' Brendan sounded sure of himself and, with Jake trying this new exercise where he trusted his team, he decided to let him be. 'You still reckon they're here?'

'Only one way to find out.'

They set off, heading towards the centre of The Pit, without much of a game plan in mind. Their resources were stretched thin – across the entire borough, with half of the team searching through the remaining addresses of Henry's known associates – and they were the only ones who could be spared. It was a long shot, finding either of Henry's right-hand men in the estate, but it was worth a look. Sometimes the obvious choices, the ones staring you in the face, were the best ones.

On the way into the estate, Jake caught sight of Lewis Coyne's house. Since the young boy's hospitalisation and his father's death, Lewis's house had been designated a crime scene. But, like all things done in the Cosgrove Estate, forensic investigations had been completed in a matter of hours, and now all that remained was a police tape stretched around the perimeter of the property and a disinterested uniformed officer hovering by the front door.

Further into the estate, something in the corner of the square caught Jake's eye. The rundown and decrepit off-licence, tucked away and forgotten about like government contract cronyism. Boarded up, abandoned, covered in graffiti. The one place they hadn't thought to look in their haste the last time they'd been there.

He tapped Brendan on the shoulder. 'Is it just me or is it the first time you're noticing that?'

'You're right. I don't think anyone's bothered to look in there, you know.'

Jake started off towards the derelict shop, donning a pair of forensic gloves as he went. The shop connected the south high-rise and the west low-rise buildings, and a small alleyway that burrowed through the tower block led to the outskirts of the estate. The shop looked as though it hadn't been used in a long time. Relics of its former owner's life still hung from the walls like lonely gravestones, and bars around the windows dangled loosely from the nails that had been buried into the brick. The words SHREE NEWS were plastered across the fascia, reminding people of how proud the owner had once been.

The entrance to the shop was on the other side of the low-rise, so passers-by and residents from afar could shop without having to set foot inside The Pit. Jake slowed to a stop by a fire exit in the middle of the underpass.

To his surprise, the door wasn't quite closed, a small piece of debris jammed between it and the frame, and he pulled it open, glancing at Brendan. Bemused. Shocked.

The shop was dark, save for the light that had just flooded in, and wasn't deserted at all. The complete opposite. The middle shelves had been cleared out and replaced by row upon row of tables and desks. Around the perimeter of the room, old merchandising units and shelves remained, but with a different type of product adorning them: hundreds of soft drink bottles. All empty, all at varying angles, all waiting to be filled with class A drugs.

Henry Matheson's coveted production line. Right in the heart of the estate. The most obvious possible place it could be. Where he had complete control over it.

'Find a light switch,' Jake whispered as he stepped into the shop.

A few seconds later, the shop illuminated, the ancient lights overhead flickering into life. Jake moved deeper into the space then froze, his muscles tautening.

In the far-right corner of the room, disorientated and half-awake, was Deshawn Aubrey – or Des, as he was colloquially known. Henry's second in command. Senior gangland member, drug dealer, murderer. Half-asleep yet appearing wired at the same time, as though he hadn't slept for three weeks and the copious amounts of drugs in his system were making sure the rest of his body didn't notice or catch up with him. His hair was dishevelled and, as he gradually became aware of his surroundings, he brushed it back and rubbed the sleep from his eyes.

Jake slowly turned his head towards Brendan, exchanged a nod with the Irishman and looked back at Des.

Because he was closest to the door, Jake took a step backwards and carefully eased his way out of the shop. Once outside, he hid round the corner of the door and waited for the signal.

A moment later, Brendan cleared his throat.

Deshawn screamed in surprise. Then came the sound of a table overturning, followed by chairs, then bottles spilling to the floor, scattering across the concrete. The sound of a struggle.

And then he received the call.

'Jake, now!'

Without hesitating, Jake stepped in front of the doorway. Deshawn's massive frame collided into him at full speed, knocking both of them to the ground and punching the wind from Jake's stomach. In an instant, Brendan was on them, heaving Deshawn from Jake. Lifting himself to his feet, Jake grappled the man and pinned him to the ground, Brendan and Jake straddling either side of the dazed giant. While he was incapacitated, Brendan arrested him and explained his rights.

As they carried him to the car, Jake's phone started to vibrate. He pulled the device out of his pocket and stared at the screen. Unknown number. Eyeing it, he slowed to a halt and contemplated answering it. Usually, he avoided calls from people he didn't know or numbers he didn't recognise. But experience on the job had told him that it was better to answer than not.

'Hey,' he began, addressing Brendan, 'I gotta take this quickly. Get him in the car and I'll be with you in a second.'

Brendan nodded in response.

Jake remained where he was and waited until Brendan was out of earshot before he answered.

'Hello?'

'You ever hear the story about the boy who cried wolf?' a voice asked him. The sound was distorted, muffled, and there was nothing in the background Jake could use to identify a potential location.

'Who is this?'

'It didn't end well for him,' the voice continued. 'And I can think of a few other examples right now. Danika. Liam. Drew… Dare I go on?'

'If you've got the time…'

There was a long silence. Jake waited. Listened.

'The rules in this one are simple, Jake Tanner,' the voice said. 'Destroy the phone evidence and stop pursuing everyone else in the E11, then there will be no need for me to harm anyone you hold dear to you. Learn from your mistakes. There's still time.'

'Sorry,' Jake said, staring at Deshawn as Brendan ducked his head into the police car. 'It's too late for that.'

'Then you've made life very difficult for yourself. We no longer thank you for your silence.'

CHAPTER 83

TRIGGER

Jake forced the phone call to the back of his mind as he and Brendan booked in Deshawn at the custody suite. As soon as they took his fingerprints, his record instantly appeared on the PNC. Most of the charges were for theft and burglary and arson and anti-social behaviour from when he was a minor. But the biggest concern Jake had was about Deshawn's health and well-being. He was still intoxicated, whatever he'd taken the night before still coursing through his body, so it wasn't until he'd confirmed he was fine and the custody officer had deemed him fit for interview, that Jake was able to relax. The decision was out of his hands, so no repercussions would follow and there was no need to feel guilty if anything happened to him.

An hour later, Deshawn was sitting in an interview room with a free legal advisor present. Kevin Rowney. Again. Back for round two because Rupert Haversham still wasn't answering any calls.

'You know,' Jake began after completing the formalities. 'I was in here a couple of hours ago, and sat in that same spot you are right now was your boss.'

Jake let the comment hang in the air, but it barely registered.

'I'd like to start by asking you a few questions regarding what happened on the night of Frank Graham's death. In particular, what Henry Matheson was doing.'

Deshawn played with a cup of water in his fingers, staring at it the same way he might an expert-level sudoku in the Sunday newspaper.

'No comment.'

'What was his frame of mind? I imagine he was angry, no?'

'No comment.'

'I mean, he'd just heard that his sister had been murdered. And he'd just found out who the person responsible was. I'd say he was pretty furious.'

'No comment.'

Deshawn might have been inebriated, but he still possessed enough brain cells to say two of the most infuriating words in the English dictionary.

'It wasn't a question,' Jake continued. 'I was making a statement. What was your frame of mind on that night, Deshawn?' He leant closer to the desk and placed his elbows on the edge, lacing his fingers together. He stared into Deshawn's eyes. 'How were you feeling? Excited? Nervous? Anxious? We've got you on camera, so we know you did it. There's no hiding from that. But first, I want to know what your state of mind was.'

'Detective,' Kevin interrupted, 'this has nothing to do with the investigation and the things you're interviewing him for. Please move along.'

Jake sighed before continuing. The ball-busting had begun, just as it had in Henry's interview. But Jake was keen to make sure he didn't have a repeat of that clusterfuck.

Instead, he'd regrouped and reconfigured his approach.

'As I was saying, I'd like to know what you were feeling.'

'Detective!'

'There's no harm in building a rapport with somebody, Kevin. And there's certainly no law to break in describing how you feel.'

After shutting the solicitor down, Jake returned his attention to Deshawn. 'You can tell me how you were feeling, can't you?'

Deshawn dipped his head. Held it there for a few seconds. 'Angry,' he replied. 'I was… I was feeling angry.'

'Why's that?'

'Because I loved Danielle. She was like a sister to me. I'd… I'd grown up with her. We'd slept together a couple of times but Henry ain't know. I…' He choked and coughed. 'I wanted something serious, but she said she ain't want that, that she weren't that typa girl. Henry kept too much of a hold over her; she said it would never work. And she hated what we did, what we were doing.'

'Which was?'

Deshawn sniggered and shook his head. 'Come on. Like you ain't already know.' He lifted his head. Beside him, Kevin bent over and whispered something into his ear.

'Nah it's fine, fam,' Des continued, addressing the solicitor. When he turned his attention back to Jake, he added, 'I'm done. With everything.'

Jake felt his body warm with euphoria as he prepared himself to witness Deshawn roll over and give them everything they needed. Whether it was the drugs in his system talking or whether he'd all of a sudden developed a sense of empathy and morality, or whether it was even his new interview approach, Jake didn't know, he was just grateful that somebody was willing to assist their investigation.

Deshawn cleared his throat before beginning. 'We was selling drugs. A lot of 'em. Henry owned half the city. And with Jermaine's help, we was gonna take it to the next level. The two of 'em were gonna work together and split the profits evenly, like a partnership. Loadsa the boys told him it was a bad idea, but he ain't listen. And it worked for a while, but then Jermaine started getting cosy with Frank. The two of 'em started cutting the food and contaminating it with other shit. Lidocaine. Speed. Fabric conditioner. Mandy. Molly. Mary. All the girls I know. They was poisoning the shit outta it. But that weren't the problem. For years we'd got on fine. We had our turf and they had theirs. But when they started poaching our customers with their shit… nah, Henry weren't having none of it. He didn't like being fucked over. So we done the same thing to him that we done to Frank. Took them both out of the game. Now it's just us running East London.'

'That's a big area to cover. Would you have been able to do it all on your own?' Jake asked, hoping that nobody realised where he was taking the discussion: away from the drugs and gang war towards the jewellery heist and the bent cops helping them get there.

'We had help. And we would've had the same help going forward. That ain't no issue.'

'Rupert Haversham?' Jake asked, floating the name in the air and keeping one eye on Kevin's reaction: nothing.

'I ain't never met him. But I know of him. Henry used him all the time. Told me to get him down if I ever needed him. Said he was the best.'

Jake smirked. How the mighty really had fallen. Cock of the walk and now look.

'Who else has been involved with you?' he asked, hoping to move the conversation along.

Des shrugged nonchalantly. 'Some cop. Can't remember his name. Probably wasn't his real name anyway.'

'You met with him?' Jake repositioned himself into a more comfortable stance.

Deshawn nodded.

'On many occasions?'

'He was always over at the estate. Henry liked having him over. He told us what the rest of you lot were up to and how to get rid of you.'

'How did he get involved with you guys?' Jake asked, rubbing his thumb over his index finger.

More. He wanted more.

He wanted Martin fucking Radcliffe.

'Dunno. Bastard just turned up one day. No warning or nothing from Henry. Apparently, some other bent copper had put the two of 'em together. Think Henry called him The Cabal or something. The bent copper said he was going to help us get away with a lot of things. And he did. He was playing an undercover cop who was trying to infiltrate us; his words, not mine.'

'How did he help you?'

'If there was ever any youngers that weren't performing, weren't bringing in the money, losing their food, or if they were giving it away to Jermaine's boys by double-crossing us, then he'd arrest them. Something about him keeping the statistics positive so he could justify it to the pencil pushers if they came snooping.'

'And did they?'

Deshawn shrugged again. 'I only worried about something if there was a problem.'

Jake made mental notes of everything, building the bigger picture in his head, and decided it was time to bring up the jewellery heist.

'Tell me about the Royal Hallmark job,' Jake said. 'Did your bent copper have any involvement in that?'

Deshawn hesitated before responding. He turned to face

Kevin and then leant back. They whispered in one another's ears, a fraction out of earshot.

Eventually, after some time, Deshawn rested his arms against the desk again, looked Jake plainly in the eyes, sober as a judge now, and said, 'I didn't kill no one, all right? I never pulled that trigger.'

CHAPTER 84

ANOTHER HOLIDAY

The wind picked up while Rupert Haversham waited in the overpass, throwing pieces of gravel and sand across the concrete. Walls of scaffolding, wire fences and mounds of earth hiding behind large trucks and skips surrounded him. The meeting place, the construction site beneath the underpass on the A12, was owned by a good contractor friend. Paul had done the renovation on his home and had needed help with a few money laundering issues; Rupert had been happy to help, as long Paul agreed to owe him one. Or ten.

And this was lucky favour number seven.

Rupert checked his watch – 11:35 a.m.

They were five minutes late, and he was beginning to grow frustrated; he didn't like being made to wait. And he especially didn't like being made to wait under these circumstances, when he couldn't have cared less about being there. They were wasting his time, and in his book that was unacceptable.

The meeting had been arranged by Helen to discuss her

and Martin's next plan of action. They were running scared as their grip on things – Henry, the Royal Hallmark heist – gradually began to loosen. In Rupert's mind, the solution was simple: run and hide, and pray they were never caught. But he knew that wouldn't pacify them, that they'd want to hear something different. Martin and Helen would want an alternative to living life in the shadows and constantly looking over their shoulders.

They, like so many others, relied heavily on him for his intuition, expertise and guidance.

Like a modern-day god.

And he was going to play like him too. The power to give them accurate advice, to help them into safety, was in his hands, and he had yet to decide whether he was going to give it to them.

Two cars entered the construction site right in front of him and parked a few feet from the nose of his Mercedes. Too close for his liking.

'Morning,' Martin said nonchalantly after he made his way over, extending his hand for Rupert to take; Rupert left it and revelled a little in the way Martin dropped it by his side.

'You kept me waiting,' Rupert said, addressing Helen. She was the more senior of the two, so she would suffer the associated consequences.

'We had to make sure we weren't followed,' Helen responded. Her bob haircut looked dishevelled this morning, and two giant black clouds loomed beneath her eyes. She looked as though she hadn't slept in days; like it had been even longer since she'd last eaten. But something told him it wasn't because of a guilty conscience.

'And were you followed?'

Helen shook her head. 'Not yet.'

'We'll find out soon,' Martin added, failing to hide the smirk on his face.

'This isn't funny, Martin,' Helen screamed and raised a hand as though she were about to smack him round the head. 'This isn't a joke. This is some serious fucking bullshit that we've got to deal with. You're part of the reason we're in this shitstorm, so sort the fucking attitude out and shut up.'

She took a deep breath and turned to Rupert, calmer now. He sensed she'd been waiting a long time to do that. 'Which is why we need *you* to help us.'

'How?'

'I suppose you've heard about Henry and Deshawn?' Martin asked.

Rupert confirmed that he had.

'Then you'll know we have to try and get them out of there. You have to find a way.'

Rupert opened his mouth to respond but then caught himself. 'You haven't heard, have you?' he began. 'It's done. It's over. I'm having nothing to do with Matheson anymore. There's no way out for him. Do you know what evidence they have against him?'

Both Martin and Helen shook their heads.

'Video footage of both Frank and Jermaine being burnt alive, with Henry, Deshawn and Jamal all putting in an appearance. There's no getting any of them out of prison for that. Not even the biggest bribe could fix the situation we're in. The only way you could ever get him out is if you destroy all traces of the evidence – of which I'm sure there are several copies now because they're not *that* stupid – or the alternative is killing everyone who's seen it. Impossible. Not even worth considering. Which is why I'm done. I'm out. I'm calling it a day.'

Martin's face contorted into an unimpressed frown. 'Just like that? You're finished? You're bailing on *us*?'

Us. That word, that concept. Rupert sniggered internally. One thing he'd learnt was that there was never any us – it was always them or him.

'When the ship begins to sink, Martin, the smartest thing to do is jump.'

'So you're a philosopher now as well as a barrister?'

Rupert struggled to suppress his smile. *Cheeky prick.* 'Just an intelligent and experienced man who knows when to step back and get out before the shit hits the proverbial.'

'And what about *us*?' Helen asked, stepping closer to him.

There was that word again. And there was also a look of desperation in her eyes that he'd never seen before in all the years he'd known her. It made him smile. Not because he was a horrible person, but because it was the first time she'd shown that she was capable of being afraid, of having something tear through the harsh, resilient exterior. For a long time, he'd thought she was a powerhouse, a dictator, someone who wouldn't take anything from anybody. But now he realised that she was just like the rest of them.

Us.

And he couldn't care less.

'What *about* you?' Rupert asked. 'You need me to hold your hand? Wipe your arse for you when you get covered in shit?'

'It's the least you could do.'

Rupert sighed. It wasn't, but in that moment he realised that, if he was going to stand any chance of moving on from Henry Matheson and these two, he was going to have to do the bare minimum to get them out of his life forever. The bare minimum, and then it was up to them. If they couldn't get that far then there really was no hope for them.

'Loose ends,' he said eventually. 'Tie them off. Right now it looks like you've got two of them. Firstly, the kid who took the video. I'm told it was one of the boys on the estate. I've got friends in the hospital and they say he's in there already, admitted because he took some drugs. Apparently, Jamal has already finished off the kid's dad, but that's fucked up a few things for you, sent the place into lockdown, so you need to be careful how you play it. And the second thing you need to worry about is the money from the heist you did the other day.'

'It was jewels,' Martin corrected.

Rupert shot him a furious look. Why did people think it was OK to interrupt him while he was helping them? He should have charged for this information, that would have shut them up. Money talks, but money also silences.

He continued, 'Jewels. Money. Handbags… It could've been a bunch of dildos for all I care. That's your last link with Matheson and the E11. You've got your alibi sorted from your undercover investigation, haven't you? You've been doing it like I told you to?'

Helen took this one. 'The statistics are up, got a couple of the estate's younger dealers behind bars, so that's all anybody cares about. People are happy.'

'Good. Then you should be fine. Unless there's anything else I need to know?'

Martin contemplated for a moment and then shook his head.

'Perfect. Then you know what you've got to do.'

Martin and Helen stared at him blankly, like a pair of dogs waiting to be told they could eat their food.

'You need me to spell that out for you as well?'

'We can't afford any errors now, Rupert.'

He sighed. It was times like these he began to question why he'd ever decided to start working with bent coppers in the first place. The majority were useless, incompetent and most of the time downright paranoid, Liam and Drew being prime examples, which only compounded the first two. If they had any brains of their own, they'd be dangerous.

'Fine. It's simple. You both know it is but perhaps you're

too afraid to admit it.' He hesitated. 'One of you needs to kill the boy, and the other needs to dispose of the jewels – and I don't mean giving them away to some pawnbroker either; I mean properly disposing of them, so they don't come back again. Bury them. Drown them. Turn them into sand again somehow. Whatever you have to do. Just make sure they don't come back to haunt anyone. We've all got enough ghosts in our closets. We don't need anything else adding to it. You guys reckon you can do that?'

Helen and Martin looked at one another before responding. The expressions on their faces didn't fill him with much confidence, but then they said, 'Yes,' simultaneously, and that was all he needed to hear. He'd done his part, now it was time to forget about them and move on.

'Good luck,' he said with a smile before heading back to his car. *I'm going to need another fucking holiday after this.*

CHAPTER 85

BANG TO RIGHTS

Jake raced back to his desk. The interrogation had been enlightening, to say the least. Deshawn had all but given him the name of the bent copper who was working with Henry and the rest of the E11 gang. Martin Radcliffe. He was adamant. No doubt. The only problem was finding the evidence to prove that he was corrupt and he'd had an involvement with the killings and the jewellery heist. Experience had taught him that bent coppers were good, meticulous even, at erasing an evidence trail, at making sure the distance between them and the crime was filled with alibis and scapegoats. But something about Martin, an earlier suspicion, was telling Jake that he was different, a different breed of corrupt officer.

The blasé attitude. The confrontation. The intimidation, the discussions they'd had in the car, in the street. There was nothing subtle or genius about his movements. It appeared he thought of himself as invincible, untouchable because he had the backing of The Cabal. But so had Garrison, so had Drew, so had Liam, and look where they'd all ended up.

Martin was a loose cannon, an eager copper intent on making a name for himself, of making sure certain people knew who he was, making sure a certain *person* knew who he was. Martin had already shown that he wasn't willing or capable of thinking through his actions, his decisions, and that meant he could have left a chain of evidence behind him.

And Jake had the perfect idea on how to unearth it.

With the idea buzzing in his head like a wasp inside a bottle, he pulled his chair out from beneath his desk, flopped into it and awakened his screen. At the top of his inbox was an email from Roland.

Here you are, Jake, as requested. Also, no luck on the address. It's encrypted beyond my means of comprehension, which surprised me. Sorry. For now, we'll have to park it but let me know if they persist.

PS – please don't try to look at porn on your computer again. It reflects badly on the rest of us.

Good and bad news all bundled into one. Nevertheless, at least he now had access to the CCTV files he'd requested half an hour before the interview.

Jake scrolled to the bottom of the email, downloaded the attachment and then pressed play, watching the video at double speed. In front of him was a still image of a wall with a door on the left. Beside the door was a key-card lock system. In the bottom-right corner of the screen, the digits on the clock climbed higher and higher as the time passed. Jake inched closer to the screen, training his eyes on the key-card panel.

Five minutes in real time passed by and there was still nothing.

Then another five.

And another.

As time carried on, he was vaguely aware of the noises in the background, the hubbub of the office. The monotonous hum of conversations, the harsh screeching of the printer ejecting paper before it went on strike. The team working on finding the rest of Henry Matheson's army. He was too engrossed in his task to pay it any attention. He didn't even realise the office was virtually empty.

A further twenty minutes went by and there was still no sign of what he was looking for.

Somebody in the office whistled, distracting him. He briefly looked away from his screen, realised that nobody was calling him and returned his attention to his monitor.

And then he saw it.

There, standing in front of the door to the forensic evidence storage unit, was Martin Radcliffe. Wearing a grey blazer and a darker tie, hair flopped to one side. He reached for his pockets and produced a key card, slid it into the reader and, before entering, glanced up and down the corridor, affording the camera a clear shot of his face.

Gotcha, Jake thought.

Done and dusted. Bang to rights.

The snobbish prick'd been caught.

Wanker.

Without wasting any time, Jake took a screenshot, printed it before the printer packed in and rushed to Darryl's office. His fist pounded the door, and he waited anxiously, impatiently.

Eventually, the door opened.

Darryl was surprised to see him. 'Jake? What is it?'

Jake waved the document in front of his face. 'We need to do something about this.'

CHAPTER 86

SAFE WORD

Every part of Lewis's body ached. His neck. His shoulders. His back. His stomach. His legs. He felt almost paralysed. With fear, sleep deprivation, anger, resentment. The synapses in his brain were fried from the trauma, and he jumped at the slightest sound coming from the corridor. Even the spring in his bed creaking as he moved was enough to cover his skin in a layer of sweat. And the armed officers outside his hospital room did nothing to calm him either.

He'd watched his father die, held him in his own arms, and nothing would help him recover from that. Nothing. No matter how many professionals tried.

The events of the past day had left him exhausted. All he wanted to do was sleep, but every time he closed his eyes he was greeted with images of Jermaine Gordon and Frank Graham burning, screaming, consumed in an explosion of flames, begging for help, begging for forgiveness, and then begging for an instant death; of his father collapsed on the floor, gasping his last breath, clasping his hand; of Reece holding a knife against his throat. In the space of a few days, life had turned to death, a heavy, irrevocable and insurmountable darkness had settled over his life, and his nightmares were stalking his every living, breathing moment.

Lewis rested his head against the pillow and turned to face the empty chair where his dad should've been sitting. He wanted to hold him. To apologise. Tell him all the things that he should have said. That he loved him. That he was *sorry*, that he should have said it more often, that he was sorry for betraying his trust, for getting involved with things he shouldn't have, that they should have moved out sooner, that he should have helped more with his condition, that he should have helped him deal with the pain better, that he should have helped around the house more. That he would take it all back if he could.

Death, the master of regrets, had a funny way of making you realise where you'd fucked up in life.

A part of him wondered what the point of carrying on was. He didn't have anyone to care for, to look after him, and the guilt of the past few years was drowning him, dragging him deeper into the depths of despair. So what was the point? What would happen if he just ended it here and now? But for some reason, as he sat there, staring into the plastic cushion, he thought of Jake Tanner. The one person looking out for him. The one person currently making life worth living. The *only* person right now he could trust.

There was a knock at the door.

Lewis turned his head slowly. There was the nurse again. Emilia. The one who'd hugged him, comforted him when no one else could. She, along with Jake, had helped him, and she'd let him cry into her shoulder while she stroked his hair. Emilia, the temporary mother he'd never had.

Except this time she was with someone else.

Someone he recognised.

'Lewis…' Emilia began, a look of concern drawn across

her face. 'This is Officer Radcliffe. He's here to ask you a few questions while the armed officers have gone for a little bit. He said that he works with DC Tanner.' She lifted her hand and held a warrant card aloft. 'I've checked his credentials and he's telling the truth, OK? He's a real police officer, Leg. He's not going to hurt you.'

Lewis's body flushed cold as soon as he heard Emilia utter his nickname. Between them, after the room had emptied, and following Jake's advice, they'd decided to choose a safe word they could use if either of them ever felt like they were in danger.

And she had just uttered it.

'You can trust me, Lewis,' the man said. He wore a dirty grin on his face; one that reminded Lewis of Old Man Bill from the estate, who used to sit on the bench and watch the boys go to school every day before he suddenly disappeared and no one saw him again.

'Is that all right, *Leg*?' Emilia asked. Her eyes widened further with every passing second, the repetition of his nickname telling him just how concerned she was.

Now all he had to do was reciprocate and use the reply they'd agreed upon.

'Yes,' Lewis replied sheepishly. 'That's fine. Would you be able to tuck me in before you go?'

She closed her eyes and dropped her shoulders slightly, a weight seemingly lifting from them. She knew what she had to do next. He just hoped she could do it in time.

'Of course I can, Lewis. It'd be my pleasure.'

CHAPTER 87

NB–180

'This is a pretty big deal, Jake. Like, a pretty fucking mammoth-sized deal. And please excuse my language, but…' Darryl shook his head, overwhelmed. 'I don't even know where to begin with this. I mean…'

If ever there were a time to feel smug, it was now. Unfortunately for Jake, it was overcast by the severity of the situation. 'I hate to say it, guv, but I've been there, done that, worn the T-shirt and even treated myself to an ice cream while I was there, haven't I?'

Sometimes being the odd one out, esoteric and knowing things no one else did had its perks.

Darryl lowered the sheet of paper onto his desk. 'What do you recommend then?'

'It's simple, but you're not going to like it.'

'I never do when it concerns you.'

Jake didn't appreciate that. Even when he was about to help Darryl out of a predicament, his boss still managed to find one more stick to prod him with.

'We need to arrest him. He's committed several offences

—'

'All of which we have no credible evidence for!' Darryl's mood switched and he slammed his hand on the table, whether out of disgust at Jake's suggestion or fury at the situation, Jake didn't know, but he didn't like where the conversation was heading.

'I can read between the lines, Jake, and I know the insinuation behind this photograph, but we can't arrest him for any of the things *you* want to arrest him for without any concrete evidence. All we've got is this' – he prodded the printout with his finger – 'heavily pixelated image of him entering a forensic lab the afternoon Jermaine's body was discovered. That doesn't mean anything. It's not conclusive, and we have no real concrete evidence that he did anything while he was there.'

'But why would he be there? He's from the Flying Squad for fuck's sake. He has no business being in our building, let alone the forensic lab. And look at the time stamp. Natalie said that the evidence went unsupervised between one thirty and seven. That's not a massive window, and how many people set foot in there every day, outside of the usual team?'

Darryl sighed and dipped his head. 'Jake…'

This was ridiculous. He'd have been able to convince a chimpanzee of Martin Radcliffe's culpability. But not Darryl. Oh no, right now Darryl was being as dense as a doorknob.

'Come on, guv!' Jake threw his hands into the air in frustration. 'You've got to admit it's wrong. You know deep down that he's the bent bastard who's been helping them get away with so much. You're just in too much of a position of power to admit it.'

Darryl rose from his chair. 'Are you questioning my professional integrity?'

Jake joined him. For a moment they looked into one another's eyes, unrelenting, neither wanting to cede defeat, the stress of the past few days coming to a head. The last thing Jake wanted was to get into another spat with his manager. Not at this juncture in the investigation. But it was looking a little too late for that now.

'What are you afraid of, Darryl?' Jake asked.

'Excuse me?'

'What are you afraid of? Why won't you rip the plaster off, eh? Is it Matheson, Radcliffe? You afraid of how Rupert Haversham might react? Or are you afraid of The Cabal?'

Because believe me, nobody should be more afraid of him than me.

Darryl shook his head defensively. 'This is ridiculous.'

And if I can deal with it, so can you.

'You didn't answer the question.'

'That's because I'm not going to. I have my justifications for my actions, and they don't need explaining to you. You're a DC, Jake. Remember your place. When you've been through the ranks and stepped into my shoes for a bit, you'll know what I'm up against. Everything against Matheson, everything against anyone near him, has to be watertight. And even more so when we go after our own. Can you imagine the damage it'll do to my reputation if I accuse Martin of being bent and he isn't?'

So it was about his precious ego, pride, saving face.

'I expected better than that from you,' Jake said coldly. 'Do you think I was worried about those things when I went after Liam and Drew? Like fuck I was. I was too busy worrying about doing what was *right*. But now I understand. Thank you for enlightening me.'

The two of them remained standing for a moment. Jake resolved himself to stay, wait until he heard a response, until he heard what he wanted to, *needed* to. He wasn't leaving that easily, not without a fight. Darryl would have to throw him out.

'You're putting me between a rock and a hard place,' Darryl said eventually. 'And I don't appreciate it.' He sighed. 'But you have to be so careful with this sort of thing. One wrong move, one false accusation and not only will it fuck up that side of things, it'll also ruin any credibility we have against Matheson. We have to be absolutely one hundred per cent certain in what we say.' Darryl shuffled documents on his desk to keep his hands busy.

Slowly, he was wearing Darryl's barrier down. Rather, Darryl was doing all the heavy lifting and talking himself out of his decision. But if there was one thing Jake had learnt from the interviews with Henry Matheson and Deshawn Aubrey over the past few days, it was to save the best hand till last.

A smile grew on his face. Slowly at first, then it reached his ears revealing his teeth.

'Why are you smiling like that?'

Keeping his gaze focused on Darryl, Jake reached into his back trouser pocket and produced a folded A4 sheet. 'Suppose it's about time to show you this then.' Jake handed the document across and waited for Darryl's reaction.

As the man inspected the second screenshot, Jake broke into a chuckle. The image was of Martin Radcliffe a few seconds after the first, closing the door behind him, holding the stolen piece of evidence in his hand, NB-180 in plain view. He'd printed it out and decided to keep it in his back pocket for when the conversation didn't go his way.

For a long while, Darryl didn't say anything, and his expression portrayed no emotion, as if he were looking at a blank page.

That was until he lifted his head and scowled at Jake.

'You bastard. You had this the whole time and didn't show me?'

Jake nodded, making no effort to hide the smugness on

his face.

'Why?'

'A poker player never reveals their cards until the end.'

'That's some poker game,' Darryl responded. 'If you win, you get to keep your job, and if you lose, well... you can work it out.'

He set the printout side by side with the other and sighed heavily, absorbing what it meant.

'So this means Martin stole...'

'Yep.'

'And that he's...'

'Yep.'

'And the heist the other day, that was...'

'Yep.'

'And the murder...'

'Yep.'

'And the people they arrested, they're...'

'Innocent? Well, yes and no.'

'But they had nothing to do with the robbery?'

'As my theory goes, yep.'

Darryl's face was a picture of shock and disbelief. Jake just wished he had Elizabeth's camera to record it so he could hang it on the wall in the living room. Instead, it would have to be saved in his memory bank until the day he died.

'Now what, guv?' he asked.

As his boss looked up from his desk, all the animosity and tension from their brief skirmish flew out the window.

'Aside from finding him, we have to work out who put him up to the challenge.'

'I have a name in mind.'

'And so do I,' Darryl replied. Music to Jake's ears. Finally, they were both singing from the same hymn sheet.

DCI Helen Clements. The elusive figure Jake had never met, the one who hid behind the desk, following The Cabal's orders. She was the Flying Squad's answer to Liam. The senior official who had power and persuasion over others and who could make things happen. There was no doubt in Jake's mind that she was The Cabal's second in command.

'Where is she?' he asked.

'No idea. Haven't seen her since the other day. She could have fled the country for all I know.'

'Either that or she's trying to cover her tracks.'

Darryl held a finger in the air, as if a thought had just popped into his head. 'Speaking of which, where is the belt buckle? We need to find that as well.'

'Is that important?' Jake was dubious and aware they might go down the wrong path if he allowed Darryl to continue this train of thought. 'The belt buckle was the sole piece of evidence that connected Rykard to Jermaine Gordon's murder. Martin stole it so that he couldn't be charged with anything. But that was all for nothing when Rykard handed himself in. So it doesn't matter whether or not we find the belt buckle. The fact we've got evidence of Martin stealing it is the clincher.'

'You've thought this through.'

'I've been wanting to tell you for ages.' He smirked again. 'Trust me, I've thought it through.'

'Well, I'm glad you have.' Darryl hesitated and looked as though he wanted to say something more – offer an apology, maybe? – but decided against it. 'Back to our next and most immediate problem: finding the wanker before he does anything like this again. Any ideas?'

Jake considered a moment, scratching the side of his jaw. But before he could say anything, his mobile vibrated. It was the nurse from the hospital; he'd given her his number before he'd left Lewis in her capable hands.

'What is it? What's wrong?' he asked, his chest rapidly rising and falling now.

'You… you… you…' she began. 'You have to come quickly. There's someone here. He got rid of the armed guards – I don't know where they are. But he's talking to Lewis right now. He said his name's Martin Radcliffe. We used the code words like you told us to. Lewis thinks he's a threat. You need to get here.'

CHAPTER 88

DEFEAT

'How are you feeling, Lewis?'

Officer Radcliffe had moved swiftly towards him as soon as the door closed and was now sitting beside him, the only thing between them the ECG monitor connected to Lewis's hand.

'I'm fine.' Lewis felt something catch in his throat. Was it fear? Strength? He didn't know. Whatever it was though, he swallowed it down and made sure it didn't come back.

'Do you know who I am?'

Lewis lowered his head slowly. There was no point lying. Martin would see right through it, and he didn't want to suffer the consequences if he did. Instead, he decided to follow Jake's advice. To stall, keep him talking, agreeing to things he didn't want to agree to, and focus on keeping Martin onside. On keeping himself alive for as long as possible. 'Yeah, I recognise you. You're that nonce that hangs around the estate sometimes.'

Martin chuckled, but it was over as quickly as it had started. 'Funny little prick, aren't you?'

Martin reached forward. As his hand made its way further up the bed sheets, Lewis flinched and retreated into the pillow. A smile grew on Martin's face, because in one move, in one instant, Lewis had shown that he wasn't the brave soldier he pretended to be.

He was, in fact, scared shitless.

'There's no need to be afraid,' Martin told him.

Lewis swallowed. 'I ain't afraid.' For a brief second, he almost believed it himself.

'You've been through quite a lot over the past forty-eight hours. Would you like to tell me about it?'

'No.'

'It wasn't a question, Lewis. I need to know what happened. I'm trying to protect you.'

'No you ain't. You just wanna hurt me like the others—'

The door burst open and both of them looked towards the hole in the wall. Lewis's heart raced, hoping that it was Jake; that hope instantly plummeted as soon as he realised it was Emilia.

'Sorry to interrupt,' she said, 'but the doctor will be arriving shortly. He just needs to carry out some tests. Routine check-ups and things. Won't take too long.'

Jake Tanner was coming to save him. He was on the way!

Lewis just hoped that he came in time.

'That's brilliant,' Martin said, wearing a large, overbearing grin. 'I should be finished by then. If not then I'm more than happy to step out of the doctor's way while he conducts his tests.'

Emilia nodded and started out of the room. As she pulled the door to, leaving it slightly ajar, she gave one last look at Lewis before disappearing. The look told him everything he needed to know: remain calm, act natural and stay safe, help is on its way.

Martin cleared his throat, drawing Lewis's attention back

to the man beside him. 'As I was saying, I need you to tell me what happened. What have you told the police? Why did you show them the video of Henry killing Frank?'

Martin lugged himself out of the chair and towered over Lewis. He'd always thought that the man was abnormally short, but now, as he stood over him, Lewis felt like he was looking up at the top of the north tower.

Heart racing, chest heaving, pulse pounding, forehead and arms sweating, he lowered the bed sheet from his chest, preparing himself to run and fight back.

'I asked you a question, Lewis. It's important you tell me. Did you tell them about me, Lewis? Did you tell them that you know who I am? Did you tell them about what I've been doing for you?'

Martin placed a hand on his wrist. A thick, greasy, sweaty hand that squeezed and seemed to consume his entire arm. 'I can protect you, Lewis. I can make sure you're safe and that nobody can hurt you. Not Jamal, Des, Henry, any of them. I know people who can look after you. Would you like that?'

'Yes. Please. I'm sorry. I… I don't want… They killed my dad.'

Martin hesitated before responding. 'You won't like me saying this, but that was necessary. You'd betrayed them. Do you understand?'

He squeezed tighter, crushing the muscles and tendons in Lewis's arm.

Lewis nodded, fighting to stop tears bursting from his face like racehorses from the starting lanes. 'Now I've got no one to look after me.'

'Then what will it matter if no one cares you're alive…' Martin said, almost as if he were talking to himself.

'Wha—'

He was barely able to finish the word before Martin acted, reaching behind Lewis's head and yanking the pillow from beneath him. The force thrust Lewis onto his side, disorientating him. Before he had a chance to recover himself, Martin forced him onto his back and smothered his face with the pillow, suffocating him. He was covered in a field of darkness, the fibres of the pillow blocking his airways and he felt pressure coming in from everywhere, three hundred and sixty-five degrees of pain.

The weight of Martin's body, pinning him down, was immense, like fighting against a tree. He gasped for breath, but there was no oxygen for his lungs to cling to. He thrashed and kicked, attempting to reach for Martin's face. Every now and then, he touched something, but then instantly lost his grip as soon as he found it. He was no match.

Soon, his chest began to feel heavy, weighed down, as if he was becoming slowly paralysed, and his body surged with the warmth of a summer's day, that immediate heat you feel when stepping out of a cool supermarket. His already fatigued muscles burnt with exhaustion as he rapidly ran out of the energy and determination to defend himself. The depleting oxygen levels in his blood made the world spin, and soon, all he could hear was the sound of his heart slowing down.

And slowing down.

And slowing down.

For a moment he considered defeat: letting his arms and legs fall to the bed and allowing the pressure to crush his face until there was nothing.

This was it, he decided. This was how he was going to die. There was nothing else left that he could do. There was nobody else that could care for him or look after him.

Soon he'd get what he wanted.

And he'd be able to see his dad again.

CHAPTER 89

MARTIN

Jake was a hundred steps ahead of the nearest uniformed officer as he burst through the doors into Lewis's private ward.

In front of him, pinning a cushion over a small, limp frame, was Martin Radcliffe, his hair shaggy and shaking wildly like a tree caught in a storm.

The door crashed into the adjacent wall with a loud *crack* that distracted Martin momentarily, yanking his attention away from Lewis. They locked eyes on one another. The other man's were empty, hollow, devoid of what little emotion Jake'd thought he had. Being driven to murder was one thing, but murdering a defenceless child was another.

Martin was first to react.

He ripped the pillow from Lewis's face, allowing oxygen to flood into the young boy's lungs, and launched the pillow at Jake.

He ducked but was too slow, and it caught him on the side of the head. In the instant he was caught off guard, Martin capitalised, lunging towards him, rugby tackling him into the corridor. The man's shoulder collided with Jake's midriff, instantly winding him. And as they tumbled out of the room, Jake wheeling backwards, he bashed his head against the wall. A flash of white illuminated his vision briefly and brought with it the onset of a panic attack.

The suffocation. The sensation of feeling trapped. The heavy weight against his chest. The impending doom of the walls closing in.

The signs were all there.

But now wasn't the place.

If he didn't snap out of it, a young boy was going to die.

Jake gasped and forced his eyes open, taking in the scene: they were in the hospital corridor. No sign of armed officers. No sign of nurses, of doctors, of the twenty uniformed officers who were currently racing their way to him.

No sign of anyone.

Just the two of them.

Martin and Jake.

Like it had been in the car, on the streets. Where Martin had had the upper hand on him all those times, known things Jake hadn't.

Until now.

Martin rolled off Jake's body and clambered to his feet. As he started away, Jake reached out an arm and caught Martin's trailing foot, tripping him. Martin collapsed to the ground and smashed his temple onto the floor. He yelled and rolled onto his back, massaging the pain away, affording Jake a small opportunity to regain his stance and composure.

He did.

Jake hovered over him and bent down to grab him by the blazer. As he did so, Martin caught him off guard, buckled his leg and pulled him to the ground. Jake, his momentum too much, his balance off, fell head first onto the floor, landing on his forehead. Another flash of white. Another sting of pain.

Another reminder of the avalanche. Shifting onto his side, he noticed a hospital bed beside him and used it for support as he hefted himself to his feet.

By the time he was standing, Martin was down the other end of the corridor, bolting towards the exit, his escape growing more likely with every step. And for a moment Jake contemplated defeat. His head hurt, and he was out of breath. But then his thoughts turned to Lewis in the room behind him. How he was possibly dead, possibly fighting for his life on that bed. How he'd been through a lot in the past twenty-four hours, and how Jake wasn't prepared to let that happen for nothing.

No, Martin was his. And he was going to make sure of it.

Twenty yards separated them. And a further ten yards separated Martin from the double doors leading to the exit. If Martin slipped through there, Jake and the rest of the officers would face a mountain of a struggle to catch up with him.

He glanced down at the hospital bed and straddled it with his hands.

Then he started to run.

Charging towards Martin, he screamed until his lungs hurt, letting his opponent know that he was there and that he was coming for him – fast.

Just as Martin reached the double doors, the foot of the hospital bed collided into his hip, sending the man barrelling through the wood and onto the floor, where he remained, incapacitated, holding his head and hip.

Fortunately, the corridor was busy, and within a second a crowd had formed and surrounded him, limiting his escape routes. Jake took the opportunity to catch his breath, filling his lungs. And then the uniformed officers arrived. All of them coming from different angles, the sound of their heavy boots thumping on the floor echoing up and down the building.

One of the officers bent down to pick Martin up but Jake stopped him. No one else was allowed to do this but him. His ego needed a boost and he wanted word to spread to Helen Clements and beyond that he was coming for them, regardless of who they were and what they were capable of.

'Martin…' he panted, 'Martin Radcliffe, I am arresting you…' He paused. When did he get so unfit? 'I'm arresting you for attempted murder. You do not have to say anything, but it may harm your defence if you do not mention when questioned something which you later rely on in court. Anything you do say may be given in evidence. Do you understand?'

Martin said nothing.

Jake refrained from making a sarcastic comment. The situation was too sensitive. But then again…

'You have no idea how long I've waited to do this.'

'Trust me,' Martin replied, taking Jake by surprise. 'There are worse people out there who feel exactly the same way about you.'

CHAPTER 90

THE FULL EXTENT

The car was filled with silence. For the past hour, she and Stephanie hadn't said a word to one another for the simple reason that they'd run out of things to say. There was only so much small talk they could make before they reached the uncomfortable levels of silence they were currently experiencing.

Ashley liked Stephanie. She thought she was nice, friendly and exceptional at her job. But there was this air about her that Ashley didn't like. Like everything was a competition with her. Like she always had an experience or an occasion or an idea better than anything Ashley had ever had, like she had to win at everything, to appear better in every way. Brothers and sisters? You've only got one, well I've got three. Dad's a clerical worker? Mine's a biologist. No matter the topic of conversation, Stephanie always had something to trump Ashley with. And Ashley hated it. Not the fact Stephanie had all those *things*, but because she didn't appreciate Stephanie being a wanker about it and shoving it in her face.

People's lives were different – get over it.

They were stationed several hundred yards down the road from the Handy Man Scrap Services warehouse in Tilbury Docks, Ashley at the wheel, Stephanie riding shotgun. They were under strict orders from Darryl to wait there until they heard or saw anything that caught their interest.

'You got a boyfriend?' Stephanie asked, scaring Ashley.

Miraculously, this topic of conversation hadn't come up in their hour of small talk. Ashley hated talking about her love life and always clammed up whenever someone broached the topic.

'No. I-I...' she stuttered. Before continuing, she swallowed. 'No, I haven't.'

But I bet you've got like ten of them on the go.

'Not really looking for one?' Stephanie asked inquisitively.

'Never really thought about it. Not important to me right now.'

'Career first, is it?'

'Suppose you could say that.'

'I used to be like that. I used to want to put my career first, and I'm grateful I did. I accomplished everything I set out to do in the IPCC. And now that I'm in the MIT with you and Jake and everyone else, I couldn't be happier. It's a brand-new exciting opportunity, and I feel like there's some stability here... But I'm beginning to think it might be time I finally settled down with someone.'

Or ten.

Ashley didn't respond. She didn't know what to say. She'd often thought about getting into a relationship, even though she wouldn't admit it to anyone else, but, after trying unsuccessfully, she'd realised there was never enough time to make anything work. She'd been on a couple of dates and even those had been arranged and rearranged several times due to the complexities of the job. She never had any free time, and whenever she did, she was always doing something related to work. It was in her blood and had become a permanent part of her life. That was her priority. And there was no room for anyone else.

'What do you think of Jake?' Stephanie asked abruptly, breaking yet another silence. Ashley was beginning to find them peaceful.

'Jake?'

'Yeah, you know the one. The arsehole who seems to think he's the boss around the place most of the time.'

'I… er…' Ashley looked away and down into her lap.

'You like him, don't you? Oh my God. No… I was just joking! I didn't really think that… I mean, yeah, he's a good-looking guy, and all. But… *really*?' Stephanie looked out of the window and then returned her focus to Ashley.

God, fucking kill me now.

When she didn't respond, Stephanie placed a hand on her arm. 'Don't worry. You don't need to be embarrassed about anything. I won't say anything. You have my word.'

Ashley said nothing. She hated it when people jumped to the wrong conclusion, but she couldn't be bothered to convince Stephanie she was wrong. Sometimes it was better to let people believe what they wanted.

Hoping that the ground would swallow her up – or, even better, Stephanie – Ashley glanced over at the warehouse.

Then something caught her eye.

In the distance, a car had just turned in.

Ashley tapped Stephanie on the shoulder and together they watched the car pull into the warehouse's car park.

'I recognise that,' Stephanie said. 'It's the same one from the other night when Jake and I followed Henry Matheson to a construction site.'

A few seconds later, two figures stepped out. A man and woman.

'I don't believe it,' Stephanie said, her voice a whisper.

'What? What is it? *Who* is it?'

'That's Helen Clements. The chief inspector from the Flying Squad.'

Ashley skipped across the pavement towards the warehouse. Helen and Jamal, who they both recognised from the photo pinned to a wall in the incident room, had entered a few moments earlier. And now was their only time to strike. She'd been looking forward to this moment. Her first arrest with her new team. The satisfaction. The ego boost. The excitement of it all. The adrenaline. It reminded her of her days on the beat.

She was first to arrive at the metal gated entrance, with Stephanie following close behind, and they gave each other a quick nod before continuing. Breathing rhythmically, in through the nose, out through the mouth, Ashley sidled towards the reception and knocked hard, her knuckles hurting as they pounded on the windowpane.

She waited.

'I'll check round the side,' Stephanie whispered, already setting off. 'Just in case.'

Ashley watched her disappear. As she rounded the corner of the building, the door opened.

Standing before her was DCI Helen Clements. Slim, well dressed, proper. Surprisingly good-looking for her age. But none of that mattered when she was a police officer fraternising with the enemy.

Ashley introduced herself. 'I need to check out a few things if that's all right with—'

Helen held a hand out in front of her, pressing it against Ashley's chest. 'I'm afraid I can't allow it.'

'Why not?'

'Because… You're interfering with my investigation into the jewellery heist that took place a few days ago.'

'But this company, property and address is all registered to Henry Matheson. What's he got to do with the raid? Didn't you arrest some of Jermaine Gordon's gang only yesterday in connection with the same investigation?'

Helen stuttered, nothing but air and broken syllables falling over her teeth. Ashley had caught her out, and she knew it. But before Helen could respond fully, a sound erupted from around the side of the warehouse, followed by a shout.

'Hey!' Stephanie's voice called. 'Come back!'

Ashley glanced in the direction of the sound, and by the time she turned to look back at Helen, the woman had already gone and was disappearing deeper into the building.

If there was any doubt as to Helen's guilt, it was immediately quashed. Guilty people ran. Scared people ran. Innocent people stayed put.

Without hesitation, Ashley gave chase. She rounded the reception desk and stormed into the main warehouse. The entire space had been cleared out, as it had been the other day when she and Brendan had searched it, when there'd only been bits of leftover scrap metal and machinery, reminders of what the factory had once been used for. But what caught Ashley's eye was the table pressed against the back wall, and the piles of trinkets that hadn't been there the other day scattered across it, sparkling and twinkling in the artificial fluorescent light overhead. *Bingo*.

But there was no time to acknowledge it because Helen was still charging towards the far left of the warehouse, where Ashley saw a small door that had been left ajar. Brilliant sunlight flooded in through the hole in the wall.

Both women sprinted towards it, Ashley clawing back the

inches with every step. She might have been smaller, but at least her legs moved faster. Not to mention she was wearing her flats, her trusted flats, compared to Helen's heels.

Rookie mistake.

They reached the door at almost the same time. Helen was only marginally in front of her; a finger length away. Ashley reached for her, extending her arm as far as possible. As she stretched, her foot caught on something and she slipped. Her body fell heavily into the side of the door frame, smashing her hip, and she cried out in pain. But there was no time to waste. She'd suffered worse in life.

She staggered to her feet and hobbled out of the building, the fire of determination numbing the pain in her body. In the time it had taken her, Helen had distanced herself by twenty yards or so. They were hemmed in by the car park. A metal fence, six feet high, ran around the perimeter. Ashley had no frame of reference for where she was, or where she was headed.

At the fence, Helen reached a small hole, covered by a thin panel of corrugated metal. She grabbed at the metal and yanked. But it wouldn't move, no matter how hard she tried. She was trapped with nowhere to go.

Except a custody cell.

Ashley took her chance. She pressed her legs harder, pumped her arms faster, ignored the searing pain rocketing up and down the right side of her body, and within seconds, she'd cornered Helen. The woman looked exasperated, defeated. But there was no sign of fear in her eyes. Only anger and vengeance.

'Helen Clements, I am arresting you for perverting the course of justice, corruption, conspiracy to commit murder and collusion to commit robbery—'

'You don't have anything on me,' Helen said.

'That's for the CPS to decide,' Ashley said, in no mood to

be intimidated. 'Might I remind you that you have the right to remain silent.'

'Oh, don't worry. I plan to exercise the full extent of my rights.'

CHAPTER 91

SAFE

Outside Lewis's ward, Jake was becoming restless, pacing up and down the corridor. After Martin had nearly suffocated him, Lewis's body had gone into shock and he'd needed resuscitation. Nobody was allowed anywhere near him until he came round.

And it was killing him. He wanted to check on the boy, make sure he was OK.

As he waited, his phone vibrated. He answered it and found a seat nearby. Something told him he was going to need to sit down. He rested his elbows on his knees and ran his fingers through his hair with his free hand.

'Guv?' Jake answered. 'What's the latest?'

'Are you sitting down?'

Jake told him that he was.

'Martin's just been booked in. We're waiting for his police friend as well as a solicitor and then Brendan's going to interview him. It'll be quite a difficult one, given his role.'

'He attempted to commit murder,' Jake began, 'I don't think it gets less complicated than that. Who did he want as

511

his solicitor?'

'One guess.'

Jake sighed and rubbed his head even harder. All this time, Rupert Haversham had been pulling the strings. With The Crimsons. With Liam. With Drew. With The Farmer and Nigel Clayton. With Jermaine. And now with Henry and Martin. He was everywhere. And he wasn't going away, like a bad case of genital herpes.

Could *he* be The Cabal? Jake wondered. It was plausible, sure. Telling everyone what to do, when to do it and how to do it, while simultaneously keeping his nose right under the spotlight when someone needed bailing out. It was plausible. But, on the other hand, there was nothing to prove that Rupert was behind everything. And Jake knew it would be almost impossible to find something against him.

But then he realised one important thing. The voice of the man he'd spoken to numerous times on the phone was not the same voice as the man who'd sat opposite him in the interview room. The first was deeper, huskier, laced with a hint of a common accent. And there was an experience behind his voice; years of delivering threats and making good on them. The hint of power was rife in his intonation. Whereas the latter was the quintessential Queen's English and sat on the opposite end of the spectrum. And possessed a bellowing quality to it like it was fit for a performance in the opera.

'What happens now then?' Jake asked, looking up and down the empty corridor.

'Uncharted territory for me, kid. But since you've been gone I spoke with Roland and he managed to find CCTV footage of Martin discarding the evidence in one of the bins outside Bow Green. Luckily for us, they haven't been emptied yet and we found evidence number NB-180 still in there. And there I was thinking he was a criminal mastermind.'

'That'll teach him? What about Henry?'

'Oh, he's gone. Escorted to Belmarsh about twenty minutes ago.'

'Ashley? Stephanie? Where are they?'

'Posted out in Tilbury Docks like you requested.'

'And?'

Darryl hesitated before responding.

'And?' Jake repeated.

A long sigh. 'I don't want to tell you. If you find out you're right too many times, it'll start going to your head.'

Jake chuckled. 'Come on. Tell me.'

'They were on a stakeout when Jamal Bennet turned up at the warehouse. And who should be with him? None other than Helen Clements. After they'd called some uniform down, Ash and Steph searched the warehouse and found everything in there: drugs, money, the jewellery from the raid earlier this week and a whole stash of weapons under a trapdoor in the floor.'

'Sounds like they hit the jackpot,' Jake remarked.

'Yeah. They're bringing her in for interview now, but I've got a feeling she'll put up a fight. She's not stupid, she's been doing this long enough. In the meantime, the rest of the team are desperately trying to find some other concrete evidence against her.'

'She could walk?'

'Fifty-fifty. Her unannounced arrival with Jamal could complicate things. She could argue that she was there on official police business as well. Jamal's already claiming he was an informant for her and knew where the diamonds were being kept. Apparently, he was just showing her where they were.'

'Shit,' Jake whispered. He wasn't worried about Jamal. The man was stupid enough to let himself be recorded burning someone to death, so he deserved whatever sentence he was given. But it was Helen Clements that concerned him. The noted and respected chief inspector. Just like Rupert and The Cabal, she'd kept her fingers out of sticky situations, so finding anything against her would be tricky.

But nothing was impossible.

'Can we get the IPCC involved?' he asked.

'I'm considering it. But like I said earlier, I have to play it carefully. We have to be absolutely spot on, and as soon as the Directorate of Professional Standards or IPCC get involved, they'll hijack the case.'

Jake sighed. He had nothing else to say. He'd made it three for three. Henry, Martin and Helen. Names he could add to the list. But it had come at a cost. He was tired, exhausted, and now that it was over, he just wanted to go home to Elizabeth and the girls, where they could enjoy a nice film together without having to worry about Henry Matheson's goons or any unwanted drugs packages on his doorstep. And then he and Elizabeth could enjoy their evening together after the kids had gone to bed. For the first time in a long time. Like they used to. Like they deserved.

'All right, guv,' Jake said, 'thanks for letting me know anyway. I'll speak to you soon.'

'One thing before you go, Jake.'

'Oh?'

'Ashley told me about what you said in the car the other day. That you... er, are finding it hard to trust people. I don't want you to be angry with her because she came to me in confidence. And I'm not stupid, Jake, I knew that something was wrong. The past twelve months haven't exactly helped you. And I'm not going to ask if you still feel that way, but I hope you realise that this couldn't have been a success without them. Without Brendan, you might have missed Deshawn. Without Ashley and Steph, you definitely wouldn't have either Helen or Jamal. And I hope you realise now that you *can* trust them. All of them. Including me. After all, teamwork makes the dream work.'

Jake smiled as he hung up, and he was grateful that no one could see it. He lowered the phone from his ear and spun it between his fingers. Contemplated for a while. Realised that Darryl was right and that it was probably the only time Jake would let him be. But hindsight was a wonderful thing. He'd been wrong, too quick to judge his colleagues, mistrust them, and he was grateful for every one of them.

Who knew Liam Greene could be relied upon for good advice?

He lifted himself out of his seat and headed towards the water fountain protruding from the wall. Arresting people was thirsty work, and as he reached the end of the corridor, a voice called behind him.

'Excuse me?' It was a nurse. Not Emilia. Male. Smaller. He wore a face mask that protected his mouth and nose, leaving only his eyes visible.

'Are you Detective Tanner?'

'Yes,' Jake replied.

'He… he's awake if you want to see him?'

Jake didn't need telling twice. He hurried down the corridor, striding at double speed, and within seconds he was at the door, standing side by side with the nurse.

'He's very weak,' the man began. 'Go easy on him. No questioning just yet, if that's all right with you. He said he wanted to speak with you first.'

'Understood,' Jake said. 'Thank you.'

Jake opened the door and stepped into the room. For some reason, unbeknownst to him, nerves consumed him and made him shake, turned his palms sweaty. The same way he'd felt when Ellie and Maisie were born. But this time it disconcerted him. He needed to act professionally and detach himself from the emotion of what had happened. Yes, he had a duty of care towards his witnesses and those involved in his case, but nothing like this. Jake was here for personal reasons when he knew he shouldn't be. The paternal instinct in him was too strong, something he couldn't suppress.

He moved about the room, rounding Lewis's bed so that he was facing the door, lest any potential attackers come in.

Lewis lay there with his arms by his side, the steady rise and fall of his chest moving in tandem with the bleeping from the ECG monitor. His eyes were closed, and as Jake pulled the chair to, he stirred awake.

'You should be sleeping, kid,' Jake whispered gently.

'You should be working,' Lewis replied. His voice was weak, faint, barely a whisper.

'Well we can both break the rules this once, what do you say?'

Lewis nodded slowly. He was too weak, and his throat too sore to talk, and he fluttered in and out of consciousness. Meanwhile, Jake sat there silently, watching over him.

A few seconds later, Lewis opened his eyes and turned his head.

'Thank… thank you.'

'Hey,' Jake said, leaning forward slightly. 'You don't need to thank me, but you do need to rest up. It's all right. I'm not going anywhere any time soon. And if I do, there will be people I trust and respect watching over you. You're safe now, kid. Nobody's going to hurt you anymore.'

CHAPTER 92

POOL OF SUSPECTS

The first thing Jake did after the madness of the previous few days had died down was book a day off from work. Darryl, much to Jake's surprise, had been more than accommodating. It was because of all Jake's hard work and perseverance, he'd said. And then he'd ruined the sentimental moment by reminding Jake again that, without the team, the result wouldn't have been the same. Something Jake was fully aware of.

On the morning of his day off, he tried to force all thoughts of work and Henry Matheson and The Cabal from his mind. He was spending time with his family. Precious time. And he needed to be present, right here in the now.

'Where we going, Daddy?' Maisie asked as he buckled her into her car seat.

'It's a surprise!'

'Yes…' Elizabeth said in a hushed tone from the passenger seat, speaking out the side of her mouth. 'Where *are* we going?'

Jake hopped in the front and kissed her on the lips. 'You'll have to wait and see for yourself too.'

Then he started the engine, pulled out onto the road and headed into the town centre. The drive to Croydon train station was filled with anticipation, which was only heightened when Maisie stepped onto the train heading into London. She quickly became restless and badgered Jake for answers. Where we going, Daddy? What we doing, Daddy? When we get there, Daddy?

As soon as the Underground train set off for London Waterloo, he leant over to Maisie and whispered, 'Do you want me to give you a hint?'

'Yes!' She smiled up at him, her eyes bright.

'Well, you'll need to be a good girl today, otherwise, they'll put you in with the rest of the cheeky monkeys!'

As soon as she'd worked it out, with a little help from Elizabeth, Maisie's face illuminated.

'This'll be a pricy day out,' Elizabeth murmured. 'Though I suppose you have got a lot of making up to do.'

'This is the making up for the kids. Yours comes later.' He gave her a wink and then turned to his girls, his precious girls, who had quickly become distracted and were currently staring out of the window at the wonders of the tunnels rushing past them. In that moment he was content. His entire world was sitting with him, happy, energised, safe.

'Why don't we make it bigger?' he whispered to Elizabeth.

'Excuse me?'

'Us. Our family. Why don't we make it bigger?'

'You've changed your tune.'

'I've been doing a lot of thinking. I think it would be a nice addition to the team. Maybe a boy this time round though.'

'You don't get to pick.' Elizabeth placed a hand on his knee and slowly moved it closer to his crotch. 'But if you're lucky, we'll see what we can do.'

It was dark when they arrived home. After a long day of excitement and walking and sightseeing, the girls were asleep and had passed out in the car. After the zoo, Jake had taken them on a tour of the city, ending with the London Eye and a nice dinner at Pizza Express. Jake didn't want to think about how much it had all cost him, because it didn't matter. There was no expense spared when it came to his family, he was quickly realising. Especially when he got to see the big smiles on their little faces. That made it all worth it.

Now, though, he was beat. And ready for bed.

Jake pulled the car to a slow stop outside the front door, unhooked the girls from their car seats and wandered to the house. He was first to enter, and as he did so, he stepped on a small package that had fallen through the letterbox. It was a small Jiffy bag with no name on it, no address. Jake bent down to pick it up along with the rest of the envelopes on the floor.

'Come on,' Elizabeth said, prodding him in the back of the leg with her foot, 'let's put these two to bed first.'

And so they did, settling the girls in for the night so they could dream their wonderful dreams of fairy tales, witches, wizards, and dwarves. And maybe a few elephants and lions and penguins while they were at it.

At the bottom of the stairs, Jake grabbed the mail again and followed Elizabeth into the kitchen; she switched on the kettle as he moved into the living room, eyes focused on the package, his mind working on autopilot. As soon as he shut the door behind him, he set the rest of the letters on the sofa and held the Jiffy bag in his hand. It was blank, almost pristine. A single piece of Sellotape had been used to seal it. Jake tore it easily and tipped the contents into his hand.

A small SD storage card fell out onto his palm. The same

make and model as the one that Darryl had snapped.

A peace offering perhaps? An apology?

And then a small Post-it note fell out and slowly danced to the floor, landing face down. Jake picked it up and read the message.

WE NO LONGER THANK YOU FOR YOUR SILENCE

He read the message twice. A third time. A fourth. Before he was able to read it again or contemplate its meaning, Elizabeth entered the living room and distracted him.

'What's that?' she asked.

Jake spun on the spot, concealing the envelope and note. He held the SD card in the air. 'I forgot,' he said, 'I meant to give this back to you. Turns out it was in my pocket the entire time.'

Jake handed it to her but knew he shouldn't; he'd gone past the point of no return. The contents of the card could be harmless, blank, empty. On the other hand, it could be filled with incriminating images of himself, of him and Henry by the river. Or it could be images of his family taken as a threat.

As the two of them headed upstairs to bed, Jake ticked off the names on the list in his head.

Liam Greene.

Drew Richmond.

Pete Garrison.

Mark Murphy.

Danika Oblak.

Elliot Bridger.

Martin Radcliffe.

Helen Clements.

All of them had been bent coppers in one way or another. All of them either arrested or dead.

And then there was the criminal list too.

Danny Cipriano.
Michael Cipriano.
Luke Cipriano.
The Farmer.
Vitaly.
Nigel Clayton.
Henry Matheson.
Deshawn Aubrey.
Jamal Bennet.
Reece Enfield.
Rupert Haversham.

It wasn't the end of it, by any means, but the names on the list were increasing. The one missing, however, was The Cabal, identity still unknown.

But the pool of suspects was shrinking incredibly quickly, and Jake couldn't wait for the day when, perhaps during one long hot summer, the pool would dry up and nothing of The Cabal's influence would remain.

EPILOGUE

Shortly after his arrest, Henry Matheson was charged with murder, attempted murder, conspiracy to murder, conspiracy to commit armed robbery, supply of drugs, and countless more. All his assets, including Handy Man Scrap Services, were seized, and he is currently in HMP Belmarsh where he is awaiting trial. The trial is not expected to take place for another eight months.

Thanks to poor record disposal and the hard work of the team, it was soon revealed that DCI Helen Clements was a high-ranking corrupt official, responsible for facilitating the armed robbery at Royal Hallmark Jewellers. She was charged and her case is currently being investigated by the IPCC.

An arsenal of evidence was quickly gathered against Martin Radcliffe, who'd protested his innocence throughout interview. Like Helen Clements, he was charged with conspiracy and corruption, and his case is being looked after by the IPCC. He will never work for the police again.

Deshawn Aubrey was later charged with two counts of

murder, armed robbery and conspiracy to supply class A drugs. He, along with Henry, is awaiting trial. Deshawn is staying in Winchester Prison.

Following his arrest, Jamal Bennet committed suicide in his custody cell before any charges were brought against him. A handful of members from the E11 gang attended his funeral.

Rykard Delawney, during his time in remand, was transferred to a different prison, where he is awaiting trial for the murder of Jermaine Gordon. It is hoped the judge will look favourably upon his sentencing in light of the support he offered to Operation Deadwood. He hasn't seen or heard from his daughter in months.

Lewis Coyne quickly made a full recovery and was released from the hospital within a few days. With the help of social services, he is now living in foster care. If he is deemed fit, he will give evidence against Henry Matheson. No charges have been brought against him.

After several attempts at tracking him down near the Cosgrove Estate, Reece Enfield was declared a missing and vulnerable person. His mother hasn't seen him and campaigns daily for him to come home. He is wanted for murder, but his current whereabouts are unknown.

The body of Matilda Browning, the young girl held at knifepoint by Reece and the E11, was found a week after Frank Graham's death in the back of Henry Matheson's Range Rover. The vehicle had been abandoned in an underpass north of Stratford. She was bound and gagged but had died of dehydration and suffocation.

Ashley Rivers received high praise from Darryl for her esteemed work in Operation Deadwood, and she was later treated to a round in the pub, the highest reward the team could give her. Enthused by her own determination, she endeavours to assist the team in any way she can.

Stephanie was pleased with her performance during the investigation and believes it puts her in good stead for promotion to detective superintendent one day.

The following day, Jake checked the SD card using his personal computer and was relieved to find it blank. The threat of The Cabal, however, remains and is growing closer every day.

Rupert Haversham, less than a week after Henry was arrested and charged, booked a holiday for himself and his family to Jamaica. They are there for the next three months.

* * *

Jake, Stephanie, Darryl and the team return in *The Company*, the next instalment in the series. Coming soon.

Enjoy *The Cadre*? You can make a big difference.

Reviews are the most powerful tools in my arsenal when it comes to getting attention for my books. They act as the tipping point on the scales of indecision for future readers crossing my books.

So, if you enjoyed this book, and are interested in being one of my committed and loyal readers, then I would really grateful if you could leave a review. Why not spread the word, share the love? Even if you leave an honest review, it would still mean a lot. They take as long to write as it did to read this book!

Thank you.

Your Friendly Author,
Jack Probyn

ABOUT JACK PROBYN

Jack Probyn hasn't experienced the world. He's never even owned a pet. But he'd like to; there's still time. His twenty-two years on the planet have been spent in the United Kingdom, with a few excursions overseas — a particular favourite of his was Amsterdam. Or Norway. Both of which were lovely.

But what Jack lacks in life-experience, he more than makes up for in creative ingenuity. His Jake Tanner series is the birth child of a sinister and twisted mind, and a propensity to assume the worst will happen in even the most mediocre situation.

Finding himself pigeon-holed as a millennial, Jack decided to stick with the stereotype and do things his own way. After all, he felt entitled and he wanted to destroy industries.

Enter: writing.

The love of writing was rekindled in Jack's life when he (briefly) entered the corporate world, and the passion snowballed from there. No more will the millennial writer find himself working 9-5, indulging in the complexities of business life, or wearing a M&S suit.

He will take the world by storm with his pen (keyboard) and his ability to entertain and enthral readers.

Why not join him (and his future dog)?

Keep up to date with Jack at the following:
- Website: https://www.jackprobynbooks.com

- Facebook: https://www.facebook.co.uk/jackprobynbooks
- Twitter: https://twitter.com/jackprobynbooks
- Instagram: https://www.instagram.com/jackprobynauthor

Printed in Great Britain
by Amazon